Editor: Jenny Sims and Amanda Rash
Formatter: Melissa Cunningham (To.All.The.Books.I.Love)
Cover model: Mick Maio
Photographer: Michelle Lancaster
Cover and interior designer: Melissa Cunningham
(To.All.The.Books.I.Love)

PLAYLIST

"Dethrone" by Bad Omens

"S & M club remix" by Rihanna

"Hungry Eyes" by Eric Carmen

"Just Pretend" by Bad Omens

"Bleed On Me" by Daniel Seavey.

"Wicked Game" by Lusaint

"Panic Room" by Au/Ra

WARNING

Things to know about **The Sacrifice**
- Secret society
- Arranged marriage
- Revenge seeking H
- Virgin h
- It is MF (no sharing of the h)
- J/P (jealous/possessive) H
- OTT (over the top) H
- Told in dual POVs

The Sacrifice is set in the Lords' world introduced in **The Ritual.** They can be read as standalones in no particular order.

THE SACRIFICE

USA TODAY & WALL STREET JOURNAL BESTSELLING AUTHOR

SHANTEL TESSIER

PROLOGUE
L.O.R.D.

A Lord takes his oath seriously. Only blood will solidify their commitment to serve those who demand their complete devotion.

He is a **Leader**, believes in **Order**, knows when to **Rule**, and is a **Deity**.

A Lord must be initiated in order to become a member but can be removed at any time for any reason. If he makes it past the three trials of initiation, he will forever know power and wealth. But not all Lords are built the same. Some are stronger, smarter, hungrier than others.

They are challenged just to see how far their **loyalty** will go.

They are pushed to their limits in order to prove their **devotion**.

They are willing to show their **commitment**.

Nothing except their life will suffice.

Limits will be tested, and morals forgotten.

A Lord can be a judge, jury, and executioner. He holds power that is unmatched by anyone other than his brother.

Chosen one:

A Lord must remain celibate during his first three years at Barrington University. Once he is initiated into the Lords, he is gifted a chosen for his senior year.

A Lady:

After they graduate from Barrington, they are to marry a Lady— a wife to serve him. If he shall die before her, she is then gifted to another Lord to ensure the secrets are kept within the secret society.

ONE

TYSON
INITIATION

LOYALTY
FRESHMAN YEAR AT BARRINGTON UNIVERSITY

"**A**s a Lord, one must prove to us that we can count on you. No matter the situation. No matter the cost." Lincoln paces in front of me and the other Lords. I guess you could say he's our leader.

We're all required to live in the house of Lords for the next four years of our lives, and he runs it. I've heard rumors that some call the HoL a fraternity on crack. But no one really knows what happens inside that mansion other than the badass parties we throw. Only the Lords who attend Barrington and are going through their initiations know what we really do.

It's freshman year. Our first time to show just how far we're willing to go in order to be the best.

"You will not be punished for your actions, only rewarded," Lincoln continues. "A Lord is willing to take a life without any questions asked." He comes to a stop and opens his arms out wide. "You will be given an assignment each year to show just how far you are willing to go for us." He crosses his arms over his chest. "Not all of you will make it, gentlemen, but those of you who succeed will know a life that others can only dream of."

My father's voice echoes in my head. *"Joining the Lords is not an option; it's an honor. And you want to honor the Crawfords, right, Son?"*

"Yes, Father."

He has prepared me the best he could for this day. For this life. And I will do whatever I can to be the son he raised me to be —ruthless.

"Tyson, you're up." Lincoln's words have my head snapping up to look at him.

I stand from the spot where I was kneeling and see a guy enter the makeshift ring. He's got to be in his late thirties with at least six inches of height on me, and who knows how long of a reach. He's wearing a hoodie and jeans with black combat boots.

Reaching up, I yank on the top of my shirt and pull it over my head before throwing it to the side, knowing the fewer restrictions I have, the better. I've also got jeans on but am wearing tennis shoes. They won't help me in a fight. But technically, I'm not supposed to win. They want us to fail. It's their way of weeding out the weak ones as quickly as possible.

The guy shoves his hand into his back pocket and removes a pocketknife, flipping it open. I see dried blood on the blade, and my eyes meet his as he smiles, showing off his crooked teeth. "You're dead," he states.

The words make my heart race. Not with fear but anticipation. This is what we're bred for. This is why they make us show our worth. Not just anyone can be in this society. It only accepts the best of the best. And I am the motherfucking best at everything I do.

You have to be born into this world—your blood makes you a

Lord—but they can remove you at any time. Some would be so lucky to get this chance to prove they can live up to their name.

I glance at Lincoln, and he shakes his head, knowing my silent question. The only way I'll get a knife is if I take his.

Challenge accepted.

The guy rushes me, and I jump out of the way just in time. Throwing my arms up in the air, I barely miss the knife he holds out in front of him. I kick my leg out, making contact with the side of his knee. He goes down but rolls at the same time I try to stomp on him, missing my shoe to his face.

Recovering quickly, he jumps to his feet with the knife out in front of him once again. He swings his hand in front of my face, trying to cut me, but I duck while moving out of the way. The quicker I am, the better my odds. Keep him guessing my next move.

"Do your job, Clarence," Lincoln calls out to the guy, sounding bored. These men have been Lords for a long time. They should be able to take us down without thought.

I've got a split second to make a decision. It's not the best, but it's all I can think of.

I rush him, getting low enough to wrap my arms around his waist and pick him up off his feet. I feel a sharp pain in my back as he screams out, but the adrenaline coursing through me overrides it.

The weight of his body pulls us both down to the ground, slamming him onto his back. It knocks the wind out of him, and I take the opportunity it gives me and fist both my hands, hitting him in the face.

"Motherfucker," I hiss, feeling the skin on my knuckles split from the contact. But it doesn't stop me.

Fellow Lords are yelling for me to succeed. They will be up next. If I lose, it sets a tone. Right now, I represent all of us. I'm not fighting them; I'm fighting for them. For us as a team.

Blood splatters on my face, and my fists start slipping from it, covering his face and my sweaty hands. He fights back or tries to, at least. His eyes start to swell shut, so he's fighting blind. I've got an advantage.

I slam my fist into his jaw, feeling a crack. My next swing hits high on his head, making my arm go numb for a brief second, so I hit him with the other, knocking his head to the opposite side. Getting to my unsteady feet, I kick him, rolling him over onto his stomach. He's coughing up blood, and his body starts to convulse. I yank him back over, fall to my knees again, and wrap my bloody hands around his throat, squeezing with the little strength I have left. Now is not the time to show off. It's time to finish what I started.

He doesn't even fight me.

An arm wraps around my neck from behind, restricting my air, and I'm yanked off the guy. I start kicking, and my hands grip the arm holding me in place.

"Calm down, Tyson," Lincoln says in my ear. "He's dead. You're done."

My body instantly relaxes in his hold, and he releases my neck. I fall to my knees, my bloody and busted hands slapping the concrete floor. I'm having trouble catching my breath. Looking down, I notice blood dripping from my mouth. Did he get more hits in than I thought?

I cough, and more blood splatters across the concrete floor. The room starts to sway.

"Gavin," Lincoln calls out to our doctor, who is among those in the audience.

The last thing I see is the guy's knife on the floor, covered in my blood, before I pass out.

TWO

TYSON

INITIATION

Devotion
Sophomore year at Barrington University

I hold the knife down to my side, and blood drips from the tip onto the once pristine white marble floor. I had to kill the two guards to gain access to the house. They never saw us coming.

The woman lies on her stomach, hands tied behind her back with duct tape over her mouth, silently sobbing. Pathetic, really, if you think of why we're here. Don't ever let a pretty face and tits fool you. A woman can be just as ruthless as a Lord. She's as bad as they come, or so I've been told. We weren't given much about why we're here. Other than to collect another Lord and do whatever needed to be done to fulfill the assignment.

I kneel next to her, using the bloody blade of the knife to push her bleach-blond hair away from her face. "Where is he?"

She shakes her head quickly, informing me she doesn't know. *She's lying.* "Bring me the girl." I stand, snapping my fingers.

The woman starts screaming behind the tape, her body

thrashing on the floor. She goes to get up, but I place my black boot in the middle of her back, holding her down.

A fellow Lord, Miles Hopper, was given this assignment with me. He enters the living room, his arm wrapped around the girl's upper arms. He shoves her into the room and she trips, falling to her knees. Her arms are also tied behind her back. She leans forward, her long, dark hair shielding her face from me.

I step into her and place the tip of the knife under her chin, forcing her head up. Bright blue eyes glare up at me. "Where is your brother?" I ask her.

"I'll never tell you," she says through gritted teeth.

Sighing, I crouch in front of her, my elbows resting on my thighs. "You understand that I have to hurt you if you choose to protect him, right?" I run the blade over her heaving chest.

Her brother has betrayed the Lords. There's always someone who can't fulfill their oath. That one Lord who risks it all and then runs, leaving behind a family to take his punishment. It's a shame, really. We're taught to rule the world, but no one wants to take responsibility when we fuck it over.

"Do what you have to do," she spits out.

Standing, I shake my head at her. "What a waste."

"You're the waste." She pulls her lips back with a growl. "Doing whatever the Lords tell you to do. You're nothing but a fucking puppet."

I throw my head back, laughing. "What's that make your brother?"

"He had the balls to stand up for himself," she snaps. "To get away from them."

Smiling, I wonder, "Why didn't he take you and your mother with him?" The poor thing has no clue as to why he really left them. Or why we're here. Not like it matters. Her knowing won't change the outcome.

"He'll come back for us when the time is right." The way she lifts her chin, I think she truly believes that. But why wouldn't she? He's her brother. He's supposed to protect her.

But rules are rules. I have an assignment to complete, and they are at the top of my list. If we don't retrieve the Lord, we're not to leave anything for him to return to.

I move over to her mother lying on her stomach and pick her up by her hair, making her scream into the tape over her mouth. I stab her in the chest. Yanking the knife out, she falls to the floor dead.

"MOM!" Her daughter jumps to her feet to rush over to the body.

I step in front of her, wrapping my hand around her neck, lifting her feet up off the floor. Placing my face in front of hers, I say, "Still want me to do whatever I have to do?" I arch a brow.

She's sobbing, body shaking. I loosen my grip on her neck, and she chokes out, "I ... don't know anything."

Miles enters the room, and I didn't realize he had left. He holds up the girl's cell phone. "Let's see if we can get him to come to us."

I tighten my hand on her throat once more, and she thrashes in my hold as I watch her face turn white, lips blue. When her eyes start to roll into the back of her head, I let go and step back. She falls to her knees, coughing and spit flying from her mouth, sobbing once again.

Moving to stand behind her, I grip her dark hair, yanking her head back as Miles stands in front of her and holds up her phone. "Smile for the camera," he tells her, and it makes her sob harder.

He types out a message and sends it. I yank her to her feet by her hair and drag her over to the couch, forcing her down onto it. I sit across from her, on the coffee table, and grip her chin, forcing her to look up at me. "You better hope he's as loyal to you as you are to him."

The cell in Miles's hand rings and he looks at me. "Blocked number."

"That's not a good start," I say, and her shoulders shake while she rocks back and forth on the couch.

He hits answer and places it on speakerphone. "What the fuck?" her brother's voice demands.

"Help me!" she cries, jumping to her feet as if he's here in person to save her.

I leap forward, shoving her onto her back on the couch and I straddle her chest the best I can, placing my hand over her mouth to shut her up. He's seen the situation she's in and understands her life is in our hands. We want him to talk.

"Who the fuck is this?" her brother shouts. "What the fuck do you want?"

"You," I say simply.

He goes silent, and her muffled cries grow louder while her small body tries to fight me.

"The Lords sent us to collect you," Miles says. "Either you're here in an hour or your sister is dead like your mother." He hangs up the phone and turns it off, tossing it into the vase filled with red roses on the end table by the couch.

I get up off her and make it back to where I was sitting across from her on the coffee table. I watch her slowly get up and try to stretch her arms that are still tied behind her back.

"Don't worry," Miles begins, walking behind the couch. He pulls back the slide, cocking his gun, and her body trembles at the sound. "If he doesn't come to your rescue, we'll show you mercy and make it quick." He grips her hair, yanking her head back, and pushes the end of the barrel into her temple.

She's gasping for breath, her black mascara running down her face. "Please ... I didn't do anything." I watch her neck work as she swallows.

I get up, and she must hear my movement because she starts

thrashing around on the couch, trying to get up to see what I'm doing, but Miles has her head pinned to the cushion by her hair. I open the bag we brought and remove what I need.

Walking back over to her, I fall down onto the couch, straddling her legs, making her scream at the top of her lungs for anyone to help her. But no one is coming. I know it, and she knows it.

She'll die tonight for her piece of shit brother. He's willing to kill others to be initiated into the Lords, but he'll willingly let his family die for his mistakes. He's a fucking coward.

"Please ..." she sobs, her small body trying to throw me off of her, but it's useless.

I shove the cloth into her mouth, silencing her, and then I rip off the duct tape, tearing it with my teeth, and roughly place it over her lips. Her tear-filled eyes meet mine and the life fades out of them, knowing it's over. Nothing is worse than not being able to plead your case. Especially when you're innocent. She'll have less than an hour to come to terms with facing her death.

Getting up, I find myself wandering over to the fireplace to look over the pictures that sit in various sized frames of her and her mother. Not one has a father figure in it. Or her brother.

I'm not surprised. There's a reason he isn't going to return to try to save anyone in this house. But I'm still in initiation and I must do what is required of me. I won't go soft to save someone else's ass. Not when mine's on the line.

"Fuck!" Miles hisses behind me.

I turn to see he had taken his eyes off her for a second, and she got up off the couch to run. He grips her hair and yanks her back into him. Her feet come up off the floor as she kicks them out, fighting him with all she has.

"Goddammit," he growls, throwing her face down on the floor next to her mother's body. "Fucking bitch." He falls to straddle her back, grips her hair, and yanks her head up off the marble.

Her bloodshot eyes met mine while she tries to breathe through her nose.

"I was going to make it quick." He grabs his pocketknife out of his jeans and flips it open. He places it against her neck, pushing it into her skin, and she closes her eyes tightly. Her face scrunching as blood trails down her neck. "Now I'm going to take my time. Split this little body of yours open one slice at a time. You'll be begging for us to kill you soon."

Looking over, I see her ruined cell phone while it sits in the water at the bottom of the vase. I walk toward them and kneel, pulling mine out. "Look at me," I command.

She opens her eyes, her wet lashes clumped together from the makeup she had on when we arrived. I take a picture of her once more, making sure not to get Miles's face.

"Just a little something for us to jack off to later." Miles laughs, reaching around with his free hand and pinching off her nose, making her buck wildly underneath him.

I pull up the phone number in my cell and send the picture, knowing it will get the reaction that I want.

THREE

TYSON

INITIATION

Commitment

Junior year at Barrington University

I sit tucked back in the dark corner of the hotel room when I hear the door open. A woman giggles, followed by a man's voice. "You're so sexy." He sounds in awe of her. Like it's impossible he could ever have a woman her age be interested in him.

He's right.

But men get stupid when they see a pretty face with tits and an ass. I picked the perfect one for this job.

"Make me a drink?" she slurs. Sounds like she's already had too many.

"I'd like a drink of you," he counters, and I roll my eyes when she giggles at his stupid comment.

Part of being a Lord is that we have to abstain from sex for our first three years. So I'm not even embarrassed that I'm hard at the moment. At this point, it has a mind of its own, and I don't even try to control it. No amount of porn or jacking off helps.

"Get undressed," he orders, his voice changing. He's no longer in the mood to wait. He wants to fuck his little bitch's cunt right here, right now. I get it. *Why wait?*

I don't hear her argue with him, but the sound of the zipper on her dress follows before a light comes on when they enter the bedroom. I sit up straighter to see he's got his hands in her strawberry-blond hair. She's lost the dress but still has her heels, underwear, and strapless bra on. His dress shirt is unbuttoned, showing off his defined abs. For an older guy, he's in pretty damn good shape.

"Gorgeous." He pulls his mouth from hers to look her up and down. His hands aggressively run over her ribs and to her hips, yanking on her underwear.

She tosses her hair over her shoulder and spins him around to where his back is to me. She rises up on her tiptoes and leans in, her teeth latching onto his earlobe, making him hiss in a breath. Her brown eyes land on mine across the room. She can't see me, but she can feel me watching them. It won't stop her.

He grabs her upper arms and throws her onto the king-sized bed, her body bouncing on the white duvet. Usually, the room is covered in fresh flowers and champagne. But this woman isn't his wife. This is his fuck. His plaything for the next few hours. "Spread your legs. Show Daddy that pussy," he orders.

She opens her legs, her hand sliding into her thong that still covers what he wants to see.

He slaps her inner thigh. "I said fucking show me, you little whore."

Whimpering, she grips her thong and pulls it to the side, not making him wait any longer.

"Yes. Yes. That's what I'm going to fuck." He undoes his slacks. Grabbing her ankles, he yanks her to where he stands at the end of the bed, her ass almost hanging off the edge.

"Wait," she gasps, her hand going to his chest. "Maybe we should—"

"Shut the fuck up." He slaps her face, making her cry out.

"Get the fuck off me." She manages to twist onto her stomach and tries to crawl away, but he yanks her back, getting onto the bed himself.

"Like to play hard to get? I like that." Laying his heavy body over the back of hers, he pins her down while gripping a handful of her hair. "Scream my name." Spreading her knees with his, it arches her ass up in the air into a better position for him.

"No. No. No," she cries. "Stop!"

"I'm going to fuck this tight cunt, sweetheart. Then I'm going to come all over that pretty face of yours."

"Please." She begins to sob. "Don't do this. I don't want to."

"Too bad, bitch." He shoves her face into the bed, silencing her cries, and with his free hand, he reaches into his unzipped slacks to pull his dick out.

I stop recording and stand from the chair in the dark corner. "That's enough."

"What the ...?" He jumps off the bed, spinning around to face me just as I step into the light. "Who the fuck are you?" he demands. "How the fuck did you—"

"About time." She smirks, wiping the fake tears from her face.

"You may go," I inform her, nodding to the bedroom door.

She jumps off the bed and pushes her hair over her shoulders, exposing her big tits, and my eyes fall to her hard nipples. I wonder if that turned her on. Does she get off on that kind of shit? I've watched some fucked up shit over the past few years when it comes to porn. And even I've been amazed at what some women are into. Or found what I'm going to be into once I can fuck again.

Giving the man one last look before winking at me like she knows what I was thinking, she exits the room.

"What the fuck is going on here?" he barks. "She never said

anything about a fucking boyfriend." Pointing at the door, he goes on, "She fucking begged me."

"I know." I agree with him. "That's what she was paid to do."

His face pales, and I lift the cell in my hand.

"What ... You ... What is this? You want money?" he asks through gritted teeth. "Did you two set me up for a payday?"

I give a rough laugh. "Even you couldn't afford to pay the Lords what they charge." It's never money. No, they demand your soul.

His knees give out, and he falls to the edge of the bed. Bringing both hands up, he buries his face in them. "Fuck," he hisses.

"This is how it's going to go." I pocket my cell and walk over to the end of the bed, closing the distance. "You're going to pull out of the race for senator."

His head snaps up and he glares at me. "I will do no such thing."

"If you refuse, the video I just took of you forcing yourself on an underage girl will go live on every social media outlet. I can only imagine what that would do to your reputation, much less your marriage." He clenches his jaw. "I also have this ..." I pull out the vial and shake the contents inside. "Drugs. She will willingly drink it before I anonymously call 911. Making sure she tests positive for GHB after they pick her up from a room that's registered in your name."

"You son of a bitch." He jumps to his feet.

"I can send you a copy of the video so you can watch it whenever you'd like, if that's what gets you off," I offer.

His fist swings out to hit me in the face, but I see it coming. Mine connects with his jaw before he gets the chance. He falls back onto the bed, groaning.

I sigh. "Do you really want to return home to your family tonight having to make up a story about how you were mugged and didn't get a good enough look at the man who beat the shit out of you?" I rub my knuckles.

He sits up, eyes blazing fire at me. "You will not get away with this."

"You've got twenty-four hours to pull out, or the Lords will make sure you don't win," I inform him, then turn and exit the room. Walking down the hall, I can hear him cursing back in the bedroom.

I enter the living room to see the woman, back in her dress, standing at the floor-to-ceiling windows. She hears me and turns around. Her brown eyes light up, falling to my jeans and slowly running up over my T-shirt. She licks her lips, following me to the door. "You paid for the night. Sure you don't want to use me?" she asks when I push the button for the elevator.

I shove my hands into my pockets, avoiding her question. "You did good."

"Baby, that was nothing." Coming up next to me, she slides her left arm through mine, pulling me closer into her side. "Your cock isn't the only thing I can blow."

"I don't doubt your skills," I tell her, pulling away when the door slides open. "But I can't."

She pushes out her bottom lip, stepping into the elevator with me. "You know I'm twenty, right? I'm not underage."

I nod. "I'm aware." I said that to add to the fear factor. Nothing is more terrifying than a man thinking he fucked an underage girl. If I let this leak, they'd seize all of his electronics to see if he's been searching for underage porn. It would be humiliating to say the least. And even if they didn't find anything, the media would twist it enough to ruin any future he might have in politics. The man is already a powerful Lord, but now he's getting greedy, and the Lords aren't having that.

We each have a purpose in this secret society. Some need the power and are willing to test the Lords to see just how far they can go. Those Lords are shown that they were given their life, and it can be taken away just as quickly. That's why they have us kill for initiations. They say it's to control the numbers, but I think it's to show us just how easily we can lose everything.

She crosses her arms over her chest, pushing her tits up even more. My cock is still hard, imagining how good it would feel to shove her to her knees right here and now and fuck her injected lips while drool runs down her enlarged tits. "You have my number if you need me." Winking, her tongue runs across her top lip.

The elevator doors open, and I step off, not even bothering to look back at her. Instead, I shove open the glass doors to the five-star hotel, and the valet stands there with my car already parked up front. "Thanks." I give him a couple of hundreds on top of the three I gave him when I arrived to keep my car ready for me.

"Of course, Mr. Crawford." He nods.

Falling into the driver's seat, I smile, knowing I just finished my last initiation. The Lords have decided who they want to sit in as a senator, and my task was to make sure he wins. No matter the cost. It worked just as I planned. No man can pass up pussy.

I remove my cell and pull up the video, emailing it with the subject **DONE**. Throwing my car in gear, I squeal the tires and pull away from the curb.

FOUR

TYSON

INITIATION

ONE OF THEM
SENIOR YEAR AT BARRINGTON UNIVERSITY

I kneel with my arms cuffed behind my back, a metal collar is around my neck and attached to the wall behind me. It allows us no wiggle room. We are secured for a reason, so we can't fight them. It signifies our trust. We must willingly give them our bodies to mark. It's a privilege we've made it this far.

"Lords," Lincoln calls out to our audience that is dressed in their cloaks and masks. "These men have completed every task we've asked of them. Tonight is the night that we celebrate them and their loyalty to us." He turns to face me and the other men who are secured to the wall inside of the Cathedral on the second-floor balcony.

A fire roars to life where the baptism pool usually is. They've drained it, filled it with stacks of wood, and lit it on fire. I can feel the heat from where I kneel. The sweat rolls down my back and forehead.

The men place the branding irons into the fire to heat them. I try to pull myself off the wall, but all it does is choke me. Wiggling my arms, I try to relieve the tightness in my shoulders really quick. It's also useless. They've been doing this for years. Each one is different, but the result is the same.

I knew going into this that it would be painful. They push you as far as your body and mind will go just to see how much you can endure. It's the ultimate test. Every Lord that is present in this room is here because of their last name. The blood in their veins got them this ticket, but we have to prove we deserve it. My freshman class at Barrington started with fifty. We're down to twenty-two. They're the lucky ones though. They got to walk away.

Once I'm branded, the only way out is death. And it will come. The question is, will it be because of me or them? Only time will tell.

The lower classes of Lords at Barrington watch from the pews. It's a way to remind them why they can't fuck for three years. This is where they want to be. What they're training for.

The man standing in front of me turns and holds the branding iron by my face. The blazing end heats up my skin, and I pull away the best I can. My body tenses, every muscle already aching. It's that natural fight or flight kicking in.

"Tyson Crawford, are you ready to be a Lord?" Lincoln asks.

"Yes, sir." I nod, taking in a deep breath, ignoring my heart pounding so hard I fear it may rip through my chest.

"Silence him," he orders, snapping his fingers. A man walks down the row, shoving a cloth into my mouth to bite down on. I've watched it enough over the past three years to know what's coming.

Without warning, he shoves the hot iron onto my bare chest—a reminder that I will now live and die for them.

FIVE

TYSON

THE CHOSEN ONE

UNKNOWN: Cathedral 2 a.m.

I check my messages while sitting in my car. I received the text three hours ago while lying in bed. Now I'm back at the Cathedral. I was just here a week ago getting my brand, and it still hurts like a bitch.

Getting out, I walk up the stairs and push the two heavy doors open. Two Lords stand inside the dimly lit entrance. Both have their black cloaks on with white masks. I'm not supposed to know who they are. There are thousands of Lords all over the world, but you aren't given a list of who everyone is. Especially the founders. They're kept a secret.

The one on the left pushes open the next set of doors and pauses for me to enter. I step in and come to a stop. My eyes scan the large, open space. I've never been here when it wasn't full of Lords. Usually, they fill the pews, but right now, it's empty. It has a haunting feel to it. Cold and lifeless. It's not a place where you hang out. It's for business. They perform all their rituals and confessionals here.

Each Lord behind me grabs an arm, and they escort me down the aisle to the front of the room where the altar and the Lords' table sit. A staircase on either side leads to the second-story loft that overlooks the congregation below, where I was just days ago.

They take me over to the right set of stairs and dig their fingers into my upper arms, pushing me to the top. Then they shove me forward.

I catch my feet before I trip and look at the Lord who's dressed the exact same. I feel his gaze on me, as hot as the branding iron they used to bind me to them.

"Tyson Riley Crawford." He states my name, stepping forward.

"Yes, sir." I do the same.

He nods his head, the mask—white with black lines through it, making it appear cracked—moving up and down slowly, and then I'm grabbed from behind. One of the guys that brought me up the stairs kicks the back of my legs, knocking me to my knees. Then I'm shoved down face-first to the cold floor. My arms are brought behind my back, and I hear the cuffs before I feel them wrap around my wrists. Tightened to the point that I grind my teeth at the pinch of my skin.

My shirt is grabbed, and I'm dragged over to where the baptism pool is that faces the congregation down below. It's where they perform their vow ceremonies for their chosens.

I'm brought to a stop with my head hanging off the edge. The water is filled to the brim. My heavy breathing makes it splash up on my face. The smell of chlorine fills my nose.

Someone sits on my back, straddling my cuffed wrists, and my teeth clench.

"You do what they say," my father told me. *"You were born to serve. No matter what they ask of you, you do it."*

"You've got promise, Son," he goes on, now standing behind me.

My heart races while looking over the pool. Three stairs are on either side for entrance and exit. I look down at the glass front that shows the congregation down below what's in the water. It's so they can see their fellow Lords get pussy. So they can see us being rewarded for our devotion.

"Then why do I feel like you called me here to kill me?" I grind out, struggling, but the guy on top of me has me pinned down into the uncomfortable floor, making it hard to breathe with his heavy weight. The fresh brand on my chest burns from the pull of my skin and the pressure.

"Only those who disobey their oath are terminated. Do you intend on doing that?"

"Not today," I joke.

The silence that follows proves they don't find it funny.

"Tell me, Son, have you picked your chosen?"

Why the fuck would that matter? A chosen is a daughter of a Lord. It doesn't matter if you're female or male because we're all born to serve. But a chosen has to be gifted to a Lord. The Lords believe we should be rewarded our senior year at Barrington University for our devotion and hard work, so we are given a list of women. We are to choose which one we want. A Lord can take on as many as he desires and can share her with whoever he wants, but she is devoted to her Lord and cannot step outside of who he shares her with. "No."

"That's good to hear."

I let out a sigh, watching the water ripple from my breath. If I stick my tongue out, I could drink it as if I'm a cat and the pool is my water bowl.

"We have a chosen for you."

"So you're going to tell me who I can fuck?" I snort, the water splashing my face some more. *Why not?* They dictate every other aspect of our lives.

"Well..." He pauses. "She has a sister. You can have them both if you like?"

Isn't that kind of them. When I realize he won't offer any additional information, I ask, "Who is it?"

"Whitney..." Another pause. "Whitney Minson."

Fuck! My teeth grind. "Her father will never allow it."

"If she chooses you as her Lord, then his opinion will not matter."

"And Whitney? How the fuck am I supposed to make that happen?" I know her. She goes to Barrington. Am I close with her? No. Not to mention, her father hates my guts.

"Tell her she's pretty. Tell her you love her." They all laugh at that. "If that doesn't convince her, then force her."

"You can't force a chosen," I snap, fighting the guy sitting on my back. "That's why it's called a chosen. She chooses her Lord."

He drops to the floor next to me, gripping the back of my neck, his lips by my ear. "Drug her, rip her fucking clothes off, and take her. Do whatever you have to do to make her your bitch. Do you understand me?"

"Why her?" I demand through gritted teeth.

"The question is, can you do it? Yes or no?"

"I—"

He shoves my head down into the water, and I fight, screaming into it, sucking some up through my nose, making it burn. Gripping my hair, he yanks my head up, and I gasp through a cough.

"Yes or no?"

"Yes," I grind out. "I can do it."

"That's a good Lord." He taps the side of my wet face, and I pull away the best I can.

I'm yanked to a sitting position, and I take in a deep breath now that the weight is finally off my back. Water drips from my head and hair onto my clothes, and I look up at the man dressed in

24

his cloak and mask. No founders ever reveal themselves. Their lives would be in danger.

"You will be protected," he assures me.

Why the fuck would I need protection to fuck a chosen? "And the girl?"

"What about her?" he asks.

"Will she be protected?" I demand, getting my breathing under control.

"Depends."

"On what?"

"How useful she is."

I hang my head, my wrists pulling on the cuffs. I'll make sure of it.

He drops a folder in front of me, and it slaps on the floor, echoing through the high ceilings and framed arches. "Do your homework, Tyson. You've got three weeks before you're back in this very spot getting wet."

I got WHITNEY MINSON.

It wasn't all that hard, really. I watched her, followed her. Made her see me. Want me. Crave me. I made sure to put myself in every aspect of her life for the past three weeks.

For three years, I've had to get myself off. Now she'll be the one doing it. This very reason is why they make us abstain from sex until our senior year. They want to reward you for your loyalty. What's more rewarding than saying *here, take this girl and fucking use her however you want?*

Three weeks ago, I was up here on the second floor of the Cathedral with my hands cuffed and head shoved into the water. But this time, I'm standing in it. It comes up to her chest, and I watch her nipples harden behind her white dress. I push her hair back, my fingers lingering a little longer than I should, just taking in the way her breathing picks up. I love the smell of fear.

"I vow." Her voice trembles as much as her body does against mine.

Her arms are tied behind her back with a zip tie so she can't fight me when I push her under the water. "You vow," I announce.

"We vow," we both say at the same time.

I grip the back of her dark hair so tightly she gasps, making her lips part, and I shove her down into the water—it's to cleanse her from past sexual partners. A chosen should be as clean as her Lord.

She's gasping for breath and coughing when I pull her up. I grip the hem of her dress and yank it up all the way to expose her body to the Lords below. She's not wearing a bra or underwear. I prepared her beforehand. Told her what we must do in order to be together. For me to make her mine.

Grabbing her waist, I spin her around so the front of her body is against the glass that faces the Lords below. Wrapping one arm around her waist, I pull her hips back and use my free hand to grab my cock. I push into her pussy and start to fuck her in front of everyone, knowing that I'll get to do this all year. Of course, I have ulterior motives as to why I'm here with her today, but only I know that.

Her soft cries and heavy breathing fill the large building. I slap my hand over her mouth, silencing her. Right now is all about me. She's mine to fuck. A chosen one is a slave to her Lord, like the Lord is a servant to his society.

My teeth grind, my breath hitching, remembering how fucking good pussy feels. It's like I'm getting it for the first time again.

My least favorite place to fuck is in water, but when you've been deprived of something that brings so much pleasure, it's earth shattering.

I feel my balls tighten, and I can't help but come. Not able to hold out, I don't care if she got off.

The vow ceremony is to show ownership over our chosen. Not please her.

Pulling out, I remove my hand from her mouth and yank her from the water. We're both dripping wet. I leave her dress pulled up, exposing her body to my fellow Lords as I walk her down the staircase where we go to sit in the front pew. "Eyes on the floor," I order in her ear, and she drops her head like the good slut she is.

We'll wait until every last senior has completed the vow ceremony for their chosen. I'll take her home and use her all night long. However I want.

Come tomorrow morning, I'll tie her facedown, naked, with a gag in her mouth and a blindfold over her eyes and leave her there while I go to my classes and pretend they matter. All while livestreaming it to my phone from all the cameras I have set up in my room, just like I was instructed to do.

Make it public.

Use her, fuck her, claim her. She is mine to use as I see fit. Typical chosen, really. Most Lords treat their chosens like slaves. But it's what I'm supposed to do when I'm not with her that's so important.

It's a distraction. Watch me do this while I'm really doing something else.

SIX

TYSON

THREE YEARS LATER

My father always says life is made up of choices; depending on which one you pick will determine what you get out of life.

M y hands curl around the metal railing, looking down over the four-story nightclub. Blackout is a consequence due to one of my life choices.

I was supposed to be a powerful Lord, wear a three-piece suit every day, run a multibillion-dollar company, marry the Lady my parents wanted through an arranged marriage, have kids and a dog. All of that bullshit we're forced to do to appear "normal" to the public eye.

It's all a fucking lie. In my world, you can't believe a damn word you're told or anything you see. It boils down to this: you'll live until you die. It's that simple.

The lights flash, and the music vibrates the breezeway I stand on. It's a Friday night, after midnight, and the place is packed. I've run Blackout for three years now. The Lords gave it to me when I saw an opportunity and chose a different path than what I was meant for. They're always willing to give you something in return for your servitude. So I allowed them to chain me to this club for the wife of my choosing.

She hates me. Too bad I don't give a fuck.

How many marriages do you know where the husband and wife love one another. Not many in my world. It does happen, but it's rare.

Pushing off the railing, I walk down to the doorway and enter my office, closing out the sound of the bass and the flashing lights. I walk over to my desk and sit down, leaning back in my chair.

I pull out the picture of my soon-to-be wife in my top desk drawer. She stands there with a smile on her face, her brown hair up in a messy bun, and bright blue eyes. This was before her life went to shit. Before my life took a change and I decided to take her *choices* away from her.

From here on out, I will decide her fate and how her story goes. It's for the best. However, she'll never see it that way. To her, I'll be the enemy, but I'm okay with that. Sometimes the villain is the only one who wins because no one else is ruthless enough to fight him.

A knock sounds on my door, and I put the picture back. "Come in," I call out.

Colton, Jenks, Finn, and Alex enter. "What's up, boss?" Finn asks.

"I'm about to leave," I tell them. "I'll be gone for the rest of the night."

One thing about Blackout is I get to run this place how I want. Which means I answer to no one. As a Lord, you serve them for the rest of your life once you get your brand. You will be called to do assignments until one of them eventually kills you. But not me. Blackout guarantees that I do whatever the fuck I want.

That's why I decided to hire an army of my own. Colton,

Jenks, Alex, and Finn aren't Lords. But they're as close as they'll ever get to being one. I even gave them their own brand. They work for me until I release them. And that will be the day I die.

"What do you need us to do?" Colton asks, crossing his arms over his chest.

"Keep the place from burning down," I say seriously, but they laugh like I'm joking.

The sound of my cell ringing has them all turning and exiting my office to give me some privacy. I look down to see **Ryat** light up my screen. He's a senior this year at Barrington and one of my best friends. He was a freshman during my senior year there. "Hey?" I answer.

"I'm on my way," he announces in greeting.

"Okay. I'll be ready."

Exiting my office, I lock it up and go down to the first floor. Making my way down the back hallway, I enter the basement, grabbing a bag from a shelf and filling it with the things we'll need.

The naked guy chained to the wall mumbles nonsense through his gag, but I ignore him. I'll take care of him later. Not like he's in a hurry to die.

Zipping up the bag, I throw it over my shoulder and lock up the basement as well. As I run up the stairs, the floor vibrates from the music coming deeper within the club.

Shoving the back door open, I walk out into the pouring rain to see a black SUV parked nearby. I open the passenger door and hop in, tossing the bag into the back seat.

Ryat looks over at me, his green eyes then sliding to the bag. "Ready?"

I nod, shutting the door. "Yep." I've waited for this day for too long. The Lords didn't make me the Lord of the underworld for nothing. They knew I'd do their bidding as long as I got my chance at revenge. They're handing it to me on a silver platter, and I'm going to make him choke on it while my wife is on her knees swallowing my dick.

LAIKYN

YOUR WEDDING DAY IS SUPPOSED TO BE ONE OF THE MOST exciting days of your life. Just like my mother, I'm about to marry a man I didn't choose and who I don't love. I actually despise him and everything he represents—money, greed, and power are just a few of them.

My mother hates my father, but there was nothing either one of them could do. Their fate was decided, their destiny sealed. Same as mine. Same as my children's. And my grandchildren's. We are bred for the sole purpose of power. Control in numbers.

Fuck that!

Women in my world—the secret society of the Lords—should not reproduce. I don't want children. The cycle will end with me. It has to. The Lords will only find a way to use its members. They marry us off to ensure we add to their army. The next generation of Lords and Ladies will help them take over the world.

I stand in the middle of the room, overlooking the white dress in the mirrored wall, running my hand down the mulberry silk—some of the finest silk available in the world. I take in a deep breath. It cost a whopping two million. Two million dollars for a fucking dress? My soon-to-be husband had it custom-made by a designer in France. I know this because my mother reminds me every chance she gets.

Why would I get to pick out something so important in my life? That's insane, right? To think I should have any say in what I wear on the day I give my life to another.

It's as if she thinks his wealth will impress me. It's blood money. I know this because it's the same fortune I grew up with. I never did want the finer things in life. I know a poor person would roll their eyes at that statement, but it's true. Give me a beer, a cheap hoodie, and a hat to hide my three-day old mop of bleach-blond hair, and I'm happy.

But no. That's unacceptable. The one percent aren't allowed to look anything less than perfect. Not in public anyway. I'm surprised they even let us speak. We as women might as well walk around with duct tape over our mouths dressed in nothing but chains.

A Lord needs a Lady but not because of the reasons you may think. It's a way to hide who he really is. He'll have fucks all over the world, but we're expected to cook, clean, and spread our legs for him when he's home. Worship him like he's God himself and birth his children.

I've never been religious, and I'm not going to fall to my knees and start worshipping a man now.

My brother comes up behind me, his eyes scanning over my dress in the mirror. "At least he has good taste."

I roll my eyes. "As if that matters."

"Just pop out some kids and get fat." He shrugs. "Then he'll screw anyone but you. Oh! Hire a hot, much younger nanny." He nods to himself. "Let me try her out first, though. Make sure she's good enough."

His words just prove that all Lords are the same. He's been a Lord for years but has yet to marry. He has the privilege of fucking his way around the world while I'm forced to sign my life away.

A cell rings, and he pulls it out of his tuxedo jacket to answer. "Hello?"

Sighing, I pick up the dress and walk over to the stained glass window. You can't see shit out of it. This place is ancient. The Cathedral is to a Lord as a church is to a religion—their sanctum. It holds a hundred years of secrets like a sarcophagus encloses a mummy.

It was handed down to them years ago—a place to perform their sick and twisted rituals. There's nothing fancy or special about it, if you ask me. I could be walking down the aisle in blue jeans and a T-shirt or lingerie. Doesn't matter.

Not all Lords and Ladies are required to wed here. But it's where my future husband picked. Our parents wanted it to be as traditional as possible. It's a bullshit reason. They just want to make a spectacle of handing me over to him. We might as well be standing in a courtroom with a judge sentencing me to life in prison without the chance of parole for a crime I didn't commit.

I place my hand on the cold glass, listening to the rain fall. It's been storming for the past two days. It's like the world knows I've been destined for a lifetime of servitude to a man I'd rather kill than kneel and suck his dick.

I blame my mother. She raised me to be strong-willed and determined. But now, I'm just supposed to turn it off and believe that I'm to devote my life to a man that will neglect me during the day but demand I spread my legs at night.

I won't accept that. I deserve more. I want more.

My brother ends his call, getting my attention, and looks at me. "We have a problem," he states.

My whole life is a fucking problem. "What?"

"Luke is missing."

I snort. "Don't toy with me like that." That's not a problem; that's a prayer answered.

"I'm serious." He swallows, looking around the large room nervously as if Luke's going to appear out of thin air. "He's not here. He never arrived. He's also not at his house. He's missing. No one has seen him."

"I'm not sure why that's a problem." I don't want to marry the sick bastard. Luke Cabot is the highest-ranking Lord you can come by, which just makes this even worse. Lords are like anything else in this world. You have some at the bottom, and others at the top.

34

There are different tiers. But honestly, it doesn't matter; they're all sick fucking bastards who will kill anyone to get to where they are. Even the bottom feeders will destroy anything to get a chance at serving.

He steps over to me. "Laikyn ..."

The door opens, and my father enters with my mother. I cross my arms over my chest. "I'm guessing this good fortune has nothing to do with you two?"

My mother's injected lips seem to thin a tad at my comment. She's told me a million times that this is just the life we live. That it's a "tradition" and I just have to accept it. That as far as Lord and Lady goes, we're royalty. Bull-fucking-shit. I'd rather be someone's bitch than a Lord's Lady.

My father, however, stares at the floor while running a hand through his dark hair. "Daddy?" I step over to him, holding my dress in my hands so I don't step on the hem. "What's going on?"

His throat works, swallowing before his eyes find mine. There's a look of regret in them, and hope fills my chest. Maybe he's realized that I don't want this life.

He clears his throat. "I just received a call ..."

"Please tell me you did this—called off my wedding?" I rush out, my words hopeful.

"I'm sorry, Laikyn, but the wedding is still on." He sighs.

And what little hope I had is now smothered. "But Miller said Luke's missing." I point at my brother. Had my father received the same phone call that my brother did? Or was it someone else?

"You are no longer to wed Luke." He yanks on the collar of his tux.

Picking up the dress so I don't trip over it in my six-inch hooker heels—that my soon-to-be husband also picked out—I take a step back, my heart picking up speed. This is good news. Why does he look so concerned? "I don't understand. If he's not here—"

"A new Lord has chosen you," he interrupts me.

My mother places her hand over her mouth, trying to quiet a sob.

"No," I argue. "That can't be." It was decided that Luke would be my husband when I was eighteen—three years ago. Things like this aren't just changed at the last minute. I've lived the past few years preparing for this day. To be his wife. What he wanted. A Lord can't choose to marry me, not when I'm already promised to another.

"Who?" my brother demands. "Who in the hell would make this change?" He fists his hands at his sides.

I reach up and grab the pearls my mother gave me. She thought they would give me some kind of comfort, and I laughed, but now I hold on to them as if they're an anchor to a lifeline.

"I—" The door swings open once again, this time hitting the interior wall and making me jump.

A set of baby-blue eyes meet mine, and my stomach drops. The wind knocked out of me. I haven't seen them in years, but they've haunted my dreams ever since.

Three years ago

*"W*HERE IS SHE?" MY MOTHER DEMANDS, ENTERING THE *hospital. She received a phone call that my sister was brought in tonight, but no other information was given.*

"Ma'am—"

"Where is my daughter?" she screams at the nurse, pounding on the check-in desk.

I turn around to see my sister's boyfriend walking toward us. His white T-shirt and jeans are covered in blood, and my chest tightens to the point it restricts my air.

My mom's legs give out when she sees him. "N-o," she chokes, placing her shaking hand over her mouth.

Tyson catches her and holds her body to his, but his baby-blue eyes meet mine, sending a chill down my spine so cold, it's paralyzing. "I'm so sorry," he whispers. "She's gone."

"Tyson," my brother growls, shoving me to the side and pulling me out of that memory, and steps in front of me. "What are you...?"

Ryat, Tyson's best friend, slams the door shut just as hard as he opened it.

I take a step back, tripping over the dress, but thankfully, the stained glass stops me from falling to my ass.

"How?" my father demands, turning to face him.

Tyson just gives him an evil smile that reminds me of how fucked up he really is. "Leave us," he orders.

Just the sound of his voice makes my legs want to buckle, but I manage to stay standing.

"I will not!" My father sidesteps to block their view of me.

Tyson takes the steps to close the small space between them and leans in, whispering in my father's ear. His cold, baby-blue eyes are on mine, and even if he were screaming at my father, I wouldn't be able to hear him over the pounding in my chest and the blood rushing in my ears. Sweat instantly beads across my forehead, and I'm having trouble catching my breath at the sight of him. Suddenly, the extravagant dress is too tight. The expensive material an anchor, pulling me down into a bottomless sea.

My father grabs my mother's hand and pulls her from the room, leaving me. My brother goes to step out, but Ryat grabs his tuxedo jacket, yanking him back into the room. "You may stay," Ryat tells him.

"Get the fuck out!" my brother yells at them. "Or I'll call security."

"Go ahead." Tyson shrugs. "I replaced your guards with my own."

I raise my sweaty hands. "What ... what are you doing here?" Luke would never invite them to our wedding. He hates Tyson. I'm not sure how he feels about Ryat, though. But I can almost guarantee he's not a fan due to the fact that he's Tyson's best friend. It's that guilty by association thing.

"Ryat." Tyson snaps his fingers at his best friend, who reaches into his tux and pulls out a folded piece of paper. He slaps it to my brother's chest.

Letting out a huff, my brother opens it up and his eyes scan the paper, his body stiffening, and my breathing picks up. "What?" I ask nervously, my sweaty hand gripping the pearls around my neck.

"No," he growls, shaking his head quickly.

"What is it?" I step forward, and Tyson moves in front of me, his large frame towering over mine. I try to step away, but the glass is at my back again.

My brother's face pales, and he whispers, "You are to marry Tyson."

"Wh-at?" My legs threaten to buckle, my heart stopping altogether. "No. There must be—"

Tyson's hand wraps around my neck, and he pins me to the cold glass. My hands shoot up, my nails digging into the sleeve of his black tux. I try to kick him away, but he's standing on the skirt of the dress, restricting my movements.

"Laikyn!" My brother drops the paper and runs for me, but Ryat grabs his hair, yanking him back while kicking the back of his knees and forcing him to kneel. Reaching into his pocket, Ryat pulls out a pocketknife and flips it open. The sound of the click makes my breath catch before he holds it to my brother's throat.

"No!" I shout at Ryat, and my eyes find Tyson's blue ones. They're cold. I'm not even sure if the man feels anything. He's as bad as they come in the Lords. Most of the Lords are placed strategically out into the world to fit in while they take what they want. But not Tyson. No, he openly runs the underworld for them. "What do you want, you fucking bastard?" I demand. My body twists under his grip.

"Just you. Forever," he answers simply.

My teeth grind and I lift my chin. "You sick fuck! You really think I'll marry you?" He's the reason my sister is dead. All Lords are evil, but something about him has always been off. "Over my dead body."

A smile spreads across his face, telling me he expected this. He knows how I feel about him and that I'd never willingly give myself to him. I'd marry Luke a thousand times over before giving myself to Tyson. "Either your brother walks you down the aisle and gives you away to me, or Ryat slits his throat, and he hands you over to me himself with Miller's blood on them."

"Don't do it," my brother growls at me, and Ryat yanks his head back, forcing him to look up at the ceiling. Bringing the blade across his neck, he pushes the tip into my brother's skin as if he's about to slice it open.

"Don't," I cry out, knowing that he'll kill him right here in front of me. I don't know Ryat personally, but I know enough to know that he's not the joking kind. He's here for Tyson and will do whatever he tells him just to prove a point. I wasn't able to save my sister, but I'll do anything to save my brother. "I'll ... do it." My chest tightens on the words, making it hard to get them out. I just signed my death warrant. But I will not lie down and give him the satisfaction of accepting it. He may run the Lords' hell, but I will make sure I burn it down with me.

"That's a good girl," Tyson praises, running his free hand down the side of my face. He gently caresses me as if he thinks it'll give me some sort of security. It's all a fucking lie. I know how the Lords work. I've seen my father manipulate my mother over the years. But she allowed it. I, however, won't. "Ryat, let our guests know we'll be ready in ten minutes." He steps away, releasing me, and I rub my sore neck where the pearls were digging into my sensitive skin.

Ryat exits the room, dragging my brother with him and leaving me alone with the monster who ruined my life.

SEVEN

TYSON

I forgot what actual power felt like. It's been a long time since I've used it for my own benefit. I hide in Blackout like a bat to a cave. I prefer the neon lights and pounding music to fresh air and sunlight.

But this? This is refreshing. Although I didn't think it would be all that hard.

I walk over to the bag that Ryat dropped when we entered. Watching her rub her neck, I see her eyes dart to the stained glass window and then the door. She wants to run. To get as far away from me as possible. "This is going to happen," I say, unzipping the bag and pulling out what I need her to see. "And just in case you think you have an exit in mind, let this be a reminder." I drop the stuff to the floor, and her eyes widen when she sees what I have.

"Ty—"

I step back into her, making her inhale sharply. "You've got two choices here, Lake." Her pretty tear-filled blue eyes search mine. "You either willingly walk down that aisle to me, or you crawl on your hands and knees with a collar around your neck while I drag you by a leash."

Her bottom lip trembles at my words as reality starts to set in. "Please," she begs softly, her bare shoulders shaking.

"Ah, begging me already?" It's like fucking music to my ears. If only her father was in here to witness it. I knew it wouldn't take much. She's not as strong as them, but that's not her fault. She's a product of her parents. Laikyn has no clue she's been conditioned to be obedient. To beg for the simplest things in life.

Reaching up, I cup her face, and her lips part. I run my thumb over the nude-colored lipstick. "Don't underestimate my ability to humiliate you, darling. It will happen. But right now, I'm giving you the choice of it being another time in the privacy of *our* home, or in front of everyone you love."

A tear falls free of her black-painted bottom lashes. I catch it with my knuckles before it runs down her face, wiping it away. "Don't cry, Lake. You'll ruin your makeup. I'll do that later."

It's been three years since I've seen her, and she looks nothing like she used to. She once had dark hair, now it's bleach-blond. She has it pulled into a tight bun at the nape of her neck, showcasing her Barbie-doll face, pouty lips, and bright blue eyes. Her wedding gown is strapless and dips down between her breasts into what gives the illusion of a heart. My eyes drop to look, and I can tell she's had her tits done.

That's Luke's doing. The Lord knows what he likes, and he had time to transform his future wife into exactly that. She's been groomed to perfection just how he wants her. I wouldn't say I don't like it, but it's not what I would choose for her. Not like it matters. Laikyn Grace Minson is nothing more than a doll to be played with. A toy to be used and put on display for the world to see.

"I do have a gift for you," I tell her, stepping away, and I hear her take in a deep breath now that I've put some space between us.

Walking over to the bag, I pull out a rectangular black velvet box. Walking back toward her, I open it up and her eyes drop to it before slowly meeting mine. "Turn around," I order, ignoring the questioning look in her wide eyes.

Swallowing, she gives me her back. I have to help her with the train of her dress so she doesn't fall over it. I don't want her to hurt herself before she takes my name. Reaching up, I grab the pearls and yank, breaking the thin Tiffany necklace. The sound of them bouncing on the old wooden floor makes her inhale sharply.

Removing her gift from the box, I toss the box and reach around her slender neck, pulling the black velvet around it before fastening it at the back. It fits her perfectly, just like I knew it would.

My eyes meet her watery ones in the mirror, and I step into her back, smashing her dress in the process. Lowering my face next to hers, I ask, "What do you say, little darling?"

Her shaking hand comes up, and her fingers run along the thin material.

"It's one of a kind. Had it made just for you," I go on at her silence. The outside looks dainty and feminine. It's black velvet with various sized diamonds. From the outside, it looks like any other choker. It's the inner leather lining that makes it so unique.

She sniffs and lowers her hand to her side, her eyes falling to the floor.

I lower my lips to her ear and whisper, "You can thank me later." And with that, I turn and exit the room, going to get ready.

LAIKYN

I CAN'T BREATHE, AND MY HEART POUNDS IN MY CHEST SO hard it's painful. I feel around for a chair, anything to grab, but I end up falling to my knees in the tight dress. I hear the sound of something ripping, but I no longer care if I ruin it. Not like Luke will, either.

The door opens, and my brother reenters. "Lake." He runs over to me and kneels. "Lake, are you okay?"

I shake my head, gasping for air. My hands go to the choker Tyson just put on me, and I tug at it. But my hands are shaking too much. They fall, slapping to the silk and gripping it, and I feel my brother's hands on the back of my neck.

"It won't come off," he growls, yanking on it. "Fuck, Lake." He pulls me back by my neck, choking me. "I don't know how—"

"Leave us." My father's voice interrupts us when he enters the room once again.

"Dad, you can't be fucking serious," Miller snaps. "Tyson?"

"I said get the fuck out," our father commands, pocketing his cell. "I won't say it again."

My brother huffs, and then the door shuts with his departure.

My father bends down in front of me and grabs my hands, pulling me up on my shaking legs, also not seeming to care if I ruin my dress by the way he yanks me to my feet. "Daddy, do something."

His eyes drop to the choker, and he swallows, his Adam's apple bobbing before he looks away from me. His eyes fall to the things that Tyson dumped out of the bag he brought. A thick black collar that has a silver ring on the front, a chained leash, and something else that I can't quite place. The threat he made was real. He will make me crawl on my hands and knees like a dog down the aisle and force me to be his wife.

"It's done, Laikyn." My father finally speaks.

"No." I shake my head, refusing to believe that. "I can't ..."

"The Lords have given him a choice. And he picked you."

A choice? Why would he want me? I yank my hands from his. "No. I won't do it." I storm over to the door, but he grabs my upper arm, pulling me to a stop. His fingers pinch my arm, making me cry out.

"I won't let you bring our family shame!" he yells, making my chest tighten.

"What does our family have to do with it?" I ask, but he doesn't respond. "Daddy—"

"The Lords have spoken, and that's final. You will walk down that aisle with your brother, and you will marry Tyson."

Why do I have to give myself to Tyson when my own father won't give me away? "Please"—a single tear runs down my face—"don't make me do this." My knees shake, and I shuffle from foot to foot, the heels hurting my feet.

"I will not take the fall for you having too much pride." He straightens his shoulders.

"Pride?" I gasp. How can he even think it has to do with that?

I stand paralyzed as I watch Tyson place my mother in a chair in the waiting area. She's sobbing, hands covering her face.

Walking over to me, he reaches out and wipes his knuckles along my cheek, and I realize I'm also crying. "H-How?" I choke out.

He doesn't answer. Instead, he tilts his head to the side as if I asked how my sister died in a foreign language.

"How?" I grind out.

"Lake—"

"Tell me how she died!" I shout, my fists hitting his bloody chest, making him flinch. "It was you, wasn't it?"

"I tried to ..." He stops himself from telling me the truth.

"You tried to what? Save her?"

"Lake—"

"You killed her!" I shove him, but he pulls my body into his, hugging me tightly. I smell her blood on his clothes, feel it soak into my own shirt, and I start to gag.

"Lake?" He pulls me away from him.

It's too late. I feel the bile start to rise, and my wide eyes meet his.

He grabs my arm and yanks me over to a trash can. Gripping the back of my neck, he shoves my face into it, and I vomit as he gathers my hair, holding it.

"Yes," my father snaps, bringing me back. "The last thing you need is to let your pride get in the way."

"This isn't about fucking pride." I fist my hands. "He killed Whitney—"

He slaps me across the face, cutting me off. "Do not mention her name!" he roars.

I cup my throbbing cheek, staring at the floor as fresh tears blur my vision. He's never hit me before, and I try to hold in a sob, but everything is falling apart so quickly. I just thought today was going to be a horrible day. It's gone from bad to worse faster than I could have ever imagined.

The door opens. "Lake?"

"I told you to get the fuck out, Miller," our father snaps, and the door slams shut, once again leaving me alone with him. "Now, where were we?"

EIGHT

TYSON

Three years ago

I stand tucked back behind the tree line, staring ahead at the family. I wasn't allowed to come, but I slipped the security guy watching the gate a few hundred-dollar bills, and he let me enter the cemetery.

Whitney's favorite color was pink, and they got her a white casket. She had a fear of burning to death, and they cremated her. Not sure why they chose to do a traditional funeral and bury her ashes in a twenty-thousand-dollar box, but I didn't have a say.

I feel someone come up next to me and I look over to see Ryat by my side, hands in his slacks and eyes on the service. "I thought I'd find you here," he says softly. He's a freshman at Barrington this year while I'm a senior. It's his first year of initiation, and he's become a close friend.

My eyes look ahead, and I watch the service come to an end. The family kept it small. Only immediate family were allowed to attend. Which, again, I find odd. Whitney was loved by many. She had a lot of friends at Barrington. Everyone who loved her should have been given the chance to say goodbye.

"You didn't have to come," I say.

"I know."

Her mother hasn't quit sobbing, and her sister, well, I'm surprised she's even able to walk. Her older brother is holding her up. Their father hasn't shed a tear. His children mean nothing to him. They are something to be used. A way to grow his own wealth and power.

I'll make sure he remembers who I am.

"Are you sure this is what you want?" Ryat asks softly, knowing what I'm going to do.

"It's done," I answer. I've made up my mind, and I'm not going to change it.

Her father helps her mother over to the black limo, and I watch it drive off. My eyes go back to the burial site, and I see Laikyn now on her knees in her black dress. I can hear her cries over the howling wind in the trees. Miller rubs her back, trying to help her up, but he, too, decides to kneel next to her.

If I had a heart, I'd say it feels for them. But I don't. I was raised to believe I live for the Lords. But they've failed me, making me even colder than they already taught me to be.

My cell vibrates, and I pull it out of my pocket to see it's my father. "Hello?" I answer, turning my back to them and walking toward my car.

"What in the fuck have you done?" he demands.

Guess he got word of my career change. "What I needed to do," I answer simply.

"Tyson," he growls my name. "You have a responsibility to this family. You cannot give it up for fucking pussy." His voice rises to the point he's screaming at me.

"I don't expect you to understand." He doesn't love my mother. The Lords have always come first to him. His side pieces a close *second. He thinks I fell in love with Whitney, and it made me weak. He has no clue what I did and didn't do or how I feel.*

Letting out an aggravated sigh, he lowers his voice. "What happened to Whitney was unfortunate, Son. But you don't need to give up your life as well." He pauses. "It won't bring her back."

A sob gets my attention, and I turn around to see Miller stand, picking up Laikyn and carrying her off to their Town Car. She clings to him, her cries growing louder the farther he walks away from the casket. "I don't ... want to leave her," Laikyn sobs.

"She's gone, Lake," he tells her, placing her in the car. Her sobs are no longer heard once he shuts the car door.

"I've made up my mind," I say to my father, watching them drive off.

"Ty—"

I hang up on him and shut off my cell, not in the mood to hear his opinion about how I should live my life. That's all I've ever done. I was raised knowing I would one day serve the Lords. I've devoted the past four years to them. That has changed.

While attending Barrington University, you can be stripped of your title at any time while going through initiations. But once you're branded, the only way out is death.

I was raised to believe that being a Lord is something special— nothing but endless wealth and power. Now I realize they are their own kind of prison, collecting us as prisoners. They chain us to them with no escape.

I took their offer and made one of my own that they couldn't refuse. It's a different level of hell, but I have all the control. I'm the devil now and will choose who burns.

LAIKYN

I'M LOOKING AT MYSELF IN THE MIRROR AFTER MY FATHER leaves me, making sure tears haven't ruined my makeup. I don't understand. Why me? Why now? Why today?

I was promised to Luke. What could have changed that he would give me over to Tyson? Why would the Lords allow this?

Stepping closer to the mirror, I tilt my head back and look at the choker he placed around my neck. It's so tight that I can't even fit my finger between it and my skin. I can feel my pulse throbbing against it.

I'm powerless. As a Lady, I don't have any say, to begin with, but for the Lords to make such a change at the last minute? I'm fucking doomed. It's like a plane falling from the sky. Nothing can be done. I have no parachute. No escape plan.

If I run, they'll find me. If, for some reason, they don't, my family will pay the price. I refuse to let anyone else die because of Tyson. He's taken enough from our family already.

The door opens, and my brother steps into the room. "I'm sorry, sis. I don't know what's going on. Dad said—"

"It's fine." I straighten my shoulders. I will not cry in front of these elitist assholes. I won't give Tyson the satisfaction of letting the world see how much he terrifies me. I'll wait until I'm alone.

He runs a hand through his dark hair nervously. "Lake."

"I'm ready," I say, turning to face him. The longer I wait, the longer Tyson has to get angry. After I say my vows, he'll get me to himself. And I don't want to give him any more reasons to beat me.

Miller's mouth is set in a hard line as his eyes drop to the choker and then to the floor to look at the scattered pearls. It was the only object to remind me of who I was. Tyson's already making me what he wants me to be—his slave. A piece of meat to fuck and torment.

"Let's go." I grab the silk fabric in my hands, lifting it off the floor as my brother gathers the long train, and walk out of the room with him following behind me. We're on the second floor of the

50

Cathedral. I walk over to the old railing that looks like if I pushed too hard, I'd fall to my death, which, right now, doesn't sound so bad. My luck, I'd just break a leg or something.

The high stained glass windows remind me of a birdcage. Just another way for the Lords to trap you. Across the way, on the second-story loft, is where the vow ceremonies are performed for chosen ones. I was never allowed to be one. My sister was. She was Tyson's chosen. After she was killed, my parents set up my marriage to Luke. I was to be an offering to a Lord. The last Minson female in my family to bring honor to our name.

It's all bullshit.

It's sex trafficking at its finest without money being trans-ferred. Well, not physical money, but funds are still involved in a way. Families are forged, companies combined, and the Lords involved just get richer. More powerful.

Wrapping my hands around the balcony, I look down to the first floor. Rows and rows of pews are full of Lords. All dressed in their black cloaks with their hoods up and masks on. Only my parents, my brother, and the wedding party are allowed to show their faces today. Ladies aren't even invited. And I have no brides-maids. When you're kept prisoner in your own house, you aren't given the opportunity to make friends. Even if I had any, Luke would have had to approve them, and I know he wouldn't have. Tyson will likely be much the same.

The storm outside makes the place darker than it would normally be this time of day thanks to the gray clouds and rain falling from above us.

A white-carpeted runway runs the long length of the aisle. It signifies my innocence. White as a winter snow. The rest of the inside is lit up with red lights, giving the place a bloody feel. It's part of our marriage oath. I have to bleed for him. And he will bleed for me.

I might give my life over to him in front of all these people, but

I won't mean it. He has to know that, right? Because I know he sure as fuck won't. He doesn't love me. He doesn't even fucking know me. Not like he knew Whitney.

My eyes move to the front of the altar and see a set of baby-blue eyes already staring up at me. Even from this far away I can see him as clear as day. He stands there, his arms behind his back, legs wide and shoulders pulled back. A look of malicious intent covers his hard features.

My father gave me an ultimatum—marry Tyson or else. The *else* being far worse than becoming Tyson's wife, I'm sure.

"Lake?" Miller gets my attention from behind me.

I turn to look at him over my shoulder to see him holding my veil. It's tacky and over the top. I hate it. My mother ordered it. Said it would make me look the part. Of what? Not sure what she meant, and she never answered. I left it behind and stashed it in another room on purpose.

He reaches down, picks up my train, and moves it to the side to get closer to me. Sighing, I turn back, and my eyes find Tyson again before my brother places my veil on.

NINE

TYSON

I stand at the front of the Cathedral, my eyes dropping when she pushes away from the railing. I half expected her to jump to her death. But to my surprise, she glared at me as if she's ready to hand her life over to me.

My eyes drop to scan the rows and rows of pews filled with Lords. I can't see who is who through their masks and cloaks, but I can hear their gasps and hushed voices follow as they all stare at me, trying to figure out what the fuck is going on.

Ryat stands next to me with his arms crossed in front of him. He will be the only other Lord standing with me today. He hasn't even asked or questioned my motives. It doesn't even matter, really. He understands I'll do whatever needs to be done because he's the same way. He had his own reasons for doing what he needed to do when it came to Blakely. And I was there for him to help however I could.

The pastor I hired to replace the one that Luke had comes to stand next to me at the front of the altar and nods, letting me know he's ready.

"Wicked Game" by Lusaint begins to play throughout the high

ceilings and I smile at the song I chose for her to walk down the aisle to. Luke had something completely different. I thought this would be more fitting.

As the double doors open, the guests rise to their feet to welcome my wife. She and her brother stand side by side. Her long train fluffed to perfection behind her. The dress is form-fitting, showing off her large breasts and thin waist. It flares at the bottom, making it look like she's walking on a cloud. A veil covers her pretty face. If she didn't need to say her vows, I'd have made her open her mouth and filled it with a ball gag. Wouldn't that have been a sight? Her standing in front of her parents with drool running from her painted lips and onto her expensive dress. The thought alone makes me hard.

In time.

The song plays on a loop as they make their way up the long aisle. Miller comes to a stop as the pastor asks, "Who gives this woman away?"

Her brother's eyes glare at me. "I do, Father."

I chose him to give her away for a reason. I want to laugh but refrain. Instead, I hold out my left hand, and he slowly places hers in mine. When I yank a little too hard, she trips over her dress, but I keep her up.

Her brother takes his seat next to their parents. There's absolutely nothing they can do. The Lords have arranged marriages for multiple reasons, so the fact that I get to have her should terrify them. It proves just how far I'm willing to go to get what I want. I've been biding my time. I went three years without sex and then waited three more years for this moment. I've always prided myself on my patience.

I reach out and lift the veil, pushing it over the top of her head to see her bloodshot eyes meet mine. She drops them to the floor, and it shows me just how submissive she'll be. She'll crawl if I tell her to. Won't that be a sight? She's pretty in that fake 'I'm insecure' kind of way, so she bleaches her hair, whitens her teeth, and has big fake tits. Too bad Luke made her that way. The Laikyn Minson I remember had more self-respect than that. I'm going to test her every chance I get just to see how much it'll take for her to break.

It took three years for Luke to make her what he wanted. I'll do it in much less.

LAIKYN

HE HOLDS MY SHAKING HANDS IN HIS WHILE I TRY TO CALM my breathing. My watery eyes look at the floor, unable to meet his or anyone else's in the building. Shame washes over me like a tidal wave carrying me out to sea with nothing to grab. I'm going to die —a slow and painful death.

I blink, and tears run down my face when I see him slip a ring on my finger. He already wears his wedding band.

The Lords do everything their own way. They are each given a path and are allowed to do whatever the fuck they want with it. Not every wedding is performed this way. Take Ryat, for example. I know from talk that he and his wife didn't have a big wedding in front of fellow Lords.

We're only here because this is how Luke wanted us to exchange vows. Tyson just hijacked it.

The pastor steps to the side, allowing Tyson access to a long rectangular wooden table—the Lords' table. It has a black runner that hangs off each end with white rose petals covering the surface and tapered candles sitting in their own individual crystal bases. The building is so large that the flame gives no light to it. They hold no meaning other than decoration for the table.

Tyson releases my hands and they drop to my side while he reaches out to pick up the dagger that sits in front of the candles.

He pulls it from the old worn-out leather sheath with their crest engraved into it—a circle with three parallel lines through the middle—and lifts it to my chin, forcing me to look up at him. The cold sharp edge pressing into my flesh is enough to pinch but not enough to break the skin just yet.

My eyes meet his, and I hold my breath. He steps into me, the tip of the blade gently running along my jawline to the base of my ear. The metal is cold but smooth against my burning skin, making me break out in goose bumps.

"Recite your vows," the pastor announces, making my heart skip a beat.

"I ... vow," I say with a heavy tongue. My breathing is ragged, and my pulse races.

The tip of the blade punctures my skin, making me hiss in a breath before I feel the warm liquid rolling down my neck.

His baby-blue eyes watch it slowly trail down my chest and fall between my breasts.

Taking the dagger, he pokes the tip of his thumb and cups my jaw, gently running it along my shaking lips, smearing his blood on me. "You vow." His deep and assertive voice holds power. That thought makes me whimper.

"Together," the pastor adds.

"We vow," I whisper to myself, while his commands our audience.

Tyson steps into me, closing the small distance. His eyes stay on mine while he lowers his lips to my collarbone. A tear runs down my cheek when I feel his warm and wet tongue run up my neck, licking along the trail of blood. A shiver runs through me.

I feel his lips slowly running along my jawline as he speaks softly, "As blood is my oath, you will forever belong to me and I to you." He reaches my lips and captures mine with his.

I taste something metallic—our blood—when his tongue enters

my mouth and I swallow, knowing that if I don't, I'll vomit. I've already embarrassed myself enough.

I go to stop the kiss and pull away, but his hand flattens across the back of my head, holding me in place. The other slides around my waist, pinning my front to his hard body.

I try to fight him, but his lips pry mine open easily and he dominates my mouth, making my body react to him even though I don't want it to. My thighs tighten, and my heart races. My eyes fall closed, and he swallows what I can only think is a moan from me. I've been kissed before, but it was different. I actually liked that guy.

His fingers dig into my hair, and I feel him pulling the tight bun loose. Tilting my head, he deepens the kiss, and his tongue caresses mine in the softest way even though I know it's anything but. Heat runs up my back, and my body begins to tingle with electricity.

When he pulls away first, ending the kiss, I hate that I don't step back. That I willingly stay close to him. He gives my lips a gentle peck before he breathes into my ear so only I can hear. "Welcome to hell, little darling. You'll only be able to crawl as far as my chains will allow you."

I bite my tongue to keep from sobbing. My body is shaking, my heart racing, and my breathing is ragged. I can't think straight right now. He pulls back and licks his bloody lips while watching me silently cry.

"I now pronounce you Mr. and Mrs. Tyson Crawford," the pastor announces to the silent audience.

The words are like a door slamming shut, locking me in my cage.

TEN

TYSON

My wife stands before me in the very spot I signed my life away for her three years ago. Her watery eyes meet mine, and I smile at the blood smeared across her lips. I felt her body stiffen when I kissed her at first. The way she tried to fight me. But a part of her, the best part, melted into me. Her body is going to crave being mine. I'm going to parade her around as my own personal fucking trophy for all to see. For her father to be disgusted and ashamed.

The bell is rung, slicing through the silence of the Cathedral. She jumps at the loud intrusion, trying to take a step back, but I hold her in place.

My eyes drop to the blood trail that makes its way from her neck to her chest. She will bleed for me in more ways than one tonight.

"Tyson." My name is spoken softly on her trembling lips.

"Yes, little darling?" My eyes lift to meet hers.

"Go to hell," she whispers, referring to my last statement.

I smile at her. "It's going to be so much fun bringing you to your knees, Mrs. Crawford."

She swallows.

LAIKYN

HE GRABS MY HAND AND HELPS ME OFF THE ALTAR, AND immediately pulls me down the aisle covered in the white carpet. Everyone stands on either side to watch us go. My parents don't even try to catch up and speak to me. But what is there to say?

It's too late. I'm now married in the eyes of the Lords. The pastor didn't even ask those who opposed to speak now or forever hold their peace. Because he knew it wouldn't have mattered. Once a Lord chooses his Lady, there is no going back.

We make our way outside and rain instantly drenches me. I squeal, throwing my free arm over my head. He's already got a black limo parked right in front of the Cathedral, and he holds the back door open for me to jump in.

That's probably the most gentlemanly thing he'll ever do for me.

I get as far away from him as I can, which is hard, considering my dress is in the way. Finding a seat, I yank on my train just as he shoves it into the car and gets in. Placing my hands on the now ruined silk, I don't even bother looking out the window to see if my family came out to see us off.

It doesn't matter.

There was a big and elaborate wedding reception planned that was also supposed to take place at the Cathedral but I'm guessing that's no longer needed. He proved his point and made me his wife.

We sit in silence as the driver takes the curvy two-lane road while the rain comes pouring down. He takes us downtown and my heart races when he pulls under the awning of the hotel, knowing why we're here. I was hoping that he'd skip this part. The valet opens the back door for us, and Tyson exits. It takes me a moment to get back by the door, and I mumble a thank you as a man at valet helps me out.

"Congratulations." The guy smiles when his eyes land on my wedding dress, and I feel my shoulders slump, unable to thank him this time. No matter how rude of me that is.

Tyson takes my hand and drags me up the black velvet stairs and through the glass door. I feel eyes on us, so I keep mine on the white marble floor with the black diamond inlay design.

My heels get caught in the dress, and I almost trip, but he yanks on my hand, keeping me up.

We make our way through the elaborate lobby of the luxury hotel and to the elevators. We have to wait for ours, and I try to calm my breathing. I've spent a lot of my childhood here at the Minson. My father owns it. He has over five hundred locations in the United States alone. People check in having no clue what kind of illegal activity goes down here. The Lords place their members throughout the world to benefit their society. They will take the worst kind of evil, dress it up in a ten-thousand-dollar suit and give them an expensive bottle of scotch and the ability to suck your soul out of your body without you knowing. I've seen my dad do it too many times. Poor bastards never see it coming.

Our elevator opens up, and we step into it. Tyson pulls out a card before scanning it. This is the only one that has access to the floor. H for honeymoon suite lights up and takes us over twenty-five floors up in silence.

I run my wet hands down my dress when the door slides open, and we step into the suite. On any other day, it would be gorgeous. Red and white rose petals litter the white and gray marble floor. A black circular table sits in the middle of the foyer. A glass vase sits on top with the most beautiful red roses I've ever seen, and a bottle of champagne along with two flutes sits on either side.

He walks past them, stepping down into the open living room. I slowly follow.

"Gavin will be here shortly." He finally speaks to me, making my pulse race.

I've heard that name before. I've seen him a couple of times when he came to visit my father. I'm pretty sure he's a doctor. That has to be wrong. "Who ... who is he?" That's my biggest fear. That he'll whore me out. Let others use me because I'm no use to him. Sell my body to make him some extra cash. This isn't a marriage out of love. So why would he treat me with respect?

"A doctor," he clips, removing his black tuxedo jacket from his broad shoulders while walking farther into the room. I take a look around, seeing more flowers all over. The overwhelming smell almost makes me gag.

I swallow nervously. Afraid I was right. "Why ... why do we need a doctor?"

He comes to a stop and turns to face me, his baby-blue eyes scrutinizing my smeared makeup from the downpour. I hate that I care what I look like right now. "Are you on birth control?"

My cheeks flush. Luke didn't want me on birth control. He wanted a baby straight away. An heir. A Lord is nothing if he doesn't have someone to carry on his name. I hadn't quite figured out how I was going to keep that from happening, but I wasn't going to have Luke's child. I answer Tyson. "No."

"Exactly." Turning his back to me, he goes over to the baby grand piano. A silver tray sits on top with a tinted decanter with an M in the middle. He removes the glass diamond top and pours the whiskey into one of the glasses that sits next to it. "The last thing I want to do is knock you up," he adds.

I want to be happy that he doesn't want to get me pregnant because I don't want kids either. But instead, it pisses me off because it's just one more way he'll control me. Why wouldn't he take away my ability to reproduce?

Taking in a deep breath, I remind myself it's something we agree on. But that thought also makes the hair stand on the back of my neck. *He's going to fuck me.* I knew this day would come. That it would be my wedding day when a man would take my virginity. I just never thought it'd be my sister's ex.

A part of the agreement of me being handed over to Luke was that I was a virgin. I know the Lords have to abstain from sex their first three years at Barrington. He wanted me to remain one until our wedding night. If I didn't bleed for him, then I would be considered a whore. My parents promised him my innocence, and I had to deliver. I know for a fact that Luke had been fucking women the past few years. I didn't care. I actually prayed to God, hoping that Luke would fall in love with one of them and forget about his arrangement with me. They were not answered. Instead, God laughed at me and sent me someone far worse than Luke.

"Here." Tyson offers me the second glass of whiskey, and I look from it to him, making no attempt to take the drink from his hand. "I didn't drug it," he growls.

"I don't believe you." I lift my chin. He could have very easily slipped something into it since we entered the room. It only takes a second to spike a drink. I know. I've seen it done before.

He rolls his eyes and throws the one he's offering me back, proving that it was, in fact, not laced with something. Setting both down on the tray, he walks over to me, closing the distance, and I stiffen. "Why would I drug you?"

I swallow nervously but answer honestly. "Makes me compliant. Easier to take advantage of."

Reaching up, he runs his hand through what's left of my bun, pulling bobby pins loose and letting them drop to the floor at our feet. The long, wet curls fall down across my bare back and over my shoulder, some falling in front to frame my face. "That would be too easy." He finally speaks, his knuckles brushing it off my shoulder. "I want you to feel me holding you down. I want you to

63

hear yourself gasping for breath when I force you to come. And I want your eyes on mine while I make you cry. I'll never drug you, Lake, because I don't need you *compliant*. You're now my wife, and I can take whatever I want from you."

My throat closes up while his eyes bore into mine. He's got it all figured out. I hadn't realized until just now that he's had this planned. I thought it was a last-minute thing. Like he just woke up this morning and decided he would crash my wedding and make me his wife. But I was wrong. He's had this plan for quite some time. The Cathedral, the hotel—he's rubbing it in my father's face. It wouldn't have been hard for him to figure out any of this information. It's been in the works for years. My parents and Luke making a big deal out of this day. "Tyson, please..."

"You'll do that too, little darling." His hand moves to cup my jaw and he lowers his lips to my forehead, brushing them against my skin. Words spoken as soft as the tender kiss and my pulse races at how calm he can be. How well he can hide what he really feels. He hates me and my family. I'm nothing more than an outlet for his revenge.

His cell rings, making me jump, and he pulls away to answer it. "Hello? Yes, send him up."

The elevator dings before the door opens, and he turns, giving me his back. I let my shoulders fall while trying to calm my breathing.

"Mr. Crawford. Good afternoon, sir," a man's voice says.

"Who the fuck are you?" Tyson growls.

"I'm Jackson," the man answers.

"Where the fuck is Gavin?" he snaps.

"He got caught up in surgery and asked me to fill in for him."

Tyson pauses a second before he speaks. "She's in here." They enter the open living room a few seconds later. Tyson is holding his cell to his ear, eyes on me. But after a few seconds, he hangs up.

"Hello, Mrs. Crawford." The kid gives me a big smile, and

my stomach sinks that that's what I'll be known as now until the day I die. So easily stripped of my maiden name that once meant something to me. Minson is known around the world—wealth and power are just a couple of things. Don't get me wrong, I've always hated that my father is a Lord and the life we have to live, but that doesn't mean I want to be a Crawford either. "This will only take me a second." He places a briefcase on top of the piano and pops it open, pulling out a couple of packages. He rips one open, revealing a syringe, and the other is a vial full of liquid.

"Whoa." I take a step back. "I thought—"

"You're getting on the shot," Tyson interrupts me, and I look over at him to see he's now standing at the island in the kitchen, making himself a new drink. "Too many women are irresponsible when it comes to taking the pill, and I refuse to wear a condom when I fuck my wife." He glares at me, daring me to argue.

My cheeks redden at the way he talks to me in front of this stranger in the room, but this is one fight I'll let him win.

The guy inserts the syringe into the vial and pulls back the plunger, filling it with the liquid. Once done, he looks at me. "Turn around and pull up your dress." His eyes drop down to the train, and he frowns. "Tyson might have to hold it for me."

I take several steps back away from him, my heels tripping over the silk material, and I fall onto the bench seat at the piano. "Excuse me?" I shriek, wide-eyed.

"Turn around—"

"You will administer it in her arm," Tyson snaps at the man, and I flinch when I hear him slam the glass down.

"Of course." The man nods, walking over to me. He opens the new alcohol pad before rubbing it on my arm. He lets it dry and then grabs the skin. "Small pinch," he says and sticks me.

I don't even feel it. Too many other things running through my mind right now. "How long will it take?" I ask, hoping he says days, maybe weeks. It could buy me some time to stay a virgin if Tyson refuses to wear protection.

"When was your last menstrual cycle?" the guy asks.

"Earlier this week," I answer softly, counting the days in my head. Luke planned our wedding around my cycle. I've always been like clockwork. I just recently got off it.

He smiles. "You should be good then. As long as it's five days out from when you started, it should work immediately."

Fuck my luck.

"But I also brought some morning after pills that you can take just to be on the safe side. Just remember, they aren't to be used as a form of birth control. Just last resort. You may experience some bleeding for the next couple of months but that's nothing to worry about. Make sure to schedule another shot within twelve to thirteen weeks for it to be the most effective." His eyes drop to my chest, and silence fills the large room.

My eyes shoot over to Tyson in panic. Am I payment? Will he let him fuck me now that I've received the shot? Is that another reason he's putting me on birth control? So other men can't get me pregnant when he allows them to fuck me? A Lord raising another Lord's child? Unheard of as far as I know. If it's not their bloodline, they don't want it. It's just another awful thing on a long list that disgusts me about these men.

Tyson was about to take another drink but sets it down. Not as hard as last time. "Is there a reason why you're staring at my wife's chest?" he demands.

I hate that my thighs tighten when he calls me *wife*. Like it actually means something. As if he will protect me. I could laugh at myself right now if I was alone. Tyson Crawford only cares about himself. History proves that.

"Oh no." The guy chuckles. "The blood." His eyes meet mine. "Do you need stitches?"

"She's fine," Tyson growls before I can say anything. "And your services are no longer needed."

"Just in case." He removes some Band-Aids from his briefcase and drops them on top of the piano. Like they're going to do me any fucking good.

Tyson walks him to the elevator, and then he returns. He stands with his hands in the pockets of his dress slacks. His crisp white button-up that once fit him like a glove is now wet, sticking to his skin and showing off his hard chest. My eyes drop to the way his abs flex as he breathes.

His sleeves are rolled up, showing off his tanned and muscular forearms. A Rolex watch that I know must have cost him over a hundred grand sits on his wrist. All Lords wear their crest on a ring while attending Barrington but take it off after graduation. They no longer need it. The brand on their chest is reminder enough of their devotion. My eyes drop to his wedding ring. It's simple—a silver band. I haven't gotten a good look at mine. But I feel it. It's bulky and heavy, weighing me down.

I used to think he was hot. I found him attractive when my sister dated him and was jealous of her. I was so stupid. An immature little girl who didn't understand how the world works. I hate that he looks better now than he ever did back then. How is something so stunning so evil?

He walks over to me, and with each step he gets closer, the louder my breathing gets. "Stand up and turn around," he orders.

Getting right to it.

I stand on shaky legs and turn around to face the piano. I feel him reach up and unzip my dress. My breathing is erratic, my heart hammering in my chest. The room sways as the soft material slides down my body and pools at my feet. Heat covers every inch of my skin. All of a sudden, it's too hot in here.

I tremble when he gently moves my hair to lay over my shoulder before his knuckles touch the top of my spine and slowly run down the curve of my back, making goose bumps rise all over. "Don't be nervous," he whispers, and I close my eyes tightly to keep from crying.

I'm trembling. My heels are shaking on the marble floor, and I can feel the sweat beading across my forehead.

I feel like I've turned my back on my sister. Even though I don't have a choice in the matter, she would still hate me for what's about to happen. She loved him. He just didn't love her in return. Not the way she deserved.

"Face me," he softly commands.

Taking in a shaky breath, I slowly turn to face him but keep my eyes closed.

"Look at me, Lake." His hand cups my cheek, and I open my watery eyes to meet his. His thumb brushes over my parted lips and I sniff. His eyes drop to my neck and then my chest, following the blood from when he cut me with the dagger at our wedding.

Blood is our oath. I had to bleed for him in front of his fucking cult. And I'll bleed for him now when he rips my innocence away.

His knuckles run down my sternum and outline the top of my white strapless bra. Reaching around me, he brushes his lips on my ear while I feel him undo it. The material falls to our feet seconds later, making me whimper.

When he pulls back, his baby-blue eyes darken while devouring my breasts. I hate that my nipples are hard. I've waited so long for this moment. To become a woman. I wished I could have done it a hundred times with him. Back before he took the one thing that meant everything to me.

"I'm going to take it easy on you," he speaks softly, "because it's your first time."

"Thank you," I whisper, hating that he's going to have so much power over me. That I'm going to have to thank him for every-thing. I will forever rely on him for food, shelter, fucking survival. Men like Tyson don't allow women to have their own careers or lives, for that matter. They are owned. A Lady doesn't need to know who she is. She belongs to her Lord, and serving him is all that matters in their lives.

His hand grips my chin and lifts my face, so I have to meet his cold stare. "It's still going to hurt, Lake."

My stomach ties in knots, but my pussy pulses. I don't understand it. Why is my body reacting to him when my mind knows it's not right.

"And afterward, I won't give you the courtesy of going easy," he adds. "Do you understand?"

"Y-yes." My voice wavers, and my feet shift in my heels.

He pulls away and gives me his back, ordering, "Go to the bedroom and lie on the bed."

ELEVEN

TYSON

I can hear her heavy breathing fill the room while doing as she's told. I wasn't lying when I told her I'd go easy this one time. Of course, my easy isn't soft, but it's better than what I have planned for her in the future. She will learn to love being whipped, chained, and gagged when I fuck her. The daughter of Frank Minson will crawl on her hands and knees while begging me to use her however I want.

Her parents hate me. They blame me for Whitney's death. I don't give a fuck what they think. They were the ones who failed both of their daughters. One is dead, and the other will be wishing that soon.

I stay in the living room, watching the heavy rain hit the floor-to-ceiling windows while undoing my button-up. Shrugging the wet material off my shoulders, I pour myself another drink and throw it back, making sure not to let it go to waste. It's Dalmore—a fifty-year-old whiskey, courtesy of her father. He had given Luke this room tonight. A sick way for him to make sure she bled when they consummated their marriage. I'll make sure to leave him a visual. Just in case the scene I put on at the Cathedral wasn't enough.

Her soft cries filter down from the hall, interrupting my thoughts. I won't let it get to me. She's a means to an end. My chance at revenge. It's nothing personal. I saw an opportunity and took it. If Lake knew what I was really doing, she'd thank me.

Finishing off the drink, I set it on the table. Toeing off my shoes, I undo my dress slacks and push them and my boxers down my legs before removing my socks.

I walk down the hallway and enter the only bedroom in this three-thousand-square-foot suite. I turn on the light. It's the middle of the day, but the storm outside makes the room darker than it would normally be at this time. The curtains are open on the far wall, which is nothing but floor-to-ceiling windows showing off the city.

Laikyn sits up in the bed, her back to the headboard. The rose petals that once covered the white duvet are now littered across the floor. Tears silently run down her face. Making my way over to the bed, I stand beside it, and her eyes meet mine through her watery lashes.

I reach out, my knuckles brushing her tears. "Lie down, little darling. Flat on your back. Let me see what's mine."

She sniffs, but slowly pushes off the headboard to lie down, her eyes on the ceiling. Mine run over her body. All she wears is white lace underwear that sit high on her narrow hips and a matching garter up on her thigh.

Her skin is flawless, no tattoos, no piercings, no scars. She was sheltered. After her sister died, her family put her on lockdown. Her parents aren't stupid. The fact that their father is a Lord should be reason enough to protect your children. Both her mother and father knew the possibility of either one of them being hurt. They just didn't give a fuck.

I reach out and place my hands on her legs, and they shake

while she takes in a deep breath. I slide my hands up her smooth thighs and grip her underwear before pulling them down her closed legs along with the garter and tossing them onto the floor. "Spread your legs," I order.

Her shaking hands come up to her face and covers herself from me. I should tie her down, restrain her to the bed so she can't hide. But even I understand that may be too much right now. I've got the rest of my life to degrade her, use her. Honestly, I'm not even in the mood to fuck her, but we're here to prove a point.

That she's mine.

I reach up and wrap my hand around her fragile neck, squeezing until her eyes pop open. Her hands grip my wrists, trying to free herself with no such luck. Her hips lift off the bed, trying to get any kind of leverage to get free. "I gave you an order, little darling. You don't want me to say it twice."

Her heels dig into the white duvet that she lies on as her trembling legs part. I release her neck and run my fingers down her heaving chest, over her flat stomach and look at her shaved pussy. For someone so innocent, she's been groomed for what her husband would like.

The bed dips at my weight as I sit between them. She sucks in a shaky breath as I hold them wide open with my knees. I run my thumb over her pussy, spreading her lips. She's not wet, but I didn't expect her to be. I lean over, and spit falls from my mouth onto her cunt. She makes a gagging sound.

Spit is the least of her worries. When I'm done with her, she'll kneel with an open mouth, begging for me to spit down her throat like it's on fire and only I can put it out.

I rub my fingers over it, pushing one into her.

She whimpers, her hands reaching out to the side and grabs the bed. Her face scrunching at the invasion. "Tyson," she gasps.

I am going to use her as my toy. She will crawl, cry, and beg me to fuck her. That's what the Lords taught me to do. To take and take. Sex is power, and she will be no different. I shove two fingers into her, and she whimpers. I pump them in and out before forcing a third into her, opening her wide, and she cries out. "Feel that, Lake?" I slowly pull them out before entering them again. "That's your pussy getting wet for me."

Her cries grow louder, and her back arches off the bed.

Pulling them out, I slap her cunt, making her scream. Her body twists, trying to free itself between my legs, but there's nowhere for her to go.

Shoving her legs farther apart with mine, I grab the base of my dick and run the head along her soaked cunt. I push into her, her back bowing off the bed while a scream is ripped from her lips.

Leaning over her body, I slap my hand over her mouth, silencing her, and pull back before pushing forward, my cock entering her more. Her hands grip my forearms, her sharp nails digging into my skin.

Her thighs tighten against mine, trying her hardest to close them, but I keep them spread wide open for me.

"That's it," I growl through gritted teeth, pulling back and pushing in again, more this time. Loving the feel of her tight pussy hugging my dick. "Take my cock, Lake. Let me use you."

She tries to shake her head free of my hand, but I keep a tight grip on it. Her eyes open and look up at me as tears fall down the side of her face. Her once-perfect makeup has been smeared from the rain and more so now from crying.

"Fuck." I pull out and then shove forward, and her neck arches. Sitting up, I remove my hand from her mouth.

"Tyson," she cries, her back arching off the bed, nipples hard.

I pull out, and her body relaxes into the mattress with relief, but I'm just getting started. I flip her over onto her stomach and grip her hips, pulling her ass in the air. Looking down at my bloody cock, it makes me smile.

It's not a lot, but it's enough for me to make it messy. I stroke my dick a few times, covering my hand with it. Sliding two fingers into her for good measure, I then push my cock back into her, loving the way her cunt grips me tight. Leaning over her back, I reach around and grip her chin with my blood-covered hand.

"Taste that?" I shove a finger between her open lips, and she starts gagging. Spit flies from her mouth in the process and covers the white velvet headboard. "That's your innocence, Lake, smeared all over my cock. Isn't it sweet?"

She continues to gag while I pump in and out of her. "I'm going to take everything you have to give." She sobs around my finger in her mouth. "And then some more. You will not know who you are or where you came from."

She chokes out a cry when I slam my hips forward, her fingers digging into the now bloody sheets.

"All you will know is me." I shove into her, the sound of our bodies slapping fill the room. "All you will need is me." Pulling out, I slam into her again and she screams. I remove my finger from her mouth and release her chin to slap my hand over her face, covering both her mouth and nose to silence her. "All you will have is me, little darling."

A groan escapes my lips at the feel of her cunt tightly wrapped around my cock. "You feel so good, Lake. So fucking tight," I tell her, listening to her mumbled cries. "You're doing so good for me." She tries to take in a breath, but my hand covers most of her tear-streaked face. "Taking my cock like the good whore I knew you'd be."

She shakes her head, trying to free her face from my hand. I smile, tightening my hold, and lift her head back at an odd angle. My hips thrust forward, slamming into her, loving the way her body shakes under mine. Her hands come up and try to pry mine off her face, but it does no good. "Fight me, Lake," I tell her. "Pretend you don't want me when we both know your pussy is soaking wet."

Her hands drop from mine as I feel her body starting to go soft, and I finally remove my hand from her face, allowing her to suck in a deep breath. I don't want her passing out. Not today.

Sitting up, I grip her hips with my hands, smearing more blood on her body. I want her covered in it along with this bed. I don't need her to bleed a lot. A little can go a long way when done right.

"I ... hate you." She sobs, her hands pushing against the headboard.

Smiling, I pause, my dick buried deep inside her cunt. "That's not going to keep you from coming on my cock."

LAIKYN

FIRE IS ALL I CAN THINK OF. I'M BURNING FROM THE inside out.

I've never experienced anything like this before. I was never allowed toys. The fear of touching myself made me sick to my stomach. If I made myself bleed, I'd be a disgrace to my family. Luke would have thought I wasn't a virgin. Now I wish I would have just done it myself so Tyson wouldn't have that satisfaction.

I cough and spit on the bed, not caring what he thinks of me, just wanting to get the blood out of my mouth. He holds me down, one hand in my hair, the other on my hip while his cock continues to tear me apart.

My hands grip the sheets, the headboard—anywhere I can get ahold of.

My face is covered in tears, drool, and my blood. I can't stop sobbing. I feel like twenty-one years were just ripped away from me, but my body is enjoying it.

His grip in my hair tightens and he adjusts my head, shoving my face into the blood-stained comforter. I try to push myself up but he's too strong. I can't breathe. The taste of blood fills my mouth once again and bile rises. I have to force it down, so I don't drown in my own vomit.

"Goddamn, Lake." I hear him groan, and my pussy tightens around his dick at the sound.

He lets go of my hair, and I lift my head, sucking in a sharp breath, my lungs burning. He pulls out of me, and I sag against the bed, trying to catch my breath. But he grabs my hips and throws me onto my back once again, forcing me to look up at him.

He spreads my legs wide with his, and my eyes drop to his dick. It stands straight up, long and hard. A barbell piercing through the bottom of the shaft. It's covered in blood and so is his lower abdomen.

"Please," I beg, placing my hands on his bare muscular chest. "It hurts."

He tilts his head to the side, his hand going to his dick, and he strokes it slowly. His eyes soften but quickly harden and it makes me wonder if I'm seeing shit. The lack of oxygen is making me delirious.

Reaching out, he grabs my hips and yanks me farther down the bed and pushes into me once again. I arch my neck and let out a scream as that burning sensation intensifies at his roughness. He wraps a hand around my neck and squeezes, digging the choker into my skin and cutting off my air.

Leaning over my body, he thrusts into me over and over. His eyes staring into mine, watching the tears run down the side of my face while he fucks me. "You're doing so good, Lake. So fucking good. Look how well your pussy is taking my cock."

My arms fall to my sides, and dots take over his features. I'm going to pass out. Or he's going to kill me. Either way, all I can do is take it.

But something else is happening. I feel a different kind of heat. That fire burning inside me starts crawling up my legs to my stomach. That is quickly replaced with a numbing and tingling sensation. Chills cover my entire body but I feel hot at the same time. *Is this what it feels like to die?*

"That's it, little darling." He lowers his mouth to my face and licks my innocence off my lips before growling. "Let it go. Be a good girl and come all over my bloody cock. Show me how much you like it."

I don't know what he's talking about. I can barely hear him over the blood rushing in my ears. Then everything goes bright like a burst of energy shoots through me. My body tenses, my back bows, and my eyes shut. Or I lose my sight completely. I'm not sure.

My body rocks back and forth a few more times before his dick pulses inside me. I'm gasping for breath when I look up and see he's hovering over me. One bloody hand cupping my face while the other is on the comforter by my head.

"You're okay," he tells me, and I don't understand why he would say that.

My hands slap at his chest, and he sits up, grabbing both wrists and holding them captive to stop me. "Breathe, Lake." His eyes are on mine. "Deep breaths."

I'm shaking uncontrollably. My body sweating and still tingling. I feel like I've been struck by lightning. "I—"

"Don't talk," he orders. "Just breathe."

He releases my wrists and pulls his cock from my pussy, making me flinch at how sore it is. Everything hurts. My hips, my throat, my jaw, my back. My fucking teeth are chattering, for Christ's sake.

Cupping my face, he wipes his fingers across my cheek, and I realize I'm still crying. "Sit up." He doesn't even allow me to do it. He grips my shoulders and pulls me to a sitting position.

Getting off the bed, he bends over and slides one arm under my shaking legs, the other around my back, and he lifts me up off the bed, carrying me to the bathroom. We enter the glass shower that takes up the large corner, and he sets me on the cold tiled bench seat before turning on the showerhead.

Adjusting the water, I sit silently staring at the floor. I had an orgasm. I've read about it but never experienced it before. I've heard that it's hard to get off your first time, but I didn't have a problem.

What does that say about me? Why did my body enjoy something so wrong? So painful? It betrayed me. My mind knew what we were doing was wrong, but that didn't matter. Sex is manipulation, and he just found out how much he can use that.

Warm water hits my chest, and I lean into it, my body freezing.

"Let's get you cleaned up."

I lift my head and look up at him. He's got his hand out to me. "Can you stand?" he asks.

Not really sure. I make it to my shaky legs and pray that I don't give him the satisfaction of falling to my knees.

TWELVE

TYSON

I take the sprayer and wash off what's left of her innocence. She bows her head, watching it go down the drain.

The poor thing had never orgasmed before. She didn't know what the fuck hit her. I can say I was surprised. I was sure she had fooled around with herself before and gotten off. A woman doesn't have to fuck a dick or dildo to come. Has she never touched herself before?

What twenty-one-year-old woman has never used a vibrator on her clit? Or rubbed one out with her fingers?

Her entire body is still feeling it. She stands before me shaking and still trying to catch her breath. Of course, that could be from me choking her as well.

"You've never gotten yourself off?" I break the silence.

She wraps her arms around herself and shakes her head, staring at the floor.

"Turn around," I order.

Happy to do so, she almost trips over her own feet. Before she can fall into the wall, I wrap an arm around her thin waist to hold her up. She whimpers in my grip.

I lean down, my lips next to her ear. "Spread your legs and place your hands on the wall in front of you."

She sucks in a shaky breath but does as she's told.

I smile. My wife is already being a greedy slut. Fuck, I couldn't have planned this better. Gripping her chin, I lift her neck so she has to arch her back while my other hand comes around her body, lowering the sprayer to her pussy.

She cries out, trying to get away from me, her hands gripping my forearm, but I tighten my hold, keeping her in place. "Hands on the wall, Lake," I command.

After a long second, she reaches out and flattens her hands on the white tile.

"Good girl," I tell her, and she sucks in a deep breath. "There are so many ways I can get you off, little darling," I inform her.

I know she's hurting, but I'm not going to show her any mercy. I'll work through her soreness. She fights my hold, but I don't let up. I keep the showerhead on her pussy. I can't see what I'm actually doing from this angle, but the way her breath hitches, I'd say I'm close enough.

She begins to moan, and I lower my lips to her neck and suck the blood and water off her skin while her hips start to rock back and forth. "That's it, Lake," I whisper, pulling away just enough to speak before biting down on it.

Letting go of her chin, I lower my hand between her legs and spread her pussy wide open. The new position allows me to feel where the water is hitting. I make a little adjustment, and she begins to pant once again. Her back pushes against my front, trying to step back, but my body is enough to keep her in place. "Come again for me. Show me how much you like getting off."

Her voice rings out in the shower as she does exactly that. I let go of her and she turns around just in time to fall down onto the bench.

"That's two," I say.

She lifts her eyes to meet mine, and they're shooting daggers at me. What makeup is left runs down her face. Pulling her lips back, she lets out an audible growl.

I bite back a smile. *This'll be easier than I ever thought.*

SHE'S SITTING ON THE END OF THE BED WITH A WHITE towel wrapped around herself. Her fingers have a death grip on it as if the material will keep me from having my way with her. It won't.

"Get dressed," I order, going over to the closet and grabbing her bag.

Luke already had a bag packed and delivered earlier this morning. I could have just taken her home, but I wanted her father to have a physical reminder that I fucked her after our wedding. The white comforter, sheets, and pillowcases are covered in her blood along with the headboard. I made sure to smear that shit everywhere.

It looks like a crime scene. They'll either have to burn the bed or replace it.

"Where are we going?" she asks softly, opening the bag.

"Home," I say, and she flinches.

"But the hotel room—"

"Was to prove a point," I interrupt her. "I proved it. We're done here." I never planned on staying here all night. I've got a business to run.

She grabs a pair of underwear, shorts, and a T-shirt. Standing, she walks back to the bathroom but comes to an abrupt stop. Her eyes meet mine and widen.

"What is it?" I ask.

"Nothing." She drops her head and hurries to the bathroom, but I jump in front of her. She whimpers, taking a step back.

"What. Is. It?" I demand, gripping her chin and forcing her to look up at me.

She licks her lips nervously. "I, uh ..." Her hand goes between her legs, and I let go of her chin to grab her wrist.

"You're not allowed to get yourself off." If she wants to know pleasure, she will have to beg me for it. "Drop the towel."

Placing her arms out wide, it falls to her feet. I reach down and run my fingers over her pussy, feeling the wetness not only there but also coating her inner thighs. Lifting them up in front of her, she pulls her face back. "This is my cum, Lake. It will leak from your cunt when I come inside you."

Her cheeks flush. I love how innocent she is. I'm going to teach her so many things. It'll be fun turning her into my whore. Sex will always be on her mind. Her first time might not have been that enjoyable, but it'll get better. Sex is like a drug. A high. She'll beg for it.

"Of course, there will be times that I force you to swallow it," I inform her.

Her lips part, her large, round eyes meeting mine.

"I'll also choose to come all over your face, tits, and inside of your ass."

"Tyson." My name shakes on her lips.

"I'm going to use your body as it was intended, Lake," I say truthfully.

Her lips thin. "Like you used my sister?" she demands.

I should be mad that she brought up Whitney so soon, but I'm not. I expected this from her. She blames me like the rest of her family. And I can't even be mad about that. I blame myself too.

Gripping her hair, I spin her around and shove her body over the side of the bed, spreading her legs with mine while pinning the side of her face, chest, and stomach to the blood-covered duvet.

I lean over her back and whisper into her ear, "If I remember correctly, you liked the way I used her."

"Fuck you!" she spits out, and I chuckle, a memory surfacing.

"Ty-son." Whitney breathes my name while lying on her back. Her head hangs off the edge of her bed.

"Open up, Whit." I groan, feeling like I'm about to explode already. It's been six weeks since our vow ceremony at the Cathedral, and I can't get enough of her. I wouldn't say it's her, but just the act of coming and not having to do it myself.

She parts her painted lips and sticks her tongue out. I slide my cock into it, my hand going to her throat to feel my dick push to the back of it. Fuck, it's amazing. Her mouth is hot and warm.

She tries to lift her hips but her legs are tied to the bed spread eagle, so she doesn't get far off the mattress.

I pull out, and spit flies from her mouth, covering her face, and I slap the side of it, making her moan before shoving back into her mouth. "Fucckkkk." I throw my head back while she swallows me whole. "I'm going to come if you don't stop doing that," I warn her. The woman knows how to suck dick. Guys talk, and I've heard rumors at Barrington about how good she is in bed. Chosens don't have to abstain from sex at any time, so I didn't expect her to be innocent. I knew she'd be a good fuck, and she did not disappoint.

I open my eyes, and they land on a set of blue ones that stare at me in the mirror hanging on the wall in front of me. Laikyn, Whitney's younger sister, stands at her sister's cracked bedroom door watching us.

She doesn't pull away and run. No, instead her eyes fall to her sister's face that I'm fucking.

I pull out and Whitney gasps, body jerking in the restraints. I slap her face again, and she whimpers while her sister watches like she's in a daze. It makes my cock jerk. Not because I want both of them but because I like having the audience. As a Lord, we are taught to put on a show.

"Open your fucking mouth," I order, shoving my cock back into it. I don't give her the chance to breathe this time. Instead, I reach down underneath her neck and hold the back of her head, tilting it more at an angle while I lean over the edge of the bed and fuck her mouth until I'm pulling out and coming all over her face.

"Did that make you wet, little darling?" I ask my wife. "When you watched me fuck your sister's mouth?"

She fights me harder at the mention of Whitney. If she's going to bring her up, then so will I. No matter how inappropriate it once was. She's why we're where we are right now anyway.

"You're disgusting," she yells at me over her shoulder.

Leaning over her back, I lift my hips enough to reach between our bodies and grab my hard dick. I spread her sore pussy with it, making her cry out. "You'll learn to beg, cry, and come for me just like she did."

Her fingers grip the bed and I grab them, yanking them behind her back and holding her forearms parallel with one hand while the other grips her hair, pinning the side of her face to the bed.

"I told you, little darling. I'd only go easy on you the first time," I grind out, shoving my cock into her while my feet hold hers open. "From here on out, you will be reminded who the fuck you belong to."

LAIKYN

I sit at the kitchen table with my parents as Tyson and Whitney enter the room. He pulls the seat out for her, and she thanks him.

My cheeks blush when his eyes briefly meet mine. I watched him fuck my sister's mouth. My bedroom is across the hall from hers, and I could hear her. They've been going at it for six weeks now. All I hear is her screaming his name and him telling her how good she feels.

Our parents have raised us to understand what sex is and what is expected of us. My sister and I are both meant to be chosens. She got to be Tyson's—without my parents' permission—and I hope when my time comes, the Lord I want, also wants me in return.

I watch my sister fix the collar of her shirt to hide a hickey that he's obviously given her. I also don't miss the fact that she's washed her face after he came all over it. When he started, she had makeup on. Now she looks like she just woke up.

My sister slides her arm through the crook of his and pulls him closer to her. My mother frowns at the PDA but doesn't say anything. My sister tends to get dramatic. She and my mother have had several very intense conversations that have turned into yelling matches over Tyson. My sister wants to marry him. My parents have shut that down. She is his chosen, but she will be another Lord's Lady.

They are two very different things.

I lean against the table, my eyes looking over Tyson. His chiseled jaw, baby-blue eyes, and broad shoulders. His muscular arms and chiseled abs. He's fucking gorgeous. And the fact that I've seen him in action just makes him that much more attractive.

My clit is swollen, pussy wet just from watching them in her bedroom. Some would say eighteen is too young to be interested in a twenty-one-year-old, but at least I'm of legal age. Plus, my father is six years older than my mother. Her father gave her away when she was seventeen.

There are no age limits when it involves the Lords. I've heard of girls marrying as young as fifteen. We have our own laws. Our own traditions. That any outsider would disagree and look down on.

. . .

Tyson holds me pinned over the side of the bed and wetness runs down my legs while he fucks me once again. I can't fight him, and the worst part is, I don't want to. It hurts so bad, but I'm also already craving that sensation that takes my breath away. I'm still shaking from the other two he gave me.

"Ple-ease?" I beg through a sob. My shoulders are screaming while he holds my arms to my back, pressing me into the bed. I'm having trouble breathing from the pressure.

"Please what?" he commands, thrusting into me.

"I need—"

He pulls out and slams forward, making me scream, and his body tenses against mine before his cock pulses inside me. He comes, not letting me.

Pulling out, he lets go of my arms, and they fall to my side as a whimper escapes my lips. My legs can't hold me up and I fall to the floor, twisting so my back leans against the side of the bed, pulling my shaking legs to my chest. I look up at him through watery lashes as he stares down at me.

Kneeling, he pushes my wet hair from my tear-streaked face. "You will have to earn to come from now on, Lake." Then he stands, giving me his back and exiting the bedroom.

Valet had his blacked-out Bentley Continental GT V8 Coupe waiting for us when we exited the hotel not even thirty minutes after he left me shaking on the bedroom floor. We ride through the city in silence once again. We haven't spoken to each other since he told me I'd beg him to get off.

Being this close to him in such a confined space has my breathing ragged. I'm trying to calm my racing heart, hoping he doesn't hear how worked up I am while "Just Pretend" by Bad

Omens softly filters from the speakers. I wish he'd turn it up to drown out any chance of hearing me.

I can feel his cum leaking out of my sore pussy and soaking my underwear. He's proving a point. Dominance. Not like I needed a reminder. I'm very well aware of how powerful Tyson Riley Crawford is. He might not have taken over his father's multibillion-dollar company like he was supposed to, choosing a nightclub instead, but he is still a Lord. And they're all the same—ruthless.

The rain continues to fall, but it's not as hard as before. He takes an exit, and I run my hands over the shorts my mother had packed in my bag. Tyson didn't even bring it. I picked out what I wanted to wear at the hotel, and he made me leave the rest behind. I'm guessing he'll make me sleep naked at his house. Hell, will he even let me wear clothes during the day while at his home? Doubtful. Visions of chains, cuffs, and leashes come to mind. I'll be his personal pet. A slave to serve him. I'll be lucky to sleep on a bed. He's probably had a cage made just for me. The thought makes my chest tighten. Lords are all about humiliation. It makes them feel powerful to belittle others.

I once overheard my mother's friend telling her that her husband threw a party for his three best friends and made her wear a gag in her mouth while she served them food. That was all she was allowed to wear. After they were done with dinner, she was ordered to lie on the table where they tied her down and each took their turn with her for dessert. I was disgusted at how turned on I got at the thought. All she could do was tell my mother how amazing it was to serve them. And how her husband's one friend had the biggest dick she had ever seen. It was the best night of her life.

Slowing the car down, Tyson pulls into a parking lot, and I read the white sign outside of a redbrick building—*Walls Dentistry.* "What are we doing here?" I ask.

He comes to a stop in a front-row parking spot and shuts off the car. Without answering, he gets out, and I let out a huff, doing the same. Taking my hand, he drags me into the front glass double doors. It looks closed. There isn't a single person sitting at the front desk, and it's a weekend. The row of chairs up against the far wall is also empty. A black coffee table is in the middle with a stack of magazines.

Tyson pushes open a door, pulling me down a hallway, passing room after room where the hygienists clean their clients' teeth.

We pass another reception desk, and he then comes to the last room on the right. A man sits in a chair, his back to us. A dentist chair sits in the middle of the room. "Sit," Tyson orders, pushing me toward it.

"Ty—"

"Good afternoon." The man turns around to face us. He gives me a warm smile and looks to Tyson. "Congratulations on the wedding. It was beautiful."

I shift uncomfortably in the chair. *He's a Lord.* Of course, he is. "Tyson?" My wide eyes find his as he sits down in a chair in the corner. "What are we doing here?" I ask, licking my lips nervously.

He doesn't answer. Instead, he pulls his cell out of the pocket of his jeans and drops his eyes to it while he types away. The guy I assume is the dentist chuckles softly. "We'll have you guys out of here in no time." He places the blue paper bib on my chest, fastening it around my neck, and I try to even out my breathing. I've never been a fan of the dentist. And to be here, not knowing why, makes my heart race more so than it already was.

Turning his back to me, he resumes whatever he was doing when we arrived, and Tyson continues to type away on his phone as if he's writing a fucking novel to someone.

I close my eyes. *Deep breaths, Lake.*

"Open wide," the guy says, and my eyes spring open just in time to see him leaning over my chair from behind. He's shoving something into my mouth, and I don't even have the chance to fight him.

It's big and bulky, filling my mouth, and he presses it to the top, his fingers making sure to pull my upper lip around it. I start gagging as something touches the back of my throat.

"Breathe," he tells me. "Through your nose."

I pull my knees up, my back arching off the chair, but no matter how much I try to move, he keeps his left hand in my mouth, his fingers holding the device to the roof of my mouth. Tears sting my eyes, and just when I think I'm about to puke, he pushes down on it. I feel suction before it pops loose, and I watch him remove it. It's a paste of some kind. I realize that I've done it before. He's having molds made for whitening trays. Luke had me bleach my teeth. He wanted a Barbie for a wife. Small framed, glowing white teeth, and big tits. He always told me things that needed to be changed about my body. How he *wanted* to be attracted to me. He's spent the last few years of my life altering what needed to be changed.

Why the fuck would Tyson care what color my teeth are?

I sit up, coughing. My tongue feeling the small pieces left around my mouth. I dig my fingers around and spit them out, not caring what I look like. Tyson has already seen me come and cry. I'm sure his plan is to make me feel humiliated in my everyday life.

I'm grabbed and pulled back down before I can fight the dentist again. He pushes my lips apart and does the same thing to the bottom. It's not nearly as bad as the top was.

I stare at the clock on the wall, watching the secondhand make its way around sixty seconds before he removes it. "When was the last time you went to the dentist?" the man asks, placing the small mirror inside my mouth and looking around.

Hell if I know. "Six months ago," I say, trying to think when the last time I had a cleaning.

He removes the mirror and mumbles a, "Hmm," to himself.

91

Looking up at the ceiling, I run my tongue over my teeth, spitting out the chunks of the leftover mold.

Then his fingers are back in my mouth, pulling my lips apart. "Let that sit there," he says, removing his hand, and something remains in my mouth.

"Wh—"

"Don't talk," he scolds me. "That numbing cream needs to set up. You've got a cavity that I'm going to fix. Afterward, I'll clean them, and you kids will be on your way," the dentist now sings, tapping my shoulder.

My eyes go to the corner to see if Tyson is still on his phone, but he's no longer there.

THIRTEEN

TYSON

I pull up to Blackout and turn off my car. She hasn't spoken to me since we left the dentist's office thirty minutes ago. Getting out, I open her door and grab her hand, pulling her from it.

"Why are we here?" she asks softly when we enter through the back door.

All the lights are on, but we're the only ones here at the moment. "This is where we'll live," I inform her.

"But your house—"

"We'll live here," I repeat, and she lets it go. I'm at Blackout most of the time already, so I figured it'd be best if we just lived here. I don't want her at my home right now. It'll raise too many questions that I refuse to answer.

We enter the elevator and ride it up to the fourth floor, where the apartment is. I unlock the door and we step inside. "You have three hours," I say, glancing at my Rolex.

She turns to face me, a look of concern in her blue eyes. "Three hours until what?" she asks slowly. I'm sure part of her mouth is still numb from the dentist.

"Until the club opens."

"Why would that matter to me?" she wonders.

I smile, stepping into her. "Because you're going to work here."

Her eyes widen and her lips part. "Tyson—"

"You will work for Blackout."

"But I don't want to."

I snort. "Doesn't matter what you want." I step away and turn my back to her. This is part of my plan. A Minson working as a cocktail server at a nightclub is beneath them. Just another way to drag their name through the mud. I want her father to be disappointed. Embarrassed. This is one way of many to do it.

"Tyson—"

"Get ready. Meet Beau down at the bar, and he'll help you get your uniform." I turn to exit the bedroom.

"You're leaving?"

I face her once more, and I can't tell if she's excited to be alone or terrified. "I'll be in my office. I have work to do." With that, I turn and leave the apartment.

Entering my office on the second floor, I sit down and pull out my cell when it starts to ring. "Hello?" I answer.

"Hey, man. Nice wedding," the familiar voice says in greeting.

I lean back in my chair. "Glad you were able to make it." Smiling, I add, "Didn't know you planned on attending."

He snorts. "When they require cloaks and masks for attendance, it's easy to hide in plain sight."

"True." I agree.

If the Lords had seen *them* there, they'd have had a fucking fit. The Spade brothers are Lords in a sense, but not what you'd think. They run their own hell, their own way. Just like I do with Blackout. They don't have to answer to the higher-ups because you don't get any higher than them. Not all who rule choose to watch peasants from their thrones. Some of us like to keep our hands dirty.

"I just wanted to congratulate you and let you know we're

94

making a quick trip out of town. We'll be back soon, though. I'll reach out when we return."

LAIKYN

I didn't need a shower, but I decide to take a long, hot bath. It feels good to relax. To be left alone with my thoughts and actually get to breathe without feeling like he's watching me.

My body aches everywhere, and I'm sore between my legs. Will it always feel like this? I remember watching my sister and Tyson have sex in our parents' media room once, and she didn't cry. She enjoyed it. Begged him to fuck her harder. Will it be like that for me? Is my body broken because of how much it hurts? Tyson has already proven that it won't matter if it's painful. The only thing that matters to a Lord is themselves. And he had no problem getting off. Told me I'd have to earn to come from now on. How will I earn it? And how long will I be able to hold out until I beg him to hurt me again?

Is that his plan? Make me beg for bruises by his hands? To be treated like his personal whore? He just gave me a little taste and now wants me to beg for each bite.

Lifting my hand out of the water, I take a deep breath and finally look at my wedding ring. It's a heart-shaped red diamond ruby, or maybe it's a red diamond with a double diamond band. It's exactly what I expected, large and over the top. Another way for him to own me and show off that I'm his. I hate that it's gorgeous.

Dropping my hand back into the water, I lean my head back and sigh. Tears prick my eyes, and I close them. Letting my body relax, I slide down into the water to drown out my mind, the voices screaming at me to run. You don't run from men like Tyson. That's how you end up chained to a wall in a basement.

I walk down to the main bar, knowing the club opens in less than thirty minutes. I made sure to take my time. Honestly, I'm surprised that Tyson didn't come up to the apartment and fuck me again. Then I told myself to shut the fuck up. The only reason he slept with me at the hotel was to prove a point to my father. I'm no longer a virgin. He'll probably choose to fuck anyone other than me now.

If I'm lucky, he'll never touch me again. Hell, that may be why he wants me to beg him for it, just so he can have the power to turn me down. It's all mind games when it comes to a Lord. It's only my first day of being a Lady, and I'm already mentally exhausted. At least my mouth is no longer numb from the dentist, and I've stopped drooling on myself. Now my mouth is just sore. A dull reminder that, once again, he'll control everything I do.

I stop to see men and women running around the club with the lights on. It's four stories tall, the apartment being on the top floor. It's got a dance floor in the middle, and tables and booths line the far walls. A hallway leads to the entrance and exit, where a security guy stands next to the coat check. His hands hanging on his bulletproof vest. I've never been here before, but I've heard stories of people getting shot, beaten, killed. It's like a free-for-all. Then add alcohol and drugs to the mix, and it's a recipe for disaster. But I expect nothing less when it comes to a Lord owning a nightclub.

Cages stand on platforms in various places on the dance floor. They're high enough that if you got into one, you'd be able to see out over the entire club.

I look over the men and women setting up chairs and carrying trays, getting ready to open. I run my sweaty palms down my thighs. I had to put my clothes back on that I had taken from my luggage at the hotel after my bath. I don't even have any makeup on right now. I don't have mine with me. He did have a hairdryer, though, so I was able to at least dry my hair. There was also a curling iron under the sink. I don't even want to ask who it belongs to, but I used it. Might as well look halfway decent. I understand that to make money as a cocktail server, you must look presentable.

"Laikyn?" a guy asks, stepping out from behind the main bar.

"That's me," I say softly.

"Follow me." He takes me down a hallway and to a back room. It's a locker room. Open with lockers lining each side, a bench in the middle, and a few showers against the back wall. Each one has a curtain for very little privacy. "This will be yours." He points at a black locker that has *Mrs. Crawford* across the top.

I sigh. He's going to shove it down my throat. As if I could ever forget that I was forced to marry the enemy. Like I could ignore the rock on my finger that feels like an anchor.

"Here is how to set your combination." He holds out a folded piece of paper and I take it. "Your uniform is in the locker. And Tyson told me to tell you to see him before you start your shift. His office is on the second floor." With that, he turns and exits, leaving me all alone.

I open the piece of paper and follow the directions on how to set the code. Once done, I open it up, and my shoulders slump when I see my uniform.

You're a trophy, Lake. What did you expect?

I should have known I'd be dressed as the others. Not sure why I didn't think of it before. He might as well tattoo *Tyson's slut* across my ass cheeks.

97

FOURTEEN

TYSON

I'm sitting at my desk when a soft knock sounds on my office door. "Come in," I call out.

I'm too busy staring at my computer to pay any attention to whoever enters. I finish typing out the email and look up when I'm met with silence to see my wife standing in my office.

Her head is down, her eyes on the floor, her bleach-blond hair is curled in big waves flowing down over her shoulders, and she's wearing her uniform. It looks like lingerie. I've never really paid much attention to what I have the staff wear until I see it on her.

Getting to my feet, I walk around my desk and lean back against it, arms crossed over my chest. My eyes drop to her black Vans and slowly take in the black Charmnight fishnet tights—they have rhinestones on them to shine while working under the neon lights—up to her black booty shorts that I know show off her bubble ass with a form-fitting matching leotard that has a deep V showcasing her large breasts.

Fuck, I'm hard just looking at her. I wonder if she's still bleeding. The thought makes me smile.

"Come," I command, and her head snaps up at my voice.

"Excuse me?" she whispers.

"Get down on your hands and knees and crawl to me," I say, testing the waters just to see how far I can push her so soon.

She stares at me, eyes large for a moment, and then she bursts out laughing, doubling over with amusement. "I'm not a dog, Tyson." She turns, giving me her back, and reaches for the door to leave.

I pick up my cell off my desk, unlock it, and open the app. I push the button before she can open the door.

A shrill scream comes from her as she drops to the floor. Quickly, she scoots backward to where her back is up against the wall to the left of the door. Her knees to her chest. Locking my cell, I set it down and make my way over to her.

Kneeling, I listen to her gasping for breath while she holds her neck. Her eyes swimming in unshed tears. *So pretty*. "You're right, you're not a dog. But you are my pet, Lake," I say, reaching out and cupping her face.

She cowers, trying to pull her body away from me, but she's up against the wall with nowhere to go. I lower my hand to run my fingers along the velvet wrapped around her delicate neck that I gave her before we got married earlier today. "This is a shock collar."

Her eyes widen, and she gasps, the color draining from her beautiful features. "Wh-at?" The single word trembles on her plump lips.

"You may not have willingly crawled to me, but you will, little darling. Until then, I don't mind forcing your hand."

I grab her upper arm and yank her to her feet. I push the long curls off her chest and shoulders, watching the way it rises and falls with each sharp intake of breath.

Her watery blue eyes meet mine. "Tyson ... please." They plead with me as much as her words. I can't even explain how turned on I am when she licks her lips, trying to catch her breath.

I lower my hand so the pads of my fingers run along the top of her leotard, gently feeling the softness of her cleavage, loving the sound of the whimper she makes with such little contact. Her body shakes, and her hands reach out to fist my button-up, preparing to push me away at any second.

"I can't wait to come all over these, little darling," I say, my eyes lifting to hers.

She's staring at my shirt, avoiding me, but I feel the way her chest heaves at my words. I reach up and grab both straps on her shoulders and slowly pull them down her shaking arms, exposing her chest to the room. She isn't wearing a bra. She doesn't have one here. I smile, my hand dropping and slowly running my knuckles over her breasts.

"Your nipples are hard." I make sure she knows I'm aware of her reaction to my touch, to my words. No matter how much her mind fights it, her body enjoys it.

She closes her eyes in shame.

"Did you like that?" I ask her, and she whimpers. "It's okay, Lake. There will be lots of things that I do to you that your body will like." I cup the side of her large breast and run my thumb over her hardened nipple, making her hiss in a breath.

Grabbing her arm, I pull her over to the couch and place my hand on her back to bend her over the side of the armrest. I yank the leotard farther down, and it falls to her ankles, pulling down her shorts and fishnets in the process. "Are you still bleeding?" I ask.

"I ... I don't know," she replies softly, her ass and pussy up in the air for me to use.

Doesn't matter if she is or not. It's not going to stop me. I drop my hand between her legs and push her thong to the side before I run my fingers over her cunt, making her flinch. "You're wet," I say, loving the sound she makes. She already knew she was, but I liked making her feel uncomfortable.

I unzip my slacks and pull my hard cock through my boxers, not even bothering to take them off. I need to order her a new uniform. Nothing but snaps on the leotard will suffice. I require easy access to my wife at all times.

As I rub my cock against her pussy, she whines, her ass wiggling back and forth, silently begging to be fucked. Smiling, I grab both her arms, pulling them behind her back parallel. I cross her small wrists, one hand wrapping around them to hold them in place while the other guides my cock into her cunt.

She cries out as I push my way into her, and I bite my lip to keep from groaning at how tight she is. Fucking incredible. "Before every shift, you will come to my office, and I will fuck you," I tell her. "You will feel my cum leak out of *my* pussy while you work. Do you understand me?'

"Yes," she gasps, her body trying to fight me, but I've got her pinned in place.

She will serve men who stare at her all night, but I will be the one who fucks her. Who owns her.

My free hand grabs her hair, yanking her head up, and I don't take it easy on her. It's a quickie, just to prove a point, no matter how much I want to take my time fucking what's mine.

Her whimpers and cries turn to moans and gasps. I hold her pinned down while my eyes fall to watch my cock slam into her soaked cunt until I can't hold off any longer. I shove my hips forward one last time and come inside her. Pulling out, she flinches, and I release her arms.

She remains lying over the armrest, breathing heavily, and I shove my bloody cock back into my boxers. She's still bleeding. Less than earlier, but it's still there.

I make my way over to my desk, and she slowly rises, pulling up her fishnets, leotard, and shorts. "You're dismissed, Lake," I inform her, in case she hasn't caught the hint, and place my attention on my computer. A moment later, the door opens and closes with her departure.

LAIKYN

I RUN TO THE PUBLIC BATHROOM ON THE FIRST FLOOR, looking at myself in the mirror. I wrap my fingers around the choker and try to pull on it. Tears run down my face, and I sniff. "Fucking sick bastard." I yank on it some more, but there's no use. All it does is pinch the skin on the back of my neck. It's irritated, red, and itchy. "GODDAMMIT!"

My hands slap the counter, and I bow my head, trying to stop the tears that want to fall. I'm not this fucking weak. I told myself after Whitney was killed that I would not be this helpless girl.

Yet here I am with a fucking shock collar around my neck and my husband's cum leaking out of my bleeding cunt. Once again, he didn't let me get off. He told me in the hotel suite that I'd have to earn it. Fuck that. I've gone twenty-one years without getting off. I can go another twenty-one. Hell, fifty if it takes me that long to kill him.

I wonder what the Lords will do to me if I shoot him in his sleep. Surely, they won't care. Tyson Crawford was meant for greatness, but he gave it up. For what? I don't know but I don't think they'd hold a trial for me if I offed him.

I'm sure I wouldn't be the first Lady to kill her husband and sure as fuck not the last. But they would hand me down to another—when a Lord dies, his Lady is gifted to another Lord. It's how they keep us in line. We've seen and know too much, so we must stay within the society. Who says he won't be worse? Is there worse than my dead sister's ex-boyfriend that killed her? I'm not sure I want to test that theory.

Lifting my face, I look at myself in the mirror and wipe the tears out from underneath my eyes. I never thought I'd be glad that I wasn't wearing makeup. Otherwise, I'd look far worse. But who the fuck cares what I look like. Right? I'm here because I have to be not because I want to be.

The door opens, and I avert my eyes to hide the fact I've been crying.

"Laikyn, right?" a woman asks.

Letting out a slow breath, I lift my head. "Yeah." At least she didn't call me Mrs. Crawford.

She comes to stand next to me, looking at herself in the mirror. She's pretty, dark hair fixed in a high pony, full makeup on with pink glittery eye shadow and matching lipstick. "I'm not sure what he sees in you." Her brown eyes meet mine in the mirror.

I stiffen at her words. "Excuse me?" I ask, hoping I heard her wrong.

Turning to face me, I do the same, curious as to what she meant by that. "Tyson." She crosses her arms over her chest and her eyes drop to my ring. "Now your sister ... that made sense."

My heart pounds in my chest. "You knew my sister?" I can't help but ask.

Instead of answering, she just smirks before she turns and walks out of the bathroom, making me wonder what the fuck that was about. Just one more thing to add to this fucked-up day.

THE NIGHT HASN'T GONE ALL THAT BAD. I SPILLED A COUPLE of drinks but nothing serious. They just tipped over on my tray when I tilted it too much. I haven't broken any glass, so that's a plus. I did however have problems answering customers who asked what we serve.

Alcohol, dumb ass, is what I wanted to reply with, but instead, I smiled brightly, bent over and shoved my tits in their faces, and said, *"I'm new. What do you usually drink?"* One guy gave me a twenty and said to surprise him. The other guy got hit in the arm when his girlfriend caught his eyes on my chest.

I've never been allowed to party, so unless it's a rum and Coke or Red Bull and vodka, I don't know what goes into these mixed drinks. And anyone who asks is stupid. You came to the club; you should know what you like.

I've flirted with everyone at my tables. Thankfully, Tyson isn't a complete idiot and only gave me two tables tonight, knowing I didn't have any experience. But it is a Saturday, and it's been slammed nonstop. He also didn't put with me another server to train me. He just threw me to the wolves. I feel like it's a test, and I'm failing.

The lights hurt my eyes, and the blaring music has given me a headache. I don't know how he chooses to work and live here.

Making my way over to the main bar, I step up to the wait station in the corner and hold up two fingers and call out *"Bud Lights."* Beau is pretty cool. He's been the most helpful. The other servers kind of stay away from me. There's nine of us here tonight and I think they're mad because two of them each lost a table. And one girl was already complaining about the schedule change when she demanded to see which section she has tomorrow night.

I briefly glanced at it, and I work every night for the next seven days. I have a feeling that's how it'll be from here on out. My husband owns it, so this is where I'll be. I know he'll make me hand over my tips to him every night once we close because that'll just be another way for him to control me. I'll work for him day and night and have nothing to show for it, except for bad eyes and migraines. *Living the life.*

"Here you go." Beau sets the open bottles on my tray, and I thank him.

He gives me a huge smile and winks at me. "You don't have to thank me every time, Lake."

I blush when his eyes drop to my chest, and I nod my head in understanding. *I'm sorry that I have manners.*

Walking over to my table, I turn, and someone runs into the side of me. Beers are knocked over, and I gasp at the feel of the cold liquid splashing my face, neck, and hair.

"Watch where you're fucking going!" Bethany snaps at me, before throwing her long dark ponytail over her shoulder, pushing her nose up in the air, and storming off.

I could tell from our first encounter in the bathroom that she was going to hate me. She's made sure to remind me of that every chance she's had tonight.

Turning back to the station, I set my now wet tray on the surface, and Beau gives me a sympathetic smile. "Here you go." He passes me a handful of bar napkins, and I blot my face and lick my lips, tasting the nasty beer.

Well, so much for having a good night. Now I need another bath.

FIFTEEN

TYSON

I sit back in the corner booth inside of Blackout, reviewing paperwork while my staff picks up after closing. Every man who works for me is training to be a Lord.

The lower part of the totem pole, but a Lord nonetheless. Unless you're like Ryat, Sin—another Lord I'm close with—or myself, high up in rankings, you have to provide a service as you go through your initiations while attending Barrington University. When I took on Blackout, the Lords came to me and asked if I could employ some while they went through initiations. I didn't see why not. They saved me the trouble of going through the hiring process.

I look up to see Lake sitting at the bar, her back to me. "Come here," I call out, not even bothering to use her name. She knows I'm referring to her.

Her back stiffens, but she makes no move to acknowledge me.

I pick up my cell off the table to turn on her collar but stop myself. Instead, I sit back in the booth and cross my arms over my chest. I watched her all night on the cameras, and she did better than I thought she would. "I'm going to give you to the count of five to crawl your ass over to me."

That does it.

Her head whips around, her hair slapping her in the face in the process. She jumps to her feet, glaring at me. "I'm not fucking crawling anywhere in this place. That's disgusting."

As if she'd crawl anywhere else. "One."

She huffs, her large tits rising with the action, and then places her hands on her narrow hips. My eyes drop between her legs, and I wonder if her underwear is as soaked with my cum as her leotard is from the beer that got spilled.

"Two."

"I'm not fucking doing it, Tyson," she snaps, her voice ringing out through the silent club.

"Three."

"Fuck you." She turns her back on me to storm off and up to the apartment, but she runs face-first into one of my bartenders, Walter. Everyone is aware she's my wife. I sent out an email before we opened this evening. It wasn't for her to get special treatment, but to see if they picked on her more. Some chose to ignore her. Others chose to show her just how much they don't want her here, and I will say she handled it better than I expected.

"When your husband gives you an order, you follow it," he tells her.

"Fuck you, Walter." She slams her hands into his chest and shoves him out of the way, but instead, he grabs her hair and yanks her toward me while she screams, trying to untangle herself from him.

My skin instantly begins to burn. My teeth clench, seeing his hands on her. I shift in the booth but stop myself from getting up. I wait to see what she does. How far will she allow him to go? Just how much fight does she have in her?

Finally, she manages to slam her hand into his face but not

before he pushes her to the floor. "Don't fucking touch me, you piece of shit!" she screams at him, shoving her now tangled hair out of her face.

"Four." I keep counting, my eyes on her while my hands are fisted on the table.

Her narrowed eyes are on mine while she's gasping for breath.

"You're already on the floor." I add to her already pissed-off attitude. "Crawl to me."

Walter reaches down for her again, and she scrambles away from him. Pressing her back into the side of the bar, she knocks over a barstool in the process.

Everyone just stands around watching the exchange. I look over at Beau—another bartender—and arch a brow. He wants my wife. I also watched the way he looked at her tonight on the cameras. I've noticed the way all the men who work for me look at her. I understand that they are all horny boys who haven't had sex in years, but I still don't like how they look at what's mine. As if they think they'd have a chance with her. That I might be nice enough to strip her naked and tie her down to the bar for all to sample. Offer her up as a bonus. Over my dead body.

Beau throws his hands up. "Respectfully, sir. She's your problem. Not mine."

I smile and get up from the booth. She huffs, gets to her feet, and pretends to dust the dirt off her already dirty uniform.

Stopping in front of Walter, I remove my knife from my back pocket and flip it open. Grabbing his wrist, I slam his hand down onto a table and stab the knife through it, pinning it down.

He screams, trying to jerk it away, but the knife is in the wood.

"Apologize," I order.

"Wh-hat?" His shrill voice fills the open club.

I grip his hair, yanking his head back. "Apologize to my wife. Now." My eyes go to hers, and she's looking at me wide-eyed, her body frozen in shock.

"I'm … I'm sorry," he growls through gritted teeth.

I remove the knife from his hand. He drops to his knees, holding it to his chest as it bleeds everywhere. Running the blade across my thigh, I close the knife and slip it back into my pocket. "Walter?"

"Yeah?" He lifts his head to meet my glare. I remove my gun from the back of my slacks and shoot him right between the eyes.

Lake's scream follows the sound of my gun as blood splatters her uniform, and his body falls to the floor where she has been lying. She places her hand over her mouth, and silence follows as everyone stands paralyzed at what I just did.

"This will be your only warning. Don't put your hands on my wife. Ever." My voice rings loud and clear. Reaching out, I grab her shaking hand and yank her to me. "Clean this shit up," I order, and everyone scrambles, getting back to work.

I pull her into the hallway, and she yanks her arm free of my hold. "Why don't you just whip your dick out and piss on me," she growls. "It might help get your point across." Her palms hit my now bloody shirt.

I wrap my hand around her throat and shove her back into the wall, pushing my hips into her to pin her in place. "Nothing is off the table, darling."

Her nostrils flare, her pretty blue eyes swimming in tears that she hasn't allowed to fall yet. "You're disgusting."

I lower my lips to her ear, and whisper, "I am, but I will make you crave everything I choose to do to you."

LAIKYN

I'M NOT SURPRISED TYSON JUST KILLED THAT GUY. I'VE known my father was a Lord since I was young, and I also knew what that entailed. What I am surprised about is that he killed

Walter because of me. I don't want that on my conscience. Another dead body because I couldn't save them. Even if the man was a fucking prick.

Tyson steps back, grabs my hand, and I look over my shoulder to see the body already gone. Beau is on his hands and knees, cleaning up the blood that remains with towels and a bucket of water.

We get into the elevator and ride it up to the fourth floor in silence and step off. We enter the apartment, and he pulls me through the master bedroom and into the bathroom. "Get undressed. We're showering and going to bed." He lets go of my hand, and I come to a stop, watching him undo his blood-covered button-up and then shrug it off his shoulders. He removes his gun from the back of his slacks, pulls back the slide, and removes the magazine. He places them all on the countertop by his sink.

If I knew how to use a gun, I'd take the opportunity to shoot him, but I know I'd fail or end up shooting myself. Then he toes off his shoes and removes his socks. Last, he undoes his belt before unbuttoning his slacks, shoving them down his legs along with his boxer briefs.

This is the first time I'm actually paying attention to his naked body. The last time we showered, I was too embarrassed to even look at him. And thankfully, he demanded I turn around. When I watched him with my sister, I never paid much attention to it. But now, I couldn't look away even if I wanted to.

He's got scars on his back, above his right shoulder blade. Looks like a small circle. Bullet wound, maybe? I hate that I want to ask what it's from. Another on his arm, and a third scar down on his left lower back. Possibly a stab wound?

My eyes drop to his ass and my breathing picks up at how chiseled it is. His muscular thighs flex when he opens the glass door and steps into the shower, turning it on.

I sigh, removing my clothes, knowing I'm covered in blood and alcohol and need to clean off before I go to bed. I'm exhausted. It's been a long day, and I never stay up this late.

Getting naked, I step inside and pause for a second, remembering he's got a fucking shock collar around my neck. I'm afraid to get it wet, but then I remember I already took a shower with it on before I even knew what it was. I highly doubt he'd kill me this soon. He married me for a reason. Whatever it is, I'm sure he's playing the long game here.

He turns to face me, and I step back until I'm up against the cold tile wall. He cages me in, a smile tugging at his lips. "What's wrong, little darling?"

I snort. Way too many things to answer that question.

"Afraid of me?"

Squaring my shoulders, I say, "If you think I'm going to bow down to you because you're my husband, you're wrong."

He reaches out, hands on either side of my face, tilting my head back so I have to look up at him as he presses his slick and firm body into mine. My hands come up instinctively to grip his wrists, trying to pull them free of my face, but it doesn't work.

I expect him to choke me, slap me, grip my hair, yank me under the sprayer and drown me. Instead, he lowers his lips to mine and kisses me. A slow and soft sensual kiss that makes my heart race with unease while my body melts for him.

My eyes fall closed as a tingling sensation slowly runs up my spine, making me shiver. I moan into his mouth, my body going soft and pushing into his. My arms drop from his wrists to wrap around his waist, my fingers digging into his wet skin.

It's in this moment I realize just how fucked I am. I've never considered myself to be fragile. But he's taking my body to places it's never been before. He's forcing it to experience things it didn't know existed. And I can admit that I don't know how to fight that.

He pulls away, my lips stay parted, gasping in a shaky breath, and my heavy eyes open. His thumb runs along my upper lip before tracing the bottom. "I can't wait to see you on your knees, crying for me while you choke on my cock."

My thighs clench on their own at his words, reminding me how sore my pussy is. They're just fucking words and I'm already going weak. They're not even endearing, they're vulgar and disgusting, yet my body likes the way they sound.

He pulls back just enough to separate our bodies, and my eyes drop down his chiseled abs to his deep V, and I see his dick. He's as hard as my pussy is wet. Or that could be his cum from when he fucked me before my shift.

"You want that, little darling?" he asks, and my eyes snap up to meet his. His left hand leaves the side of my face to trail down over my heaving chest until he gets to my breast. He's gentle, his thumb running over it. "Tell me, Lake. That you want me to fuck your mouth."

I realize my lips are still open, so I close them, swallowing the saliva and water from the shower before they open again on a gasp when he pinches my nipple, making my hips rock forward involuntarily. It's like he's got a map straight to my pussy. He knows exactly what to touch, what to say. Are all women like this? Or am I just a stupid bitch? I hate how inexperienced I am.

I can't make the words come out no matter how much I want to. So I reach up and grip his wrist once again. Out of amusement or curiosity, he allows me to guide his thumb back to my lips. I pull his thumb into my mouth and close my lips around it, sucking on it.

His baby-blue eyes grow heavy, a growl comes from deep in his throat, and I feel a small sense of pride, but it's gone immediately when he yanks it free from my mouth. "Ty—"

He shoves his middle and ring finger both into my mouth, interrupting what I was about to say, and it makes me gag. My body jerks involuntarily.

"That's it, Lake. That's the sound I want to hear you make.

Suck on them, little darling. Pretend it's my cock. Show me how good you're going to be on your knees." He splits his fingers inside of my mouth, one on either side of my tongue, and I close my lips the best I can to swallow. "That's it." He slides them out, and I keep my mouth open for him, waiting for whatever he wants to do next. My tongue is out and ready like a hungry slut begging to be fucked.

He pushes his fingers back into my mouth, and I gag once again. My hips push forward, and my eyes start to sting with unshed tears. I arch my neck, trying to pull his fingers from my mouth, but he just pushes them farther down my throat, and I choke on them.

"Gorgeous," he murmurs, eyes on mine. "Such a good girl."

My thighs clench while my pussy throbs at his words. I want to hear them again, so I open up for him the best I can.

He adds a third finger, making me whimper around them filling my mouth.

"You're doing so good, Lake," he praises, and drool runs out of the corner of my lips. "Look how needy you are."

I blink, trying to nod.

He gives me a smile. "Your body is begging me to fuck it."

I'm having trouble breathing and I can't swallow, but I look up at him through my lashes, unable to look away from the hunger in his eyes.

He removes his fingers from my mouth and steps back. I sag, dropping my head and sucking in a ragged breath, needing a moment, but he grabs my arm, yanking me across the shower, and pushes me down onto the bench. I gasp, the tile freezing against my ass, legs, and back. He stands in front of me before I can get back up. He reaches over and grabs a bottle of soap and pours some onto his hard dick, then lets the bottle drop to the floor.

"Wrap your hands around my cock, Lake. Show me how much you want me in your mouth."

Licking my wet lips, I drop my eyes to his dick right in front of my face. I do as he says, wrapping my hands around the long and veiny shaft. There are still inches that they don't cover. I don't know how big he is compared to others, but I'd say he's on the larger side. His cock is the only one I've ever seen, let alone touched.

I start to move both hands up and down, smearing the soap. I've never done this before, so I have no clue what I'm doing.

His hands gather in my wet hair, and he holds my head in place, making my scalp tingle while I jerk him off in the shower.

"Fuck," he groans, lifting his right foot on the bench next to me. I release his dick with my right hand and start massaging his balls. His body jerks, and he sucks in a deep breath through his teeth.

I smile to myself. He likes it. I'm controlling him right now. He's my puppet. Sex is a two-way street. I never thought about it this way. I was afraid he'd use me, but I can use him.

"Tyson," I moan. My mouth waters, imagining being on my knees for him just like he described—crying and gagging.

"Yes, little darling. That's it." He groans.

I look up and watch him slap his free hand on the wall behind me. He throws his head back, showing me his chiseled jawline, and I watch his Adam's apple bob when he swallows. "Goddammit."

My hand goes back to his dick, and I move them faster, grip him harder. I'm in awe of the way his muscles tense and his hips thrust forward. I can only imagine what he'll look like when I'm on my knees for him.

I slow them down and run my fingers over the barbell at the bottom of his shaft. I want to lick it, pull it into my mouth to see what kind of sound he makes when I suck on it. Running my hand up to the head, I twist my hand, and his breathing becomes erratic. Then all of a sudden, he steps away from me, yanking his dick from my hands. He holds my head in place with his hand still in my hair while his free hand grips the base of his hard cock. He runs it up and down his shaft a few times before he comes all over me.

I close my eyes just in time to feel it hit my chest, neck, and bottom half of my face. He tugs me to my feet and slams my back against the wall. "Open your eyes," he demands.

I do as I'm told and look up into his eyes blazing down on me. I'm not sure if it's anger or want. I'm hoping the latter because I'm so turned on right now, I can't even be ashamed.

He runs his thumb over my lips, and he smears his cum before he lowers his to mine and kisses me once again, forcing his cum into my open mouth with his tongue. The texture is thick, but I don't really taste anything. My arms wrap around his neck on their own, both his hands grip my hair, forcing me to cry out into his mouth.

He swallows it, devouring me, and I let him.

My hips push into his, and I'm desperate. My extremely sore pussy throbs, begging to be used. Fuck, I'm pathetic. This man is a monster. A killer. I haven't even been married to him for twenty-four hours, and he's already got me trained. Just like he said he would.

All of a sudden, he pulls away, leaving me gasping, and my arms fall to my sides.

"Get cleaned up," he commands and turns, leaving me in the shower all alone and needing him. I don't know if I should cry or beg him to come back.

SIXTEEN

TYSON

Fuck, she's smarter than I thought. Or I'm dumber than usual. Either way, that can't happen again. I gave her control. I felt it, and so did she.

I'm supposed to be manipulating her, not the other way around. She wears the collar, and soon the leash, a gag, and this club will be her cage. She'll be the doting wife begging for attention. Not me.

I run the towel over my hair as I enter the master suite. I open the nightstand and grab what I need out of it. Placing all three items on the bed just as she turns the shower off.

For someone with no experience, her willingness to try something new was refreshing. She didn't want to beg to suck my cock, so she tried a different tactic. I don't like that it worked. But she deserves the small victory that it was. If I reward her for good behavior, she'll be more willing to make me happy.

She enters the bedroom and comes to a stop when she sees the items on the bed. "Drop the towel and come here," I command.

Her eyes narrow on me, but she does as she's told. The towel falls at her feet, and my eyes fall to her cunt. I want to taste her so bad right now. Even I can't deny the fact that my wife makes me hard. She's addicting in the worst way. I love to hear her moan my name and beg me to let her come. Fuck, I love it when she's needy.

She walks over to me, and I gesture toward the bed. "I want you facedown with your ass in the air."

Her breath hitches and she looks up at me, eyes now wide with concern. Her tongue comes out to run across her lips nervously, but all it makes me think about is her sucking my cock. "Ty—"

"Now, Lake," I interrupt her. She thinks I'm going to fuck her ass. I reach out and push her wet hair off her chest so I can see her breasts. Her nipples are hard, and I see her soft skin covered in goose bumps. She's cold, water still dripping off her. "You've earned a reward, little darling."

A smile spreads across her pretty face before she masks it, and I like the way her eyes light up with happiness. She crawls onto the bed, and I grab her ankle to stop her from going too far because I'll be standing right here on the side of the bed. "I want your feet at the edge," I tell her. "No need to go to the middle. I want you to lay across it."

She places her chest and face on the bed and spreads her knees wide, showing me her shaved cunt and ass like the needy slut I'm making her. The shower got her all worked up. It's amazing that just yesterday she was crying and trying to hide her body from me, and now she's practically begging me to touch her.

I reach over and gather her wet hair off her back. "Sit up for a second," I say, getting a thought now that I see her in this position. She does so, her back to me. "Place your arms between you and the bed. I want them underneath you and your hands down by your feet."

She thinks about it for a second and then lays her arms down her chest and stomach before lying down once again.

"That's it. Good girl." I open the nightstand and grab something different from what I originally wanted.

Looking back at her, I grab her wrist by her leg and pull it farther down to where her hand is by her foot. The position pushing her legs farther apart. I pull off the end of the duct tape and hold her wrist to the inside of her ankle, wrapping the duct tape around the two, taping them together.

"Tyson," she whimpers, her ass lifting up in the air only to push it back down.

I rip it off once I'm satisfied she's not going anywhere. Then I go over to her other wrist and ankle, doing the same. Once done, I stand back and look at her. She's fisting her taped hands, her body rocking from side to side, trying to loosen the tight spot I've got her locked in.

I toss the tape to the floor and step up behind her, running my hand over her pussy. She jumps, and I push my finger into her. She cries into the bed, and I thrust a second one into her cunt. "Does that hurt?" I ask her, not caring if it does. I'm committed at this point. Even if it hurts, she's going to come.

"Yes." She pushes against me. "No." Her voice changes to a moan as she shifts on the bed, and I smile.

I pick up my pace, pushing them in and out of her harder, faster. She's rocking back and forth the best she can, and she cries out when I add a third, opening her up. I reach over and grab the Bodywand and turn it on. The sound of buzzing fills the room.

I place it on her clit, and she jumps. "TYSON!" My name rings out, and I rub it against her clit while my fingers continue to fuck her.

Pushing the dial, I turn the wand up a little more and she wiggles, her body thrashing and gasping. Her hips rock back and forth as if she's fucking my cock. She's screaming my name into the mattress in no time. I knew it wouldn't take her long. She's never played with toys before.

I turn off the wand, toss it to the floor next to the tape, and step back, removing my fingers as well, watching the cum drip out of her pussy. I run my knuckles over it and bring them to my lips, sucking on them, tasting her like I wanted. "Fuck, you taste so good, Lake."

She lies there with her ass up, shaking uncontrollably, gasping. I place my thumbs on either side of her pussy, opening up her cunt. Leaning over, I'm unable to stop myself, and I run my tongue over her pussy, licking up her cum like a starving man.

"Ty-son," she whimpers my name.

I push my face into her, sucking on her throbbing clit, feeling her try to pull away from me as she screams. I grab her thighs and dig my fingers into her skin, holding her in place, knowing I'm going to leave reminders tomorrow of what I do to her tonight, but I don't care. She's mine to mark. To claim.

I fuck her with my mouth and fingers until she's crying out my name once again and she's coming in my mouth while I devour her like she's my last meal, loving the way she tastes like a peach—sweet and oh, so juicy.

Standing, I open the top drawer and grab a knife. I cut the tape, freeing both of her wrists from her ankles, and she stretches out, softly crying at how sore her body is from being bound so tight. She needs to get used to it.

That was just a quick reward. I'm looking forward to putting her in uncomfortable positions and watching her come over and over while she begs me to stop. I'm going to show her what her body was made to do.

She rolls over onto her back, and her heavy eyes look up at me. Leaning over the bed, I place my fists on either side of her head and lower my lips to hers. I kiss her, pushing my tongue into her mouth, and she doesn't pull away. She's too exhausted; her body has no fight left in her. My tongue meets hers, and she sucks on it, making me groan into her mouth. My cock is hard once again. But that's all she gets tonight.

Pulling away and standing, I walk over to the door and go to flip off the light when I see her now sitting naked on the side of the bed. Her eyes dart around the room. "What are you looking for?" I ask.

She crosses her arms over her large chest as if I haven't already seen her naked and looks up at me through her long dark lashes. "I don't have any of my stuff here." When she licks her lips, I refrain from smiling since I know that she can taste herself on them. She adds at my silence, "Like clothes or anything."

I only allowed her to wear one outfit from what her mother packed and left her bag at the Minson Hotel for a reason. I wanted her father to find the suitcase and know exactly what I'm doing with her. "You'll sleep naked," I inform her.

Her shoulders slump. "I need clothes—"

"Your things will be delivered tomorrow," I interrupt her. The stuff I think she'll need anyway.

She nods and gets up on shaky legs, and starts to walk toward the bathroom. I step away from the wall and grab her upper arm, bringing her to a stop. "What are you doing?" I can feel her body still shaking against mine from her orgasms.

"I'm going to clean myself up," she replies softly.

I place my hands on either side of her face. "You will do no such thing."

"Ty—"

"You'll sleep next to me, your husband, naked, with cum between your thighs." She inhales sharply. "Do you understand?"

Nodding, she whispers, "I understand."

I allow her to pull away, and she crawls under the covers. I flip the light off and do the same thing, leaving some space between us. I interlock my fingers behind my head and stare up into the darkness, smiling to myself.

Part one of my revenge is complete.

LAIKYN

I LIE ON MY SIDE, MY BACK TO HIM, TRYING TO GET MY breathing under control. Once again, my body is shaking, and I'm soaked between my thighs.

I should be embarrassed at how quickly he's turned me into such a slut. I pushed my pussy into his face and practically begged him to let me come. I needed it. My body craved it. When I felt his tongue on me, I about lost it right then and there. Then the vibrating toy? I couldn't stop the wave that washed over me. Then I didn't want it to stop. Even now, my nipples are hard and my pussy still throbs.

Tears prick my eyes, and I sniff. Pulling my knees up to my chest, I pray that he's fallen asleep and can't hear me cry like a little bitch. I don't even know why I'm upset. I mean, it's been a long day and I've got a million things to cry over. I'm just not sure which one it is right this second.

My mind wanders back to the hotel room after the wedding. Has my father seen it? Does he know we were only there for a few hours? I knew that my father would see that I had bled for Luke, but Tyson? It was so messy. Blood everywhere. The thought of him seeing it makes me want to vomit.

I close my eyes and take in a deep breath. Speaking of Luke, what happened to him? Is he dead? My guess is that Tyson killed him. That's why he went missing before Tyson showed up at the Cathedral and forced me to marry him. Even though I didn't want to be with Luke, it doesn't mean I wanted another dead body on my conscience.

The sound of a cell ringing fills the room, and I open my eyes when Tyson shifts in bed.

"Hello?" he answers, getting up. "Yeah..." He trails off, not wanting to speak any further with me lying next to him.

I watch him exit the bedroom, but he leaves the door open as he walks down the hall to the living room, out of earshot so I can't hear his conversation.

Who would be calling him this late? Early? Blackout didn't close until three in the morning. Then we cleaned up the club, plus our shower. The sun has to be coming up soon, if it's not already.

I sit up and reach for the nightstand to look at the time but realize I don't have a phone. I left the Cathedral immediately after the ceremony. My phone was in my purse in the room where I was getting ready. I left it all behind. If I can't have clothes to wear, I highly doubt he'll allow me any communication to the outside world. He wants me secluded. One hundred percent relying on him for everything.

Not like I have anyone to call or text anyway because I've never had any true friends. My mother can't save me, and my father has made it very clear where he stands. The only person who could potentially be on my side is my brother. And I can't even trust him anymore. My father will make sure he doesn't help me. He controls everyone in our family. He has the power.

"I'll call you when I get up," Tyson says. His voice gets closer as he walks down the hall back to the bedroom.

I shut my eyes and lie as still as I can, listening to him set his phone down and get back in bed.

The last thing on my mind is why he left the room to take the call.

TRUE TO TYSON'S WORD, I WOKE UP THIS MORNING TO HIM ordering men around in the living room who were delivering my things. Now, it was only clothes and bathroom essentials. I didn't get my king size bed that I love or any of my furniture. But it's all replaceable, right? People get their entire lives taken away in a matter of minutes in house fires and have to start over. The fact that they got out alive is most important, right?

Now, I'm not comparing my life to a house fire. I'm just trying to convince myself not to cry that I've got a rock on my finger, given to me by my sister's ex-boyfriend, and that he's making me his personal whore.

Everything is fine. I'm fine.

I walk out of the bathroom from hanging some clothes up in the closet when I see a black box on the bed. Tyson stands next to it at the dresser, putting on his watch. He looks up, seeing me in the mirror, and turns to face me. "Open it," he orders, nodding to the bed.

Picking up the box, I push the lid open and pull out a cell phone. My eyes shoot to his, and he walks over to me. "What happened to my cell phone?" I wonder, knowing this isn't it.

He doesn't answer. Instead, he pulls it out of the box and hands it to me. "It's already been charged."

I swipe the screen and see the background of us standing in the Cathedral at the altar in front of the Lords' table. "Who took this?" I ask.

Again, no answer. It was probably Ryat. He was the only one there who Tyson actually liked. Going to my contacts, I growl, "You're the only name in my phone."

"I'm the only person you need to call," he replies simply.

I throw the cell onto the bed and cross my arms over my chest. "What about my family?"

He gives a rough laugh. "Yeah, you won't have any contact with them."

"Tyson," I growl.

He walks over to me, and I stiffen when he reaches out and wraps his hand around my throat. It's not tight enough to restrict my air, but it pushes the collar into my neck. "Do not contact them. I will know and you will be punished, do you understand?"

"But—"

His hand tightens, and I stand up on my tiptoes, my hands gripping his wrist in a silent request to let go of me. He doesn't. "They don't give a fuck about you, Lake."

His words are spoken softly, but he might as well have yelled them in my face because even I can't argue that. "Like ... you do." I manage to get out through gritted teeth.

He pushes my back into a wall, slamming me into it, knocking what little breath I have left in my lungs out of it. "Go ahead, little darling. Communicate with them in any way, and I'll show you just how much I care." He releases me and steps back.

I rub my sore neck and begin to cough as tears fill my eyes. Without another word, he leaves the room. Picking up the cell, I sit on the edge of the bed. I have no doubt that he has an app downloaded that tells him every person I contact on here.

Refusing to contact him for anything, I place the phone in the top drawer of the nightstand and head back to the closet to finish putting away my things.

SEVENTEEN

TYSON

I enter my office, shutting the door behind me. I make it over to my desk, sitting down just as my cell phone rings. **Unknown** lights up the screen. "Tyson," I answer.

"Congratulations on getting your bride," a man says in greeting.

I lean back in my chair, getting comfortable. "You sound surprised."

He gives a dark laugh. "I knew you'd get what you wanted. You've been putting in the work for it anyway. Those devoted get rewarded," the Lord reminds me.

"And you?" I ask. "Are you keeping up your end?"

"Of course." He snorts, sounding offended.

"And?" I dig deeper, expecting an answer.

"And nothing yet. But we're getting closer," he promises.

I roll my eyes. They've been telling me this for years, but I'm a patient man, and things like this take time. "Keep me updated," I say and hang up, not even bothering with a goodbye.

Pulling up the cameras on my computer, I watch her in the apartment upstairs. She's on her knees in the middle of our closet, going through her clothes that arrived today. My right hand twirls my wedding ring around, feeling the weight of what I've done.

This was the only way I knew to save her. But I'm no saint. I'm going to make her hate me more than she already does. Is one devil better than the other? No. Evil is evil. It doesn't matter who dishes out the punishments. She'll still see this as her hell.

It's taken years to get to this point. I'm not stupid. I didn't expect her to accept her future with me overnight. She's not like her sister was.

I LIE IN MY BED AT THE HOUSE OF LORDS NEXT TO WHITNEY. It's well after two in the morning. She's naked, hands tied behind her back while she lies on her stomach. I brought her right back here after the vow ceremony at the Cathedral.

I fucked her until she passed out. Literally. I was on a mission to make sure she was so fucking drained she had to stay the night. Not like she was planning on going home anyway.

Getting out of my bed, I walk over to where her wet dress lies on the floor next to her purse. I pick it up, and dump out the contents, finding her cell. Climbing back into bed, I lean my back up against the headboard and press the button on the side to light up the screen to find it locked.

I want to laugh at the fact she thinks that'll stop me.

In a matter of seconds, I've got it unlocked and download the app I want that grants me access to her cell. If I'm going to complete my assignment, I need to know everything she knows.

SITTING BACK, I WATCH MY WIFE GO THROUGH HER THINGS and wonder just how much she knows. She and Whitney were close, but I highly doubt she knew everything.

Picking up my cell, I send her a text. When I don't immediately see her responding, I get up from my chair and storm out of my office.

LAIKYN

An hour later, I'm sitting in the middle of the closet still, sorting out my summer clothes when I hear the bathroom door open. The sound of it hitting the interior wall has me jumping to my feet just as Tyson enters the walk-in closet.

"Where is your phone?" he demands.

"In the nightstand," I answer honestly.

"Why?"

I bite my bottom lip, unable to answer that question. Telling him that I refuse to use it sounds stupid right now, considering how mad he seems over it.

Storming out of the closet, he returns seconds later, holding it out to me. "When I message you, I expect a response. Immediately. Do you understand?"

"I understand," I answer softly, reaching out to him and taking it from his hand.

He turns and exits just as quickly as he entered.

Standing, I look around at the mess I've made. My clothes are everywhere, but I decide I'll work on it later. As much as I want to say *fuck you* to my husband, I also don't want to piss him off. If he wants to see me so bad, then why didn't he just tell me what he wanted while he was in here.

Turning the cell on, it pings immediately with a text.

Your husband: My office. Now.

I roll my eyes. Seriously? He could have told me to go to his office in the first place when he was just in here. But I'm not surprised. I saw him do this with my sister once.

"W HERE IS YOUR PHONE?" TYSON DEMANDS AS I STAND IN THE *hallway, eavesdropping.*

"It got wet at dinner," Whitney explains.

"How does that happen?" he wonders, his voice telling me he doesn't believe a damn thing she just said.

"I accidentally knocked over my drink right on top of it. I've got a new one coming. It should be here tomorrow."

"Why didn't you use your sister's to call me when you got in last night? I've been calling you all day," he asks, letting out a growl.

My breathing picks up when I realize I could have his number in my phone.

"It was late when I got home. She was asleep."

I frown, wondering why she's lying. She didn't get home until after seven this morning. I was awake, eating breakfast downstairs, when she came running into the house dressed like she just came from the club with her makeup smeared and hair wet. I thought it was odd, but it had rained last night. The storm had woken me up around four in the morning.

"Babe..." I hear her soften her voice and imagine her wrapping her arms around his neck. "I'm sorry. Let me make it up to you."

"How do you plan on doing that?" His voice has dropped as well, huskier, sexier.

My heart starts to race as I listen with my back against the hall-way, trying to stay quiet and unseen. Her door is to my right, open just enough for me to hear but not able to look inside.

"You can choose." I hear them start to kiss and then they're moving around, followed by the sound of her bed hitting the wall as he slams her onto it. "My mouth or pussy?" she asks breathlessly.

"Both," he answers without hesitation. "I'm going to fuck your cunt until you come all over my cock, and then your mouth, so you lick it clean."

Sighing, I pull myself out of that memory. Careful what you wish for, right? I was excited that his number might be in my phone, and now it's the only contact I have. I place the phone in my pocket, leaving my mess behind to go see what he wants.

EIGHTEEN

TYSON

She enters my office and I look up at her dressed in nothing but a pair of cotton shorts and a T-shirt. Same thing she was wearing moments ago up in our apartment. "You wanted to see me." Her snarky tone tells me that she's holding back rolling her eyes at me.

"Come here." I stand and push my chair back, giving us both enough space to do what I have planned.

She walks over to me, and I grab her hand, bringing her around the desk and spinning her to face away from me. "Hands behind your back," I command, and she takes in a deep breath, dropping her head but doing as she's told.

I remove my belt from the loops of my jeans and wrap it around her wrists to hold them in place. Placing my palm on her back, I push her facedown across the side of the desk. I hook my fingers into her white shorts and pull them down her legs along with her black thong.

Opening the desk drawer, I remove the two things that I need and pop the top of the lube. I squeeze enough over my two fingers and rub them up over her pussy to her ass. She jumps, her body making the desk rattle.

"Do not move," I order, pressing my free hand on her back to hold her down.

"Please, Tyson." Her breathing has picked up as she begs. "Don't—"

"I'm not fucking it. Not yet," I inform her, and she whimpers. "Just relax, and it'll slide in much easier than if you try to fight it and tense up."

"What will slide in?" she rushes out.

I don't answer. Instead, I push my thumb against her ass, and I hear her start to cry. I pour more lube over it, making sure to coat it so much that it's running down her pussy and inner thighs. I push my finger into her, feeling it opening up for me.

"Tyson," she cries, her body still trying to fight me. Her tied hands clenching.

I remove my finger and enter it again, giving her a few seconds to get used to it before I push a second one in. "You're tense." I remove my fingers and slap her ass cheek hard enough to make her yelp in surprise and leave an instant handprint.

"I can't help it," she whines.

"Spread your legs," I order, needing her to open up more for me.

When she doesn't do as she's told, I pull her from the desk, her back to my front. I reach around, gripping her chin and whisper in her ear, "You're going to get on your knees and place your cheek on the floor with your ass up in the air. Do you understand, Lake?"

She softly cries but nods the best she can. I let go of her to see what she does, and she steps to the side of the desk, slowly gets to her shaking knees and bends over, placing her ass up in the air.

"Spread your legs. Wide open for me, little darling."

Quietly crying, she spreads them for me, and I fall into my chair and place my shoes inside of her calves on the floor, to hold them in place, and pick up the lube. I place some more on my fingers and begin the process once again of getting her ready for what I'm about to do to her. She cries, body rocking back and forth, but she stays open for me. Taking it, knowing there's no way out of what I have got planned for her.

Removing my fingers, I watch her body relax as if it's over and pour the lube over the butt plug. I begin running it over her ass and push the tip in, and her crying gets louder. "Almost done, Lake," I tell her, bending over in my chair and pushing a little more in each time. "You're doing so good, little darling." My free hand rubs her ass cheek, then slaps it, making her yelp.

I push it halfway in and hold it in place. "Rock back and forth," I order.

She pulls forward and slowly pushes back against it. "That's it, Lake. Fuck it. Show me that you want it."

Whimpering, she repeats the action and this time, I push against it, forcing more into her. She arches her back, her legs trying to close against my shoes, and I slap her outer thigh with my free hand as I push it in farther.

Watching the tapered tip disappear into her ass has my dick hard. I'm not normally an anal guy, but this needs to be done. If I'm being honest, I prefer a mouth over a cunt. There's just something about a woman on her knees, drool running out of the corners of her mouth while she gags on your dick that turns me on.

But what I've got going on with my wife isn't like any other woman I've fucked in my past. I will use every part of her. Over and over. To the point I don't have to tell her to spread her legs, open her mouth, or put her ass up in the air. She will just know which hole I want to use, and she will beg me for it.

Sitting back, I look over the black silicone butt plug in place. It's not big by any means. It's not meant to stretch her wide enough to take me just yet. That'll come later.

"You may stand," I tell her.

She lowers her ass, closing her legs, and stands. Turning to face me, she has her head down, her hair covering her face. I rise from my chair, pushing the long bleach-blond strands back and cupping her cheeks to force her to look up at me. "Go shower and get cleaned up."

Her bloodshot eyes meet mine. "How long do I have to keep it in?" she asks softly.

"Until I take it out."

She sniffs and nods once in understanding.

"You've got two hours to get ready," I inform her. I'm not really sure how long it'll take her. I know some women take more time than others. But now she's got everything she'll need to do her hair and makeup since her stuff was delivered today.

Her brows pull together. "The club doesn't open for another four."

"We're going to dinner."

"Tyson?" she gasps, realizing what that means. "You can't expect me—"

"I do, and you will." I interrupt whatever she was about to say, knowing exactly where she was going with that argument. "Now, go get ready. I'm going to finish up here and then I'll be up there." Letting go of her, I sit down, dismissing her.

LAIKYN

I MAKE MY WAY OUT OF HIS OFFICE ON SHAKY LEGS. IS THIS what they call the walk of shame? I'm having trouble catching my breath, I'm so embarrassed about what he just did to me.

I can feel the plug inside me. It's not uncomfortable, just awkward. My body wants to push it out. My thighs and legs are slippery from all the lube he used to make it fit.

Making my way into the apartment, I close the door and go

straight to the bathroom to start a shower. He said I had two hours to get ready for dinner. He has something planned, but I don't think Tyson Crawford does anything that isn't intentional.

I get undressed and turn to face away from the mirror and bend over because I can't not know what's inside me. I run my finger over the black rubbery base and jump when it's pushed inside of me.

The urge to remove it is strong. My hands are shaking and sweaty. But I know if I do, I'll get in trouble. Punished. I could always take it out and put it back in myself before he gets up here, but I'm not sure I have the strength to place it back in myself. It doesn't hurt right now, but it did when he pushed it inside me. Plus, I don't have any lube.

Shuffling from foot to foot, I know I have no other option. This is where he wants me. Uncomfortable and humiliated. Letting out a deep breath, I open up the glass door and start getting ready.

I'M IN AND OUT OF THE SHOWER IN LESS THAN FIFTEEN minutes. The longest part was scrubbing all the lube off my skin. It felt oily and didn't want to come off, even with the amount of soap I used.

Standing in the bathroom, I'm leaning over the countertop putting on my lipstick when I see Tyson enter. My breathing instantly picks up. I'm not sure if it's fear or anticipation. He's steered clear of me most of the day other than when he had me meet him in his office. I have a feeling that's how this marriage will be. I'll only see him when he needs me.

If I'm that lucky.

Trying to avoid his stare, I keep my eyes on myself in the mirror, but I can't help but feel the plug in my ass. Reminding me that it's there.

He comes up behind me and hooks his fingers into my shorts, and I drop the lipstick from my hand. It hits the counter before rolling onto the floor. Closing my eyes, I take in a shaky breath. I expect him to fuck me every day because he told me to meet him in his office before every shift, but I figured he'd wait until after our dinner. Guess that's stupid for me to assume it'll only be once a day. Men like Tyson need to be *serviced* as often as possible.

My pussy is still so sore, but my clit is throbbing. It's like it's begging for punishment. And the plug in my ass has me wet.

My cotton shorts drop to the floor at my bare feet, and a whimper escapes my lips. He runs his hands up the back of my shirt, pushing it up in the process, and he leans over, kissing my back tenderly and making a shiver run through my body. *Tyson Crawford is good.* I'll give him that.

When the shirt tugs on my underarms, I take the hint and raise my arms, letting him lift it over my head. I go to turn around to face him, but he stops me.

"Bend over," he commands, and I do as he says, knowing there's no other choice.

My naked body lies across the cold surface while he stands behind me fully dressed. "How's it feel?" he asks, his fingers pushing on the plug, making me whimper.

"Like you give a fuck." The words come out before I can even process them. It grants me a slap on the ass cheek that makes me yelp in surprise. The lingering sting has my pussy clenching.

He grips my freshly dried hair, jerking my head up off the countertop, and slams his hips into me, pinning me to the sharp edge and making me hiss in a breath. The plug pushes deeper inside my ass. "Tyson—"

"Just wait until I start fucking that mouth, Lake. You'll think twice before you open it."

I swallow at the threat, and he pulls his hips back from my ass just enough for him to reach between us. The sound of his zipper being lowered makes my breath quicken. The head of his dick is at my entrance moments later. No foreplay. I didn't earn that. One thing about Tyson is he doesn't need me. He wants me for some sick plan that I'll never know the secret to. I'm a toy to use, to fuck, to get him off and I hate how much my body likes it.

My breath is taken away when his large cock spreads my sore pussy wide open. He's so big, it hurts. "Feel how wet you are, Lake?" he asks. "How much your body likes being used?"

I hate how turned on I am from the plug, his words, and the way he wants me. It shouldn't be this way. I should be repulsed by the very thought of him and me together. I should be screaming nonstop and fighting him. Make him take it from me. But I'm bent over the counter, biting my tongue to stop myself from making any noises to show him how much I like it.

There's nothing soft about how he fucks me. His hand in my hair holds my head up so I have nothing to do other than look at myself in the mirror while he pounds his cock into my pussy and my hips into the side of the counter.

The sound of our bodies slapping fills the room and my lips fall open, a moan escaping that I can't hold in. Don't want to hold in. My eyes grow heavy as they watch him in the mirror. His are narrowed as if he's angry with himself. Or maybe he's mad at me. It doesn't matter. Every time he thrusts forward, he pushes on the plug. I feel so full. The combination of pleasure and pain takes my breath away while my soaked cunt tightens around him. The sound of his heavy breathing and grunts turns me on even more, and I'm reminded how much I hate myself over the fact that I actually like this vile man.

I'm so close, my body climbing that high that is right there...but he shoves his hips forward one last time, and he pulses inside of me, filling my pussy with his cum. I didn't get to. Again, it's not something I earned. I'm sure he just wants me to feel him dripping out of me while we sit at dinner.

Pulling out, he lets go of me, and I drop my cheek to the cool surface of the countertop, trying to catch my breath.

He pulls up his jeans. "Your outfit is on the bed."

I push myself up and slowly stand to turn and face him. "You picked out my outfit?" I'm not surprised. Like I said, I'm a doll to him. Something to show off to the town.

He doesn't answer and I walk out of the bathroom to the bedroom to find a dress, underwear, and heels laid out for me. My brother's words come to mind. *At least he has good taste.* But of course, he was talking about the other guy I was supposed to marry.

NINETEEN

TYSON

She sits next to me in my car, wearing the red dress I picked out for her along with matching six-inch Gucci heels. The butt plug in while my cum coats her black lace thong. The wedding ring and collar top off the look that screams MINE.

I watch her out of the corner of my eye, noticing the way she keeps moving in the seat. The butt plug doing what I wanted it to do—turn her on. Her cunt was soaked when I fucked her in the bathroom. Even now, she keeps running her hands up and down her bare thighs. She's silently begging to get off. To get a release that I'm going to make her earn.

She sits up straighter when she sees me pulling up to our destination. "Do we have a room?" she asks, her breathing picking up.

"No," I answer honestly. "We'll only be here for an hour." Less, if I have my way.

I come to a stop, and a guy opens my car door while another opens hers and helps her out. "Have a good evening, Mr. Crawford," one says as I take her hand and pull her up the stairs and into the Minson Hotel. We ride the elevator up to the twentieth floor and step out into Marble, the elite restaurant, that overlooks the city.

"Hello, Mr. Crawford. Your party is already seated. Please follow me." The blonde smiles at me brightly, completely ignoring the fact that I'm here with a woman.

"*Party?*" my wife whisper-shouts in my ear. "Who the fuck are we meeting for dinner, Tyson?"

I ignore her and follow the hostess to the back room. We're not here for an audience. Well, none other than who I have called to join us.

The hostess opens the double doors and steps aside to allow us to enter the dimly lit room. "Here you go, Mr. and Mrs. Crawford."

Lake stops, and a small gasp escapes her red-painted lips when she sees who we're dining with tonight.

The man stands from his chair and clears his throat. "Laikyn, Tyson." He nods to us, but I see the sharpness in his tight jaw. He doesn't want to be here, but he also couldn't turn down my request to meet us for dinner. I'm pretty sure he just agreed to have proof she isn't dead yet.

"Dad," she whispers. "Mom."

Her mother rolls her eyes and then throws back most of the wine in her glass. She also didn't have a choice to be here. Like her daughter, her husband informed her she'll attend. My father-in-law refusing my request to dine at his hotel would make him look foolish. And Mr. Minson is anything but a fool.

"I'll let your server know you've arrived," the hostess states, exiting the private room. She closes the tinted black glass double doors at her departure, silencing the chatter in the main part of the restaurant.

I help my wife over to the table and pull out a chair for her to sit in. I take the one next to her while we both face her parents. A silence lingers over the room, and I feel for the object in the pocket of my dress slacks. It's the icing on the cake for tonight.

The double doors open, and our server arrives, approaching the table. "Hello Mr. and Mrs. Minson. Mr. and Mrs. Crawford. What can I get you all to drink tonight?"

"Scotch." Her father answers first.

"Bring me a bottle." Her mother speaks, lifting her now empty wine glass. She's obviously had a head start.

"Of course. For you, Mrs. Crawford?" He looks at Laikyn.

She swallows nervously. "I'll take a glass of what she's having." She nods to her mom.

The server looks at me. "She'll have a water, and I'll take a whiskey—neat," I inform him.

"Perfect. I'll get those right out to you." He turns and takes off.

Lake's mother snorts at the fact I won't allow their daughter to drink. Her husband prefers her drunk all the time, but I'm nothing like him.

Reaching under the table. I rub my hand up and down Lake's thigh, making her jump. Her knees hit the table, causing it to rattle, and she clears her throat as if that's going to distract them from what really just happened.

"So Lake," her mother starts, "are you ready for your initiation?"

Her body tenses under my hand. "I, uh—"

"Lake won't be doing initiation." I interrupt my wife's rambling and calm her unease. There's no reason for her to be worried about that.

"All Ladies must participate in initiation." Mr. Minson looks over at his daughter. "Don't worry. I highly doubt that it'll be anything too drastic. It goes by level of power."

I refuse to acknowledge that he just tried to make a dig at the fact that I no longer hold the powerful title I was supposed to have before and gave it up for the opportunity to be sitting here with his daughter as my wife.

The server reappears and passes out our drinks. I pick up my whiskey. "Rules have changed for some," I decide to say, not wanting to give too much away but also making sure he understands he's not right.

He looks at me and then at his daughter. His jaw sharpens and he slams down the drink he was just given. Is he mad that she's not going to be initiated? If so, I don't know why he'd care.

"You're not a Lady unless you pay your dues," her mother adds, throwing back her now full glass of wine.

I look at Lake, and she drops her eyes to stare at her glass of water. It's like they want her to fail, which would make sense. They don't want her with me, and if she were to fail initiation to become a Lady, then she'd no longer be my wife. Would they rather her be shunned by the Lords? Killed? Than be with me? Abso-fucking-lutely.

To them, a dead daughter is better than one serving me. I know. History proves that.

"Are you ready to order?" the server asks.

We each take our turn ordering, and then he's gone. We sit in silence once again and I feel it's time to prove the point that I came here to prove.

I reach into the pocket of my slacks and push the button.

"FUCK!" Lake slams her hands down on the table, her body jerking in surprise.

"Laikyn," her mother scolds her. "Language."

She starts to stand, but my hand on her thigh tightens to prevent it. She stays here, where I want her. When she realizes that, she reaches out, grabs her mother's glass of wine, and takes a big gulp, coughing through a gasp when she pulls it away. I know she's never been a drinker before.

I bite back a smile at the thought of what she's feeling right now. She had no clue that the butt plug vibrated because I hadn't turned it on until now. I have it on the lowest setting, but it was still a surprise nonetheless. Not only does it vibrate but it's not called the rimmer for nothing.

She's rocking her hips in the chair, and she sets the now empty wine glass down. "Tyson?" She growls my name. Her hand drops to wrap around mine that sits on her thigh, and she digs her nails into my skin.

"Yes, little darling?" I ask, unable to stop my grin.

"May I speak to you for a second?" she asks tightly. "Privately?"

I push my chair back and stand, letting go of her thigh. "Of course."

She shoves hers back and jumps to her feet. Then she turns and all but runs off to the private restroom that's provided for this section of the restaurant.

I follow her. The moment we enter the restroom, she spins around on me. "You son of a—"

I wrap my hand around her throat and shove her back into the now closed door. I press my body into hers, and she whimpers, her eyes falling shut before they open to meet mine.

"That's no way to talk to your husband," I tell her.

She lets out a shaky breath, and I hold up my free hand with the remote in it. "Especially when he has the control."

"Please, Ty—"

I up the intensity, and she cries out, her hips pushing into mine. "Oh my God." She gasps, her hands gripping the sleeves of my crisp button-up.

I lean forward, my lips gently kissing her parted ones, tasting the lingering wine on hers. "I am the only god you will worship, little darling. Ready to get on your knees for me?"

"Please," she begs, her pretty, plump lips trembling. "Turn it off. Or I'm…"

"You'll what? Come?"

She closes her eyes tightly and whimpers once more, but her body presses into mine as her fingers dig into my arm. She's holding on for dear life.

I step back, pull her from the door, and turn her to face the bathroom mirror, wrapping my arm around her neck from behind. "Watch yourself, Lake. Watch yourself get off with nothing but a butt plug up your ass." I hold up the remote and turn it on full blast. I also take away her air at the same time, knowing if I don't, she'll be screaming so loud they'll hear her.

This part of the restaurant is reserved for her family. Her daddy fucking owns this hotel. I'm sure her parents are out there right now trying to hear whatever we have to say. And although I want them to know I've made her my whore, now that we're here, I'd rather not have them hear her come for me. That's for my ears only.

I lean down, whispering in her ear. "It's okay to like it, Lake. It won't be long before you beg me to fuck your ass." This is also why I didn't allow her to come earlier when I fucked her pussy in the bathroom. I wanted it to build and for her to explode when I finally allowed her this privilege.

She swallows, her hands coming up and gripping my shirt once again. This time trying to pull my arm away so she can breathe. I hold it in place.

Her lips are parted, her hips rocking back and forth, and the thin material of her dress displays her hard nipples. I want to bend her over and bury myself inside her pussy, but that's not what tonight is about. It's to prove just how much power I have over her without my dick. With a simple flick of a wrist, I can have her begging me.

Her eyes grow heavy, dark, thick lashes fluttering, and her body stiffens against mine. Her arms drop to her sides, and I loosen my hold on her neck just as she comes. She's gasping for air when I remove my arm from around her neck completely, and her head sags as her hands flatten out on the counter.

I gently gather her hair off her back, and she raises her head, her narrowed eyes meeting mine in the mirror. "You're a fucking bastard," she says through gasps, trying to catch her breath.

I pull on her hair, not enough to be rough but enough that she stands. I turn her to face me and cup her cheeks, loving how flushed her face looks. "That's no way to talk to your husband, who just got you off."

She bares her straight white teeth at me, and I smile.

"What do you say?" I ask her.

"Fuck you," she snaps, panting.

I bite back a smile. Leaning forward, I kiss her forehead and say, "You'll learn to be more appreciative of my kindness, little darling."

LAIKYN

I FALL INTO THE PASSENGER SEAT OF HIS CAR THAT THE VALET had waiting for us outside the Minson Hotel. After I came in the bathroom, we sat back down with my parents. All I could think about was the cum-covered underwear I had on. It was more awkward than it had been in the beginning. I felt like they could see it written all over my face. My father couldn't stop looking at my choker. My mother drank herself into a drunken stupor, but that was nothing new. She's been drunk most of my childhood. It got worse after Whitney passed, though.

Tyson gets into the car and drives off.

I cross my arms over my chest, pissed at him. But what did I expect? I should have known he had an ulterior motive to even take me out in public. Some of me thought he was taking me out on some kind of date. Fuck that. He wanted to show me off. Show his power off. He only married me in the first place to throw it in my parents' faces.

For a second, I was the dumb bitch I swore I'd never be. The same one that he turned my sister into. Well, that won't happen again.

Thankfully, he remains silent while we drive back to Blackout. I want to ask him about initiation but refrain from doing so. He'd probably lie to me anyway. My mother was right—a Lady has to be initiated. I'm not sure if he was telling the truth or not about me not having to. I'd rather not know, honestly.

If I'm given an assignment, I'll make sure to do whatever the fuck it is. That'd be an easy out for him—me failing at initiation. I would never willingly give him that kind of gratification.

Pulling up to Blackout, he parks in his designated spot and turns off the car. I get out and make my way over to the door. I have to wait for him to punch in the code to open the back door because I don't know it. The thundering bass vibrates my heels, and I make my way to the elevator, knowing I've got to go upstairs to change into my work outfit.

He grabs my hand as we step off the elevator, and I let him pull me down the hallway to the door to the apartment. Once we're inside, he lets go, and I make my way to the bathroom.

"Bend over the counter," he orders, entering as well.

The hairs on the back of my neck instantly rise, and my breathing picks up. Doing as I'm told, I bow my head and stare at my heels. My hands on the cold marble surface.

He comes up behind me, and I shiver as his knuckles run up my thighs, lifting the soft material of the dress in the process. My heart starts to pound when I feel my ass exposed to him. He bunches the dress at my waist and abandons it to pull my thong down my shaking thighs.

"I love how much my touch affects you, little darling," he says, sounding amused.

A whimper escapes my lips before I can stop it.

"Your body practically begs me to fuck it," he goes on, and I shuffle from foot to foot, knowing he's looking down at the butt plug in my exposed ass.

I jump at the feel of his hand between my legs, his fingers running over my soaked pussy before he pushes two into me, making my breath catch. When he pulls them out, I sag at the sound of his zipper. He told me he'd fuck me each night before my shift started. I guess he's getting it over with.

It's part of his plan to humiliate me. My family's name.

My breath catches when he pushes his cock into my already sore and sensitive pussy. Stretching me wide open to accommodate his size, he doesn't waste any time. Immediately, he starts fucking me. The sound of my heavy breathing fills the bathroom, along with the sound of his body hitting mine.

He places his finger over the butt plug, pushing on it, and it makes my pussy tighten around his dick. I bite my lip to keep from begging him to turn it on. I can't show how much I like being used by him. He already knows how much my body enjoys it.

"Tyson." His name slips from my lips, and I am unable to stop it.

His free hand grips my hair, and he yanks my head up, forcing a soft cry from my lips as I stare at him in the mirror over my head. "Don't you dare come," he demands.

My eyes fall closed. "I can't stop it."

He slams his dick into me, and I snap my eyes open when he lets go of my hair, reaches around, and wraps a hand around my neck, pulling my back to his front. He lowers his lips to my ear, his hard eyes still holding mine in the mirror. "If you come on my cock, you will be punished. Do you understand?"

I swallow against his fingers, crushing the choker into my sensitive skin. "Please—"

"Begging will only make it worse, Lake," he warns, and my

pussy once again clenches around his dick that is resting inside of me.

I need him to move. "Yes, sir." I manage to get out.

He growls, his hand tightening to the point it takes my air away. I don't fight him. I'd rather pass out than come on his dick. I don't want him to think that a part of me wonders what kind of punishment coming will get me. Instead, I grip the edge of the counter tighter while his hips start to move again.

He's brutal, shoving mine into the counter, not giving a fuck if he leaves bruises. Or maybe he's doing it on purpose. Either way, I let him take what he wants. My body, my dignity, my fucking mind.

I've only been Mrs. Crawford for two days, and already I'm his little bitch to treat as he pleases. He shoves his hips forward one last time with a grunt as his cock pulse inside me.

Letting go of my neck, it falls forward, and I suck in a ragged breath as he pulls out of my dripping pussy. He places his hand on my back, pushing my front onto the counter, and I go willingly, unable to meet his stare right now.

I want to cry from how sore I am, but I also want to beg him to let me come again.

I feel his fingers on the butt plug, and I try to relax, not sure what he's going to do with it, but a second later, I feel him pulling on it. I surprise myself as a moan escapes my parted lips when he pulls it free of my ass.

Trying to calm my breathing, he grabs my hair and yanks me to my feet, spinning me around to face him. I watch him bend down and grab my underwear bunched around my ankles. Standing, he pulls them up my shaking legs and places them on me.

Leaving my dress up around my waist, he steps into me, his hands on either side of my face. "You will not shower before your shift."

I lick my dry lips, already knowing this was coming. He wants me to feel him running out of me all night. "I understand."

"Good girl."

I don't know why those two words make me feel butterflies in my stomach all of a sudden. I shouldn't like pleasing him. I don't need praise or validation for something that I didn't even have a choice on. But he's shown me that when I'm good, he rewards me. And I'd love to get to come again tonight.

"Get changed. Your shift started an hour ago." With that, he lets go of me and walks out of the bathroom.

I take a second to collect my thoughts before entering the bedroom to find him already gone, and I take in a calming breath. My leotard, boy shorts, and fishnets are on the end of the bed. I pick them up to notice this isn't the leotard I wore last night. It looks identical except it snaps between the legs. It only takes me a second to understand why the change.

Trying to ignore those butterflies that flutter again, I quickly get changed before he comes back to punish me for taking my sweet time.

I'M DRESSED AND DOWN AT THE BAR IN LESS THAN FIFTEEN minutes. The club isn't packed just yet since it's not quite ten, but it is busy. I wonder just how busy it'll get since it's a Sunday night.

"Hey, Laikyn," Bethany yells at me over the music. "Tyson wants to see you."

I frown but set down my tray and start to walk toward the back hallway I know leads to the elevator for his office.

"He wants you in his back office," she calls out, taking a turn down a hallway that I've never been down before. There's a door at the end. She pushes it open, and I step inside.

I turn around when she chooses not to enter with me and

instead shuts the door. "Hey!" I try to open it, but it's locked. What the fuck? "Bethany?" I shout, knowing she can't hear me over the music. I yank on it, but nothing. "Open the damn door."

"You know..."

I spin around at the sound of a familiar voice. "Fuck." I place my hand on my chest, leaning back against the door and letting out a long breath. My heart now hammering in my chest. "You scared the shit out of me."

His brown eyes narrow on me. "Watch your language, young lady."

I stand, straightening my shoulders.

"Married for forty-eight hours, and he's already got you talking like him," my father growls.

What just happened hits me, and I gasp. "Dad, you can't be here. I can't be here." I turn back to the door and try again, but we're locked in here. "She'll go tell Tyson." I don't trust Bethany as far as I can throw her. I haven't gotten close enough to her to find out if she and my husband have a past or not, but the comment she made about my sister tells me she's known him for quite some time. Her loyalty will lie with Tyson, not me.

"She will not."

"Dad, she—"

"Works for me," he interrupts me, making me frown.

"What does she do for you?" I inquire, but he doesn't answer. Instead, he just stands there staring at my neck to the point it makes me nervous. I reach up and rub the shock collar. It's irritating, to say the least.

"God, you're a disgrace," he growls.

My stomach sinks at his words. I've never been one of his favorites. I was actually the only one he didn't care for. My sister was his *baby girl*. And my brother was going to run the world like my father does. I was the leftover who didn't matter.

"I don't have a choice." I try and justify what I've done. I try to think of what he's seen. Blood all over the bed in his hotel. Me almost coming at the table while at dinner. The way I'm dressed right now to go work at a nightclub. "Dad—"

He backhands me across the face, making me cry out. It wasn't as hard as the day of my wedding, but it still stings.

"At least your sister was willing to do what needed to be done," he snaps.

Cupping my throbbing cheek, I look up at him through my lashes. "What do you mean?"

"It doesn't matter." He fixes his tie and has the audacity to look annoyed. He steps closer, and I cower against the door as he towers over me. "You will do whatever needs to be done for this family. Do you understand me?"

I nod and whisper, "Yes, sir."

Adjusting his shoulders, he sighs as if momentarily satisfied with my answer. "That means if he wants to pass you around like the whore you've become, then you spread your fucking legs and let whoever he chooses fuck you."

I flinch at his words. The fact he's talking about me having sex with men makes me want to vomit. Even if I know Tyson won't do that. He's too possessive. His point is that *he* owns me. He proved that when he shot his employee for just touching me. "Yes, Father," I say to please him, knowing the only person who will fuck me is my husband. I never thought I'd be thankful for that. Because what my father just said proves he'd force me to whore myself out if need be.

"This is for you." He removes a cell phone from the inside of his suit jacket.

I take it from him with my shaking hands.

"Hide it but have it on you at all times. Do not let Tyson find it."

What? Tyson is so hands-on; I'd never be able to hide it on my body. "How am I supposed to—"

"Figure it out!" he shouts, interrupting me. Taking a deep breath, he lowers his voice. "You will receive your initiations through this phone."

"Initiations? I thought there was only one?"

"You'll have as many as they send you," he snaps. "And they will be completed, do you understand? Tyson wants you to fail. To be even more of a disgrace." His eyes drop to my black Vans and move up my fishnet tights to my booty shorts and leotard with a look of disgust. "Our family name would have been better off if you had been the one to die."

His words hurt me more than the slap to my face ever could because I've thought of them more times than I can count over the past few years. As a Lady, you are raised to serve. We were meant to bring our family pride by making the next generation of Lords and Ladies.

Only Tyson and I are aware that I'll never reproduce. Again, I'm thankful that my husband is too ashamed to knock me up. Even if my father doesn't want me to birth a Crawford, not having a child is a worse kind of failure in the Lords' eyes. Because to them, I can have a daughter that could one day marry up. It's a vicious cycle that I can't put on an innocent child. The women are to be used and the men rule.

"I'll be checking in frequently," he informs me as if I thought he wouldn't.

"Yes ... Father." I manage to get out without sounding like I'm about to cry.

"In the meantime, when I'm not around, just know Bethany will be watching."

She'll be his bitch. I wonder what he has on her to make her willing to be my babysitter. Or maybe she just hates me that much that she went to him and offered her services. "I understand," I whisper.

He knocks his knuckles on the door three times and then it

opens, letting him out. I take a second to collect my thoughts and get my breathing under control, unsure of what to do with the phone he gave me. I decide to run to the locker room and hide it in there for now before I make my way back to the side of the bar and grab my tray. I ignore Bethany, but I can feel her stare on me. I'm outnumbered. If I betray Tyson, there's no telling what he'll do to me. But if I betray my father? He'll have me killed. I've seen him do it for less. No one stands in a Minson's way. Not even blood.

I've got to pick a side and hope it's the right one.

TWENTY

LAIKYN

It's almost two in the morning and Blackout is slammed, which surprises me. I really didn't expect it to get this busy tonight. It looks like last night. Don't these people have to work tomorrow? Or go to class? It is a party town. Barrington University is a college for kids from all around the world. It costs families millions for their kids to go to college here. It's full of the elite and the one percent.

I've already watched two guys puke in trash cans. One guy had to carry his girlfriend out over his shoulder because she was passed out drunk. I had one table full of guys offer me a line of cocaine. It was right there on the table.

Blackout is known for drugs. If you want to get fucked up, this is where you come. I honestly don't know how Tyson keeps this place running. The cops have to give him a hard time. Maybe he pays them off, or perhaps they just don't care because a Lord runs this place.

"Lake?" Bethany yells at me, and I hold in a sigh.

"Yeah?" I ask, approaching her at the server station on the side of the bar.

"Tyson needs to see me upstairs; can you watch my section for me?"

I shouldn't care that she's going to be with my husband up in his office. But the first thought that enters my mind is that he's going to bend her over his desk and fuck her. And then there will be two of us working with Tyson's cum running out of our pussies.

"Laikyn?" She snaps my name, making me flinch. "Yes or no?"

It's not like I have a choice, right? If Tyson expects her to be in his office and she doesn't go, then I'll be in trouble for keeping her. Then I have to explain to him why I wouldn't watch her section for her. I nod. "Sure."

She turns, flipping her hair so it slaps me in the face, and practically runs across the floor to the elevator. My shoulders slump that I care if my husband is cheating on me already. I mean, I shouldn't be surprised. Lords aren't faithful. They don't have to be. Tyson didn't marry me because he loves me. Only stupid Ladies think their husbands will be faithful.

Our world teaches us to be nothing more than baby factories and sex dolls. And Bethany just asked me to watch her section to make it known that she will be in his office. She wants me watching the clock that Beau has behind the bar. She wants me to be aware if she spends five minutes or thirty with my husband.

"Lake, that table is looking for Bethany," Beau calls out, lifting his chin behind me.

Picking up my tray, I turn and walk over to the table with three guys and one woman. There are only three chairs, so she's sitting on one guy's lap. He's got one hand wrapped around her throat with her head back while he speaks into her ear. The other rests on her bare thigh that her mini dress shows off. It reminds me of Tyson.

He's so hands-on that it makes my mind race with all the possibilities of him and Bethany up in his office right now. "What can I get you guys?" I call out over the remix of "Hungry Eyes" by Eric Carmen vibrating the floor under my feet.

He lets go of her, and she lowers her head to look at me. Her heavy blue eyes are unfocused. She's probably on drugs, or already drunk. They don't have any drinks on their table, so they have just arrived.

They each give me an order before he slides his hand between her thighs, and she pushes it away. "Can we get another chair?" she asks me over the pounding bass.

I look around quickly. Their table normally has six chairs at it, but others have taken them to accommodate their overcrowded tables. "I'll see what I can do," I tell her and walk back over to the bar to place their order.

Once done, I return and give them their drinks, informing her that there are no other chairs at the moment, but I'll keep an eye out for one.

"It's fine. You can stay on my lap," the guy tells her, his hand slipping higher up underneath her dress. She goes to push his hand away, but he grabs her neck with his free hand, yanks her head back to where she must look up at the flashing lights, and lowers his lips to her ear, where he says something to her, making her legs fall open to give him access.

I turn, giving them my back and walking away, planning on coming back to check on them later. My husband is upstairs in his office possibly fucking another woman, so the last thing I want is a visual of what I think they're doing.

THIRTY MINUTES HAVE GONE BY, AND I HATE HOW PISSED I AM that I'm still watching her section. The guy and the girl abandoned their friends at their table and are probably fucking in a hallway or the bathroom at this point. He was practically finger fucking her just minutes ago when I checked on them.

I'm standing at the bar, checking Beau's clock once again, and I look away when I see him catching me.

My body tingles, and my skin feels hot and sweaty. I have no right to be this mad, right? He may be my husband, but he definitely doesn't belong to me. He never has, so I'm not sure why I think he should now. He wants everyone to know that he owns me, not the other way around.

I turn to go check on the tables once again but stop when I see Bethany walking across the floor toward the server station. She's fixing her hair up into a high pony and pulls on her leotard. She spots me and winks. "Thanks," she says, and my hands fist the sides of the tray.

"Did you just fuck my husband?" I turn and demand. I'm not sure why I even asked. Or why I even care. But he's fucked me like five times in the last forty-eight hours. How much sex can the guy have? I know I'm not an experienced whore, but fuck, I don't think I'm that bad. It's not like he allows me any control when it comes to him fucking me. And I have a feeling that Tyson always has to be in control in the bedroom.

She throws her long ponytail over her shoulder, smiling at me. Stepping in, I hold in my breath when she lowers her lips to my ear and speaks over the music. "I'm just doing what your *daddy* asked me to do." Then she pulls back and gives me a fuck you smile. "I can't help it that your husband didn't turn me down. He loves a woman on her knees with an open mouth." With that, she picks up her tray and goes to check on her table.

Tears sting my eyes. Why would my father want her to fuck Tyson? To prove that he doesn't love me? I already know that. Why is he proving it? The Lords won't care that he's being unfaithful. I can't divorce him. I have no fucking choice but to do what he wants when he wants it, so why make him fuck Bethany?

In front of me? Why does my father want to make my life more miserable than it already is?

Slamming my tray down on the bar top, I march my ass across the floor and to the elevator. If he's going to fuck around, I'm going to make sure he's aware that I know it.

TYSON

I'M SITTING AT MY DESK WHEN MY WIFE COMES BARGING IN, shoving my door open so hard that it hits the interior wall.

"Your shift isn't over." I lean back in my chair, crossing my arms over my chest.

Storming over to my desk, she slaps her hands down on it, glaring at me. I can't help the smile on my face at her little attitude. It's cute.

"If you fuck other women, I'm going to fuck other men."

The smile immediately drops off, and I stand. She pushes off the desk, taking a step back. Her shoulders pulled back, but I watch her swallow nervously. Making my way around the desk, I reach out, grip her fragile neck, not restricting her air just yet, and yank her to me, forcing a gasp from her plump lips.

"What the fuck did you just say to me?" I demand, my face so close to hers I can see the fear set into her eyes. *Just who the hell does she think she is?*

"Why did you marry me?" she asks, her voice much softer this time.

Her pulse races under my fingers. "If I have to ask you again, you'll answer from your knees," I growl, tightening my hand around her throat, hoping she understands that I'm referring to her shock collar. I want to know why she has an attitude all of a sudden. Even though I'm hard at the fact she's jealous of me fucking other women. The fact she wants to fuck another man

161

makes me want to hurt her. Fucking brand my name into her soft, flawless skin so every man who looks at her will know she belongs to me.

Her hands grip my forearms, and she tries to arch her neck to get in a breath, but I don't allow it. Her red-painted lips open and close before she finally gives up and her hands drop to her sides. I relax my grip just a little but still hold her in place.

"If you ... fuck other women ... I'm going to fuck other men." She manages to speak through gasps.

I let go of her, and she steps back, rubbing the sensitive skin and sucking in a deep breath.

"Look at me, Laikyn," I command.

Her watery eyes snap up to meet mine at the use of her first name, and I step into her. She doesn't retreat, but she's lost some of that confidence she had when she entered my office. "If I even think you're going to fuck another man, I'll kill him. In front of you. It'll be slow and painful. You will see his bloody corpse in your dreams for years to come." She swallows nervously. "And then I'll make you wish I did the same to you," I say honestly.

Her eyes narrow, and she lifts her chin. "But you'll fuck whoever you want?" She slams her hands into my chest, but I don't budge. "Why did you marry me if you're going to fuck around? To throw it in my face?" She slams her hands in my chest once again. "Like you did my sister?" her voice rises. "Huh? Just divorce me," she goes on. "You've proven your point."

I stare at her while she tries to catch her breath. She's panting, the anger evident all over her pretty face. "Just do us both a favor and divorce me!" she screams.

I grab her arm and yank her forward while spinning her to face my desk. I grab the back of her neck and shove her facedown, making her cry out at my force. "Remove your shorts," I snap, stepping back and letting go of her.

Reaching behind her, she shimmies out of them while

remaining bent over. Her soft cries now filled the room. As they fall to her Vans, I step forward and reach between her shaking legs, undoing the snaps that hold her leotard in place.

"I knew these would come in good use." I yank the material up to rest on her lower back, giving me a full view of her round ass and fishnet tights. "Hands behind your back, and don't move."

Sniffing, she does as she's told while I walk over to my desk. I open up the top drawer and grab what I need before going back to stand behind her. I wrap the zip tie around her wrists, pulling it tight, pinching her skin and making her whimper.

I reach out, grabbing a hold of her fishnets and ripping them over her ass, but allow her to leave her thong on. Then I undo my belt and yank it free of the belt loops on my dress slacks. I double it over and bring it down across her ass, getting to the point.

She screams, her body jerking. Standing to the side of her, I place my hand on her back, shoving her down when she tries to stand. "Count," I order.

"One," she cries out.

I let go of her back and do it again a little lower, hitting the top of her thighs this time, right across her fishnets, and they rip a little more.

Her body shakes. "T-wo."

Whack.

"Th-three." She's sobbing, and she's got several marks from my belt.

Whack.

"Four."

Whack.

"F—" She hiccups. "Five."

I drop it, grip her hair, and yank her to her feet. Turning her around, I grab a hold of her hips and pick her up, slamming her red and freshly spanked ass down on the desk.

She cries out, and I grip her chin, stepping between her open legs and forcing her to look up at me. Her makeup smears across her face from her tears. I didn't plan on hurting her, but she needs to understand I won't tolerate her attitude. I could have given her ten more, but even I know my limits. She got the point.

"If a Lord divorces his wife, he gets to choose who she is regifted to. Did you know that?"

Her bloodshot eyes widen, and she shakes her head the best she can with my hand gripping her chin. She can't push me away because her wrists are tied behind her back.

"I can't hear you," I growl.

"N-o. I didn't ... know that." She sniffs, her chest rising and falling quickly with each intake of breath.

"Is that what you want, Lake? Want me to divorce you and hand you over to another Lord of my choosing?"

"No." She licks her wet lips. "Please. Don't."

Although she hates me, she understands that there are way worse Lords out there. Ladies have come up missing, others dead. When a Lord is forced to marry a woman due to their name, rank, or convenience, they tend to get bored. And it's easier for them just to eliminate them completely.

Letting go of her neck, I run my fingers down her sternum over her heaving chest. "I think we've got something special, Lake. Don't you?"

She nods quickly, and I refrain from smiling at how well she'll lie to please me. I'd never give her away, but she doesn't need to know that. That would defeat the purpose of marrying her in the first place.

Reaching up, I gently push her hair off her shoulders to fall down her back. "Tell me, little darling, are you going to fuck another man?"

"No," she rushes out.

"Are you going to let another man touch or kiss you?" I go on.

Shaking her head, she sucks in a deep breath. "Only you."

"And who am I?"

Swallowing, she answers, "My husband."

Leaning in, I gently kiss her forehead. "Good girl." Pulling away, I grab her hips once again and pull her off the desk. She bites her bottom lip to keep from whimpering at the movement with her spanked ass. I pull her around my desk and open up the top drawer, grabbing my knife. Flipping it open, I cut through the zip tie. "Go upstairs, shower, and get in bed. I'll be there soon."

She goes back to the front of the desk, grabs her shorts, and pulls them up before running out of my office.

Sitting down, I pull up my surveillance and sit back, watching to see what happened tonight for her to get all pissy with me about who I fuck. I come to a spot where I see her talking to Bethany and push play. I can't hear what they're saying, but Bethany walks off across the dance floor, and I watch Lake take over her section.

Changing cameras, I follow Bethany to see her enter the locker room. I don't have cameras set up in there, but I fast-forward to see she was in there for almost thirty minutes. When she returns, she goes straight to Lake, and I can tell the moment she comes onto the camera that she already looks pissed. They exchange some words, and then Lake storms off to my office.

I turn it off and sit back. It doesn't take a rocket scientist to figure out what was said between the two of them. Bethany wants her to think that she was up in my office fucking me. The question is, why?

Is Bethany jealous of my wife? I mean, we fucked around, but it was never more than sex. I used her, and she enjoyed it. That was that. Maybe she did it knowing Lake would come up here and be punished. Or maybe she was hoping Lake would find a guy and retaliate. Making me push my wife away so I'd fuck Bethany again.

Making my way down to the first floor, I get off the elevator and go over to the bar while the "S & M" club remix by Rihanna plays as the purple and blue lights flash to the bass.

Beau spots me from behind the main bar and frowns. "Everything okay, boss?" he yells as I approach the server station.

I lean over the counter and holler back, "Have Nicki take over Lake's section for the rest of the night."

"Not sure why you even gave her a section, to begin with." I look to my right and see Bethany now standing next to me. She nods to Beau and orders a bottle service for one of her tables.

I decide to keep my mouth shut for now. I want to see how this plays out. I like my wife jealous.

Bethany looks up at me at my silence and adds, "She can't cut it." Pressing her side into the bar, she pushes her tits into my face. I've never cared about them before, so I'm not sure why she'd think I do now.

"She can." I decide to say, defending my wife. "But I'd rather have her on her back than working on her feet tonight."

Her eyes widen at my words for the briefest second before narrowing at my comment.

Beau laughs, handing Bethany her order. I tap the bar top with my knuckles and then turn, walking off and making my way back up to my office.

TWENTY-ONE

LAIKYN

I wake the following day, and my ass is still on fire. I fell asleep on my stomach to help relieve the sting, but I woke up on my back. I also woke up alone. I don't remember Tyson coming upstairs last night. After he spanked me like a child, I ran to the apartment and cried myself to sleep.

I was embarrassed, ashamed, and wet from what he did to me. I'm glad he didn't make me remove my cum-covered thong and fishnets in his office to check.

But I learned a lesson. He can hand me over to another Lord. And I don't want that. I've seen Lords over the years and know what some wives have been through. Heard my mother's friends cry to her before because of what they were made to do. Tyson is a fucking bastard, but it could be worse.

Sitting up, I hiss in a breath at the stretch of skin from his belt across my ass and upper thighs. I manage to get off the bed and get dressed. He didn't even let me finish my shift last night. Not like I could have. Nobody wants to be waited on by a crying woman who looks like a mess.

When I realize I'm alone in the apartment, I make my way to

the elevator and down to the first floor. It opens, and I immediately hear voices. One being Tyson's.

I step out and the dance floor comes into view. I see the back of Tyson standing by the main bar, dressed in a new pair of dark gray slacks and a black button-up. Two police officers stand in front of him. One guy has his hands on his belt. The other hangs onto the top of his shirt, gripping his collar.

"Lake?" the one with his hands on his shirt says when my eyes meet mine.

"Collin," I say, smiling.

Tyson spins around at the sound of my voice, and the look on his face has my smile dropping.

"What the hell are you doing here, babe?" Collin asks, looking me up and down. The flirtatious smile on his face tells me he has no idea that I'm now a married woman.

Before I can answer, the other cop clears his throat. "Can we stay on track here?"

I walk over to stand next to Tyson and ask, "What's going on?"

"Ma'am," the one I don't know speaks, holding out a picture to me. "Have you seen this woman?"

I take it in my hand and recognize her instantly. "I—"

"She has not." Tyson answers for me, yanking it from my hand and handing it back to the cop. "I've already told you. The woman hasn't been here."

I look up at him, confused as to why he would lie. Maybe he hasn't seen her here.

"Lake, is this true? You've never seen her?" Collin asks, his eyes are now hard on mine as if he knows the truth.

I lick my lips nervously and nod once. "Yeah. I've never seen her." The lie burns my mouth as much as Tyson's belt stung my ass.

"I think—"

"My wife and I have answered your questions. You may leave now." Tyson interrupts the other cop.

Collin's eyes drop to my left hand, and they widen when they see my ring. I feel like Tyson said that on purpose. Once again, making it known that I'm his. Another pissing contest. Why can he do that, but I can't? It's a two-way street. I mean, he hasn't openly flirted with other women in front of me, but he also didn't deny fucking other women last night when I confronted him.

"Here's my card if you hear anything." The cop holds one out to Tyson, but he shoves his hands in the pockets of his dress slacks.

I take it. "Thank you, and we will." Dropping my eyes to it, I avoid Collin's stare. Instead, I watch their black shoes turn and hear Tyson lead them out the front exit. I don't look up until I hear him locking the door.

He comes over to me, yanks the card from my hand, and rips it to pieces before shoving them into his pocket.

"Why did you lie to them?" I demand.

"Blackout doesn't cooperate with cops. Never have, never will."

So he did know she was here? "You made *me* lie." I fist my hands.

He turns to face me. "You chose to lie."

Like he gave me a choice. "I was about to tell them that I saw her here last night when you interrupted me. Not letting me."

"I'll look into it," he says.

"You're not a cop," I snap.

"Speaking of cops. How did Collin know you?"

I cross my arms over my chest, refusing to answer. He smirks, at my silence and my thighs tighten in anticipation as to what he's thinking.

Reaching down to his slacks, he slowly undoes his belt, and my heart starts to hammer in my chest. "I dated him." I rush out, and his hands stop. No matter how turned on it made me last night, I can't take another right now. It's still too sensitive.

"Dated him?" he repeats slowly.

Nodding, I add, "Back when you were with Whitney." He stiffens at the mention of my sister's name, but he wanted to know.

Stepping into me, he reaches up, running his thumb over my lips, and I hold my breath at the action. "What did you two do?" he asks, and I know exactly what he's referring to.

He knows he was my first when it came to sex. But there are other things I could have done. He's never asked about my past experiences until now. For some reason, he seems to care. "He kissed me," I say softly.

"On the mouth?"

I nod.

"Anywhere else?" His thumb pulls down my bottom lip, and I breathe heavily.

"No," I answer, my voice shaking.

He seems satisfied with that and turns, walking away.

"What happened to her?" I ask, wanting to know.

He stops, turns back to face me, and says, "She's missing." Then he gives me his back once again and walks behind the bar.

He's lying. I can tell. The question is why?

TYSON

How did I not know that she and Collin dated? I mean, I never paid that much attention to her life when I was with Whitney, but I feel like I should have known this. All the research I did on her over the past three years should have told me they were together at some point. I needed to know what I was getting into with her. An ex-boyfriend never popped up.

There are two problems with this new information. One, I

don't like the fact that they have any kind of past. Two, I don't like that he knows she's here at Blackout.

I made it very clear that she belongs to me. But if he knows she works here, he could start appearing just to see her. And the fact that she's barely dressed while working makes that thought worse.

"You are not allowed to speak to him," I inform her as she walks past the bar.

Stopping, she turns to face me, hands on her hips, and she lets out a huff. "Excuse me?"

"You heard me." I'm not repeating myself.

"Jesus, Tyson. We didn't fuck." She rolls her eyes.

"I don't give a fuck what you did and didn't do with him." Her cheeks flush at my words, even if they were a lie. If he had slept with her, he'd be dead. "He's a cop. And I don't want him trying to get any information from you."

"Like what?"

"Lake," I growl.

"You going to kill him?" She gives a rough laugh.

"If need be."

Her laughter stops, and her lips thin. "Don't be stupid, Tyson. You just said so yourself, he's a cop."

"I've killed more important men for less." I shrug carelessly. Walking over to her, I reach out and run my hand through her bleach-blond hair. Her large blue eyes look up into mine at my confession. "We both took a vow that you belong to me and I to you. That means I will eliminate anyone who I think may be a threat to our marriage."

"But you're free to fuck whoever you want," she snaps, referring to Bethany.

I still haven't informed my wife that she's the only woman I'll be fucking. And I don't plan to. I like her jealous. I don't see how sleeping around on her proves anything. The point is that she belongs to me. Besides, her cunt, mouth, and ass are all I'm going

171

to need. "Just stay the fuck away from him. And if he comes in here, you tell me. Understand?" I'm busy when the club is open. I don't have time to sit and watch the cameras a hundred percent of the time. It's never bothered me until now. Especially after what I saw last night between her and Bethany.

She glares at me for a long second but finally nods. "Understood." Turning, she starts to walk off but pauses once more and faces me. "Why haven't you asked me about the girl?"

"What's there to ask?" I avoid her question.

"If I spoke to her? Who I saw her with?"

"None of that matters."

"Of course not. If you're not a Lord in this world, no one gives a fuck about you." With that, she turns and stomps off to head back upstairs.

SHE'S AVOIDED ME MOST OF THE DAY. AFTER SHE CAME DOWN when the cops were here, she went upstairs and hid from me in our apartment. I've had too much to do to chase her down or to care whether she's mad at me.

It's now eleven and I just realized that she didn't come into my office before her shift started. She'll get punished for that. I highly doubt she forgot like I did. She's just trying to prove a point. Well, I'll prove my own.

I stand at the railing on the breezeway on the second floor, looking down over the club. My eyes are on my wife. It's after midnight, and we're packed. I stepped out of my office for a breather. I see someone walk up out of the corner of my eye and look over to see it's Ryat. He looks down to where I was looking and sees Lake laughing at a table with five men sitting at it.

Ryat pulls a sucker out of his mouth, leaning his forearms on the railing. "You let her wear that?"

"It's her uniform," I answer.

"Yeah." He sucks on the sucker once more before pulling it free from his mouth. "I get why you're doing it, but how are you doing it?"

I push off the railing and turn to face him.

He shrugs at my silence. "Even before I loved my wife, she was mine. And I don't like anyone seeing what belongs to me." He pulls his cell out of his pocket to reply to a text he just received, and I turn back to look down at my wife.

She's bent over, her face in front of the guy's face while he says something to her. I know the music is loud and she can't hear what he wants to order, but it makes my fingers curl around the railing. I'm supposed to put her on display. That's the point of what I'm doing. But Ryat is right. I don't like how close he is to her. Or how when she pulls back and walks away, his eyes are on her ass while his friends smile, all of them knowing exactly what he's thinking about.

I push off the railing and stomp off to my office. Ryat enters behind me.

"Why are you here?" I ask, picking up the remote to my cameras and placing them on the big screen to watch my wife.

He leans over and looks up at the TV hanging on the wall above his head. Once he sees what I'm watching, he straightens and smirks at me.

Dick.

"I was on my way home and thought I'd drop by." He finally answers.

I pull my cell out of my pocket and send her a text.

My office. Now.

Setting it on the desk, I watch her on the camera, seeing her cell light up on the counter next to the server station. She reads over my message and then places it back on the bar, picks up her tray, and walks over to the table where the guys are seated, ignoring me.

Okay, Lake. Let's play the game your way.

"What are you doing out this late?" I ask him.

"Had to stop by the house of Lords," he answers vaguely.

I nod, knowing that's all I will get from him. Ryat and I have been close since his freshman year, when I was a senior. But we're not girls who share everything.

His cell rings, breaking the silence, and he answers. "Hello?" He nods to himself. "I just stopped by Blackout for a second. I'm about to leave and will be home soon. Need me to stop and get anything for you?" He listens as the person—I'm guessing his wife —on the other end speaks. "Love you." He hangs up and stands. "I'll call you tomorrow."

TWENTY-TWO

LAIKYN

I'm avoiding my husband. I'm mad at him, and although my ass reminds me that he's probably going to spank me once again, I just don't care.

How can he be mad at me for something I did years ago, when he's fucking other women now? That doesn't make any sense to me. I guess it doesn't have to. He's Tyson and does whatever he wants. I'm Laikyn, who has to obey her husband's every demand.

The club has closed, and I'm standing at the end of the bar counting out my tips. I'm really surprised at how much I make here. And Tyson hasn't taken my money away. Yet. Which means there's hope that I can put some away for a rainy day if I ever get the chance to run away from this place and this life. I've always dreamed of something different.

I hear laughter and look over my shoulder to see four guys walking through the empty club, talking to one another. They make their way across the dance floor and over to the round booth where Tyson always sits while we're cleaning up. He hasn't even looked my way.

He's proving a point. I know he saw that I read his text and chose to ignore it. My punishment will come later when we're alone.

"Fuck, those guys are all fine." A cocktail waitress by the name of Starla sighs. She hasn't spoken directly to me, and she's not now either.

Bethany snorts. "They're all pretty much spoken for. So don't waste your breath."

"They can choke me any day," Starla goes on. "Especially Colton Knox."

I watch them all slide into the booth and talk to Tyson, wondering what they're saying and who they are. Why is he allowing them in here after hours? I haven't seen them here before, so I know they don't work at the club.

"He's definitely not available," Bethany tells her.

"What? He's a fuckboy. He's not saving himself for marriage." She snorts.

"He's secretly in love with his stepsister." Bethany rolls her eyes. "Everyone knows this. And Alex is in love with his high school sweetheart. That's how they got their job working for Tyson to begin with."

"They're Lords?" I ask without thought.

Bethany and Starla both spin around to look at me. Their eyes narrow as if they had no clue I was standing right by them. I'm used to that—being invisible.

"No," Starla answers, surprising me. "They work *for* a Lord. There's a difference."

I nod as if I understand. But I don't. What does this Alex guy and his girlfriend have to do with Blackout and Tyson?

We all go about our business, cleaning our sections, tipping the bartenders, and putting everything away. When I finish, I look over to see Tyson sitting in the booth with the four men. I make my way upstairs and enter the bathroom. Yawning, I get undressed and step into the shower. I'm exhausted and just want to go to bed.

The warm water stings as it runs down over the belt marks on my ass, and it makes it hard to wash my hair, but I manage as quickly as I can.

Stepping out, I walk over to the mirror and run my hand through the steam on it. I stare at myself and sigh. I hate how I look. I don't even recognize myself anymore. Over the past few years, I was transformed into someone that I'm not. It's changed me. I felt myself slowly slip away every day.

My eyes look sad, my lips frown. Dropping the towel, I see my fake boobs, and I want to cry. I allowed a man to change me. Well, not like I had a choice, but I didn't even end up with him. Now I'm stuck with this person that I don't want to be.

Being told that you're not good enough over and over gets to you. No matter how much you try to ignore it, you start to tell yourself that maybe one day it'll get better, but it doesn't.

I miss my dark hair, small boobs, and smile that I used to have. I always knew I'd be someone's Lady, and although I didn't love the idea, I was okay with it. I accepted it. Then everything changed.

Three years ago

"I got you something," Luke says, entering my bedroom at my parents' without even knocking. Good thing I'm dressed. My own mother won't even alert me when he comes over to visit me or my father.

"What is it?" I sit up straighter on my bed.

He walks over and sits down on the side, holding out an envelope for me. "Go ahead, open it."

I gently pull apart the seal and remove the card inside. I read over it and frown. "I don't understand."

He rips it from my hands. "It's a gift card."

"To a doctor. What's wrong with me?" I'm not sick. Why the hell would he get me this?

"It's for your tits, babe." He points at my chest. "He's the best plastic surgeon in California. He's booked out for the next year, but I got you in, in three months."

"Oh." My shoulders slump.

"I've already told him the size I want. And I've already spoken to your mother. She's going to go with you, and you guys will spend a few nights there. They're going to look amazing."

I stare down at my hands, and he grips my chin, forcing me to meet his eyes. "What's wrong?"

Why wouldn't I be okay with him wanting to change my body? I mean, how dare I be confident and like how I look? I didn't get to pick who I spent the rest of my life with, so I shouldn't be surprised. My sister was killed, then this guy shows up in our lives, and I'm just handed over like a piece to be traded. "He's going to be power-ful," my mother told me. "You'll be set for life." That doesn't matter when your life is hell.

"Nothing." I lie because he won't care, just like the rest of them.

THAT'S WHEN I KNEW I'D NEVER HAVE A SAY IN HOW I LIVE my life. If I refused anything that Luke wanted, my parents would make sure he got it. After that, he just kept changing things about me. My father joined in on it too. I always walked into a room and was already greeted with things that I needed to work on. A personal trainer to stay in shape. A diet. It was never-ending. I had to drop eight pounds for the wedding. The dress was designed in the size that Luke wanted it. Then I had to make sure I fit into it.

Maybe Tyson could be different in this aspect. He doesn't want me to look a certain way, so it seems. It never hurts to ask.

TYSON

I ENTER THE APARTMENT AND MASTER SUITE TO FIND HER walking out of the bathroom. She comes to a stop and looks down at the floor for a long second before her eyes slowly lift to look at me through her long lashes. She's already showered, her hair still damp and makeup off her face, dressed in one of my T-shirts. My cock instantly gets hard noticing her hard nipples through the thin fabric.

"Can I color my hair?" she asks softly.

"No."

"You didn't even consider it," she growls, her eyes narrowing on mine as she lifts her chin.

"Why do you want to change it?" I ask my own question, curious of her answer. I'm pretty sure I already know, though.

"Never mind." She turns to walk to the bed, but I grab her upper arm, bringing her to a stop.

"Did Luke make you bleach it?" I wonder. Maybe he prefers blondes.

She bows her head, biting on her lips nervously. I reach out, letting my knuckles run over her breasts, noticing how she pushes her chest into my touch. I bet she's begging to get off right now. "I asked you a question, Lake."

"No," She answers softly.

"Then who?" I ask.

She looks up at me, her eyes red. "My dad."

"Why would he care what color your hair is?" I snort at the thought.

She swallows. "He said I looked too much like Whitney," she whispers. "We weren't even allowed to mention her name. So the fact that he thought of her every time he looked at me disgusted him."

Lake and Whitney looked nothing alike, other than they were

179

both brunettes. But even that wasn't identical. Whitney's was darker, and she kept it shorter—just below the shoulders. Why would it bother him how Lake looked? That doesn't make sense.

Reaching out, I take a piece of her hair and twirl it around my finger. I step into her, letting go of it. I slide my fingers through the damp strands to the back of her head and I gently tug, forcing her eyes to meet mine. "If you want to change your hair, then change it." I don't want to give her permission to change something that she doesn't like about herself. Her body has already been altered because a man told her it wasn't what he wanted.

Her eyes light up, our earlier fight forgotten, and her plump lips pull into a big smile. She throws her arms around my neck. "Thank you." She presses her lips to mine to give me a kiss. It's innocent and thoughtless on her part. Just an action of gratitude.

She goes to pull away, but I use my hand that holds onto her head to keep her in place. I part my lips, forcing hers open as my tongue enters her mouth, wanting to taste my wife. My free hand wraps around her waist, holding her to me. Fuck, I want to bend her over and run my tongue along the slashes on her ass. Hear her gasp as my teeth sink into her skin and listen to her cry as I make her beg me to let her come.

But not tonight. I pull away and give her my back. Walking into the bathroom, I shut the door behind me. This is just the beginning of her punishment for avoiding me tonight. If she doesn't want to come see me, then she sure as fuck isn't getting off. And as hard as my cock is right now, I'm not sure I'd be able to do a quickie and finish before she could.

TWENTY-THREE

LAIKYN

I fell asleep last night after Tyson left me in the bedroom wanting more after that kiss. I was so turned on and my pussy was dripping for him. But he turned me down. I know why. He was mad at me, which is crazy because I was the one who started the fight. I was supposed to make him suffer, not the other way around.

I don't even remember passing out in bed, but I woke up this morning all alone and was excited to change my hair color only to realize I have no car and no way to get it done. So his answer was probably just to fuck with me. He's not going to take me to get it done.

He spent the entire day in his office, and I slept most of it away. I only got to fix myself something to eat and then went back to bed. Now it's another night and another shift at Blackout.

I exit the bathroom and walk into the bedroom, where I see several boxes on the bed wrapped with white ribbon. Tyson stands at the foot of the bed with his hands shoved in the front pockets of his gray slacks.

I pull the towel tighter around myself as nervousness sets in.

He hasn't spoken to me all day. I was mad at him and ignored the fact he wanted me in his office before my shift. Then I also avoided his text. I shut off my phone and pretended it had died. But I knew better. He'd retaliate. I felt good about it last night, but now I'm on high alert. I've been waiting for him to attack all day. "I need to get dressed for my shift."

"Come here." He ignores me.

Knowing that I can't do the same to him, I walk over to stand in front of my husband and let go of the towel. My hands slap my bare thighs as my arms fall to my sides. It's crazy how comfortable I am with him seeing me naked now. Another choice I didn't have but am now used to.

He grabs a pair of black fishnet tights. These are different from the ones I usually wear. They don't have the rhinestones on them. "Sit on the end of the bed. I'm going to dress you."

This is new, but I expect Tyson to be this way—unpredictable. I sit down and lift my right foot off the floor. He kneels, sliding the rough material over one foot and then the other. He slowly moves them up and over my calves. Standing, he pulls me to my feet and continues pulling them up over my thighs, and when he makes it to my ass, I hiss in a breath. It's still sensitive. He keeps pulling them up and over my stomach. They're high-waisted and come up all the way to my belly button. I realize he didn't let me put any underwear on first. I never wear fishnets without them. I have a feeling they'll be rough against my pussy as I run around the club working, and that's what he wants—all my attention between my legs.

He opens up one of the smaller boxes and removes a pair of black leather booty shorts. I place my hands on his shoulder while he helps me into them as well.

Turning, he zips them up the back, and I glance at my ass in the mirror on top of the dresser. Half my ass cheeks hang out of the bottom. They too are high-waisted—more than the ones I usually wear—and if you look close enough, you can see the belt marks on my ass.

He opens another box, and it's a black silk corset. "Grab the dresser," he orders, and I reach out, gripping the edge, wondering why my uniform isn't what we normally wear.

He bends down and has me step into it, pulling it up carefully so as not to tangle the black nylon strings. Once he gets it in place, he starts tightening it. So much that it makes me whimper. "I won't be able to breathe," I say, flattening my hand across my stomach while he jerks my body back and forth as he laces it up.

Again, he ignores me.

Once done, he goes to another box and pulls out a pair of black Dior heels. They're gorgeous. Platform style with at least a six-inch skinny heel. Bending down, he lifts one foot at a time, sliding them on.

"Tyson." I grip his shoulders once they're in place. "I can't work in these all night." Is he punishing me for last night? For ignoring him? God, I'd gladly bend over, remove my clothes, and let him spank my ass instead of having to serve in these tonight. But that's the point of a punishment.

Standing, he goes over to the dresser and grabs what looks like black leather cuffs.

"What are those?" I ask him, confused.

He kneels once again, and I look down to watch him wrap the black cuff around my ankle, fastening the buckle in place. Then takes the skinny black leather strap underneath my shoes where the top of the arch meets the heel. He fastens it to the black leather cuff that is attached and wraps around my ankle.

My heart starts to pick up when he pulls a silver lock out of his pocket and slides through both straps where they meet on the outside of either ankle, securing the heels to my feet. "Tyson, I can't—"

He stands, baby-blue eyes staring down at me and cutting my

words off. "Tonight, you will willingly crawl to me, little darling." I whimper, understanding what he means. "How long until you do, depends on you."

He removes his cell and then undoes the choker from around my neck. Opening up the last box, he steps behind me where I can't see what he's doing. But seconds later, he wraps a thicker black leather choker around my neck. It forces my neck up and comes to a point at the top of my chest between my breasts, covering my entire neck. I feel him fasten it and lock it as well. He lets my hair fall down to cover the back.

Placing his hands on my upper arms, he meets my eyes in the mirror. "I'll see you soon." He gently kisses my cheek and then exits the bedroom.

By the time I make it down to the club, my feet are already killing me. My calves burn, and my neck is sore. It's hard to turn it from side to side. How the hell does he expect me to work like this?

He doesn't. That's the point. He wants me to abandon my shift and crawl to him in his office.

"Someone's in trouble." Bethany laughs, looking me up and down.

She's dressed in a black leather catsuit, but I notice she's wearing platforms. Looking around, I see Beau dressed in black leather pants, a mesh black top, and cuffs around his wrists. It's a theme night. BDSM. I knew about it. I overheard Starla talking about it last night, but thought it was for the customers, not the employees.

"You've already got two tables, Lake," Beau informs me. His eyes drop to my tits. This corset has them shoved up to my fucking neck. My chin can practically rest on them. Then add the collar

184

I'm wearing. They definitely can't be missed. "VIP is going to be crazy tonight," he tells me.

Bethany was about to walk away with her tray, but she pauses. "I have VIP," she states.

"No." He nods to me. "Lake does." He places a glass of what looks like a mixed drink next to my tray and nods behind me. "Table twenty asked for this. He hasn't paid for it yet."

"No, she doesn't." Bethany slams her tray down on the edge of the bar. "I do."

He rolls his eyes and rips the schedule off the back wall, placing it down in front of us. I bite my bottom lip. Sure, as fuck. Tyson must have changed it sometime today and given me VIP.

"What the fuck, Lake?" she snaps, turning her angry eyes on me. She looks like she wants to hit me with her tray.

"I didn't ask for it," I growl back at her. Pissed at not only Tyson but now her too. She makes it sound like I have to double-cross her. I'm not after anyone in this club, and I sure as fuck didn't ask to marry her boss that she obviously has a sexual past with.

"No, you just fucked for it." She reaches out, grabs the glass of mixed drink, and takes a step back from me, dumping the contents onto my legs.

I gasp, jumping back as it runs down my calves, and into my high heels that are cuffed to my ankles. "What the fuck, Bethany!" I shout.

She slams the empty glass on the counter and smiles at me. "Have a good night. We're going to be slammed." Then she tosses her hair over her shoulder and storms off with a fucking smile on her face.

I wiggle my toes, feeling the drink at the bottom of my heels. My feet already sliding, shoving my toes to the end. The heels have a high arch, making the alcohol puddle inside. I pick one foot up at a time, kicking the heel to my ass, trying to tip it upside down to let the drink run out. It works but some remains. So I grab some bar napkins and start shoving them into the side of the heels, trying to soak up whatever I can.

"What can I do?" Beau asks me with a sigh.

"Get me a new fucking drink," I snap, picking up my tray. I turn, heading to VIP, and realize why Tyson gave it to me. It's elevated up off the main floor. I have to go up and down ten stairs. Each fucking time. In these heels. That are now wet. I already want to cry.

Goddamn him.

Tyson was right. I'll be crawling to him tonight. And it won't take me long.

TYSON

I SIT AT MY DESK WHEN THE DOOR OPENS. I LOOK UP TO SEE Lake enter, wobbling like Bambi, and I sit back in my chair as she shuts the door and leans back against it. I refrain from smiling.

Tears silently run down her pretty face. She's been crying for a few minutes because her makeup is already ruined. She doesn't say anything. Instead, she drops to her hands and knees, a cry ripping from her parted lips. I don't know if it's from relief or pain. The way the collar is made, she can't avert her eyes in shame. She has to look up at me while she slowly crawls across my office floor to my desk. I stay where I'm at, enjoying the small victory.

She comes around my desk and looks up at me with red-rimmed eyes and trembling lips.

I lean forward and run my thumb over her lip before pulling it down to show me her perfectly glowing white teeth.

You don't get more royalty than her in my world. A queen of sorts forced to marry the riff-raff—a man who gave up his high-ranking title to slum it with the peasants.

186

"Was that so hard?" I ask, and she whimpers. "You'll learn that your pride will get you in trouble, darling."

"Pl-ease?" she chokes out.

"Turn around, remove your shorts and put your ass up in the air. Face on the floor."

Her face falls. "Ty—"

"Go back to work, Lake." I dismiss her at her refusal to do as I say. Turning to my computer, I start responding to an email I have when I hear her softly crying. Looking out of the corner of my eye, I see her turning her back to me. She pushes her shorts down her legs, places the side of her tear-streaked face on the floor, and spreads her legs, placing her ass and cunt up in the air.

I turn my chair once again to face her while she sits impatiently. She rocks her hips back and forth, trying to get comfortable. Nothing will work. This is a punishment.

Reaching out, I push my fingers through the holes of her fishnets and run two fingers over her cunt. "Do you enjoy pain, Lake?" I ask. I'm met with silence. "Because you're wet." To prove my point, I plunge them into her pussy, and she rocks back against them. "You will learn that I will always win, Lake. No matter if I have to cheat."

I unlock both of the locks and remove the shackles from around her ankles. Then I pull the heel off, and she cries out in relief. I hold up the shoe, turning it upside down, and liquid runs out of it. I frown. "Why is your shoe wet?"

She remains facedown, and I pull the other one off. Same thing.

"Lake?" I bark her name.

"I knocked my water off the bar and spilled it on my heels," she softly answers.

I lift the shoe to my nose and sniff. It smells like Red Bull. *Why is she lying?* "Turn around and face me. Stay on your knees."

Lifting herself off the floor, she does as I say and looks up at me. I reach out and cup her tear-streaked face. "Last time. Why are they wet?"

She blinks her watery lashes, and whispers, "I spilled my water..."

"Get up, put your shorts back on, and sit on the couch," I command, cutting her off. She's not telling the truth.

Getting to her feet, she slides on her shorts and manages to walk over to the leather couch and plops down, her arms wrapping around her chest, but her chin is lifted high due to the collar still in place.

I go back to my computer and pull up the security footage.

I rewind it until I see my wife coming up to the side of the bar. I watch her, Beau, and Bethany exchange some words. Looks like they're arguing. He shows them the schedule, and I smile.

Then Bethany grabs the drink on the counter and tosses it onto my wife's legs. The smile drops off my face. Bethany storms off, and I watch Lake try to get the drink out of her heels unsuccessfully.

Turning it off, I sit back in my seat, looking back over at Lake. She sits there as tears silently run down her pretty face. I thought she was crying when she entered my office because of her pride. It had nothing to do with that. It was because she'd been walking around with wet high heels on.

Glancing at the clock on my computer, I see she's been working for over an hour. It had to have been painful. I mean, the point was for it to be painful, but not like that. I wanted to force my hand. Show her that I was in charge here. But not like this. I control my wife, not anyone else.

I pick up my office phone and push five for the bar. Beau answers and the sound of the bass filters through the phone. "Yes, sir?" he calls out.

"Send Bethany up here," I order.

"On it." He hangs up and I sit back in my seat, staring at the heels on my desk.

"Tyson." Lake jumps to her feet, her face scrunching at the pain she feels, knowing exactly what I'm about to do.

"Sit down, Lake," I order.

"But—"

"Sit. Down," I bark out, pissed off. Not at her but the situation. She is my wife. Mine to own. I can do with her as I please, not some little bitch who thinks she owns this place.

Lake falls into her seat and closes her eyes, letting out a deep sigh as my door opens. "You wanted to see me, sir?" Bethany enters with a naughty smile on her face as if this is a booty call. It drops off the moment she sees Lake sitting on the couch.

"I'm going to give you one chance—"

"You little bitch. You snitched on me!" she yells, turning on Lake, interrupting me.

My wife jumps to her bare feet once more. "I didn't say shit."

"Enough!" I shout, and the room falls silent. "This is your one chance, Bethany, to tell me what happened." I stand, placing my hands in the pockets of my slacks.

She lets out a huff and crosses her arms over her chest. Silence follows.

I nod in understanding. "Sit on the couch, Bethany." She takes in a nervous breath before doing as she's told. "Lake, come here."

I turn, giving them both my back to pick up what I need off my desk and then turn to see my wife standing in front of me. "Bethany will wear these tonight." I hold out the shoes and cuffs to my wife. "Put them on her."

Her wide eyes stare up into mine as her shaky hands take them. "Tyson," she whispers. "Please don't." Her voice trembles as she begs me not to make her do this.

I don't give a fuck.

She sniffs, taking them from me, and I can't help but reach out

189

and rub my thumb along her cheek, smearing the black mascara that has run down her pretty doll-like face. "You've been given an order, little darling."

Her shoulders fall, and she turns to a pissed-off Bethany who sits on the couch. She reaches out, snatches them from her hand, and puts them on, slamming her feet down on the floor. My wife kneels at her feet and places the cuffs on. Just like I did hers. I smile at the fact that I don't even have to tell her to place them on tightly.

Once done, my wife stands and turns to face me. I walk over to her. "Go upstairs and wait for me."

She turns and exits the room, more than happy to obey that command.

"Ty—"

I turn and face Bethany, who now stands in front of me.

"It was an accident," she says, her eyes desperately pleading with me. "I didn't mean to."

Ignoring her, I go over to my mini fridge that I keep in my office and open it up. I unscrew the top of a bottle of water. I step into her, and her breathing picks up as I lean down, making sure to pour the water directly into the heels until it's spilling over the closed toe.

I stand, tossing the empty water bottle across the room. Reaching out, I grip her neck and slam her back into the nearest wall. "This is your only warning. Leave my wife alone. Do you understand me?"

"Tyson—"

Gripping it tighter, I pull her from the wall and slam her back into it. "Don't fucking touch her. Don't talk to her. Don't even look at her. Do you understand?" I'm shouting in her face.

Tears run down her cheeks, and her lips are parted as she tries to suck in a breath. Stepping back, I let go of her, and she falls to her knees, gasping for air.

I ignore her and walk over to my desk where I sit down, putting my attention on my computer. "If that is something you can't do, then you can quit right now," I offer.

It takes her a second to get to her feet, and she makes her way to the front of my desk. Sniffing, she speaks, "I understand, sir."

Looking up at her, I say, "You will keep your section and add the VIP." She whimpers, knowing what I'm doing. "After closing, come up to my office, and I'll remove the cuffs." Dismissing her once again, she turns to leave my office. "Oh, Bethany. You'll be buying my wife a new pair of shoes with the tips you make." My wife isn't going to be wearing a pair of designer heels that have had alcohol spilled on them.

Nodding, she opens the door and exits my office.

TWENTY-FOUR

LAIKYN

I sit on the end of the bed, naked. It wasn't easy getting myself undressed, but I managed. It's hard to breathe with this large collar around my neck. He placed a lock on it so I couldn't get it off.

The apartment is dead silent, other than the pounding of the music below in the club. The bedroom light is on so he can see what a *good girl* I'm being. I'm fucking shaking at what he made me do to Bethany. A part of me thought it was a victory. The other part reminds me that she's working for my father. She's going to tell him what happened, and he'll find a way to punish me too.

It's never-ending. At least Tyson gets me off. I'd take his punishment over anyone else's.

The sound of the apartment door opening and closing has my breathing picking up. He enters the bedroom a moment later and I stare straight ahead, unable to look him in the eyes.

"You lied to me," he says.

I say nothing. It wasn't a question. I lied because I thought that was my only option. Telling on Bethany wasn't going to do me any good.

"Lie on the bed. Facedown," he commands.

I turn around and crawl onto it, lying on my stomach, praying that he doesn't spank me. I'm still too sore. But that's the point, right? Punishments aren't supposed to feel good. Even though it'll hurt, I'll still get wet. Hell, I'm wet now. I've been soaked all night. He's already trained my body to want him. To beg for him.

I hear him behind me in the bathroom and the closet. He comes back moments later and doesn't even bother to tell me what to do this time. He just does it himself.

He spreads my legs far apart, and I feel something wrap around each ankle. I pull on them, but he's tied them, wide open. I groan, pushing my face into the comforter.

The bed dips as he gets onto it. He straddles my lower back and grabs my arms, pulling them behind me. I have to arch my neck due to the high collar, and I realize he's not going to take it off.

My breath hitches when the cold metal wraps around my wrists before they click into place. They're tight, and I twist my wrists just to test them out. They're the real deal.

He gets up off me, and I feel his fingers between my spread legs, making me jump. He pushes two into me and starts to roughly fuck my cunt.

I moan, my body rocking back and forth on the bed the best it can. I try to lift my hips to give him better access but that's hard to do in my position. He removes his fingers and I sag against the bed only to feel them back in moments later.

Pushing my pussy open, I feel something slip inside, and I begin to pant when a soft buzzing begins. "Tyson." I bury my face into the comforter so I can lift my hips.

He grips my hair and yanks my head back, making me cry out. His face now by mine. "You'll lie here until I get back, Lake."

I whimper. He's going to leave me like this. "I'm ... sorry."

"You won't lie to me, little darling. Otherwise, you get fucked.

And not the way you like." He lets go of my hair, and my face falls to the bed once more.

Without saying another word, he turns off the light and shuts the bedroom door, leaving me in complete darkness.

TYSON

I'VE JUST SAT DOWN AT MY DESK WHEN THE DOOR OPENS, AND I look up to see Bethany enter. She looks worse than Lake did earlier when she came in crying and wobbling.

"You didn't cover all of your tables," I inform her, letting her know I was watching on the cameras.

She sniffs, walking to the couch and sitting down on it. She whimpers, getting off her feet.

"Come here," I command, and she bows her head. Using her hands, she pushes herself up off the couch and makes her way over to stand beside my desk. I grab the key and unlock the cuffs; she falls off the side of the heels onto her ass to the floor.

With shaking hands, she reaches into her pouch and pulls out her tips from tonight. "I'll ... bring the rest ... tomorrow," she chokes out through her soft sobs.

I count the cash. She only made three hundred tonight, further proving my point that she passed most of her tables off. "You'll bring me your tips after every shift until they're paid for," I inform her. Bringing money from home isn't going to count.

She nods, getting to her shaky feet. "Yes, sir."

"Get the fuck out of my office and go home, Bethany," I order, and she hobbles out as fast as she can.

I close down my office and make my way back up to the apartment. Turning on the bedroom light, I find her right where I left her. Tied facedown and moaning into our bed. "Miss me, little darling?" I ask, removing my belt from my slacks.

She doesn't answer me. Instead, she buries her face into the sheets. I smile and undo my slacks. I remove them along with my boxer briefs and button-up.

I tied her so her legs are wide open, each ankle to each bedpost of the footboard. Reaching out, I grab her thighs and pull her toward the edge. "Bend your knees. Ass in the air," I command.

It takes her a second to get where I want her, but she manages with my help. She's making whimpering noises in this position, considering that the posture collar around her neck is probably making it hard to breathe.

"Let's see how wet you are." I tug on the vibrator, pulling it free from her cunt and she cries out, her body sagging now that she can finally relax.

I position myself between her legs and grab my hard dick. I slide it into her soaking cunt and start fucking her hard and fast. Her voice rings out into the room.

Grabbing her hair, I yank her head back and fuck her into the bed like the whore I'm turning her into.

TWENTY-FIVE

LAIKYN

I t's been two weeks since Tyson hijacked my wedding to Luke. Thankfully, my father hasn't made any more appearances at Blackout. And actually, the more I think about what he did, the more concerned I get. Why would he come here? Why risk being seen? I'm guessing that Bethany helped him sneak in and out. But still, if Tyson saw him, I have no doubt he'd kill my father without thought. Then I'm sure Bethany would rat me out about the fact I was aware he's been inside of Blackout. She's been avoiding me and won't even make eye contact. It also makes me nervous. It's almost as if Tyson set me up for her to come after me only to get onto her and force her back. My head is spinning from the possibilities of what the fuck is happening. If I could drink, I'd stay drunk just to slow down my mind.

I'm lying in our bed watching TV, eating a bag of chips, when the bedroom door opens. Tyson enters. He's left me alone most days since he punished me for lying to him about what Bethany did. It's been weird actually. I visit him before my shift, and he fucks me and sends me on my way. I'm up here and asleep before he's done with what he needs to do, and then I wake up the following morning alone. It's all part of his head games. Nothing but sex, then total isolation. I don't exist to him unless he's using my body.

"Throw on some clothes, we're leaving in ten minutes," he announces.

"Where are we going?" I ask, sitting up.

"Our house."

It's not the fact that he actually answered that makes me pause. It's how he called it *our* house. I swallow nervously, getting out of bed, and I run my hands down my bare thighs. "I'm already dressed," I say, looking down at my cotton shorts and tank top. Not like I need to look my best just to go to the house. "I can get ready when we get back," I say, knowing my shift doesn't start for five hours.

"We'll be staying there tonight," he informs me.

"Oh," I say softly. "So I'm not working tonight?"

"No." He enters the bathroom, closing the door behind him. The act pisses me off.

I turn the knob to find it unlocked and open it. I push harder than I meant to, and it slams into the interior wall.

He's standing in front of his sink, washing his hands, and his eyes meet mine in the mirror.

I flinch and mumble, "Sorry." I didn't do it on purpose. "Why are we going there?" I haven't seen daylight other than through the windows of this apartment since our wedding day, and even then, it was raining. So why are we leaving all of a sudden?

He turns off the water, picks up the towel, and spins to face me, wiping off his hands. "We're going to get ready for a party tonight."

My frown deepens. "A party at your house?"

"It's *our* house." He tosses the towel and walks over to me. "And no. The party is at the house of Lords."

My eyes widen. I've always wanted to go there. I used to hear my sister talk about it to her friends all the time. They threw some wild parties, and crazy shit went down there. "What kind of party?" I ask nervously. If he's allowing me to skip my shift, then it must be something important, especially if he won't be working tonight.

"The senior Lords are graduating from Barrington soon. Tonight is the night they are celebrated for that." His eyes search mine before he adds. "Your parents will be there."

I swallow nervously at that thought. I haven't seen my father since he was here at Blackout, and I haven't seen my mother since our dinner at the Minson Hotel when I had a vibrating butt plug shoved up my ass. "Will other Ladies be there?" I ask.

He frowns, wondering why I would ask that and avoid the conversation about my parents. "Yes."

At least I can try and make some friends. I never had that problem growing up. I wasn't quiet, but I also wasn't a social butterfly. Not until after Whitney died. Then I had no one. It would be nice to have someone to talk to other than the man I was forced to marry.

A knock sounds on the apartment door, and it makes me jump. No one is ever up here with us.

He turns, exiting the master suite and closing the door behind him.

TYSON

I OPEN THE DOOR TO THE APARTMENT TO SEE COLTON AND Finn standing there. "You wanted to see us, sir?" Colton asks.

"Come in." I take a quick look down the hall to make sure she's kept our bedroom door shut. "I won't be at Blackout tonight," I say, facing them.

Colton crosses his arms over his chest while Finn jumps up

and sits on the barstool. "Going to the house of Lords for the graduation party?"

I nod. "And we'll be staying at the house tonight. I'll be back here in the morning. So you four are in charge."

Finn's eyes go large, and I narrow mine on his. "Don't fuck it up."

"Wouldn't dare." He raises both of his hands in surrender.

"If anyone causes any problems, put them in the basement and lock them up. We'll take care of it tomorrow."

"Yes, sir." Finn jumps off the barstool.

"And the cop?" Colton asks.

I've filled them in on the situation with the missing girl and Collin. And that he is not to be around my wife. They're not here every night, but when they are, I like the extra eyes on Lake. "What about him?" I snap.

"If he shows up again?" His eyes slide to the hallway as if he knows my wife is back there.

"He won't stay long." Not once Collin finds out Laikyn isn't here. He won't want to be associated with this place unless it was for a good reason. My wife is the *only* reason. He is a Lord, but I highly doubt he's going to the house of Lords party tonight. He's not required to be there.

The bedroom door opens, and we all look down the hallway to see Lake walking toward us. Her brow furrows as she looks from Colton to Finn and then to me. "Everything okay?" she asks.

"They were just leaving." I open the front door and nod to the guys as they exit. "Ready?" I ask her.

"Yeah," she answers slowly while eyeing me. She expects me to say something about the guys, but I'm not going to. Laikyn may be my wife, but she doesn't need to know anything about how I run Blackout. Or what they do for me.

"Let's go."

TWENTY-SIX

LAIKYN

I've never been to Tyson's house. When my sister dated him, he lived at the house of Lords, which is where all the Lords are required to live while attending Barrington. Lords come from all around the world to attend Barrington during their years of initiation, so they make them all stay under one roof where they can be watched twenty-four seven. That is until their senior year. They have more freedom then once they're given their chosens.

So when he pulls through a wrought-iron gate and up to a house that could only be described as a haunted mansion, my eyes widen in surprise.

It sits back in the woods, hidden from the road. It's white with black trim and a matching roof. He brings the car to a stop, and I get out. I wonder how long he's even had this place. He seems to live at Blackout.

Tyson walks up the stone steps to the black double doors and opens them. It doesn't surprise me that they weren't even locked. "I've got some work to do," he says. "I'll be in my study." He checks his watch and adds, "You've got an hour before they arrive."

"Who?" I ask nervously. Hopefully, he's not talking about my parents. I don't mind seeing them at the party where there will be a lot of people. I can try to avoid them or let Tyson do all the talking. I'm not sure I can face my father after all the things he said to me in the hallway closet at Blackout. But here? In this house? I don't want to be alone with just the four of us.

"I've got some ladies bringing you a few dress selections," he answers.

"Oh," I say, surprised. "Is the party that important?" The Lords have always gone all out for their parties and celebrations. But I'd think they would have the party at the cathedral if it was that big of a deal.

He reaches out and takes a strand of my wild hair between his fingers. I look up at him through my dark lashes as his pretty blue eyes search mine. "It is for us. It'll be our first public appearance as Mr. and Mrs. Crawford."

I swallow nervously, wondering what he'll do before we leave here tonight. Will he have me bend over so he can put a butt plug in my ass? Will he make me wear my shock collar? Or will he make me wear wrist cuffs? A leash? Maybe he'll take a marker and write *Tyson's bitch* on my forehead. My parents will be there, so it would make sense for Tyson to claim me in front of them.

A smirk appears on his handsome face as if he's reading my mind, and he leans forward, gently kissing my forehead. I don't know why I whimper, but the action feels too intimate. I'd rather him bend me over and fuck my pussy until I'm begging to come than show love and affection. I think he knows that, and that's why he does it. He has to throw in a little tenderness with the fucks to keep me constantly guessing his intentions.

"Mr. and Mrs. Crawford. Welcome home."

Tyson pulls back, and I look over to a man standing in the foyer. He's dressed in a black and white tux with a kind smile and his arms behind his back. He looks to be in his fifties with dark hair and green eyes.

"Lake, this is William. William, this is Laikyn." Tyson introduces me to who I can only guess is his butler. Of course, he has one. Why are we staying at Blackout when we could be living here?

"It's a pleasure to meet you, Mrs. Crawford." He reaches out his right hand.

I place mine in his, and he brings it to his lips, kissing my knuckles. "Please call me Lake."

Tyson's cell rings, and he pulls it out of his pocket. "I have to take this."

"Go. I'll show Mrs. Crawford to the master suite." William informs him, obviously going to ignore the fact that I want to be called Lake.

Tyson answers his cell and immediately starts walking up the grand staircase to where I'm guessing his study is. I look over the black banister and the pristine white carpet. This place is gorgeous. The white walls have different sizes of black-and-white abstract art hanging in various places. There's none of himself or anyone else from what I can see.

"Please follow me, Mrs. Crawford," William says, turning and walking down a hallway.

"How long have you worked for Tyson?" I ask, being nosy. Tyson isn't going to tell me anything, so I might as well try my shot with William.

"Since he was a young boy," he answers, and I come to a stop.

He worked for Tyson's parents. I'm sure when Tyson bought this house, he moved with him. Meaning he probably knew my sister.

"Everything okay, Mrs. Crawford?" he asks, noticing I've stopped walking.

I meet his stare. The question on the tip of my tongue is to ask if he knew Whitney, but I can't get the words out. He steps closer to me, and I break the stare and look to my right. There's an open door. I frown, stepping into it. There are boxes everywhere. But it's what I see hanging from the ceiling that makes my heart skip a beat. "Where did you get that?" I point at my wedding dress.

"Your mother had all these brought over for you," he answers. "I ordered a display case for it. It should be here next week." William smiles proudly at me. "It was made to fit your dress."

"What?" I ask wide-eyed. "What-what is in all of these boxes?" How did my mother get this stuff here? I left the dress in the honeymoon suite.

"Items from your wedding, ma'am."

"Items from my wedding?" I repeat, whispering to myself. I rip open a box that sits on top of a table and look inside to find black tapered candles. They're from the Lords' table at the altar. There has to be more than twenty inside. There's a smaller box, and it has my heels from that day.

I open another box, and my chest tightens when I see it's nothing but pictures. They're of my sister and me; they were in my room back at our parents' house. "Does Tyson know this stuff is here?" I ask numbly. Looking over, I see the bag that Tyson had me leave behind in the hotel room.

"Yes, ma'am." He nods. "He arranged it."

Why is all this here? What am I supposed to do with it and why did Tyson not tell me? "I don't understand why he'd do this," I say softly.

"If I may ..." William clears his throat, and I look at him, trying to ignore the way my heart races from all my stuff in this room. "Mr. Crawford isn't a bad man. He's just the type who does whatever needs to be done," he says simply as if I'm supposed to know what that means.

He looks at me expectantly, and I lick my lips, remembering my manners. "Thank you." The way he frowns tells me he's not buying my gratitude.

"Of course." He nods and walks over to the door, holding it open for me. "This way."

I follow him down a long hallway and take a right toward a set of black double doors. He pushes them open. "Your master suite, Mrs. Crawford."

I step inside to see the large room. A black four-post Alaskan king-size bed sets up against a dark gray wall with black silk sheets and duvet. White and red decorative pillows have been fluffed and strategically placed. It's obvious more than just William takes care of this place. No man cares that much about their bed, especially one that doesn't live here. A white leather couch sits at the foot of the bed with a blanket draped across the armrest.

"I'll leave you to it, Mrs. Crawford. Our guests should be arriving soon," he reminds me, closing the bedroom door behind him.

I enter the bathroom to see all of my products that Tyson had delivered to the apartment at Blackout are also here. From my shampoo to my soap. From my razor to my favorite lotion. I hate that it makes me smile.

Getting undressed, I enter the shower, starting to get ready and trying not to think about the spare bedroom that has all of my stuff in it.

"Mrs. Crawford?" a woman says.

"Yes?" I exit the bathroom to find three women standing in the master suite. One looks to be fifty, dressed in an all-white suit with fire-engine red heels on. The other two look to be her daughters around my age. They all three smile at me. They're whispering and giggling with one another. "Please call me Lake."

"Ladies." The older woman says tightly when she sees me. The two others straighten and clear their throats.

"Lake." She gives me a soft nod. "Mr. Crawford wanted us to show you some dresses." The older woman smiles at me brightly. "We've brought quite a selection for you. Is it okay to set them up in here? Or would you like them somewhere else?"

"Here is fine," I answer nervously.

"We'll have everything brought in and set up for you," she says, and they all three turn to leave the bedroom.

"I can't believe we're in Tyson's house." One of the girls squeals.

"Right?" the other agrees. "God, she's so pretty. They make a perfect couple." Their whispering voices trail off as they walk down the hallway, and I stand nibbling on my lip, not sure what I'm supposed to be doing.

They return with garment bags hanging on racks that are on wheels. More than I can count. And they wheel in trunks that are full of heels when they open them.

"May I ask you a personal question?" the young brunette asks me.

The other's eyes dart around the room, making sure their mother isn't close enough to hear it.

"Sure."

"Can I see your ring?" She looks down at my hand.

I lift my left hand, and she gently holds it, looking at the ring. I've never really paid much attention to it other than that one time while in the bathtub on our wedding day. It's been an annoyance, a reminder of my life sentence.

"It's gorgeous," the girl says in awe, staring at it.

"It is." I agree. Even I can't deny that.

"I heard he flew to Paris and had it specially made just for you," she continues, her eyes coming up to meet mine.

I shake my head. "Oh, I—"

"I heard that he paid millions—with an s—for it."

I laugh at that. "No..."

Her face goes serious, and I stop talking. "A red diamond is the rarest diamond color in the world," she informs me.

"Oh," I say. It reminds me of a bleeding heart with its intense crimson color. Or blood since we had to bleed for one another. I highly doubt Tyson picked this ring for anything other than a sick reminder that I'm bound to him until one of us dies.

"They are also the most expensive diamond per carat of all colored diamonds," the other adds.

"Ladies," their mother snaps, entering the room, and they scramble back to face her.

"Yes, Mother?" they ask in unison.

"Do not bother Mrs. Crawford," She scolds them.

"Oh, they weren't bothering me," I assure her.

She gives me a tight smile, and I avert my eyes, afraid I'm now in trouble. "Let's get started." She claps her hands.

As they start pulling out dresses for me to look at, I examine my ring. It really is gorgeous. But they have to be rumors. Tyson wouldn't go that far out of his way to have a ring made for me or pay that much money for a woman he doesn't love.

TYSON

I'm in my study when my cell rings. I'm about to turn the fucking thing off because I'm not in the mood to deal with it tonight. "Hello?" I ask, holding in a sigh when I see who it is.

"Son." My father's voice sounds just as dead as it always has. "Your mother wanted me to call." Of course, she did. I haven't heard directly from my mother since she found out that I wasn't going to live the life that her and my father raised me for. "She's expecting to meet our daughter-in-law tonight."

I love how he said *she*. Because I know he doesn't give a fuck. "We'll be at the house of Lords," I say.

"I will let her know." He hangs up. Nothing else for him to say.

He could have done that in a text. I drop my phone to my desk and run my hands through my hair as a knock sounds on my door. "Come in."

William enters. "Can I get you anything, sir?"

"I'll take a whiskey. Neat," I say. "Thank you."

"My pleasure, sir." He goes to leave but turns back around to face me. "Mrs. Crawford found her things in the spare room, sir."

"How did she find them?" I growl.

"I apologize, sir. I had left the door open."

So what if she knows I brought her things here? It doesn't mean anything. Her parents already had her stuff packed up, ready to be delivered to Luke's house. I just intercepted them. "Thanks for letting me know." I wave it off, and he shuts the door.

My cell goes off once more and I grind my teeth. "What?" I bark out, not even bothering to look and see who it is.

"Hello to you too," the voice says coldly on the other end.

I pull the phone from my ear to see **BLOCKED** on my screen. "You better have something for calling me."

"I do."

"Well?" I'm not in the mood for games tonight. At least, not the kind they want to play. I do, however, have some that I'm going to play with my wife. And they're keeping me from that.

"I'm calling to confirm."

I lean back in my seat. Surprised but also pissed off about it. My body heat instantly rising as I fist my hand around the phone. "And?" I growl through gritted teeth.

"No location at this time," he answers before hanging up, knowing I don't want to speak to him if he has nothing to give me.

I let the phone drop to my desk and then slam my hands down onto it. *I fucking knew it!*

My door opens, and William enters, setting my drink on the desk.

"Bring me another one, please," I say, knowing I'll need several tonight.

TWENTY-SEVEN

LAIKYN

When he walks in, I'm standing in front of the mirror about to apply my mascara.

I pause, straightening my back, and turn to face him. He's leaning up against the doorframe to the bathroom. One hand is shoved into the pocket of his slacks; the other holds a glass with nothing but ice left in it. He's already finished the drink.

He's dressed in a three-piece suit; every inch is black, even the silk tie. His blue eyes are on mine, and it makes me squirm, wondering what he's thinking.

"Did you pick out a dress?" he asks, his voice sounding on edge.

"Yes," I answer softly. Unsure. I hate that I hope he likes it. I feel like him giving me the choice was a test. And I'm afraid to fail. I had way more than a *few* options to pick from. They brought an entire store to the house full of designer dresses and heels.

Pushing off the doorframe, he walks over to me, and my pulse starts to race, knowing he's in here to do something to me. He's already told me tonight is a big event—our first public appearance as husband and wife. I can only imagine what he's got planned for me before we leave this house. My body tingles in anticipation.

"There's no reason to be nervous, Lake," he says, noticing the change in my breathing.

I swallow and lie. "I'm not."

A smirk plays across his lips. "So you're saying you're this worked up over nothing?" He arches a brow.

No reason to lie again, so I don't respond.

Reaching out, he unties the sash holding up my robe. I didn't want to put clothes on, fix my hair and makeup, then mess it up getting undressed. That's what I tell myself anyway. In the back of my mind, I was screaming easy access in case he came and fucked me beforehand.

He gently pushes the soft, fluffy material off my shoulders and it falls to my feet. Once again, I stand naked before him while he's fully clothed, and I wish he'd get undressed.

His fingers run down my heaving chest, and the metal from his rings makes me shiver when they run over my breast.

"Gorgeous," he whispers, and it makes my breath catch and butterflies flutter in my stomach. He's such a good liar. And I'm the dumb bitch who believes it. Luke made me get my boobs done, but he hated them. Said they were too small. That he should have made them go bigger. I weighed a hundred and ten pounds and was a small A. I'd say a full D is damn well big enough on my body size.

The tip of his finger lazily circles my nipple. My eyes lift to his and he grips it, pulling me into him, and I gasp at the pinch. The moment my body knocks into his, his hands lower to my ass, his fingers dig into my hot skin, and he picks me up, setting me on the countertop where I was just doing my makeup.

I open my legs, wrapping them around his hips and pull him into me without thought as he stands in front of me.

My mind has been racing about what William told me. *"Mr.*

Crawford isn't a bad man. He's just the type who does whatever needs to be done.

He felt the need to marry me. Why can't I enjoy it? Because it will end in a fiery crash. We're not meant to be together forever. My father will see to it.

He lowers his head to my breast, and I lean my head back against the cold mirror when his lips wrap around my nipple. He sucks on it, softly, tenderly.

"Please," I beg, my fingers gripping his dark hair. I'm rough and needy, my body is already prepared for this. I've been getting ready for the last two hours just waiting for him to come find me. I've got myself all worked up about it.

Letting go, he does the same thing to the other.

I'm panting, my pussy throbbing.

He pulls away, and my legs sag off the side of the counter. Still standing between them, he reaches into his empty glass and picks up a piece of ice, rubbing it over my nipple. I gasp at the coldness. It's melting so fast the water runs down my stomach and between my legs. And then he does it to the other.

Leaning over, he gently blows on them, and I arch my back. My hands grip his suit jacket, needing more. Reaching into his pocket, he removes what looks like clear cylinders with black handles on the end.

"Lick it," he orders, bringing one up to my lips.

I do so without thought. I run my tongue along the outer edge of the small circle and even close my lips around it.

His eyes darken, and his free hand grips my thigh. When he pulls it free of my mouth, there's a thin line of drool that falls on my chin. Lowering the device to my breast, he presses it to my skin, covering my nipple, and starts to twist the dial on the end. I cry out when it begins to suck my nipple into the cylinder.

"Tyson," I gasp, reaching for it.

He swats my hand away. "Again," he commands, placing the

other one in my mouth and I suck on it. The action makes me moan, and he smiles. "Such a needy fucking slut," he murmurs, his free hand grabbing my other breast before slapping the side of it, making my hips buck involuntarily. I can't even be ashamed. It's so true.

He pulls it free of my mouth, and I suck in a deep breath, bracing myself. Arms out, I curl my hands around the edge of the countertop I sit on. I arch my back for him as he presses it to my other nipple and repeats the action. They both hang off my breasts like a vacuum, holding them hostage.

I go to get up, to fall to my knees in the middle of the bathroom for him, but he wraps his hand around my throat and holds me in place. "You'll stay right where you are until I tell you to move."

My eyes roll back into my head, and I'm gasping for air. Fuck, my nipples are on fire, but it feels so good. Opening my eyes, I see his free hand has his cell in it. He sets it down on the counter.

"You've got ten minutes."

He set a timer. I moan impatiently. "Are you going to fuck me?"

He chuckles. "What kind of husband would I be if I only gave you ten minutes?"

I whimper. "Please." My hips rock, my ass sliding on the cold marble countertop.

"That what you want, Lake? For me to turn you around, bend you over, and fuck your cunt? Hmm? You want my cum dripping out of your pussy the rest of the night?" He slaps the side of my breast, making me whimper. The action has the cylinder jerking at the movement and pulls on my nipple.

"Yes."

"Want everyone to see how desperate you are to be fucked like the slut you are?"

That's exactly what I am—desperate. My nipples feel like teeth are nibbling on them, and my clit is pulsing. "Please, sir..."

His hand tightens around my throat, and he leans his face into mine. I look up at him through my lashes. "What did you just call me?" His low and dark growl only fuels my need for him to fuck me.

"Sir," I say, my lips parted, trying to breathe. He hasn't cut off my air completely, but he's close.

I've never been the girl who got turned on by the thought of role-play. But right now, I'd drop to my knees, pucker up my lips and call him *Daddy* if it meant he'd let me suck on his dick like it was my own personal pacifier. So I say, "Please, sir, fuck me."

His lips attack mine, and I wrap my legs around him once more. My hands grip his ass while his free hand massages my breast. He takes my air away with the one around my throat, and I don't even care. There's no fight for survival in a single bone in my body right now. Just raw fucking desire. A needy bitch for cock.

He pulls away, arm stretched out, holding my head in place. "Don't move," he commands, letting me go. My neck and back arches while I suck in a deep breath.

He grabs the small bench underneath the countertop for the vanity. He then grabs my ankles and places my bare feet at each end, my legs open wide for him. My soaked pussy on display.

He runs his thumb over my wet lips, and I close my eyes in victory.

"Is this what you want?" He pushes one finger into me.

"More," I breathe. My nipples are throbbing. The sensation seems to intensify with every second.

He enters a second. "My wife is soaked."

"Yes." I nod, practically crying.

I open my eyes, lift my head, and see him fall to his knees on the bench between my open legs. His hands go underneath my knees, lifting them, and he pulls them to drape over his shoulders. Yanking my ass to the end of the counter, he keeps his eyes on mine as he runs his tongue over my pussy. He gets to my clit and sucks it into his mouth and I'm saying things that don't make sense.

My chest rises and falls fast with each rapid breath, and it makes the cylinders jerk, pulling on my nipples while he sucks on my clit. I'm so close to coming when he pulls away.

I slump on the countertop, and he stands, placing my feet back on the bench. Reaching out, he grabs my right breast and twists the end once more, intensifying the sting of my nipple, and I'm gasping. He then does the other. "Ty-son." My back arches, trying to reach out for him, needing him to come kiss me.

I'm shaking violently. I never knew a body could need something so much. It's an addiction. A high that I'd beg him for.

He grabs my arms, yanks me from the countertop, and turns me to face the mirror. "Knees on the bench. Spread them wide open for me."

He helps me, my legs shake so much, and I get up on the white leather bench and spread my legs as wide as I can. The action pushes my ass out behind me.

Picking up the mascara I had dropped when he entered, he hands it to me. "Finish your makeup, Mrs. Crawford."

I don't know why, but the way he calls me *Mrs. Crawford* makes it even sexier. I watch him in the mirror as he drops his eyes to my naked body, and he steps up behind me. His hand falls between my parted legs and gently rubs his fingers over my pussy. His fingers lazily play with my cunt, teasing me, knowing I want his cock. Removing them, he slaps my ass. "Makeup, Lake."

I quickly unscrew the lid and lean over to get my face closer to the mirror, making sure not to knock the things stuck to my nipples on the counter. I try to concentrate on my lashes, but his fingers pinch my clit, and I jump, dropping it. "Oh God." I moan at the pain it inflicted. Feels so good.

Dropping my head, I place my forearms on the countertop and

stick my ass out farther to him. "Pl-please." My hands are fisted, and I'm gasping for breath.

"This feel good?" He pulls on my throbbing clit. Letting go of it, his fingers run back over my soaked pussy before pushing two inside me.

"Yes." I sigh, but he just holds them in place, making me growl with impatience. I start to rock my hips back and forth, fucking them myself.

His chuckle can be heard over my heavy breathing, and once again, I'm not even embarrassed. He places his free hand across my lower back, and I feel pressure against my ass. It doesn't even stop me. As his thumb slips into my ass, he enters a third into my cunt.

I bite my lip and drop my head to the countertop. My heart racing.

"Painful?" he asks, pulling them out of my pussy and entering them again.

I shake my head, sucking in a deep breath. "No ... don't stop. Please."

I feel it building. I'm so close. My nipples are swollen and tingling, my clit pulsing, and my pussy is soaked. Goose bumps cover my skin, and I close my eyes as I feel that sensation start to build.

He does exactly what I tell him not to do. "Sit up." He removes his fingers, and I slump, doing as I'm told. He stands behind me, his hands on either hip, holding me in place. "Take the knob and twist it."

My wide eyes meet his in the mirror. "Tyson..."

"Now, Lake." He lets go long enough to slap my ass, and my hips jerk.

Taking a deep breath, I grab the cylinder with a shaky hand, while the other grips the end and twists it once, making me whimper. "Again," he orders. "I want two full turns on each breast. Understand?"

I nod, and he allows my silent response. Biting my tongue, I do it once more and my head hangs as a whimper escapes my lips. His hand slides between my parted legs once more and he goes back to massaging my clit. The other comes up and wraps around my hair, fisting it tightly. He pulls my head up and tilts it to the side at an angle so he can lower his lips to my exposed neck. "Other one," he whispers, his eyes on mine in the mirror.

Trembling, I grab the other and twist it once, feeling a sting in my nipple. Then I quickly do another and then slap my hands on the countertop.

"That's a good girl," he murmurs, sliding two fingers into me. My nipples pulse, the sting intensifying to the point it's painful but in the best way. With his hand still in my hair, he twists my head up and to the side, where he lowers his lips to mine, and I kiss him breathlessly.

Pulling away, he enters a third finger into my cunt. I bite my lip to keep from screaming his name. He removes them, and I slump, a growl of frustration leaving my trembling lips. This time he doesn't bother telling me what to do. He reaches around and twists them each two more times, making me cry out. My body shakes uncontrollably as I stay bent over, legs spread wide open.

His hands grab my hair once more, and he yanks my head up. Leaning over my back, he smiles at me in the mirror. It's not fair. He looks like he's about to go into a meeting and close a million-dollar deal, dressed in a three-piece all-black suit. I look like I'm coming off a three-day bender with my now ratted hair, lack of makeup, and I'm naked. "You're so beautiful when you're a desperate slut, Mrs. Crawford."

I whimper, closing my eyes, and he lets go of me. When I open them, I see him remove a green container from his pocket and unscrew the lid. He dips two fingers into it, and then he rubs it over my clit.

"What is that?" I ask breathlessly, feeling a cooling sensation.

"This is a little party favor," he answers vaguely.

The timer goes off, and he grabs my hand, pulling me up off the bench. He turns me around and sits me back on the countertop. I'm sweating, my body trembling.

He stands and reaches for my left breast. Untwisting the cylinder, it pops off, and I see my swollen nipple. He takes his fingers and pulls apart a small black rubber band. He gently places it over my breast, and it pinches my now swollen nipple.

My hands instinctively go to remove it, but he pins them down to my sides. "This is called nipple banding," he says softly, his lips nearly touching mine.

"Tyson, please."

"You'll wear these tonight under your dress."

I want to cry, but that'll fuck up the little makeup I have on. I lick my lips. "Yes, sir."

My words grant me another deep kiss, and I moan into his mouth before biting on his lip. He pulls away, leaving me breathless once again, and he repeats the action with my other breast, and my thighs clench at the sensation.

I stare up at him with heavy eyes and parted lips.

"Get dressed and meet me downstairs," he orders, and I swallow. "You may wear underwear, but that's it. No bra." Without waiting for a response, he lets go of me and exits the bathroom, his empty drink in hand.

I allow myself a few minutes to catch my breath, wondering how in the fuck I'll make it through this party and what I can do to get fucked sooner than he plans.

TYSON

I'M STANDING DOWN IN THE GRAND FOYER RESPONDING TO the text Ryat sent me when I hear her. My eyes lift to the top of the stairs, and I see my wife in a red dress. Her hair down and curled, my collar around her neck and ring on her finger. It's what I don't see that has me hard as a rock. The bands around her nipples.

The dress she picked out doesn't make them noticeable, but I know they're there. And by the way her eyes are heavy, the soft material of the dress reminds her they're there too.

She stops in front of me, and she's still panting. Good. I want every motherfucker there tonight to see how crazed she is for me. For my cock. For my attention. For my approval. My plan was to get her so worked up that she couldn't stand it. She was so close to coming a couple of times that I know she'd do anything right now to get off.

After what I found out earlier in my office, I want to pin her down and fuck her until she's nothing but a blubbering mess. But it'll have to wait. I had a plan for tonight, and I'm not going to deviate from it with this newfound information.

I take her left hand and raise it to my lips, kissing her wedding ring. She blushes, dropping her eyes to the floor, and I love the way her chest rises and falls with her heavy breathing. "You look breathtaking, Mrs. Crawford." It's not a lie. My wife is gorgeous, and everyone will have their eyes on her tonight.

Her eyes lift to meet mine, and I drop her hand to cup her face, needing to touch her.

"Thank you," she whispers.

Ignoring the urge to rip off her dress and say *fuck the party*, I grab her hand and pull her out of the house. We get into the limo, and I sit down next to her. I turn to face her. "You—"

Her lips are on mine, cutting me off. I don't push her away. Instead, my hands find her hair, and I deepen the kiss. I jump when I feel hers on my slacks, rubbing my cock.

Pulling away, I breathe, "Fuck, Lake."

"Yes. Please," she begs, her voice as desperate as her body is.

My hands lower to cup her face, my thumb running over her wet lips. She pulls it in, sucking on it, and I groan. "Is that what you want, darling? For me to fuck that mouth of yours?"

She moans.

I pull it out and replace it with two others, loving how wet it feels. I can't wait to have her drooling around my dick.

"Want me to shove you to your knees, grip your hair, and make you gag?"

She nods the best she can, her eyes blinking.

Pulling them from her mouth, I slide my hand into her dress, my fingers finding her swollen nipple, and I pinch it, making her cry out.

"That's it, little darling. That's the sound you'll be making for me later when you're tied to our bed."

TWENTY-EIGHT

LAIKYN

We pull up into a circle drive to what was once a hotel. I know the house of Lords was given to them years ago. It's exactly where you would expect men who think they rule the world to live.

Large and over the top.

Tyson takes my hand and leads me up a set of stairs and into the house. I'm trying to ignore my throbbing nipples and tingling clit. I can feel the bands as the soft fabric from my dress brushes against them, and it's got me breathing erratically. I catch sight of a woman walking around with a tray full of champagne flutes.

I tuck myself into his side, my free hand coming up to wrap around his upper arm. I know this is what he wants—to show me off. It's all about appearances. And I have no problem playing into his game tonight. Especially when I know it will lead to me coming all over his dick. "May I have a drink?" I ask.

He comes to a stop and looks down at me. I plead with him to let me have one. He wouldn't let me have one at dinner with my parents. I'm not sure why he's against me drinking when he does, but he wouldn't tell me even if I asked. It's not like I'm going to work afterward.

"Just one." He finally nods.

I give him a soft kiss on the lips, making sure to keep it PG. I'm afraid if I do anymore, I won't be able to stop myself from dropping to my knees in front of everyone and begging him to fuck me like the slut he's making me.

He waves down the woman and grabs a drink from her tray. She gives him a bright smile, then walks off into the crowd. It's like the hostess at the restaurant all over again. I'm invisible. Ladies always are. We're told to keep silent and look pretty. We're arm candy and nothing more. Women like me don't have minds or voices of our own.

I take a sip and swallow the sweet tasting champagne. I used to drink back in high school. But once Whitney died, my mother became an alcoholic, so my father cut back on the alcohol in the house.

Tyson leads us into a ballroom decorated in black and gold. A DJ is set up over in the corner. Round tables are positioned throughout the room with black tablecloths over them.

I'm about to open my mouth to say something when Tyson steps in front of me, making me come to a halt. I look up at him, and he's got his lips thinned, his jaw sharp.

"What's wrong?" I ask, worried. I hate to say it, but I actually feel safe with Tyson. He's proven that no one will touch me, but we're in a house full of nothing but Lords. Other than the bands wrapped around my nipples and my burning clit, my senses are already on alert being here.

"There she is," a woman's voice comes from behind him.

He closes his eyes for a brief second and then steps to the side. "Mother." His voice is as tight as his body is pressed up against me.

My wide eyes go to the couple standing in front of us. The

woman has dark hair and big blue eyes. They look like Tyson's. The man standing next to her has his dark eyes on mine.

I look down at the floor as the rush of embarrassment heats up my chest and face. It's going to be dinner with my parents all over again.

"This must be Laikyn." She steps forward, and I look up at her.

"Yes, ma'am." I reach out my right hand.

She looks at it but makes no attempt to shake it, so I drop it to my side. Whatever. I'm not here to impress her. Her son already married me. Not like she or I can change that.

Tyson makes no attempt to introduce us, so I'm not sure why I should care.

I lift the champagne flute to my lips, and she gasps, her hand flying to her mouth, and you can't miss the huge rock on her finger. I don't understand why Lords spend so much money on things that don't really matter to them.

"What?" I lower the glass without taking a drink of it. Lifting it up to my face, I look to make sure nothing is floating inside of it. Nope, just bubbles.

"Ty." Her wide eyes go to her son. "She shouldn't be drinking."

What the fuck is it with these people not letting me drink?

"She's fine, Mother," he responds tightly, and I square my shoulders and take a sip this time.

"But the baby ..."

I spit out the drink all over my mother-in-law's salmon-colored dress.

She gasps, stepping back from me. Well, that's one way to give me space. Tyson chuckles, and his father narrows his eyes on me. "Excuse me?" I ask his mother, wiping the champagne off my chin.

"Well..." Her large eyes go from his to mine. "Aren't you two trying to get pregnant?"

"No." I shake my head. I mean, I guess we're practicing, but definitely not trying.

She places her hands on her narrow hips. "I mean, I understand wanting to be married for a little while before having a child." Her eyes come back to mine. "But you're not getting any younger."

A Lady usually starts reproducing at a young age. I'm twenty-one, so to them, I'm already too old. "We won't be having children," I say when I realize she isn't getting the point.

She blinks and looks at her husband, who has still not said one word to his son or me.

"But ... but Tyson." She looks at him. "You're an only child. You need children to carry on the Crawford name."

"Maybe you should have had more yourself," I offer, taking another drink of the champagne. Why should that be put on us?

She gasps again, and I refrain from rolling my eyes at how dramatic she is. I don't want to be here anymore than she does. I just want her son to bend me over, spank my ass, and call me his good fucking slut while his cock pounds into my throbbing pussy until I come all over it.

TYSON

I CAN'T HELP THE SMILE THAT'S ON MY FACE. MY WIFE IS horny and angry. I like it. I also like that she isn't going to take shit from my mother.

"Tyson—"

"Drop it, Mother." I interrupt whatever she was about to say. I didn't marry the girl they had already picked out for me then, so I sure as fuck am not going to let them dictate what I do in my marriage to Laikyn.

They storm off and I take her hand in mine, pulling her deeper into the ballroom. I spot Ryat and Sin sitting at a round table, and they both look up to see me. Ryat nods us over and I pull out a chair for her to sit. I notice the way she slowly lowers herself into her seat. I know the clit enhancer is doing its job and driving her insane.

Next to Ryat sits his wife, Blakely. She notices us sitting and looks over at my wife, introducing herself. The moment my wife answers, *Laikyn*, Blakely's eyes slide to mine. I hold her stare as hers narrow just a tad. I'm not sure how much Ryat has told her about my wife, but he's told me that she's asked him questions about me and Whitney. So I'm assuming she knows that Lake is her sister. I had a heart-to-heart with Blakley once on a private jet, and I told her what kind of guy I am. She shouldn't be surprised to know I didn't marry my wife for love.

Easton Bradley Sinnett—Sin—sits on the other side of Ryat. Sin's wife, Ellington, sits next to him and also introduces herself to Lake. The three of them start to talk, and I jump into the conversation Sin and Ryat are having.

I jump when a hand lands on my flaccid dick under the table. Looking over at Lake, she stares at me over the rim of her champagne flute. She's teasing me. I smile at her. "Go ahead, little darling," I tell her, and she smiles like she has a chance at winning.

Finishing off her glass, she sets it down and leans in. "May I use the restroom, please?"

I want to tell her no, but then she mouths *"I have to pee."* Leaning in, I cup her face while I put my lips by her ear so only she can hear what I'm about to tell her. "When we get home, I'm going to rip this dress off you and tie you to our bed." My cock hardens at the sound of her sharp inhale. "And if you don't have two bands around your nipples, I will beat your ass black and blue with my belt."

"Tyson." She whimpers my name while her hand adds pressure to my now hard dick.

But I'm not done. "And then I'll put a vibrator up your cunt on the lowest setting so you can't get off and then sit down and watch you beg and cry the rest of the night to get you off, but I won't, Lake. It'll be a punishment, just like last time. Not a reward." I pull back and look her in the eyes. They're as heavy as her breathing. I drop my free hand and very subtly run my knuckles over her dress, and her mouth parts when I reach her nipple. "Do you understand me?"

She nods softly, her eyes telling me that she wants to disobey me just so I can punish her. A part of me hopes she does. The other part wants to see her get off over and over again.

"I understand, sir," she whispers breathlessly.

A growl comes from deep in my throat at those words. She knows they affect me so now she's going to use it against me. "Hurry back," I order.

She leans in, her soft hand cupping my face, and she kisses me. Her lips press against mine, and she opens her mouth to invite me in. I take the opportunity and swallow her moan as her body rocks back and forth in the chair. I pull away and stand, grabbing her hand to help her out of her chair as well.

TWENTY-NINE

LAIKYN

The words that Tyson said to me keep repeating in my mind. The urge to remove the bands just to see if he really does punish me is big. But I refuse to let him win. It's more of an *I can do this* type of situation.

Exiting the stall, I walk over to the sink and turn it on to wash my hands when I see the door open out of the corner of my eye.

"What the fuck are you doing?"

"Excuse me?" I look up to see my brother standing in the women's restroom. "Miller?" I look around the room to make sure no other women are in here. "What are you doing in here?"

"I asked you a question," he barks out.

I straighten my shoulders. What the hell is his problem? "I don't know what you mean."

"Don't play dumb with me, Lake."

"I don't—"

"I saw the hotel room," he interrupts me.

My eyes drop to the floor, unable to look at him any longer after his confession. I thought my father finding my blood on the bed was bad, but my brother? "I didn't have a choice," I mumble.

"Did he hold a gun to your head?"

Frowning, I look back up at him through my lashes. "No."

"Did he hold a knife to your neck?"

"No, but—"

"Did he tie you down and rape you?" He arches a brow.

Everyone in that cathedral knew I was going to be having sex later that day. It wouldn't have mattered if it was Tyson or Luke. At least Tyson didn't pay for my virginity like Luke has been doing over the last three years. He just took it. "You act like I had a choice," I snap at him.

"Jesus Christ, sis. Didn't you learn anything from Whitney? She may have been dumb enough to fall in love with him, but she was smart enough to know nothing would ever come from it."

He's not making any sense. "I don't remember you stopping it." I punch my finger into his chest. "You were the one who gave me over to him."

His jaw sharpens, and he looks away from me. Sighing, he runs his hands through his hair. "I did what I had to do."

I cross my arms over my chest and immediately drop them when it pushes against my banded nipples. I all but whimper and feel my face heat up with embarrassment. "Well, I'm doing the same thing."

He throws his head back, giving a rough laugh. "You coming all over his cock is nothing that you *had* to do."

"Excuse me?" I take a step closer to him, closing the small space. "What did you just say?"

"You know, I thought you were smarter than all the other whores who drop to their knees and beg him to fuck them, but as always, you're just another disappointment. No wonder Dad didn't try harder to stop it." He turns his back to me to walk off, but I reach out, gripping the back of his tux, yanking as hard as I can to pull him back to me. He spins around. "What the fuck—"

"What the fuck does that mean?" I bark out so loud that I hope no one on the other side hears me.

"Think about it, Lake. There's a reason why Dad did everything he could to make sure Whitney didn't end up with Tyson, but he had no problem letting me hand you over to him."

What does he mean *everything he could to stop Whitney from ending up with Tyson?* "No." I shake my head. "Dad told me he had no choice. That the Lords let Tyson pick who he wanted, and I *had* to go through with it."'

He snorts. "Dad has a plan, and you won't fuck it up."

"A plan? What do you mean? What kind of plan?" I mean, I know my father has something up his sleeve by the way he showed up at Blackout after our dinner and the fact that he has Bethany working for him. But what could it possibly be? To keep an eye on me? "Is this revenge for killing Whitney?" I ask softly.

He snorts. "You really think he killed her? Fuck, Lake. You're so goddamn stupid."

I wrap my arms around myself, feeling exactly that. "Why would Dad hate him so much, then?" After Whitney died, you couldn't even mention her name in my father's presence. It was as if she just disappeared. Never existed. Her social media pages were taken down. Pictures of her gone. All those memories we shared seemed more like I dreamed them. She just ... vanished. But my family knew the truth. No matter how much the Lords tried to cover it up, Tyson had killed her.

"Just don't get knocked up like Whitney did." He ignores my question.

My heart stops. "What?" I whisper. "Whitney was pregnant?" I never knew that.

"Why do you think Tyson *wanted* you?" He snorts, ignoring my questions. "He doesn't love you, Lake. And he sure as fuck doesn't care what happens to you. And what I just saw out there ...

you hanging all over him, just proves how much of a worthless slut he's turning you into." He exits the bathroom, and I try to catch my breath. Bile starts to rise, and I rush into one of the stalls where I slam the lid up and bend over, unable to completely fall to my knees in this tight, form-fitting dress.

I start to dry heave, but thankfully, I don't actually vomit. After a few seconds, I shut the lid and exit the stall. I come to a stop when I see two women now standing in the bathroom. Blakely Archer and Ellington Sinnett. Ryat's and Sin's wives.

"Are you okay?" Blakely asks me. Her hands on her growing belly.

Did they follow me in here? Did Tyson send them after me? Or their husbands? I'm not sure how close Sin is to Tyson, but I know that Ryat would throw me under the bus without thought. The fact that he stood next to him at the altar proves that.

I nod. "Yeah." Walking over to the sink, I turn on the faucet and cup the water in my hand to take a sip. Swishing it around, I spit it out and turn it off, trying to get the sour taste out of my mouth. I still feel like I'm about to get sick. "Did Tyson send you two to fetch me?" I'm sure my time away from him has expired.

"No." They both frown.

Ellington's eyes drop to my stomach, and I know what she's thinking. They just walked in on me about to get sick. I'm married to a Lord. It's not their fault they think the way they do; it's just how we're raised.

"I'm not pregnant," I state, and they look at one another. I hate that this is how I'm meeting them. I'd love to have friends. Like real friends. Ones that I can talk to about my day-to-day life, no matter how boring it is. But then again, they're married to Lords, so the odds of ever getting close to them are pretty impossible.

An awkward silence lingers, and I take in a deep sigh. I want to punch Tyson in the face right now but also beg him to fuck me. Shit, I need another drink.

"I'm sorry about your sister," Blakely says softly, probably overhearing my brother talking about her before they walked in.

My eyes lift to meet her blue ones. "You knew Whitney?" I ask.

She shakes her head. "No, but I'd heard about her," she answers vaguely.

"What did you hear?" I wonder.

Nibbling on her red-painted lip, she takes a second to debate if she should tell me. "Someone was telling me and my friend Sarah about the vow ceremony. Said Whitney cheated on her boyfriend with Tyson when she became his chosen."

I frown at that. My sister never had a boyfriend. Not back then.

"But then I had asked Ryat about her, and he told me not to believe everything I hear. That she didn't cheat on anyone with Tyson. That she had a stalker."

"Who was it?" I ask, stepping toward her. This is news to me. Pregnant, boyfriend, stalker? Dear Lord, did I even know my sister?

"He never told me." She gives me a sympathetic look. "I'm sorry."

"Did you know her?" I ask Ellington.

"I'm sorry, I didn't," she softly answers.

My head hangs, and I watch Blake's black heels walk toward me. "How are you doing? Are you okay?"

I look up once again and realize she doesn't mean right here, right now in the middle of this bathroom. She means life in general. I nod and lie. "Yeah." Unable to tell her that I've become Tyson's whore. Her husband was the one who helped my husband. I can't afford for her to tell Ryat anything and it get back to Tyson.

"Do you have your cell on you?" Ellington asks.

I open up my clutch and pull it out. Blakely takes it from me and after a few seconds, she hands it over to Ellington. "Let us know if you need anything," Blakely says, giving me a kind smile. "We may be married to Lords, but us Ladies have to stick together."

I pray that Tyson will let me see them again. I'm suffocating at Blackout. I'm not sure if that's Tyson's plan or what, but if so, it's working.

TYSON

A server sets another drink down for me when Ryat asks, "How are things going at Blackout?"

I look over toward the hallway that leads to the bathroom, wondering what's taking my wife so long before I answer. "You guys see the girl all over the news who's gone missing?"

He and Sin both nod, already knowing who I'm talking about. You can't miss her. Her picture is everywhere.

"Had two detectives show up a couple of weeks ago looking for her. Said she was last seen at Blackout before she went missing."

Sin raises both of his hands. "Wasn't me."

Ryat snorts at the fact that Sin had brought detectives to my club a while back for killing a man who was last seen at Blackout. And although I wasn't happy with him about it at the time, it did end up working out for him in the long run.

"One was a Lord," I inform them.

Sin frowns, his eyes glancing around before they land on mine. "The Lords gave you Blackout. Why would they send an officer that is also a Lord to investigate you? Plus, they know Blackout doesn't cooperate with the cops."

"Right? That doesn't make sense," Ryat adds.

I nod and growl. "The Lord used to date my wife." I guess *date* really isn't the correct word, but it's more than what I'd like. Lords aren't good at competition. We're taught to win. Always be the best. And no matter why I ended up marrying Laikyn, she is my wife, and I will be her first for most, if not everything her body experiences.

"Oh." Sin nods. "That makes a lot of sense." He picks up his drink and takes a sip.

"Well, that also raises some new questions. You think he's in on the missing girl?" Ryat wonders. "Trying to bring heat to Blackout?"

I shake my head. "I'm not sure he'd have the balls for that. Plus, he didn't seem to know she was my wife until he was already there." I didn't like the way Collin looked at Lake, so I made sure to mention she was mine. The atmosphere immediately changed after that.

"Think her father sent him to give you a hard time?" Ryat goes on.

I shrug and answer honestly, "Not sure. I need to find out more about the girl."

"I'll make a call," Ryat offers. "See what I can find out."

I see my wife walking toward us with Blakely and Ellington. I figured she'd make some friends while we were here. She deserves to have a couple of people in her life other than me as long as they're women I approve of.

Walking up to us, Ryat notices his wife. "Everything okay?" he asks her, his eyes dropping to her pregnant belly in her form-fitting black dress.

"Yeah." She smiles, leaning in and kissing his lips.

Sin drapes his arm over his pregnant wife's shoulders and pulls her chair closer to his when she sits down next to him. Blake and Elli aren't that far apart. Pretty sure they're due around the same time.

I look at Lake, and she's avoiding me. Her back is ramrod

straight, and she has a new glass of champagne in her hand. I'm about to ask her where she got it when my cell vibrates in my pocket, and I pull it out to see it's Colton. "I need to take this," I say to Ryat, then slide my eyes to my wife. He nods, understanding that he will keep an eye on her for me.

"Hello?" I answer, stepping away and walking out the back sliding glass door to outside.

"Sorry to call you, boss, but we've got a problem I wanted to let you in on," Colton rushes out.

"What is it?" I ask, turning to face the glass to look inside. My wife is already glaring at me while sipping on her champagne. I hold her stare, daring her to look away first. When she does, I smile to myself.

"The cop showed up."

I groan. "What did he want?"

"Well, that's the thing. He asked to speak with you. I said you were unavailable at the moment."

"He knows I'm here." The house of Lords throws a party for their seniors around this time every year. But not every single Lord attends. I know for a fact that Collin didn't even get an invite. He's nothing in our world. "Did he say what he wanted?"

"He said he wanted to see the cameras from the night the girl went missing."

"Why the fuck would he think I'd show him that? I already told him she wasn't there."

"Not sure, but he was already inside the club when I spotted him, asking around." I'm about to ask who all he spoke to when he adds, "He was trying to speak to Bethany when I escorted him out. She was too busy to pay him any time."

Sighing, I run a hand over my hair. "Okay. Thanks for letting me know. You and the guys meet me at Blackout at ten o'clock tomorrow morning. We'll review the cameras again and see if we

236

can find anything." I've already gone over them once and didn't see anything off. The girl came in with three guys and left with one of them. But nothing made me question if her life was in danger with him.

"Sounds good." He hangs up, and I pocket my phone.

THIRTY

LAIKYN

I sit in my chair, facing straight ahead. The longer I sit here, the angrier I get. At my brother, at myself. He was the only person that I thought I had left on my side. Now I have no one. But did it ever really matter? Not really. Not in the long run.

The bad taste in my mouth is finally gone. I think that's because I picked up another drink on my way back from the bathroom. My husband is going to fuck me later, and although my body is begging for it, my mind is screaming *fuck no.*

I look over to see Ryat and Blakely talking. Her elbow is on the table, face in her hand. I can't hear what he's saying to her over the voices in the room, but she's smiling at him. He reaches out and pushes her dark hair behind her ear before he leans in and kisses her. I watch shamelessly as she leans into him. Her hand drops from her face to run along his black button-up. Placing his forehead on hers, he breaks the kiss only to give her a soft one. It's like he can't get enough of her, and the way she pulls him into her says she feels the same way.

My eyes look over at Sin and Ellington. He's got his hand on the side of her growing belly and he leans into her, saying something to her. By the way her face flushes, I'd say it was what he has planned for her tonight.

Looking away, I down another gulp of my champagne. I want that. A husband who wants to be with me. One who wants me to have his children and make his house a home. Give him a family. I don't want to be married to someone who only wants to use me for some sick revenge. I'm not saying I'd have that if I were with Luke. But I'm just asking why it had to be one or the other?

I catch sight of my parents entering the room. My brother enters behind them, and his eyes meet mine. They look at me with disgust. I don't get it. Would he rather me be raped and beaten than enjoy my husband? Yep. He made that very clear. But why?

It just shows how fucked up the Lords are.

I sit up straighter when I see a guy walk up behind them. It's the guy from our hotel room suite. The one who came in place for that Gavin guy. He taps my brother's shoulder, and he turns around, giving him the one-arm handshake hug. My parents turn around as well to greet him. Another man I remember as Gavin enters behind them, and they all start a conversation.

"I told you; you could have one drink."

I gasp, spinning around at the sound of the voice in my ear to see Tyson sitting back beside me. His eyes go from mine to the champagne flute in my hand.

I lift it to my mouth and gulp it down. Once it's gone, I suck in a deep breath and put my lips as close to his as I can without touching them. He doesn't bother to pull away. A part of me hopes my brother is watching. *Yeah, I'm his whore, motherfucker.* "You can punish me later for it, *sir*." My words are as sarcastic as I can make them. But they sounded more breathless than anything.

Even though I'm mad at him, my pussy still throbs and my nipples ache. They beg to be touched. My underwear is soaked. At least he let me wear them tonight. I'd hate to have a wet spot on my dress.

He reaches up, his fingers gently running across my cheek as he pushes the hair behind my ear, and it makes goose bumps rise across my heated skin. "Be careful what you wish for, little darling."

―――――――

THE PARTY WAS PRETTY TAME FOR THE LORDS IF YOU ASK ME. There was no ritual or sacrifice made. No bloodshed of any kind. Just the Lords gathering around to slap each other on the back to congratulate each other on something that every other man has the ability to do—graduate from college. The Lords don't even go to their classes. They don't have to. They're rewarded because of their title and title alone.

I never did speak to my parents, thankfully. They steered clear of us. We told everyone at our table goodbye, and I promised to keep in contact with Blakely and Ellington.

"Want to tell me what you're so pissed about?" Tyson asks me, straightening his suit jacket as he sits next to me in the back of the limo.

"Doesn't matter," I say honestly. Nothing will change the past or the outcome of our future. What's done is done, and all I can do is take it one day at a time.

His hand tangles in my hair, and he yanks my head back. My breathing picks up as he lowers his lips to my neck, gently kissing up to my ear. "I don't like your attitude, Lake."

"Maybe you should fuck it out of me then," I challenge.

He gives a dark chuckle. "I'm going to fuck you all right. I'm not so sure it'll put you in a better mood or not."

I growl, my hips lifting off the leather without thought. He's going to piss me off on purpose. I expected this. I've been baiting him all night. This is what he wants. Me all worked up, crawling on my hands and knees, begging for him to give me the smallest amount of attention.

The limo stops at the house, and he helps me out of the back door. I stumble a bit in my heels, the few drinks I had affecting me more than I thought they would.

We enter the front door, and I head straight to the bedroom. Once inside, I slam the door shut, hoping it hits him in the face, but the sound of it banging against the interior wall tells me he was faster than I was. He expected it.

A hand grips my hair, and he yanks me back, making me scream. His free hand wraps around my neck, and he shoves me into the closed door. He comes to stand in front of me. His baby-blue eyes glare down at me. He's getting angry with me. *Good.*

I want a fight. A sick part of me likes when I make him *feel* something. It means I'm getting to him.

"Last chance, why are you mad at me?"

Lifting my chin, he smirks at my refusal to answer. What's the worst he can do, turn on my collar? Letting go of my neck, he lowers his hands to my dress and rips the thin material down the center, making me gasp. It was such a pretty dress.

The material falls to my feet, and he grips my thighs, lifting me. My legs wrap around him instinctively as he carries me over to the bed. He tosses me onto it and straddles my waist, pinning me underneath him.

Reaching over me to the corner of the bed, he grips my wrist and holds it out to the edge. Something wraps around it. He lets go of me, and I try to move my arm but can't. He's tied it down just like he promised he would.

He reaches over and does the same to the other. Then he gets off the bed and pulls my legs out wide, attaching rope around each ankle. Giving me his back, he walks into the bathroom, leaving me spread-eagle on the bed. I look up at the ceiling, trying to calm my breathing. I'm so wet. I want to be mad, but my body aches for him.

TYSON

I EXIT THE BATHROOM AND GO OVER TO THE BED. I RIP HER underwear off her hips, making her whimper, and wad them up. She sees me leaning over her, and her eyes widen. "Tyson..."

I shove them into her mouth and rip off a piece of duct tape, placing it over her mouth. She shakes her head quickly, and I grip her cheeks, holding her face in place while pushing the back of her head into the bed. "If you don't want to talk, then you don't need a voice." Letting go of her, I stand, and she thrashes on the bed, pulling on her restraints.

Reaching down, I remove my belt. "You've been begging me all night to fuck you, little darling. And although I'm going to, I'm going to play with you first." I bring the belt down across her chest, and her mumbled scream fills the room as her hips lift the best they can.

I do it again, making sure to hit her banded nipples. I'm not doing it hard; this isn't punishment. It's to see just how wet she can get.

I slap her inner thigh, and her body arches. Going across her hips, she's twisting from left to right, trying to relieve the ache between her legs.

Dropping the belt to the bed, I reach into my pocket and pull out what I grabbed from the closet. I hold it up to her face, and her eyes widen. "This goes on your clit." I flick her nipples, and her back arches.

Lowering my hand between her spread legs, I put the cylinder over her clit and twist the end, sucking her clit up into it just like I did to her nipples.

Then I make my way between her spread legs. I shove my knees into her already shaking thighs and take my hard cock in my hand. I slide the tip of my head against her and rub my precum over her soaked cunt.

I push into her while my free hand holds the cylinder so it doesn't pop off. I pause halfway in and twist it two more times, smiling at the way she screams into her gag as her clit is sucked farther into the clear tube. "That's it, Lake," I say when her pussy clenches down on me. "Show me how much you like it."

She's panting, body shaking, and chest heaving. I hold the cylinder while my cock slowly fucks her pretty shaved pussy. Just teasing her, slowly, softly. I look up at her to see tears running down both sides of her face while her neck is arched.

I twist it two more times, and she's soaking wet. Once I feel she's had enough, I unscrew it and release her clit. Her body sags into the bed, and I smile. "Not even close to being done, little darling."

Pulling my cock out all the way, I slap her pussy, and she shakes uncontrollably. I slam into her and lean over her body. I wrap my lips around her hard nipples as my cock thrusts into her hard and fast, fucking my wife so hard the headboard knocks against the wall.

Biting softly onto her nipple, I pull gently, the action rolling the band off. I spit it out and do the same to the other before sucking her swollen nipple into my mouth. She's sobbing, hips lifting the best they can to reach mine, needing to be fucked.

I reach up and rip the tape from her mouth and remove her underwear, tossing them both to the floor. I love the way her pussy feels wrapped around my cock when I'm buried inside her, but I want more from her right now. Her body isn't enough for me. I need to breathe her in.

She gasps, "Tyson—"

I cut her off when I lower my lips to hers and kiss her so deeply that I'm not sure either one of us is breathing. Sliding my hands underneath her tied arms, I tangle my fingers in her long hair while my cock fucks her cunt.

Her lips are as desperate as mine. I pull away, and she sucks in a deep breath. "Please?" she begs, her body shaking.

"Yes, little darling?" I ask, releasing her hair and moving my hands to cup her face. "Please, what?" I lick my lips, needing to taste the champagne she had earlier from our kiss.

"I...I want to feel you." She pulls on her tied wrists.

I smile at the fresh tears welling up in her eyes, and she arches her neck, letting out a growl of frustration, knowing that I won't give her what she wants.

Instead, I pull out of her dripping cunt and chuckle at the way she whimpers. I kiss down her heaving chest, over her stomach, and lower myself between her shaking legs. She lifts her hips off the bed the best she can, and I look over her swollen clit.

Licking my lips, I tell her. "I'm going to enjoy using you tonight." I place my mouth on her pussy, and I eat her out as if every man who has ever wanted my wife is watching me please her, listening to her scream my name while she begs me for more.

THIRTY-ONE

LAIKYN

W e're in the large Jacuzzi tub. He's sitting behind me, and I'm leaning on him for support. After I came three times, he left me on the bed and went to the bathroom to start a bath. Then he untied me, picked me up, and carried me into the bathroom, where he proceeded to get in with me.

My eyes are heavy, my body weak, and my mind foggy. I had too much to drink. Or maybe it's the orgasms. I don't know which one it is. Perhaps a combination of the two.

"How do you feel?" he asks, his hands rubbing my arms while they lay on his thighs as I sit between his legs.

"Sore." I'm still shaking.

His fingers massage my arms, and my eyes fall shut as a moan leaves my lips. "Oh God."

"Keep doing that, and we'll go another round," he murmurs, his lips by my ear.

I whimper at the thought of sex. "I don't think I can."

He chuckles, his hands moving to my shoulders to massage them deeply. My head falls back against him, and his hands come up to wrap around my neck. My hips lift on their own, splashing water around us.

I reach up, my hands going over my head, and grip his hair. He removes his hands from around my neck and drops one to my breasts, gently massaging them. They're so sensitive from the bands earlier. "Your body can take it, Lake. It's your mind you have to train."

My hands drop to his thighs, and I grip his muscular legs when he gets to my nipple, making me hiss in a breath. They're still swollen.

"Ready to tell me why you're mad at me?" he asks.

"Doesn't matter," I whisper.

"Try me," he challenges, letting go of my breasts, and my body sags in relief and disappointment. I want him to decide for me. *Tie me up and use me* comes to mind. Make me come over and over while I beg you to stop until I can't speak anymore. Then it helps us avoid these awkward conversations that we shouldn't even be having.

"Lake," he warns, slapping the side of my breast to get my attention. "Tell me. Why were you mad at me? What happened?" His hands are back on my neck, and I feel like he's trying to massage it out of me.

I lick my lips and close my heavy eyes. *Why the fuck not?* The alcohol is giving me some courage. "Why haven't you asked me if I want kids?" I feel like this is the only conversation we need to have right now. I don't want him to know I spoke to my brother. I'm not allowed to speak to my family.

His hands pause on my neck. "You want kids?" he asks as if that concept is insane.

I don't answer because he didn't answer mine.

He sighs at my silence and admits, "I did ... once."

My sister comes to mind, and I wonder if she was pregnant like my brother said and if he knocked her up on purpose. "And?"

I swallow. A lump forms in my throat, and I'm not sure I want to know any more.

"Things change," he says simply.

I hate that tears sting my eyes. Whitney was always the one my family wanted to succeed. They had high hopes for her. I'm the kid they didn't expect much from. And now my husband is the same. He wanted more with her than he'll ever want with me. "No." I shove his hands off me and stand, getting out of the tub on wobbly legs.

"Lake—"

"You mean you married a woman who isn't good enough to mother your children." I don't know why I care, but I do. Why, for once, can't I be good enough for something?

He stands, water running down his chiseled body. It's not fair that he looks so good. He sighs, reaching up and running his hands through his hair to knock off the excess water. "Laikyn ..."

"I don't want kids," I admit, and his eyes snap to mine. "You know why?"

He opens his mouth to answer, but I don't let him.

"Because I don't want to bring children into this world that I have to watch endure pain." His eyes soften. "I don't want them to have this life. A life I can't save them from." I suck in a deep breath. "I don't want to have to watch them marry a man or a woman who can never love them. Who they'll never be good enough for."

He steps closer to me. "Lake—"

I take a step back, and he stops. "Being alone in a world full of billions of people is hell." I wrap my arms around myself, all of a sudden self-conscious of what I've let him do to me tonight. "I just wish for once in *my* life I'd get to choose something for me." I turn and exit the bathroom, slamming the door behind me. Wet hair and all, I curl up in bed and let the first tear fall. This is why people shouldn't drink. It makes you feel things you never did before.

TYSON

Three years ago

I SIT IN THE GAME ROOM AT THE HOUSE OF LORDS. A BLONDE sits on my lap with her big tits in my face. She's another Lords chosen. He doesn't give a fuck who or what she does. He passes her around like a bong most nights. He gets off on watching other men fuck what's his.

Ryat enters the room and smirks. "Whitney is here," he states.

"No, she's not." She was here earlier but had to go home. Her parents don't agree with us being together, so she has a bullshit curfew at the age of twenty-one.

"Yes, she is. I just saw her in the hallway," he argues.

I tap the girl's bare thigh, and she reluctantly gets up. I stand, making my way to the hallway. Sure enough, I about run right into her. "Hey, babe." Whitney smiles up at me.

"What are you doing here?" I ask her.

Her smile falters, but she answers, "I snuck out."

"Come on." I grab her hand, take a sip of my beer, and pull her down the hall to my room. Once we're inside, I shut the door and lock it. "Are you staying the night?"

"Yep." She nods and pushes her body into mine.

I cup her face and kiss her, but she pulls away and slaps a hand over her mouth. "What?" I ask when her wide eyes meet mine.

She rushes into my adjoining bathroom, drops to her knees, and vomits. I grab her dark hair, holding it while she does it again. "Need me to take you home?" I ask.

Shaking her head, she stands to her feet, and I drop her hair. She walks over to my sink, opens a drawer, and pulls out her spare toothbrush. "I'll be fine. It was the taste of beer."

I frown. "Since when does beer bother you?" The woman drinks like a fish.

Placing the toothbrush on the counter, she turns to face me with a big smile. "I'm pregnant."

I just stare at her.

She wraps her arms around my neck and goes to kiss my lips, but I pull away, not wanting to taste vomit. I remove her hands from my neck, and she frowns. "You're not pregnant."

"Ty." She pops out a hip and places her hands on them. "Yes, I am."

"You're on birth control," I remind her.

"It's not a hundred percent effective." She rolls her eyes.

"It's like ninety-nine point nine percent."

"Tyson—"

"We use condoms." Other than the vow ceremony at the Cathedral, I use protection. But that's why I prefer a mouth over a cunt, because I hate having to wrap it up.

"Well, maybe they're defective."

"Whitney," I growl.

She steps into me again, and I take a step back. Her face tightens. "You knew this could happen."

"I want a paternity test," I say.

She gasps. "Are you calling me a slut?"

A chosen is given to her Lord and cannot sleep with anyone else, but as a Lord, I can hand her over to anyone I want. I have done no such thing. "You weren't a virgin, Whit. Why do you think I picked you in the first place?"

She slaps me across the face, making my cheek sting. Then turns and exits the bathroom. I hear my bedroom door slam shut moments later.

We've talked about this. I like to fuck, but kids with Whitney?

251

It's not supposed to go that far. She's my chosen, and that's that. It ends after our senior year. I get in, get what the Lords want, and get the fuck out. We're both already promised to someone else.

I didn't abstain from sex for three years to fuck up my future by getting her pregnant. It would change everything, including my future and my position as a Lord. I've been smart about it. She dropped a few hints here and there that she wants kids, but I figured she meant later in life when she's a Lady married to her Lord. Not me. Not now.

Walking out of the bathroom, I go to the top drawer of my night-stand. Yanking it open, I grab a handful of condoms and return to the bathroom. Ripping one open, I pull it out and hold it under the faucet as I turn it on. The condom starts to fill up, and I let out a long breath, but my relief is quickly replaced with anger when I watch a thin line of water fall out in multiple areas.

"MOTHERFUCKER!"

THIRTY-TWO

LAIKYN

The following morning, we woke up and headed right back to Blackout. We haven't spoken. I cried myself to sleep before he ever came to bed, but he has nothing to say to me, and I no longer want to speak to him.

If I'm being honest with myself, I'm embarrassed about how I reacted. I don't want to have a baby. That wasn't a lie, but being a mom? I'd love to have children in a different life. But I decided years ago that that wouldn't be something I'd ever get to experience. I do thank Tyson for hijacking my wedding to Luke. Otherwise, he'd already have me knocked up.

When we returned to Blackout, he left and went to his office. I didn't follow him. I also didn't visit him before my shift started. Consequences be damned. I'm hoping he's too busy to remember.

After my shift, I went upstairs and crawled into bed. Again, he didn't bother to wake me up for sex. At this point, I'm not sure if this is a blessing or a punishment.

I'm still lying in our bed, ready for another boring day in. Reaching over, I pick up my cell off the nightstand to see it's a little after noon. My sleep schedule has been screwed ever since I started working at Blackout. I'm up all night and sleep most of the day away, which is fine. What else am I going to do?

Sitting up, I see the light to the bathroom is on underneath the door. Listening, I hear the shower running. I lie back down and roll onto my side, closing my eyes. They spring open the moment I hear a cell ding, alerting me that a text message has been received.

I sit up once again and see his cell lighting up on the long dresser. Throwing off the covers, I rush over to it just as the screen goes black. I press the button to light it up and see he has a text without opening it.

> RYAT: They found the girl's body. It's not good. I'm on my way to Blackout after I make a quick stop.

Girl's body? Is this the missing girl? I haven't seen anything about it on the news in a while. It was everywhere at first, but then it was like she was just forgotten. Why do Ryat and Tyson care about what happened to her? Maybe Tyson doesn't want any heat on the club, and that's where she was seen last, and Ryat is helping him out.

Biting my bottom lip, I allow the screen to go black once more. If Ryat is on his way here, that means Blakely is free. I need a day out with someone else. I'm suffocating here. I thought being locked up in my parent's house for three years was torture, but this is a different kind.

Making up my mind before it's too late, I grab his wallet next to the phone. Opening it up, I remove his black American Express Centurion Card and then close it really quickly. The sound of the water shutting off has me setting the wallet down, jumping back in bed, and placing the covers over my face. I tighten my hand around the card, roll onto my side, and shove my arm under the pillow to hide what's in my hand.

I try to calm my breathing so he doesn't hear me when he enters the bedroom. It's so quiet in here. There's a fan going, but it doesn't make much noise.

I hear the bathroom door open, and I open my eyes to watch him in the mirror that hangs on the far wall. His back is toward me while he pulls on a pair of jeans. He picks up his cell, reads the text, and then replies before placing it in his pocket.

Then he's pulling his shirt on. He grabs his wallet and goes to turn, and I close my eyes because if I can see him, he can see me. I gently push myself farther into the covers, but I pause when they're being pulled down my body.

I hold my breath, trying not to move and give myself away. His fingers lightly touch the side of my face and run down my neck before going over my shoulder.

It's the first time he's touched me in days, and my body instantly reacts to it. Heat covers my skin, and my thighs are clenching. It only took him a few weeks to train my body to want him. To need him. Just a little touch, and my pussy is screaming to get laid. My body begs for that high that I imagine those addicted to drugs want to feel. We went from having sex multiple times a day to nothing.

Just when I'm about to pass out, he pulls the covers back up to my neck, and then I hear the bedroom door open and close. I suck in a deep breath and sit up, grabbing my cell off the nightstand. Who knows how much time I have before Ryat is here and leaves. Then Tyson will be back up here to check on me.

ME: Have any plans today?

I don't have time to beat around the bush. Either Blakely is free to hang out or she isn't. Plus, I want to ask her more questions about my sister. Nothing of what Blakely said in the bathroom at the house of Lords made sense. Whitney didn't have a boyfriend.

And a stalker? Who the fuck was stalking her, and how would Ryat know that? Tyson. He knew about it and must have told Ryat. But why?

She responds almost instantly. Her message is much friendlier than mine.

> Blakely: Hey, girl. I don't. What do you have in mind?

> ME: Know of a good salon?

My phone rings, and I see it's her. Answering it, I keep my eyes on the door, hoping that Tyson doesn't return. "Hello?"

"I thought this would be easier." She gives a soft laugh. "But yes, I do. Although I'm not sure that they'll have any appointments available for today."

True. The hairdresser that my Mom took me to bleach my hair over time would be booked out for well over six months. No way in hell would I go back to her. She'd call and tell my mother. My father will have a fit when he finds out I changed my hair back to brunette.

"What are you wanting to have done?" Blakely asks.

"I want to dye my hair."

"Oh, I know someone who can do that. I promise they're good. I'll make a phone call for you."

"Okay."

"I can be there in thirty minutes," she says.

"Be where?" I ask.

"Blackout."

"Oh no. I'll come to you," I rush out.

She's quiet for a long second before she asks, "Do you have a car?" Almost as if she already knew the answer but didn't want to bring it up.

"No." My shoulders slump. I mean, I do, but it's at my parents'. I refuse to go anywhere near there. I'm going to avoid my father as much as I can. My luck, they've already sold it anyway. "But I'll Uber to you," I say. I can't afford to waste the time it'll take her to get here. Plus, her husband will be here soon. I don't want to take the chance of her going to Tyson's office to say hi to Ryat before I even get a chance to escape. Her presence will raise too many questions.

"Are you sure? It's no problem at all."

"Positive. Send me your address, and I'll be there shortly."

We hang up, and I go to order an Uber. I have to add a card because I've never had an Uber account before, so I add Tyson's that I have in my hand. Once done, I hold it up, looking at it. Why does he even have a black AMEX? I know most Lords have these cards. My father has one himself. But not all Lords are filthy rich. Surely, Tyson doesn't make enough money owning this club. Hell, he even lives in an apartment above it. But he does have that gorgeous house. What could he possibly do on the side that would warrant him having it? Not just anyone can get one. These come with a lot of requirements. Maybe it's fake. Or maybe all Lords have one, and that's how the Lords track their purchases? Hell, if I know. But I'm willing to test it.

My cell goes off and I look down to see Blakely sent me a text.

> Blakely: She can get you in at 3.

That's in three hours.

> ME: That's perfect. Gives us some time to buy me a new car.

Let's test this baby out.

TYSON

I'M TRACKING MY WIFE ON MY COMPUTER WHEN MY OFFICE door opens, and Ryat enters. "What did you find out?" I ask, giving him my attention.

He drops a folder on my desk. "She was found three days ago."

I frown. "Three? Why haven't we heard anything about it? Collin was just in here a couple of nights ago wanting the surveillance."

Ryat sits down on the couch. Leaning back, he fans his arms across the top cushions, getting comfortable. "I'm guessing that was more of a pleasure visit. Not work related." He smirks, and my teeth grind.

But why would Collin be here when he knew my wife was with me at the house of Lords?

"Anyway," he continues. "The investigation will remain open as a missing persons case, but between you and me, they've called off the search. Per her father's request."

"So they want the world to think that they haven't given up on her even though her body has been recovered? The question is, why?"

"Because they don't want the world to know what really happened to her." He nods to the envelope.

"I'm not sure how they'll be able to hide it. She's been plastered on every news outlet and social media platform there is." I open up the envelope and remove the stack of pictures, placing them out on my desk. "How did you get your hands on all this?" I ask.

"Judge Gregory owes me a handful of favors. I called one in."

I've seen a lot of disgusting things in my life, but I've never seen a young woman so brutally tortured before. "Someone didn't want her identified."

"They removed her teeth," Ryat speaks, obviously already having gone through these pictures. "They were pulled, not knocked out. All ten fingers had been dipped into some kind of liquid. Guessing acid. Maybe."

"No fingerprints," I say more to myself than to him. But why?

"She was also raped. By the bruising, I'd say multiple times over the course of when she went missing and when she was found."

"DNA?" I wonder and look up at him.

He shakes his head. "Must have used a condom every time, but none were found anywhere near or around where the body was recovered."

I look down at the picture that shows the girl naked in a shallow grave. What's left of her body is covered in dirt, dried blood, and God knows what else.

"She had been dead no more than twenty-four hours when they found her."

"So he kept her alive for two weeks." Why? What were they trying to get out of her?

"Her wrists and ankles were both tied with what they can only guess to be barbwire."

"Guess?" I look at him, my heart skipping a beat.

"They said due to the cuts, it appears her wrists were crossed over one another, and then the barbwire was wrapped around both of them, that way when she fought the restraints, it wouldn't dig into her radial artery, resulting in her bleeding out and dying before he wanted her to. It also appears that it was wrapped around her head. Used as a gag to keep her mouth open by the looks of the marks embedded in her cheeks and mouth."

I drop my head and run my hands through my hair, letting out a long breath.

"What is it?" he asks, noticing the change in my mood.

I look up at him, and he's now walking over to my desk and sits down in the chair across from it. "You know who did this." It's not a question.

I lean back in my chair. "My freshman year at Barrington, twenty girls went missing over about five months. Five of those twenty were found raped and murdered. The bodies were recovered from different locations, but autopsies concluded barbwire was used as restraints."

"So what? The guy who did this is out of prison now and doing it again?"

I stand, shaking my head, needing to walk around. "He was never caught. The Lords assumed it was one of us."

He frowns. "What made them think that?"

"I don't know. That information was never given. My sophomore year initiation was to go to a house and remove a Lord. We were to deliver him to the Cathedral for confessional." The Lords take their confessional very seriously. They string you up in front of the congregation and force you to tell them everything. The less you speak, the more they torture you. I've seen some hold out, but every single one of them ends up spilling their secrets. Then they finish you off and toss you in a grave in the cemetery behind the Cathedral.

"So you know who this is." He points at the photos.

Again, I shake my head. "No. We never collected him."

He frowns. "But it was part of your initiation. How did you pass if you didn't deliver?"

"We were instructed to do whatever was necessary," I correct him.

"Meaning?"

"We killed two guards to gain entry to the property. There was a mother and a daughter inside. Word among the Lords was that the mother was helping her son lure these girls in so he could kidnap and torture them. If we did not get the Lord, we were to terminate everyone inside of the house. They figured if we killed those who helped him, it would put a halt to what he was doing." I begin to pace behind my desk. "I killed the mother."

"And the daughter?"

"Got rid of her as well," I answer vaguely.

"This guy is either the original killer or a copycat."

"Why her, though?" I ask, knowing he can't answer that. "The Lord back then did not choose girls old enough to be chosens, let alone Ladies. His victims were locals and didn't attend Barrington. The girls didn't even know Lords exist. This has to be personal. No one goes to that much trouble to torture and hide the identity of a body, and it not be for a personal reason."

"Her father is a Lord." He shrugs.

"I'm not sure that matters here. I mean, Lords have had their daughters kidnapped over the years and killed. But I've never seen one tortured to this extent." I start digging through the stack of papers. "What about drugs?"

"The toxicology results can take up to six weeks, but she was known to do cocaine and smoke weed. What did Lake have to say about her? Did she see anything?"

"Nothing. I told her she was missing, and that was that."

He arches a brow.

I roll my eyes. "The less she knows, the better." Plus, I didn't want to give her any reason to speak to Collin. "Who has the body?" I continue.

"Parents wanted it to be hush-hush. She was cremated early this morning."

I stiffen at his words, clear my throat, and ask, "Why are they stopping the investigation?"

"Word has it, the Lords have taken it over."

"Good luck with that." I shove the pictures back into the envelope. They didn't find him last time, so I doubt they'll have any luck this time. "What was the cause of death?"

"Exsanguination," he answers.

"So he wanted her to suffer until he got bored, and then let her bleed to death," I say. "What about the boyfriend?" I saw on the cameras that she left with the same guy she arrived with.

"He's been very cooperative with the police. He was cleared after a Ring camera showed him taking her home and dropping her off."

"She was taken from her home?" I ask. If so, that's new. Because the others weren't. They were taken while out and about by themselves. Their cars later found abandoned.

He shakes his head. "It showed her leaving fifteen minutes afterward. They seem to think she was seeing someone other than him. Phone records came up clean, though."

My cell rings, and I pick it up. "Hey, man, I'm a little busy ..."

"Tyson, I'll keep this quick," a guy I know by the name of Marlin rushes out.

"What's up?" I wonder why he's calling me. We haven't spoken in over a year. He runs one of the Lamborghini dealerships in town. He used to sell drugs in my club.

"I've got a Laikyn Minson here wanting to purchase a Urus. But your name is on the card she's using. Do I need to call the cops?"

"That's my wife," I inform him, pulling my wallet out of my back pocket to see which card is missing. He's silent for a long second making me think we got disconnected. "Marlin?" I ask.

"Sorry, man, but damn. She's your wife?" He whistles. "Good job."

"Is that all, Marlin?" I growl.

"Yeah. I'll run the card. Hey, we should get together. Have a guys' night—"

I hang up and sit back in my seat. Ryat starts to speak as it rings again.

"This is Tyson," I answer, knowing who's calling me.

"Hello, Mr. Crawford. We're calling you in regard to your AMEX card. We have suspicious activity at a Westwood Lamborghini in the amount of three hundred and fifty thousand dollars. We're calling to confirm you've made this transaction."

"You can accept the charge," I say and hang up, smirking.

"What's so funny?" Ryat asks.

"My wife just bought herself a car."

He looks around the room. "Like right this second?"

"Yeah. She snuck out this morning with an Uber and took my credit card with her."

His eyes widen. "You allowed that?"

"Of course. Sometimes you have to give them the chance at confidence. Give them a little slack to their leash so you can remind them who they belong to." She has more than usual right now because I've been ignoring her. "Plus, she's with your wife. What could go wrong?"

"What?" he snaps, digging his cell out of his pocket to no doubt check Blakely's tracker.

"It's fine. She could use a friend." Blakely is the safest friend she could have. Ryat keeps an eye on her at all times after what they've been through.

He huffs.

"Have a problem with our wives being friends?"

"I have a problem with *my* wife being Lake's friend," he answers honestly.

"She's harmless."

"It's not her I'm worried about. Her father will retaliate."

He's not wrong. "I know, and I'll be ready."

"And if he tries to kill your wife?" He arches a brow. "Just how far are you willing to go to stop that from happening?"

My body stiffens at that thought. "He won't harm Lake. He'll come after me. It's personal." I'm the one he wants. He's always

263

hated me. Picking Whitney as my chosen pissed him off, but marrying Lake was the last straw. It's war now.

"You humiliated him in front of the Lords," Ryat goes on. "Men like him will bite off their noses to spite their faces." His green eyes meet mine. "If you don't want anything to happen to Lake, I'd tighten that leash you have on her."

THIRTY-THREE

LAIKYN

I'm feeling pretty good after the day I've had. I don't know what it is about getting your hair done that puts you in a good mood, but after so long of feeling like someone else, I feel closer to who I once was.

I pull up and bring my new car to a stop in the back parking lot of Blackout. I wasn't sure if using Tyson's card would work. One, I didn't think the guy would let me use it, and two, I didn't think it'd be accepted.

It's white with black leather. I went with the most expensive one they had on the lot.

A black SUV pulls up next to me, and I exit the Urus to see Blakely get out of hers. After we had a late lunch, she messaged Ryat, and he was still at Blackout.

It makes me wonder what all he and Tyson spoke about. I've been gone for hours, shopping. So whatever they found out about the girl must have been important. I hate how much I want to know what happened to her, but I know Tyson won't tell me.

We enter the back entrance and make our way to the second

floor. We enter the office, and Ryat is sitting on the couch. He gets to his feet when he sees his wife. "You okay?" he asks her, his eyes looking over her body.

"Yeah." She frowns at his question. Her blue eyes meet mine, and she smiles. "Free next weekend? I need to do some shopping for the babies." Her hands go to her belly.

"Of course." Not like I have a life outside of my marriage or my job. Thankfully, Blackout isn't open during the day. Plus, I enjoyed spending time with her. I didn't even bring up my sister. If this is my only chance to have a friend, I don't want her to think I'm only hanging out to get information from her. And I have a feeling she's already told me everything she knows.

"Perfect. We can do lunch and then the mall. We'll see if Elli is free too. I know she wants to get a few things." She turns to kiss Ryat on the cheek and then says, "I'm going to use the restroom really quick." Laughing, she adds, "I'll be right back." Walking into Tyson's private bathroom, she shuts the door.

I look around to see it's just me and Ryat. "Where's Tyson?" I ask. I'm honestly surprised that he hasn't messaged or called me once. He must have been too busy to even check to see that I left the club today.

Ryat steps into me, his green eyes narrowing on mine. "Stay the fuck away from my wife." His voice is as cold as Tyson's can be. They're trained to be that way.

"Excuse me?" My heart hammers in my chest at his words.

"You heard me." He takes a step closer to me, and I take one back, but now I've pushed myself against Tyson's desk. "I don't trust you, Laikyn."

"I would never hurt Blakely," I whisper, my throat closing at just the thought. Why am I the bad guy here? What have I done that would make him think otherwise?

He snorts. "Tyson may think you're innocent, but I know the truth about your family. What you all are capable of."

"What's that mean?" I ask, confused.

His eyes go over to the bathroom door before sliding back to mine. "You're going to tell Blake you're too busy next weekend to spend time with her. And then you're going to leave her the fuck alone." With that, he takes a few steps back from me, and I hear the bathroom door open.

"Whew. I'm so over having to pee every thirty minutes." Her eyes go from Ryat's to mine. "Everything okay?"

I feel his eyes on me, but I keep mine on hers. "Yeah." I nod, giving her a fake smile.

She gives me a hug, and I avoid meeting his glare. The fact that he could even think I'd ever hurt his wife makes my chest hurt.

Pulling away from me, he takes her hand. "We should be going," he tells her.

As they go to walk out the door, I step forward. "Blakely?" I ask.

"Yeah?" She turns and looks at me with a kind smile on her pretty face.

"I'll see you next weekend," I say, squaring my shoulders. This time, I glance at Ryat, and he looks like he wants to strangle me.

"Can't wait." She winks at me before they exit Tyson's office.

I allow myself a moment to collect my thoughts, trying to figure out what the fuck that was. What did he mean *my family*? Tyson thinks I'm innocent. Regarding what? Ryat is the one who put a knife to my brother's neck and helped force me to marry his best friend. Why would he think I could harm his pregnant wife?

It just makes me angry. *Fuck him.* He's a typical Lord trying to control his Lady. I won't let that happen. If Blakely wants to be my friend, then I won't let Ryat stop me. Now, if she tells me she can't see me, then I'll respect that. But it'll have to come from her mouth, her words. Not some Lord who thinks he can control what I do.

TYSON

I'M STANDING INSIDE THE APARTMENT IN THE KITCHEN WHEN I hear the front door open. I step out into the living room in time to see her walking down the hallway with bags in both hands. "Nice car," I say, sipping my whiskey.

She comes to a halt, and my eyes drop to the long dark strands of curled hair that fall down her back. Slowly, she turns to face me, and I'm not prepared for what I see. The dark color of her hair against her tan skin makes her eyes bluer. They look bigger, sexier.

My cock instantly hardens inside my jeans, and I tighten my hand on the glass. She's not supposed to have this effect on me, but even I can't deny that I'm becoming addicted to her. The way her body leans into me and how she whimpers when I touch her. I just want to chain her up and play with her for hours. Explore every inch of her. Teach her things that she never knew existed to see what she likes.

She glares at me, and it makes me want to force her to her knees and mess up her pretty face. I set my glass down and walk over to her. Reaching out, I run my hand through her soft hair. "I like it."

"I didn't do it for you." She lifts her chin.

That's the confidence that I was telling Ryat about, and it's fucking intoxicating. My eyes drop to a La Perla bag at her feet. "Going to show me what I bought?"

"Didn't plan on it." She picks them up off the floor.

I laugh softly, loving this new her. Leaning forward, I gently kiss her forehead, and when I pull back, she's frowning up at me with confusion written all over her face. "Come here." I take her hand and pull her down the hallway and into our master bathroom. "Give me these." I take the bags from her hands and place them on the countertop by my sink and pull her over to hers. "Get undressed," I command and walk into the closet. I grab a few things that I'm going to need and return to see she's removing her underwear. She's needy. It's the fact that I haven't touched her since the night of the house of Lords party. "Bend over. Hands behind your back." I place the items on the counter.

Her eyes look over and widen. She takes a step back, those pretty eyes meeting mine. "I'm sorry," she rushes out. "I'll return the car..."

"Bend over," I say once more, hating to repeat myself.

"Ty—"

"Shh, Lake." I cup her face in both of my hands. Her eyes are the size of quarters, her body trembling against mine. "It's okay. The car is yours." I'll never tell her, but I'm glad she went out and purchased the SUV. *Good for you, little darling.* She deserves to have everything she wants. And I plan on giving it to her, but that doesn't mean I won't make her earn it.

Licking her nude-colored lips, she shifts her eyes to the items once more, then back to mine. "But..."

"This isn't a punishment, Lake."

She nibbles on her bottom lip, asking softly, "Then what is it?"

"Preparation," I say honestly.

Her hands grip my shirt and I kiss her forehead once again. "Turn around and lie across the countertop." Stepping back, I let go of her.

She turns and does as I say, knowing she has no other choice. I was telling her the truth. This isn't a punishment. But I can make it one if I need to. Pressing her body onto the cold surface, I rip my belt from my jeans and pull her arms behind her back, tying them together at her wrists.

Then I pop open the lid on the saline and fill the large glass bowl with it. I take the 550cc syringe and fill it up to three 300 with the saline, then add the tube to the end of it before applying the lube.

Last, I slide my fingers along her ass, making sure to push one into her. I hear her sniff and watch her close her eyes in the mirror. Removing my finger, I replace it with the tip of the small tube and slowly push the plunger on the syringe, starting to fill her ass with the saline.

"Tyson," she gasps, her hips rocking from side to side the best she can.

"You're going to feel some cramping, but it won't be painful, Lake," I assure her.

She whimpers, her body shaking. I reach out with my free hand and rub her bare back. "You're doing so good, Lake. Just relax." She takes in a shaky breath. "So good."

I hear her sniff again, and she fists her tied hands.

"Almost done," I say, glancing down at the syringe. The Lords are all about control, punishment, and humiliation.

The first time I saw an enema given was my sophomore year at Barrington while the seniors were throwing a party at the house of Lords a few weeks after they had their vow ceremonies for their chosens.

"FUCK, YOU, SAINT," THE GIRL YELLS AS I WATCH HER BEING carried over a Lord's shoulder while he walks down the hall.

He slaps her ass, making her laugh as her head bobs up and down. Her dark hair is so long it's almost on the floor. A group of guys follows them, so I do the same to see what's going on.

He kicks his bedroom door open, and we enter to fill the large space. He tosses her onto his king-size bed, and she giggles, unable to hide her excitement. Turning over onto her back, she shoves her hair from her face. "What are you going to do, Saint? Punish me?" She arches a brow, and all the guys make audible "oh" sounds, knowing that she's egging him on. The girl has balls, I'll give her that. No one fucks with Saint.

"Hold her down," he orders, and his two best friends jump onto his bed. Each grabs an arm and pins them down above her head, and her eyes widen.

"Saint..." She breathes his name.

"You asked for this, sweetheart." Reaching out, he grabs her jeans and yanks them down her legs, removing her underwear as well.

She's twisting and turning to get free, but the two Lords hold her down while Saint grabs some rope from his nightstand. "Give me her left arm," he orders. The Lord holds it out to Saint, and he wraps the rope around it before pulling the arm down by her side and tying it off to the footboard. It forces her to bend her knees. Otherwise, her legs would hang off the end.

"Other one." He does the same, tying it off to the headboard.

"Saint, please..." she cries out, realizing he isn't playing with her.

He removes his belt and bends her left knee to where her ankle is up against her thigh, then he secures it with his belt. Snapping his fingers at the guy who stands behind him, he orders, "Give me your belt."

The guy rips it off and hands it over. Saint does the same to the other leg. She pulls them to her chest.

He leaves her there naked from the waist down. Some guys in the room already have their cells out, recording her squirm. My eyes drop to her shaved cunt, and there's no denying she's wet. Some bitches get off on this shit.

Saint exits the bathroom with a bowl of what looks like soapy water, a towel, and a large syringe. He sets the bowl on the floor at the end of the bed, and he bends down, shoving the syringe into it and filling it up. "Open her legs. Hold them wide open for me." He orders to his two best friends, who are still sitting on either side of her head.

They grab her legs and pull them apart, making her arch her back and cry out into the room at the position they've got her in. Holding her wide open for the room to see. Makes me think she's about to give birth by the way they've got her spread open.

He wastes no time putting the tip of the syringe into her ass and starts to fill her with the water. She cries, begs him to stop, but he continues until the bowl is empty. Her stomach has expanded. She looks like she could be seven months pregnant once he's satisfied.

"That's my girl," he praises her. "Such a good whore." She whimpers, tears running down the side of her face. "Tell them, sweetheart. Tell them how much of a painslut you are." She can't say anything over her sobbing. "I used cooler water; it'll cause more cramping than warm water," he informs her.

Saint hands the syringe off to a friend while he keeps his fingers on her ass to hold the water in. The friend opens the tampon and hands it to him. He removes his fingers only to replace it with the tampon.

His friends let go of her shaking knees, and Saint gets up on the bed to sit by her head. "Hand me a small pillow." He points at a guy who sits on a chair over in the corner of Saint's room recording. The guy tosses it in the air, and Saint kneels, pushing it up underneath her neck and shoulders, arching her head back. "Someone start a timer," he barks out, kneeling above her head.

She looks up at him through watery lashes, tears running down her face, body shaking uncontrollably. "Saint, please. I can't..."

"I'm going to fuck your mouth," he tells her, and she shakes her head at him. "Yes. And after I come down your throat, I'm going to fuck that ass."

AFTER HE CAME, HE LEFT HER TIED THERE AND SAT DOWN TO play video games while she continued to cry and beg him to let her release the water. When the timer went off, he did just that, taking her to the bathroom, leaving us all in the room waiting. Curious to see what would happen. They were in there for what felt like forever. Once they returned, he kissed her before he tied her down once again, this time facedown with her ass up in the air. And he fucked her ass just like he promised while we all watched her get off on it. Then he let his two friends fuck her ass as well.

I get the whole *watch me fuck what's mine*. But even then, I didn't understand the concept of sharing. What's the point of having something if everyone else gets it too? But some men get off on the fact they have the power to loan their women out. That was also the first time I ever saw a painslut in action. I spent many months after that watching porn of men and women getting off on receiving and giving pain.

"Ty-son," my wife whispers my name, getting my attention.

"Almost, Lake," I tell her. "You're doing so good, little darling. Almost done." I finish off the last bit and pull it out. "Hold it in there, Lake." I only gave her 300 cc. Not much compared to the gallon I watched the girl get that night at the house of Lords party. But to someone like Laikyn, who has never done it before, it will be uncomfortable.

I gently grab her upper arm and slowly pull her to stand. I undo my belt and then turn her to where she faces me. Her pretty eyes are downcast, staring at the floor. "Look at me."

She lifts to meet mine, and she's got unshed tears in them.

"Hold it in for ten minutes."

Her shoulders shake.

"Then you can go to the bathroom. After that, I want you to shower and get ready for your shift. Do you understand?"

She nods, her eyes dropping to the floor once again. "Lake?" I command, and she raises her eyes to meet mine through her wet lashes. "You will probably need to go more than once. But you should be fine by the time your shift starts." I cup both sides of her face and lean down, kissing her lips. She doesn't kiss me back. I

273

taste her tears and my cock makes me want to bend her over and fuck her cunt. But I can't right now. I've got plans for her tonight. Another first of many to come with my new bride. "I want you down in my office before you start, understand?"

"Y-yes," she whispers brokenly.

"Good girl," I tell her, then I turn and leave her alone.

THIRTY-FOUR

LAIKYN

W hen I was in high school, I had a friend named Margaret. My parents loved her. They thought she was the best friend to have. Virgin, never partied, no drugs or alcohol. She was the only friend I was allowed to continue to have after my sister passed because she was a "good girl." Did everything her parents asked of her and wasn't *a slut like the other girls*—my mother's words.

Margaret's father was a Lord, and she was already promised to marry another Lord. He was nine years older than her. They were to get married on her twentieth birthday. One of her requirements was to be a virgin for him. So at fifteen, she started having anal.

I remember her telling me about how painful her first time was, but she expected it to be. So she did it again. And again. She ended up loving it. She told me that she had to prep herself each time. Otherwise, it would have been *messy*.

The moment Tyson said preparation, I knew exactly what he meant. I knew the time would come when he'd claim other parts of me.

He was right. I held in whatever he put inside me as long as I could. I'm not sure if it was ten minutes or not, I didn't time it. But I then poured myself a bath where I cried from embarrassment. It's humiliating. To have a guy—your husband—tie your hands behind your back and give you an enema so he can fuck your ass. Tyson told me to shower, but I didn't want to ruin my hair. It had been dyed and fixed at the salon earlier today, and it looked too pretty to mess up, so I put it up in a big clip and took a bath. I had to get out twice to use the restroom.

I had cramping, but nothing I couldn't handle.

I finish getting dressed and go down to his office. I'm more nervous now then I was after our wedding. I'm sweating. Rubbing my hands on my shorts. I was planning on asking him what Ryat meant but after I saw what he had planned for me, I decided against it. Now wasn't the time. Plus, if I say something to Tyson, he may tell Ryat and then Ryat can order Blake not to see me. I'm not sure about their marriage. I don't want to chance Ryat forcing her to stay away from me.

I open Tyson's office door and come to an abrupt stop. He's sitting at his desk, his eyes down while signing a piece of paper, and Bethany is leaning over it, her tits in his face. Her hands on the surface.

The moment she hears someone enter, she turns around and her eyes meet mine. A cruel smile instantly spreads across her face. "Well, well, well. Trying to look like Whitney?" she asks.

"Get the fuck out of my office, Beth." Tyson dismisses her. He doesn't sound mad or irritated. Just bored.

Her words make my heart race faster. My sister had dark hair and it's exactly why my father made me bleach mine. Why can't I want to be me, without trying to be my sister? Why do I have to change my appearance? I always had dark hair too.

"We'll finish this conversation later," she tells him over her shoulder before she exits, shutting the door behind her.

I look at him. He sits there staring at me, but his blue eyes give nothing away. It drives me nuts that I can't guess what he's thinking. Was she in here to fuck him? Did he call her up here because he wanted to see her? He knew I was coming to his office; did he want me to catch her in here? Another way to remind me that he can do whatever he wants.

"Stop," he commands, and I jump at the sound of his voice.

I square my shoulders. I hate that he can read my face. That my mind screams so loud that he can hear it.

"Come here," he orders.

I walk over to him, my heart still racing, but now for a different reason. Anger. Jealousy. I'm not stupid. Tyson Crawford could have any woman he wants. I'm sure women have dropped to their knees for him without him having to say a single word. Or let him fuck their ass. I watched my sister let him have his way with her— however he wanted it. I heard the stories she'd tell her friends when she called them after he left our house. Or after she'd come home from spending a weekend with him at the house of Lords. I was jealous then too. Of her. Of what he did to her.

It's been two days since he's even spoken to me. Does that mean he's gone to Bethany to fuck? If not, then someone else? Who knows how many women he's been with since he was dating my sister. I'm sure he's fucked more than half the female staff here at Blackout.

He picked me. I'm his wife. He's my husband. A man like Tyson needs a woman. A slut. His own personal whore. I'm determined to be that. I want him to see Bethany and think of me. I want her to throw herself at him and him turn her down because he knows that I can give him what he needs. Because I know for a fact Bethany isn't going to stop. My father is controlling her. But Tyson—he can control me, and I can control him.

Going over to his desk, I don't even wait for him to ask. I shove my shorts down my legs and bend over his desk, putting my arms behind my back. Taking in a deep breath, I close my eyes, knowing what's about to come. Lots of people have anal. It can't be that bad. I'm a pretty competitive person, and if they can do it, so can I.

His hands go between my thighs and undo the snaps on my leotard, pushing it up and out of the way. "You're wet, Lake," he observes.

I whimper, knowing my underwear has a wet spot. I'm always horny for him. That's what a trained slut needs. Dick.

His desk drawer opens and closes. Then the handcuffs are fastened around my wrists. I hiss in a breath when he tightens them. Then my thong is pulled to the side before his fingers run over my cunt. I moan, pushing back against him.

"How do you feel?" he asks, and then clarifies, "Your stomach?"

I blush, thankful he can't see my face. "Fine," I answer.

I think he's going to start fingering me, but instead, he runs them up and over my ass. I can't help but tense up. He removes them only to place them back, and I can feel the lube on them this time. He pushes one into me, and I suck in a deep breath. "You've got a six-hour shift tonight," he says, removing it and pushing it back in. "You will be in my office every two hours. Do you understand me?"

"Yes." I gasp when I feel him pushing a second one in. That nervousness returning to my stomach. Three times tonight he's going to fuck my ass? Dear Lord, my pussy is still sore from all the sex we've had since I became his wife.

He pulls them out, and I take in a shaky breath. "How often?" he asks, slapping my ass cheek.

"Every two hours," I answer, my arms fighting the cuffs digging into my sensitive skin.

"If you don't, you will be punished, Lake," he adds, and I inhale sharply as he pushes two fingers into my ass once again.

I rise up on my tiptoes, and when I'm about to beg him to stop, he pulls them out. I exhale and relax on the surface of the desk.

But I tense a second later when something rubs against my ass. "Tyson?" I gasp, feeling pressure against the spot his fingers just were. It's not his dick, it feels ... different.

"Take in a deep breath, Lake," he commands.

I do as he says.

"Now let it out slowly and relax." He pushes something inside me. I cry out, trying to pull away but my hips are pushed up against the side of the desk, so I have nowhere to go. I'm at his mercy.

I feel my ass open up for whatever he's making me take, and just when I don't think I can take it anymore, the pain subsides.

He grabs my cuffed arms and pulls me to stand. Turning me to face him, he cups my face. My watery eyes meet his, and he leans down, kissing me. My lips open up for him on their own, and I moan into his mouth as he reminds me that I'm his.

I want to cry that I want him. That I need him. The fact that my pussy is wet just proves that I'm trained. Just how he wants me. My hands fight the cuffs, wanting to touch him. To run all over his chest and arms, feeling his strong and muscular body.

The taste of the whiskey on his breath has me moaning. Or it could be the way he's holding me to him—both of his hands in my hair, his fingers gripping the strands so painfully my scalp stings. But I like it. I rub my hips into his, and I can feel how hard he is. He's all worked up, and I pray that it's because of me and not the bitch who was in his office when I entered.

He slows the kiss, just our lips touching before he pulls away, leaving me panting. "Every two hours, you will come to see me, and I'll change out the plug."

My eyes widen as I realize what we're doing. He's going to slowly stretch my ass to fuck it later. I knew anal was his plan, but I thought we would do it now and get it over with. Why do I feel like he's punishing me? Dragging it out by making me wait. It's a way of control.

"Do not remove it," he demands.

"What if ...?" I trail off, afraid to even finish that question.

"What if what?" he asks, running his knuckles down my neck and to my choker.

The subtle hint that, at any time, he can turn it on and shock me into submission. Maybe that's what he meant by I'll be punished tonight. The fact that I want to be his *good girl* is reason enough to turn it on and light me up. Maybe it'll help me out of this trance that he's got me in.

"What if I have to fart?" I ask softly, my cheeks heating up with embarrassment.

He laughs like I've never heard him laugh before. It makes his eyes light up and his chest shake. He looks careless and free. "That's cute." He kisses my forehead and turns me around. Uncuffing me, he pulls my leotard, snapping it, and then slaps my ass once more. "Put your shorts on and go to work. I'll see you in two hours." With that, he dismisses me, avoiding my question that was not a joke.

THIRTY-FIVE

LAIKYN

I look at the clock to see I've got twenty minutes before I have to be upstairs in Tyson's office. The plug bothered me at first, but I got so busy with my section that I eventually forgot about it.

Walking up to my new table, I see it's Collin and some of his friends that we used to hang out with. "Lake." He notices me and smiles.

My shoulders slump. I was hoping he wouldn't see me, and I could hand this table off to someone else. But this is why Tyson makes me work here. To humiliate me. To show the world I'm his bitch. So I put a fake smile on my face. "Hey. What can I get you, guys?"

His friend Timothy looks up at me. His eyes fall to my chest, over my body, and then return to my breasts again. "Well, Little Miss Lake has grown up."

"Right?" Collin reaches out and wraps his arm around my waist, pulling me into him. Much friendlier than when he's shown up here before. It's to show off to his friends, I'm sure. "I preferred the blond better, babe."

I instantly pull away and look around to make sure no one saw. That's all I need is for Bethany to go and tell my husband I'm cheating on him. That's one way for her to get him on her side. Then she'll have a plug up her ass. I ignore the comment about my hair. I don't give a fuck what Collin *prefers*.

"What?" Collin laughs, noticing, and I'm pretty sure they've been drinking for quite some time tonight by the way his eyes are glassed over. "He won't care, Lake." Rolling his eyes, he sits back in his seat.

"Don't tell us that you think Tyson married you because he actually loves you," Timothy says, making all the guys laugh.

My chest tightens at his words. It's the same thing my brother told me at the house of Lords. That had been our first and only public appearance as husband and wife. Other than that, I haven't been allowed to go anywhere, so the fact that the world is now aware of my marriage to Tyson catches me off guard. I guess I hadn't thought of that until now. "No, I—"

"He probably gave you Whitney's ring," a guy named Mickey adds.

I frown at his words and shake my head. "No. They were never engaged."

Their laughter grows. Collin looks up at me. "They were, Lake."

"No. They weren't," I argue. "I think I would have known if my sister was engaged." My parents hated that she was his chosen. They would have never let it go that far. She was promised as a Lady to another Lord. But I was never told who it was. It was kept hush-hush.

He gives me a sympathetic look. "Just because they didn't tell you, doesn't mean it didn't happen," Collin says.

"Like I said." Mickey looks at my ring. "That's probably her ring." His eyes rise to look over my face. "That's probably why he had you dye your hair. To look more like her."

I pull away, walk over to the server station, and slam down my tray. "Lake?" Beau calls out as I storm up the stairs and burst into his office, slamming the door shut so hard that it rattles the wall more than the bass that plays below us.

"You were engaged to my sister?" I shout, my heart is pounding and I'm shaking so hard. I can't get it under control even if I wanted to.

He's on his office phone. Without even telling them bye, he hangs up and sits back.

"Was this before or after you knocked her up?" I can't help but ask.

TYSON

Senior year at Barrington

> ME: She's pregnant.

> PRIVATE NUMBER: That's not what we
> agreed on.

MY TEETH GRIND. LIKE I DON'T FUCKING KNOW THAT!

> ME: What do I do now?

> PRIVATE NUMBER: Do you have what
> we want?

> ME: No.

> PRIVATE NUMBER: Then you continue
> until you do.

Fuck! Another ding and I see a new message.

> PRIVATE NUMBER: You may want to consider buying her a ring.

I watch my wife stand there with her hands on her hips. I don't need to watch the rise and fall of her tits to know she's breathing heavily. She's pissed off at me for not telling her about my past. Too bad.

She marches her ass over to my desk and slams her hands down on it. "Answer the fucking questions, Tyson!" she shouts.

I stand from my desk and open my drawer. I pull out the next size up butt plug and go to walk around it.

"You think I'm going to let you come near me with that?" She points at it and gives a rough laugh. "Fuck that. And fuck you." She turns and starts to run out.

But I grab her upper arm, bringing her to a stop.

"Don't touch me!"

I wrap my hand around her throat and pin her up against the wall, pushing my body into hers. "I'm going to fuck my *wife's* ass tonight." I put an emphasis on wife, reminding her that it's her with a ring on her finger, not her sister. Her nostrils flare in understanding. "It's up to you if it's enjoyable or painful."

Baring her straight white teeth at me, she growls, "Your cock isn't that big, Tyson. I'll take my chances." Then she pushes on my chest.

I step back, letting go of her and allowing her to storm out as fast as she entered.

Laughing, I sit back in my seat and put the plug back into the drawer. I like this side of my wife. She deserves to have some backbone at some point in her life. Too bad she'll learn that those times will have consequences.

What I don't like is that someone is talking to her about me and Whitney. I pull up the cameras inside the club and rewind them until I see her standing at the end of the bar. She walks off to a table, and my hands instantly fist. *Fucking Collin.* Should have known. And he's here tonight with all of his friends from Barrington. None of them are important Lords. They wear the crest on their chest, but it won't get them far in life. They all have jobs that make them feel powerful but fail in comparison to high-ranking Lords.

He puts his arm around her, and I stand up. I'm about to go down there and kick his ass when she pushes him away. Her eyes dart around the room, expecting me to see it. If she wouldn't have stormed her ass up here, I might not have.

Changing the cameras to current time, I watch her stand at their table, and he grabs her hand, pulling her down onto his lap. This time, she doesn't fight him to get up. Instead, she pushes her hair off her shoulder so she can lean in and speak into his ear over the pounding music, and I see fucking red. Blood rushes in my ears, and I fist my hands.

There are two ways I can go about this. One is bloody, the other is not. I've always been the kind of guy to choose violence. But that was before I had a reason not to. For the first time in my life, I'm going to choose option two. Lake won't like it, but punishments aren't meant to be fun.

THIRTY-SIX

TYSON

Three years ago

"What do you want, Ty?" Whitney asks, entering my bedroom.

I close the door and turn to face her, leaning back against it. Her hands are on her hips, one pushed out, and she's wearing a tight white minidress. She's dressed this way on purpose. She's ignored me for two days now since she slapped me and ran out of my room. She waited until after nine this evening to respond to one of my many messages. Which means she's going out tonight with her friends and she wanted to make sure she dropped by on her way. A little "fuck you, Tyson" attitude.

"How do you feel?" My eyes drop to her flat stomach. She can't be more than six weeks, if it's mine, considering she's only been my chosen for not even two months now. But the fact that all of my condoms had holes in them, I hate to say the odds aren't in my favor.

"Fine." She lowers her eyes to look at the floor.

"Going out tonight?" I ask.

"Bethany is having her birthday party."

"Sure that's a good idea?"

Her eyes narrow on mine. "I'm not going to be partying. Just going to see my friend."

I walk over to her, placing my hands on her waist, and pull her body flush with mine. "I don't think you should. It's not safe for you or the baby."

"Like you care." She scoffs. "According to you, it's not even yours."

"It better be mine," I growl, my hands tightening on her waist.

Her eyes light up with excitement at my possessiveness. Whitney is easy to read. She's explosive with her emotions. If she doesn't vocally tell you, her face will. She wraps her arms around my neck. "I promise it is." Her lips are so close to mine but not touching.

"Stay with me tonight." I press mine to hers, but she keeps hers closed, not letting me in. My hands drop to the hem of her dress and slide it up her legs.

She pulls her face back from mine. "I made plans—"

I cut her off, kissing her, this time forcing my tongue into her mouth, and I almost smile at the taste of vodka on her breath. I've been on the fence about her being pregnant, but this confirms my suspicion. I do believe she's trying to get knocked up, though. The question is why?

Gripping the material, I pull it over her head, forcing me to break our kiss. Tossing the useless dress to the side, I look over her standing in front of me with only a nude-colored thong and heels. Her nipples are hard, and her breathing is erratic.

"Let me spend all night telling you I'm sorry," I offer, my hands going back to her hips. I lift her off her heels, tossing her onto the bed.

She smiles, looking up at me, and I know she won't be leaving here until morning. I'm going to tie her little lying ass to my bed, and I'm going to fuck her mouth and her ass. But not her *cunt. I've got a plan for that, and she's going to be very disappointed.*

MY CELL RINGING PULLS ME OUT OF THAT MEMORY, AND I SEE it's Colton. "Yeah?" I answer.

"We're about to pull up," he states.

"I'll meet you down there." I hang up and pocket my cell. As I go to leave my office, I take one last look at the TV hanging on the wall and see my wife serving tables. My eyes go to Collin and he's leaning on the back two legs of his chair, his eyes on her ass as he watches her do her job.

LAIKYN

I'M SO FUCKING PISSED MY HEART IS STILL RACING. BUT I'M not even sure what I'm mad about. The fact I didn't know that my sister and Tyson were engaged? Or the fact that Collin and his friends made fun of me about my marriage to Tyson? I didn't choose this life. I sure as fuck would have never chosen Tyson as my husband.

I'm also not one of those girls who believe you marry for love.

That rarely happens in our world. Now I'm not saying that Lords and Ladies don't end up falling in love with one another after they've been married. But I've seen too many marriages where they still hate one another when their kids are forced to marry someone they don't want.

I guess I hate myself the most. The fact that I always dreamed of a different life. A special kind of love. That's for fools.

The club closed an hour ago, and we're all cleaning up. Thankfully, Bethany has ignored me tonight. The club was packed, and we've all been busy with our sections. Plus, there was a fight that broke out in VIP. Security threw three guys out and the girl they came with.

I put my tray of glasses up on the bar and look over at the round booth in the corner. It's where Tyson always sits while we clean. But he's not there tonight. I haven't seen him since I stormed into his office and demanded answers that he, of course, didn't give. I guess his silence was my answer.

"Have a good night, Lake," Beau calls out.

I wave at him, knowing that my night will, in fact, not be good. I've had a plug in my ass for six hours—is that even healthy—and I'm about to get fucked by my husband, who I insulted by saying his dick was small. Which was, of course, a lie. It's not small by any means. I know Tyson well enough now to know that he'll make it as painful as possible. Margaret bled the first time she did it. I'm guessing that will be my experience too.

Making my way to the elevator, I shake my hands and take in a deep calming breath. It doesn't work as it climbs higher. I take it to the fourth floor and enter our apartment. It's quiet, the lights off. I walk down the hallway to the bedroom with my heart in my throat.

Pushing the door open, I see the light is on, and he's already in here, standing by the long dresser with his back to me. "Get undressed," he commands without even looking up at me in the mirror.

His words instantly piss me off all over again. "I'm going to shower." And I'm pulling this damn plug out whether he likes it or not.

He turns to face me, and he has pieces of rope fisted in his hands, so long they puddle at his feet. He tosses them onto the bed. My heart picks up, but I square my shoulders, refusing to let him think I'm intimidated. No matter how much I am.

Giving him my back, I go to enter the bathroom but drop to my knees when a shock goes through my body.

I'm gasping, on my hands and knees when I see his shoes come to stand in front of me. Sitting back on my legs, I look up at him through watery lashes and suck in a deep breath. I reach up and yank on the collar, letting out a scream of frustration. *He fucking shocked me.*

"I gave you an order, Lake," he says calmly. "I expect it to be followed."

I get to my shaky legs and glare at him. I fist my hands to keep from slapping the shit out of him. It'll probably just get me a beating. But I honestly don't think he'd ever hit me. Tyson has other ways to make you do what he wants. Case in point, the collar wrapped around my neck.

Grabbing my shorts, I shove them down my legs. Then I kick off my shoes and unsnap my leotard before pushing my fishnets down my legs. I yank the leotard up and over my body before throwing it across the room and stand before him, naked and chest heaving. I'm so angry with him for making me his Lady. And mad at myself for allowing this to happen.

I hate the fact that he's fully clothed in dress slacks and a button-up. It makes me feel more vulnerable. He always does this. It's a reminder that he's superior, and I'm his slave.

I remove my wedding ring from my finger and lift my hand in front of his face before I drop it to our feet, not caring where it ends up.

A smile tugs at the corner of his lips, and what should make me terrified, gives me butterflies in my stomach. He's already decided how to make me pay for the fit I threw earlier. I'm just making it worse.

He steps into me, and I cower, my fear getting the best of me. I drop my head, unable to meet his stare. His hand softly touches my cheek, and a whimper escapes my parted lips as he gently guides my head up so I'm forced to look at him.

His free hand runs down my heaving chest and waist before

291

dropping between my legs. He gently runs his fingers along my pussy before lifting it to his lips. "You're wet, Lake." He places them in his mouth, tasting them, and my eyes grow heavy. "You may hate me for what I'm about to do to you, but I promise your body will enjoy it."

His words make my pulse race. But I manage to swallow the lump in my throat, and whisper, "I already hate you."

THIRTY-SEVEN

TYSON

Her heavy breathing fills the room, and I can't help but smile as I pick up the piece of rope I had laid out on the bed.

I tie her wrists behind her back and let the excess rope puddle on the floor. I move to stand beside her and slide one arm behind her legs, the other across her back, and pick her up. She gasps in surprise but doesn't fight me.

After I lay her down on the bed, she goes to roll onto her stomach, but I slap her thigh. "Stay on your back. I want your arms underneath you." Positioning her where her head is all the way at the foot of the bed. I don't want her head to fall off the edge, but I want it as close as possible.

She whimpers, lifting her hips up off the mattress, trying to relieve the pressure her body is putting on her arms that are tied underneath her. I get back onto the bed and grab the excess rope connected to the end of her wrists. I pull it along the bed and reach down below the headboard, slipping it through a rope cleat. I've got them placed all around this bedframe for this very reason. I can tie her up in so many different ways.

I pull the rope taut, tying it off, making sure there's no give.

"Tyson." She moans my name, and I watch the way she pulls on the rope. Her heels dig into the bed as she rocks her weight from side to side.

Grabbing the next piece of rope, I sit next to her left leg and begin doing a simple column tie around her ankle. Then I push her ankle up to her thigh and wrap it around them several times, securing them together and making it impossible for her to stretch out her leg. I make sure not to wrap the rope too high to where it can slip over her knee.

Once the other is done, I stand at the foot of the bed and look down at her. Her chest and stomach are exposed to me, both ankles tied to her thighs, keeping her legs bent. Leaning over, I grab the excess rope from her left leg and pull it to the left bedpost of the footboard. I do the same with the other, forcing her legs wide open.

"Please," she whispers.

I kneel at the foot of the bed, lifting her head off the sheet, and gently pull her hair out from underneath her to drape over the edge. "Please what, little darling?" I ask, watching the way her chest heaves as she breathes.

"I ... I can't ..." She closes her eyes.

"Can't what?" I reach out and massage her breast, which grants me a moan. "Can't move?" I take a wild guess at the way her body fights the rope. "That's the point, Lake."

A soft whimper escapes her parted lips, and my cock is so fucking hard for her. Ready to teach my wife a lesson.

"For you to be at my mercy. For me to have my way with you." Standing up, I get back onto the bed and position myself between her legs. I run my hands up her inner thighs, and she arches her back, letting out a frustrated sigh.

I unzip my slacks and grab my hard dick. Not even bothering

with foreplay, I lean forward and push the head of my cock into her. "You're so wet, Lake. So needy."

"Fuck." The word is barely a whisper as she arches her neck back.

I lean over her, pushing in deeper while my hands slide up her body. I hover my weight over her while my hands tangle in her hair, and I lower my lips to her neck. "How's that feel, little darling?" I pull out and slam into her, knowing every thrust I make also reminds her of the plug in her ass.

"So ... good," she breathes.

Her pussy tightens on my cock, and I sink my teeth into her neck before sucking on it. Pulling away, I see the hickey that I just left and smile. If she's going to act like she's single, then I'll show the world she's taken.

It's that simple.

The thought of a man even thinking he can have her has me picking up my pace. I slam into her, turning her moans into gasps and whimpers. "Tell me, Lake." I shove forward, knowing it's pulling the ropes on her wrists. I want the rope burns to be reminders too. "Who do you belong to?"

"Y-ou," she cries out.

"And who the fuck am I?" I growl, my hands fisting her hair tighter.

"My husband," she whimpers, her soaked cunt gripping my cock.

"Goddamn right, I am." I grunt. "Remember what I said I'd do to you if you let another man touch you?"

"I'm ... sorry." She takes in a deep breath. "Please, don't stop."

"You like when I use your cunt, little darling? When I make you my whore?"

Her lips are parted, her eyes growing heavy. She's close to coming all over my cock. "Fuuuucckkkk," her perfectly pouty lips say.

I smile, knowing she's right there. Pulling out, I grab my dick and come all over her stomach. She growls, knowing she isn't going to get off.

Picking up the toy that I had put out, I run it through the cum, making sure to coat it well, and then I rub it along her cunt, gently sliding it into her.

"Tyson ... what ...?" She raises her head to watch me. Her soaked pussy sucks it in, begging for more. "Please?" She sags against the bed.

I get off the bed and walk over to the footboard, kneeling once again.

Her pretty eyes look up at me and through her long lashes, they're swimming in tears. Frustrated and probably still mad. She's going to hate me by the time I'm done with her.

"Open your mouth," I order.

Her eyes narrow, and her jaw sharpens, telling me she's clenching her teeth and refusing to obey. I expected this, but I have ways to make her mind.

Reaching into my pocket, I pull out the clip and place it over her nose so she can't breathe through it. Her eyes widen.

"However long you decide to wait is up to you," I tell her.

She shakes her head, her chest heaving, needing air. I actually start to get nervous when her eyes grow heavy, thinking she'd rather kill herself than open her damn mouth. But finally, her lips part, and she sucks in a deep breath.

"That's it, Lake," I say, removing the clip from her nose. "Deep breaths."

She closes her lips to swallow and then opens them back once more to take a deep breath. I take the opportunity to place the gag in her mouth. She starts mumbling unintelligible noises as I lift her head just enough to wrap the leather strap around her head and fasten the buckle. I lay it down on the mattress, and she shakes her head from side to side.

"It's not the most attractive, but it gets the job done," I tell her, looking over the large, black gag. It covers her mouth, cheeks and chin. It's thick and bulky. "They call it the silencer," I continue. "Because no matter how loud you scream, you won't be heard."

She blinks, and tears streak down the side of her face. Her makeup is starting to run.

I pick up the bulb that is attached to the end of it and squeeze, inflating the gag inside her mouth. Her body thrashes against the restraints, and I do it again. Her wide eyes meet mine, and I do it once more. "It's an inflatable ball gag," I say, and she closes her eyes tightly. "How's it feel to have all of your holes filled, little darling?"

I remove the last thing from my pocket and hold it up to her face. Pressing the button, I turn on the vibrator I placed in her pussy. "I'm going to leave this here." I adjust it to the lowest setting and place it on her chest. Then I kiss her forehead and stand, removing my belt from my slacks. I lay it across her neck and say, "For later." Then I walk away.

LAIKYN

PAIN, PLEASURE, AND FRUSTRATION ARE WHAT I'M FEELING right now. I can't move, can't talk, and can barely breathe. I close my eyes tightly and try to calm my racing heart and ignore the buzzing inside my pussy. It's just making me mad. It's not enough to get me off but enough to make my hips move, needing more.

Opening my eyes, I arch my neck to see a clear but upside-down view of Tyson entering the adjoining bathroom. He left the door wide open, probably on purpose. The bastard gets undressed and steps into the shower.

I try to swallow around the rubber balloon that's inside my mouth while I lie back flat. My hands are going numb from how they're tied underneath me. My shoulders are screaming, and my thighs hurt from tensing. I lift my head and get a glimpse of his cum all over my stomach but have to lay my head back down because it pulls on my arms and shoulders.

Breathe, Lake. I tell myself, trying not to panic. The gag is so big that even if he hadn't fastened it behind my head, I still couldn't spit it out due to how inflated it is. And I'd hate to die here like this. That would be the most humiliating way possible.

I wiggle my hips, and it pushes the vibrator up against my G-spot and makes my breath catch. I do it again and close my eyes.

Fuuuckkkk. I'm going to kill him if I survive this.

The leather from his belt feels like sandpaper where he was kissing me earlier. He had to have left hickies on me. It felt so good when he was doing it. This is his way of marking me. Showing the world that I'm his whore. He might as well just write it on my forehead.

At this point, I'll let him do whatever the fuck he wants to me as long as I get off.

THIRTY-EIGHT

TYSON

I exit the shower, dry off, and walk into our bedroom to find her right where I left her. The muscles in her stomach flex, and her legs tense. I pick the remote up off her chest and turn it off.

She sags against the bed. "Don't want you coming too soon," I tell her, and she shakes her head. I can tell by the way her face turns red that she's screaming into the gag. I smile and run my hand down the side of her face. She pulls away, and I grab the belt from her neck. Slowly lifting it, I allow the leather to slide across her skin, drawing it out.

Once it's free of her neck, I double it over and slap it down on her inner thigh, making an instant red mark. "I'm going to spend some time marking my territory, Lake." I do it again, and her body shakes. I run the leather up her stomach, through my cum, and slap it across both of her breasts. Her nipples are hard and her chest heaves. Now there's cum splattered across her neck and face from whipping her with the belt.

"Fuck, you're so goddamn beautiful, Lake." Tears run down both sides of her face, and I watch her throat work as she tries to swallow. "I'm a lucky man." I slap it again across her breasts. Then I set it back over her neck as a reminder of what I can do with it. Reaching out, I pinch her nipples and pull up, making her breathe heavily through her nose while arching her back the best she can.

I get up on the bed, sitting between her legs, and take ahold of the base of the butt plug and turn it in clockwise motion. I pull it out just a little and push it back in. I open up the lube and pour it all over my cock and remove the plug, tossing it to the side.

I lean over her body, propped up with one hand while the other holds my hard cock at her ass. "Look at me, little darling. I want your eyes on me when I fuck your ass for the first time."

She opens them and sucks in a deep breath through her nose, and I push the head into her ass, feeling it open up for me. She arches her neck, and her body starts to shake.

"It's okay, Lake. It's not that big anyway." Then I push inside her with a growl at how good it feels.

This wasn't what I had planned for tonight, but my wife's actions earlier changed things. I'll remind them both that she belongs to me and what that means.

I pause, keeping my cock a couple of inches inside her, and pick up my cell that I had set next to her. I hit call on a number and lay it high on her chest, placing it on speakerphone. It starts to ring on the other end, and her watery eyes widen, looking up at me.

"Hello?"

"Collin," I say, pulling out and then slowly pushing my cock inside her ass—forcing it. The way her body shakes makes me think it's not as small as she thought.

"Tyson?" he asks slowly. "What's up, man?"

"I've given it some thought, and I'd like to help you out. Come to Blackout tomorrow. Five o'clock." I watch my cock slowly pull out of her ass before forcing it back in.

"Uh—"

"I'll show you the video I have of the girl in the club," I add, my eyes meeting hers once more. She blinks, and fresh tears fall from her pretty eyes.

"Why the change of heart?" he asks skeptically.

"My wife," I say, pushing deeper into her this time. She arches her neck, and I smile. "She asked me nicely." I lean down, kissing the side of her face, tasting her tears.

"Yeah. Sure. I'll be there. Five o'clock." He hangs up.

"Hear that, little darling?" I pull back before pushing forward. Fuck, I love that no one else has ever seen her like this. Fucked her like this. Even if it is a punishment, she's all mine.

Tears continue to run down the side of her face. "You're doing so good, Lake. Feel that?" I ask, pulling out and pushing in so slow it's almost painful, but I want to savor this moment. Remind her what it feels like to be mine. "That's your ass opening up for me. Taking my cock like a good fucking slut."

She blinks, and I kiss her forehead. Pulling out, I start to get more forceful. My control slips a little more with each thrust. "Does it hurt?"

She nods, her face scrunched due to the tightness of the gag fastened around her head.

"You'll get used to it, little darling," I say, lowering my chest to hers, our skin slippery from my cum that I left on her before my shower. I grip her face in my hands and tenderly kiss her forehead while my cock fucks her tight ass. Her body shakes uncontrollably against mine. "You'll learn to beg me to fuck it."

Pulling out, I push forward quickly, unable to go slow any longer. Burying my head into her slick neck, I suck on her soft skin as I fuck her ass like it isn't her first time. She lies below me, tied, gagged, and already covered in my cum while I use her.

Her throat works as she swallows, and she tenses, her neck arching. I pull away and sit up. I look down to see cum dripping from her cunt.

Smiling, I run my fingers through it. "That's my girl. Such a good fucking whore, Mrs. Crawford." She's trembling, and I dig my fingers into her tied thighs, pounding into her ass as my balls start to tighten. I come buried deep inside her ass, the force making me lose my breath.

I stay like that for a few seconds, trying to catch my breath and slow my racing heart, staring down at her heavy, watery eyes. When I pull out, I smile. "You've got cum dripping out of your ass and your cunt, Lake. I knew you'd enjoy it."

LAIKYN

My body is bound so tight that every muscle hurts from coming. Getting up, he lifts my head, so he can access the buckle. The large balloon inside my mouth deflates, and he removes the gag from my lips. I gasp in a deep breath, ignoring the drool that covers my face. Not caring how disgusting it looks.

His hands cup my sore cheeks, and I look up at him through my clumped eyelashes as he stands by my head. He doesn't speak to me, and I don't have the energy to talk. My heavy eyes close and I hear him undoing the rope from the bed over my heavy breathing. I cry out when he undoes the rope around my legs. Blood rushes back to them, making them tingle.

He starts rubbing them, and I can't stop the sobs. My chest heaving.

I'm so embarrassed. He made me come. Again. It hurt and also felt good. I don't know why or how he makes me like things that I know I shouldn't.

Rolling me over onto my stomach, he unties my wrists and picks me up off the bed. I lie lifeless in his arms, burying my face into his bare chest, not giving a fuck that his cum is smeared all over it. At this point, nothing matters.

I stay cradled in his arms while he sits on the edge of the tub and turns it on. Closing my eyes, I just want to sleep. I'm not sure I can even bathe myself at this point.

He steps into the bathtub, lowering us both to sit in the same position we were at the house after the house of Lords party. I'm thankful I don't have to face him.

"Lake, little darling." He pulls my hair off my chest to rest over my other shoulder.

A sob racks my body.

"You're okay." He wraps his arms around my chest, pulling my back into his. I bring my hands up and grab his skin, trying to calm myself. "You did so good, Lake. So good." He kisses the side of my head, and I sniff while the water fills the large tub.

The fact that he just fucked my ass isn't what upsets me. It's just the fact that I feel overwhelmed. The truth is I loved it. I hated that I was sucking on the ball inside my mouth, loving how full it made me feel. Thankfully, he couldn't hear me beg him for more. Or the way I lifted my ass the best I could so he could get deeper. Or that I loved that my hands were tied behind my back. A woman shouldn't enjoy such things.

He told me I'd be sorry for letting another man touch me, but I'm not. Because it was a punishment and I enjoyed it.

My family was right—I'm a disappointment. A sick whore who enjoys whatever her husband wants to do to her.

We sit in the bath until the water is cold, but my cries have subsided. Now I'm exhausted. The aftermath hits me like a train. I can feel my body shutting down on me, needing some rest.

He gently washes me clean and then helps me out. My legs shake so badly I can barely stand. So after he dries me off, he picks me up and places me in our bed under the comforter. I curl up into a ball away from him, still too embarrassed, and close my eyes.

He shifts behind me, and then his strong arm wraps around me from behind, pulling me into him. I wish I had the strength to push him off, but I don't. So instead, I allow him to hold me like he cares, and fresh tears sting my eyes as a sob escapes my trembling lips.

He pulls away from me, and I let him go, unable to hold onto him. I feel cold all of a sudden, but then his hands are on me, and he's pulling my shoulder, forcing me to roll toward him. "No—" I choke out, trying to push him away, not wanting to have to face him, but he doesn't stop.

"Come here, little darling. Let me hold you," he says softly. Pulling my front into his, he wraps his arm around me once again, and I bury my face into his chest. He kisses my forehead. "You're okay, Lake. I've got you."

I cling to him, hating that the very man who forced me to marry him is the same man who makes me feel safe. I'm not sure why he's being so nice. Tyson isn't the kind of guy I'd expect to cuddle after he uses you. But I don't push him away. Instead, I cling to him, loving the sense of security no matter how fake it is.

When you've been starving for affection all your life, you'll accept the least amount of effort given and turn it into something it isn't. Tyson is that man for me. He's what I wish I always had even though I know it's what I'll never find.

THIRTY-NINE

TYSON

Three years ago

Ryat and I are sitting in my car in the house of Lords parking lot about to get out when my cell rings. Whitney lights up my screen. "Hello?" I answer.

"Hey," she responds, sounding breathless.

"What are you doing?" I ask.

"Can you meet me?" she asks. Before I can answer, she goes on, "Someone has been following me all day."

I sit up straighter. "What do you mean all day?" A look at the clock says it's after six p.m. "Why are you just now calling me?"

"I didn't think it was that big of a deal. But..."

"But what?" I demand.

"Well, I got a text last night from an unknown number. I didn't think anything of it."

"What did it say?"

"It was a picture of me in my bed. Naked."

"What the fuck, Whitney?" I bark out.

"I didn't think anything of it," she repeats. "Thought it was Lake fucking with me, ya know?" she goes on. "But when I asked her about it, she had no clue what I was talking about. And today, I keep noticing this same car everywhere I go."

"Where are you?" I put my car in gear.

"I'm on my way to the house of Lords. I just finished up with my study group at Barrington."

"I'll head your way and then once I reach you, I'll follow you back here, okay?"

"Okay," she says, letting out a shaky breath. "Thanks, Ty."

I STAND AT THE END OF THE BED WHILE I WATCH LAKE SLEEP. I crawled into bed with her after our bath, and I held her while she cried herself to sleep in a matter of seconds. Her body was worn out.

Kneeling, I reach underneath the bed and pick up her wedding ring. I watched it roll under there when she took it off earlier, thinking she was making a point. She wishes it was that easy for her to leave me.

Walking back over to the side of the bed, I take her left hand and slide it onto her finger. "Sweet dreams, little darling." I lean down and kiss her forehead, letting my lips linger before reluctantly pulling away.

As I stand beside our bed, watching my wife sleep, I think about Collin. His hands on her soft skin. Pulling her into him. The fact he thinks he can do it in the first place is a problem.

The second problem is that he's telling her about my past with Whitney. I was too busy being the Lords' bitch to protect her. That won't happen with Lake. Ryat thinks her father will come after Lake, and he might. This time, I'll be ready.

She'll never understand why I married her, and I honestly

don't give a shit. I'll do whatever I need to do to prove my point. Laikyn Grace Crawford is mine. And I'll prove it to the fucking world. If I have to carve my name all over her flawless skin, I will.

———

I ENTER MY OFFICE WITH MY HAND IN LAKE'S. SHE HASN'T spoken one word to me since last night. I didn't expect her to, though. She was already mad, and I just pissed her off more. Then she broke down and was embarrassed. She woke up this morning, fixed breakfast, and then crawled back into bed, avoiding me. I won't be ashamed or remorseful for what I did to her last night. It's the first of many. I know she liked it and got off on it.

"Sorry to keep you waiting, Collin," I say and look at Lake. "Have a seat, little darling."

She falls onto the couch and winces. I refrain from smiling at her discomfort. That's why I did it the way I did. To remind her that I was there last night, balls deep in her untouched ass.

The door opens again, and Colton enters, followed by Alex, Finn, and Jenks. Letting the door close behind them, they each stay against the far back wall.

"What the fuck is this?" Collin notices and jumps to his feet.

"I have to admit," I say, falling into my seat, and he turns to face me. "I lied to you."

His eyes narrow on me. "What the fuck do you want?"

"Please forgive me, but I was a little busy last night when I called you." Lake gasps, knowing what I'm referring to, but I ignore her. "You ever had that kind of sex that just makes you do irrational shit?" I wonder.

Colton and Alex both grunt in understanding.

"I'm leaving." He goes to head for the door, but Finn jumps in front of it, blocking his only exit.

"I want to show you something," I say, picking up the envelope Ryat had brought me. "I was at the house of Lords the other night when Colton informed me you were here to see the surveillance footage."

"I'm a cop, that's my job," he snaps.

"Yes, but as you see, her body had already been found, days prior to that." My eyes slide to Lake, and she doesn't look surprised at what I just said. *Interesting.*

He squares his shoulders, readjusting himself in his seat. "I don't know what you're talking about."

"No?" I arch a brow and toss the manila envelope onto his lap. "Have a look."

He opens it up, and his body stiffens.

"But she's not the first woman this has happened to, is she?" I dig, wondering just how much he knows.

He ignores my question, or he just didn't hear it all. "Where did you get this?"

"Doesn't matter." I shrug. "What matters is I do have a video to show you." I pick up the remote and turn on the seventy-inch TV on the back wall and hit play. It's last night inside the club. "That's you, with your hands on my wife."

He jumps to his feet once again, the folder and pictures falling to the floor. He runs to the door but Alex steps out, grabs his hair and pulls him back to the center of the room while Finn grabs a chair. Alex shoves him into it and Colton takes the handcuffs from his back pocket, quickly cuffing his hands behind his back, threading the cuffs between the vertical wooden bars to secure him to it.

"You're finished!" he screams, thrashing in the chair. "You can kiss the club and your wife goodbye."

I walk around my desk, stepping into him, and lean back against the edge, letting him run his mouth.

"The Lords will kill you if you touch me," he warns.

"You think they give a fuck about you?" I ask, and the guys laugh. "You know how many people I've killed? Most were Lords." I snort. "They don't care about you anymore than they care about me. For every ten killed, fifty more are about to take their place." If I was killed right now, they'd bring someone else in to run Blackout. I guarantee they've already got a list. And they'd just continue to go down the line. That part doesn't bother me. It's the fact that my wife will be handed to another Lord. That another man would get to touch what's mine, fuck what's mine, hurt what's mine. That is something that I will not allow to happen.

"Remove his clothes," I order.

His screams fill the room as Finn and Jenks undo his pants and yank them down his legs while he tries to kick them unsuccessfully. Alex and Colton rip his shirt open, exposing his chest to the room.

I nod to Colton, and he starts digging through Collin's jeans pocket before tossing me his badge. Of course, he carries it around with him. I grab the lighter off my desk and begin to heat it. "How many are missing?" I ask.

His lips thin at his refusal to answer.

"See, I don't think she's the first one missing from my club." It was not a coincidence that she went missing from here and that Collin shows up the next day, right after I marry my wife. The question is, why Blackout? And why now? "So ... last time. How many are currently missing?" He looks away from me, and I smile. "Open his mouth," I order no one in particular.

Colton steps up to the back of the chair, placing his fingers into his mouth from behind and pries them open. I step into him, heated badge in hand and go to stick it inside of his mouth. His eyes go wide, and he tries to shake his head, mumbling unintelligible words. I nod to Colton, and he removes them. "You've got two seconds before you eat this badge," I inform him. It won't fit, but I can jam it in there enough that it'll burn the shit out of him.

"Four." He gasps. "Four have gone missing. Last seen here at Blackout." Hanging his head, he adds, "Over the last six months."

Six months? Well, there goes my theory about it involving my wife. No one knew of my plans to marry her other than Ryat and my father. Even the Lords weren't aware until the day of the wedding. When I made the deal, they never asked who I wanted. Hell, as far as they know, I didn't even know who I was giving my life up for.

"Why haven't I been informed of this?" I wonder. "Why was one girl more important than the others?"

"The others weren't reported," he growls through gritted teeth, trying to yank on the cuffs.

I frown. "What do you mean?"

He sucks in a deep breath. "After Andrea was reported missing and last seen here, we found the others via social media posts. Friends and parents looking for them. But no official police reports were filed."

"You mean they weren't daughters of a Lord." I nod my head in understanding. Now those have the same MO as the previous murders from years ago. "How many have been found?"

"Two." He swallows, looking up at me.

"The other was the same as Andrea?" I ask tightly, hating that he's not offering this information to me.

He nods, and I allow the silent answer. I mean, men and women go missing all the time, but for two to be found the same way as all the ones were years ago—that's not a coincidence.

"Hmm." I flick the lighter once again, placing the flame under the badge.

"I told you everything I know!" he screams and looks over at my wife.

"Oh, this?" I motion to the badge. "This is for touching my wife." I told her, *If I even think you're going to fuck another man, I'll kill him. In front of you. It'll be slow and painful. You will see his bloody corpse in your dreams for years to come.* She might not have slept with him, but he would if given the chance. I'm about to prove to her that I'm a lot of things but a liar isn't one of them.

"Stop him. Stop him, Lake." Collin pleads with her to save his pathetic life. "Please. You're not like him."

She hangs her head because she knows she can't help him.

"Fucking pathetic bitch," he shouts at her, spit flying from his mouth. "Your father will make sure you pay for this. For becoming his fucking puppet." She looks up at him through her lashes at that. "Just like your sister."

I just found out something that I didn't think was possible. He knows the truth about Whitney. Which means he's working for her father. That changes things.

"What do you mean like my sister?" she rushes out.

"He'll make you pay—"

I shove the heated-up badge into his mouth, and he thrashes in the chair as it burns him, not caring that it's burning my hand in the process.

Colton takes the roll of duct tape he had and starts placing it around Collin's mouth, securing it so he can't spit it out.

"No, wait." My wife jumps to her feet. "What do you mean like my sister?" Lake goes to move toward his chair, but Alex grabs her, and she kicks her feet out, trying to get free from his grip. He falls down onto the couch, shoving her down onto her stomach and pins her arms behind her back to keep her from hitting him.

I look over at Lake and she's got her watery eyes on me. "Let her go," I order, and Alex lets go of her arms pinned to her back. She sits up, rubbing them as she drops her head. Fuck, this isn't going how I had planned.

"Get rid of him," I order, and quickly pick up the scattered papers so she can't see them. That's the last thing I want to do.

I sit down and look over at her. Her eyes are on mine, and a single tear runs down her cheek. I open my mouth to speak, but she gets up and walks out, slamming the door behind her.

LAIKYN

I WENT BACK TO THE APARTMENT AND TOOK A NAP BEFORE I started getting ready for work. I thought the nap would help my mood; it didn't. Once again, I'm pissed that he didn't allow me to hear what Collin had to say. And now I never will. The guys are probably burying his body somewhere in the middle of the woods, where it'll never be found.

Making my way downstairs, I enter the locker room and open mine. I never use it because I live upstairs. So I didn't need to leave anything here. I bend down and pick up the cell my father gave me and see it's dead. Fuck! Of course, it is. It's been weeks since he gave it to me.

I haven't checked it once for my initiations. God, I've been so stupid. I don't have a charger for it. What if they already sent them to me, and I've failed.

Looking around the room, I see Starla's makeup and phone on the counter in front of the mirror. I open her bag and find an iPhone charger. Plugging it in, I thank God that it fits. I set it down and watch the battery light up.

My eyes constantly going over to the door. The club has already opened. My shift doesn't start until eleven tonight. When it's during the week, the club opens with four waitresses and then brings in more later during peak hours, breaking it up into more sections.

My knees bounce and I reach out and hold down the button, praying it's at least enough to just power on.

I clap my hands when the screen lights up, but my eyes slam to the door as my heart races. If anyone catches me, I'm going to be fucked. That thought makes my thighs tighten. I enjoyed the last punishment fuck I got.

Picking up the phone, it starts to vibrate in my hand with incoming messages. "Shit." I'm going to be so screwed.

I open one from an **unknown** number and my breath catches as fear settles over me. It's a picture of me. I'm getting into the Uber here outside of the club the day I left to go meet up with Blakely.

I back out to go to the next text. It's also unknown and another picture. It's of me at the dealership. This time it has Blakely in it.

My hands shake as I go to another incoming text. My heart is racing, and my stomach drops when there's another of me at lunch.

The phone continues to vibrate in my hands as more and more messages come through. None of which are of any initiations. Nothing but pictures of me. There is even some with me and Tyson the night of the house of Lords party. Walking out of our house, getting out of our limo at the party, and inside.

I push the button, turning it off. Unplugging it, I throw it into my locker and slam it shut. My heart is hammering in my chest, and tears sting my eyes.

"Lake?"

I jump hearing the sound of my name. "Yeah?" I push my hair off my face, taking in a deep breath when I see Bethany now standing in the locker room. "What?" I breathe looking around, trying to calm my racing heart.

She frowns when she sees my shaking hands. "I have a large table that wants bottle service. Everyone else is busy. I know you've got five more minutes until your shift starts, but can you help me?"

"I, uh," I pause, trying to decide what to do. I need to show these to Tyson, right? Tell him someone took pictures of me, but he'll ask where I got the phone. And I don't know how to explain that right now.

"Laikyn—"

"Sure," I interrupt her, needing some time to think about how to tell him.

"Beau is getting everything ready for us," she says, and then shuts the door.

I take one last breath and smooth my hands down my shorts, exiting the room. I meet her at the wait station, grabbing what we need and walking over to the table, setting the bottle of champagne in the center while Bethany sets down the glasses.

"Fuck you, man." One of the guys shouts over the music and jumps to his feet.

Bethany reaches out, placing her arm across my chest, and pulls me backward with her as the second guy jumps up across from him. "Guys, calm down. You don't want to get kicked out," she tells them.

The guy to my right picks up his glass of mixed drink and tosses it into the other guy's face. It gets on the other guy who sits next to him, and he stands too.

"Come on, babe, we're leaving." The one who tossed his drink grabs the girl's hand who was sitting next to him and turns to walk away with her.

The lights are flashing, and the music is so loud that I don't realize the guy now covered in alcohol has jumped over the table until I watch him take the other man down. They both go to the floor, and I jump back as I watch Bethany turn around. She's yelling at Beau, but he won't be able to hear her over the music. We're too far from the bar.

I go to step back out of the way but am pushed forward at the same time from a guy who enters the fight. Before I know it, I'm smashed between multiple men. My tray has fallen from my hands, and I slip on the liquid that's been spilled on the floor.

I scream as someone steps on my hand. I roll into a ball, trying to shield my body but my arm is grabbed, and I'm yanked to my feet. "Get her out of here!" I recognize Colton shoving me toward Alex who wraps his arms around me, picking my feet up off the floor. He cradles me like a baby in his arms, and I turn into his chest, holding my throbbing hand in the other.

"Fuck." His chest vibrates before I'm knocked out of his arms and back on the floor.

I look up to see nothing but fists and people flying. A guy drops in front of me, eyes closed and bleeding from his mouth. I realize Alex knocked him out. I manage to get to my hands and knees and try to crawl under the table when my ankle is grabbed, and I'm yanked across the floor.

I reach my hands out in front of me to grab at anything I can get a hold of but am unsuccessful. So I flip over onto my back and start kicking my legs out. Hell, for all I know it's Alex trying to get me out of the way, but I can't see with my hair covering half my face so I'm not taking the chance.

Someone needs to turn on the fucking lights.

Weight falls on top of me, and I can't breathe. Pain shoots up my side and I scream so loud my throat burns.

"Laikyn." I hear a familiar voice yell out my name, but I can't make out who it is. A second later, the weight is gone, and I manage to get to my feet.

I stumble over to the bar that now looks to be deserted. They've either joined the fight, or they were forced to leave. Beau looks up at me. "Lake, you, okay?"

"Yeah..." My eyes flutter shut; my hands fumble to grab anything to hold myself up.

"Laikyn?" He jumps over the bar, knocking drinks and shot glasses off. Some shatter at my feet. "Fuck ... Lake." His eyes go to my side. "Colton? Alex?" He shouts over my shoulder.

I blink again, trying to stop the room from swaying. Feels like something heavy is sitting on my chest. "I-I can't. I can't ... breathe."

Arms grab me from behind and I don't have the energy to fight them this time. But I realize it's Colton when he picks me up in his arms. "Call Tyson. Tell him to meet us downstairs."

FORTY

TYSON

I'm sitting in my office talking to Ryat on my cell when my office phone rings. "I'll call you back," I tell him, and answer the other call on speakerphone.

"Fight broke out," Beau rushes out and I sit up straighter, grabbing the remote and turning the cameras on. I've had the old surveillance on of the girl the night she was here while talking to Ryat. "Get to the basement. Laikyn is hurt. Colton—"

I hang up and am already running out of my office. I take the stairs all the way to the first floor and storm down to the basement. "What the fuck happened?" I demand as I enter.

"A fight broke out," Colton answers, laying Lake down on the metal slab we use as a table. "She's been stabbed."

I look over the knife that is still in her right side.

"Fuck," Alex hisses, entering as well.

"Call Gavin," I order to Colton, then turn to grab a hold of Alex. I slam his back into the wall, getting in his face. "Go back upstairs. Close the club down. Every door locked. Have the employees shuffle those who weren't involved out the back door one at a time. But every motherfucker that was involved in the fight stays. Do you understand me?"

"Yes, sir." He nods quickly.

"Go." I shove him toward the door, and he runs out, closing it behind him.

"Gavin is on his way," Colt states, pocketing his cell.

"Ty-son." Comes her small voice.

I rush over to the table where Lake lays. "It's okay. It'll be okay."

Her shaky hands go to her side and her watery eyes widen when she sees the knife. She grabs a hold of the handle.

"No!" Colton and I both shout. I wrap my fingers around her wrist and force her to let go. I shove them above her head and Colt takes over, pinning them to my surface.

She arches her back and starts to cry.

"Hey." I grip her face with my now bloody hands. "Look at me, Lake."

Her watery eyes find mine. "We can't remove it. Not yet." Too risky. She can bleed out and I won't let that happen. I reach up and rip the thin material of her leotard, down the center, gently removing it around the knife. Then I yank off my own shirt and wrap it around the knife, trying to apply pressure the best I can without pushing it in deeper.

She arches her back, mouth opening wide, and screams. It makes my chest tighten, listening to her. "I know, Lake. I know."

"Ple-ase." She begins to sob while Colt continues to pin her arms down to the table above her head. "Pull it out," she cries, and starts to kick her legs, making me wiggle the knife, which just makes her scream again.

"Goddammit," I hiss. "Lake, you have to—"

"Take it out. Take it out," she sobs.

"She's making it worse." Colton growls the obvious.

Letting go of it for just a second, I jump up onto the table and sit on her thighs, pinning them down underneath me. And my hands grip her upper arms, holding them down. "In the safe." I nod to it back in the corner.

Colton lets go of her wrists and runs over to it. I tell him the code and he opens it. "Black box. Bottom shelf."

He yanks it out and pops it open, immediately understanding what I'm saying. Pulling the syringe out, he holds up the vile of clear liquid and fills the syringe.

She catches sight of what he's doing, and her wide eyes meet mine. "No, Tyson. Please." Her body thrashes on the table. "You promised me," she cries. "You promised you wouldn't drug me."

"Hurry up," I shout at Colton. Technically, I never said I wouldn't. I just said I wasn't going to.

He tosses the vial to the floor, and it breaks as he rushes back over to us. Gripping her face, he pushes it to the side and plunges the needle into her neck. Her eyes roll into the back of her head, and her body instantly goes slack.

Letting go of her arms, I place my hands back on the knife, trying to control the bleeding.

I GET OFF THE ELEVATOR AND STEP OUT INTO THE CLUB, looking around. The lights are now on. The club shut down. Colton, Finn, Alex, and Jenks stand by the bar. Some of my cocktail servers sit at a table. My bartenders are behind the main bar, and my four security men stand next to it.

"How many?" I ask.

"Six total." Alex is the one who answers.

Six people were injured during the fight in some way. "How many were employees?"

"Two, but only one went for medical treatment," Colton responds.

I nod. I was told that Bethany has a broken arm and Starla drove her to the hospital. My wife was stabbed, but she did not go to the hospital. The last thing I want is her out in public. I want this to remain as secretive as possible. The less that know, the better. She's upstairs in our apartment with Gavin right now.

Turning, I make my way toward the basement, and I hear them following behind me. Pushing open the door, I take the stairs to find a guy on his knees, hands cuffed behind his back and head down. When he hears me, he jumps to his feet.

I pause, my eyes going over to the table my wife was laying on just hours ago. It's still covered in her blood. And her torn leotard lays ripped on the floor. "What happened?" I'll give him one chance to explain why my wife got stabbed tonight.

"Tyson." His wide eyes go from mine to the guys behind me when they join us. "I didn't do this. I promise. I didn't know…"

I raise my hand and he stops rambling. "Who was here with you tonight?" I ask a different question.

By the time Gavin arrived and we got Lake up to our apartment, most of the guys who started the fight were long gone. Which is fine, I'll track them down. My wife's life was in danger, and she comes first.

"My phone." He swallows. "I've got texts of everyone who was meeting us out tonight. A couple of the guys I didn't know—"

Colton grabs the back of his neck and slams the side of his face down onto the bloody, metal slab while Finn digs into his pockets, looking for the phone. "Nothing." Finn looks at me, shaking his head.

"Did you guys find any phones?" I turn, asking Jenks and Alex. They both shake their heads. I face the guy once more, shoving my hands into the pocket of my slacks. "This is a problem."

Colton lets go of him and the guy stumbles back. "I promise I didn't know she was your wife."

It's not uncommon for fights to break out at Blackout. It's usually a nightly ordeal. But I want to know if my wife was a target or not.

Removing my hand, I pull out the piece of knife that was removed from my wife's side. She's lucky. The blade had been broken so it wasn't as deep as it could have been. But someone still has to pay for it. I walk over to him, and he starts shaking his head.

"Please ... no ... I didn't—"

I stab him in the side, right where my wife was and let go of it. He falls to his knees, gasping for breath. My phone rings and I pull it free of my pocket. "Hello?" I say, seeing its Gavin.

"She's waking up," he says in greeting.

"Be right there," I say, hanging up. Turning, I walk over to the guys and nod for them to follow me up the stairs. Exiting the staircase, we step out into the hallway. I turn to face them. "Throw him outside."

Alex frowns and Finn smiles.

"Keep an eye on him. I want to know where he goes. Who he sees and who he talks to. If he survives, he'll take us right where we need to go."

"Yes, sir," they all say in unison.

Turning my back to them, I make my way up to the apartment to be with my wife. Everyone involved in what happened tonight will pay for what they did to her.

Shoving the door open, I rush into our bedroom to see Gavin standing next to the bed my wife lies in. She's got the sheet pulled up to cover her chest because she's shirtless and her arm lays across it with an IV.

Her head falls to the side, heavy eyes blinking, trying to focus.

"She's on heavy pain killers," Gavin tells me, wiping off his bloody hands. "She's going to be in and out for a while."

Reaching out, she tries to sit up. I rush over to the bed. "Stay down," I tell her softly.

"But—"

"You need to rest, Lake." I reach out and push some dark strands of hair from her face.

Her eyes fall shut.

"It's okay, little darling." I cup her bloody cheek. "Just close your eyes. I'll be right here when you wake up."

Her lashes flutter open, and she looks up at me, her pretty blue eyes look glossed over from the drugs. "Promise?" Her voice is soft, fading.

I lean down and kiss her forehead. "I promise." This time when they close, they don't reopen. I sit back, running a hand through my hair before looking up at Gavin.

"She was lucky," he states. "Another inch to the right and I would have needed an OR and even that might not have been enough."

We kept her down in the basement until he got here. After he removed the knife and stitched her up, we moved her up here to rest. "Thank you." I stand and reach out my hand. He shakes it, not bothering to care that it's still bloody.

He nods. "Of course. I'd say the knife was already broken before she was stabbed with it."

The question is, was she stabbed on purpose or by accident? I'm going to find out.

"She'll be okay. I'll come back and check on her in the morning, just make sure she takes is easy. I'd say she'll have a full recovery in no time." I thank him again and see him out of the apartment.

I go to the kitchen, grab a big bowl and fill it with warm water and soap then make my way back to the bedroom. I grab a washcloth from the bathroom and pull the comforter down to expose her chest. I place the washcloth into the bowl and then wring it out before I start to clean the blood off her chest, neck, and face along with the little makeup that remains.

"I'm sorry, little darling," I tell her, hating what happened to her. It's my fault. Even if she wasn't targeted, I put her in this club. I made her work on the floor. I should have confined her to the apartment. Kept her as secluded as possible from the world that I know wants to harm her. I should have learned my lesson after Whitney.

Senior year at Barrington University

"STILL NOTHING?" RYAT ASKS ME WHILE I STARE AT MY CELL.

"Nothing," I answer. I've been calling and texting Whitney for two days now. But she does this a lot. Goes MIA. It's because she's pretending to be pregnant while partying and doesn't want me to know.

"Just track her phone," he tells me.

"It's off," I growl. Does he think I haven't thought of that? "Been off since yesterday morning."

"Well—"

Just as he starts to speak, my cell rings and I see it's her. "What the fuck, Whit? Where have you been?" I demand.

"Tyson." She cries on the other end.

I sigh, running a hand through my hair. "What?" This is what she does, ignores me for days and then pretends to have some catastrophic reason to reach out to me. She knows how to play the damsel in distress way too well.

"Pl-ease..." she chokes out. "I need you."

I sit up straighter, the sound of her voice sounding more convincing than usual. "Where are you?"

"I—" Cough. "I don't know."

"I can track you." I pull the cell from my ear and turn on her tracking. It shows she's ten minutes away. "I'm on my way."

LAIKYN

I'VE BEEN OFF WORK FOR TEN DAYS. TYSON SAID THREE weeks, but Gavin said that I was doing surprisingly well. It didn't do any damage to any important organs. It was more superficial than anything if you ask me. I can go back to work, but I have to be careful not to lift too much too soon and tear my stitches open. Other than that, I'm good.

I haven't spoken to Tyson much. I'm pissed at him. He promised me that he wouldn't drug me, and he did. Just another reason I can't trust him. Things got hard and he just knocked me out.

Not sure why I'm so surprised.

We also haven't had sex since I was stabbed. If I'm being honest with myself, that's another reason why I'm so on edge and pissy. I never realized how much sex can affect your everyday life until now. I hate that I ever experienced it to begin with because he can cut me off at any time.

I'm not sure why he hasn't touched me. Tyson never gives you hints as to why he does what he does. He just expects you to live with it. Or I guess it could have to do with the fact that we were already kinda arguing about what went down in his office with Collin. Well, I was pissed at him, and he didn't seem to care.

"Good to see you back, Lake." Beau smiles at me from behind the bar.

I nod. "It's good to be back." Setting my tray down on the server station, I ask, "What section do I have tonight?"

He picks up a piece of paper and places it in front of me. "Sorry."

"He gave me one table," I bark out. "Seriously?" My eyes snap up to Beau's.

He raises his hands in surrender. "I just do as I'm told, Lake."

I let out an audible growl. That's why he is the way he is.

Because everyone just does as they're told. I spin around to storm off up to his office when Beau stops me. "He's not up there."

"Where the hell is he?" I bark, turning back to face him. Since he's not fucking me, he no longer requires my attendance in his office before my shifts. I haven't seen him since this morning when I woke up, and even when he left the apartment, he didn't tell me where he was going.

"Lake." His face falls. "I can't tell you that."

"Looking for your husband?" Bethany asks, coming up beside me. They thought her arm was broken but turns out it wasn't as bad as that either. He let her come back after a week.

"Yeah. Know where he is?" I ask tightly, hating the fact that I know she does.

Beau shakes his head softly, telling her no, and I narrow my eyes on him. *What the fuck?*

"Basement," she answers, trying to hide her smile. We're not best friends but she's still nicer than she was when I started working here.

"Basement? Is that like another club or something?" I wonder.

She laughs softly. "The basement. Under Blackout. He's been down there for days." Then she grabs her tray and walks off.

"How the hell do I get there?" I demand of Beau.

"Lake, don't—"

"Bethany?" I call out, interrupting him. She stops and spins around to face me, that pretty smile on her face that I just want to rip off. She got hit pretty hard during the fight and still has a black eye that she's got covered in layers and layers of makeup. I just want to make the other match right now. "How do I get there?"

She gives me a sympathetic look, and answers, "I'll show you."

I leave my tray and follow her down the hallway to where the locker room is. We pass that and turn a corner. Coming to a door, we stop, and she leans up against it. "Don't say I didn't warn you, though."

"Warn me of what?" I growl at her.

"That once you go down there, you can't unsee whatever it is you'll see. You may think you know him, but I assure you, you don't." And with that, she pushes off and sashays away down the hall.

Taking in a deep breath, I twist the knob and open the door to a set of stairs. I enter, shutting it softly behind me. Standing at the top of the stairs, I hear someone softly crying.

"You're making this harder than it has to be," Tyson speaks, sending a chill up my spine. His voice sounds so cold. Detached. Every Lord has the ability to do it. They're taught that. To destroy. To not feel.

"I'm not..." A man's voice trails off, and a scream follows.

I take a few steps down, not wanting them to know I'm here, and come to a stop once the room comes into view.

My brows furrow. I've been down here. I remember it from that night the fight broke out. There's a metal table that I remember being on. Tyson was on top of me, and Colton was holding me down. Right before I passed out. When I woke up, I was in our bed upstairs.

I see Colton and Finn first, leaning back against a metal counter. Colt has his arms crossed over his chest while Finn has his in his front jeans pockets. Taking another step lower, Tyson comes into view. He's standing in the middle of the room in front of a man on his knees with his arms tied behind his back.

Tyson yanks the knife from the guy's thigh and wipes the bloody blade across his jeans. "I'm not going to repeat myself," he states calmly, as if he has all day to torture the man.

The man looks up at my husband with gritted teeth. "Why do you fucking care anyway, huh? So what if another Minson bitch dies? It's not like it's a secret why you married Laikyn."

Tyson kneels down in front of the guy and smiles at him, it makes the hairs on the back of my neck rise. He lifts the knife, twirls it around in his hand before slamming it down, sinking the blade into the man's other thigh. "Why don't you tell me why I married her."

"Fucking ... bastard," he spits out, trying to control his breathing.

"Hmm?" He twists it just a tad, and the guy throws his head back, screaming. It's so loud I place my hands over my ears.

"Revenge," he growls. "On her father."

Tyson yanks it out and the guy sags his shoulders, his body falling forward a little more as drool falls from his lips. "And then Whitney..."

"What about her?" Tyson asks, not sounding like he cares one bit.

"She was nothing more than a pawn. Just like her sister now."

Tyson walks up to him and places the tip of the blade under his neck, forcing him to arch it back to look up at him. "Maybe I love my wife," he offers.

The guy barks out a laugh. "A Lord doesn't love anything other than their brand."

"Coming from someone who isn't a Lord." Tyson rolls his eyes, stepping back.

The guy bares his teeth. "It's not hard to win when you cheat," he spits out.

Tyson looks behind the guy to where Alex stands up against the far wall. "Uncuff him," he orders.

Alex steps forward and unlocks the cuffs that holds the guy's wrists behind his back. He brings them forward, rubbing them. He gets to his shaky legs and Tyson holds out the knife to Colton who takes it.

"I just want you to understand that if you kill me, you still won't walk out of here alive," Tyson warns him, rolling up the sleeves to his button-up. Translation, the other four men who work for my husband will make sure the guy dies.

The man snorts. "I'd gladly die a hero."

Tyson smirks and the guy rushes him, letting out a scream. Tyson ducks as the guy goes to hit him, making him miss. Tyson wraps his arms around the guy's legs, picking him up off the floor and starts running with him. Slamming his back into the far wall. Alex has to move out of the way so he doesn't get hit.

Tyson lets go of him, and the guy falls to his knees. Tyson grips his head and pushes it down while his knee comes up, smashing his face. Blood and spit cover Tyson and the floor as the man falls to it.

"Last chance," Tyson speaks. "Why did you stab my wife?"

My eyes widen. Wait? This is about me?

The guy is on all fours, looking up at my husband. He smiles. "Why would I tell you?" He falls onto his ass and wipes his bloody face. "I'm dead anyway."

"Clear your conscience," Tyson offers.

He laughs once more. "I will tell you this, though. Someone wants your wife more than you do." Tyson stiffens and my breath catches. "You're not the only monster out there, Tyson. They know every move you're going to make. And you can't save her. Just like you weren't able to save Whitney." He laughs, showing his blood-covered teeth. "Your wife will die in your arms just like her sister."

I swallow nervously. *How does this guy know all of this?*

"History repeats itself," he adds.

Tyson reaches out his right hand and Colton places the knife in it. He throws it, making contact with the guy's shoulder, knocking him to the concrete floor, screaming out once again. "Fuucccckkk," he gasps.

Tyson goes over to him and places his boot on the man's chest, holding him down on his back. "Who wants her?" he demands.

The guy shakes his head. "I don't want to ruin the surprise."

Tyson leans over and yanks the knife from his shoulder,

making the man grunt. Grabbing the man's hair, Tyson drags him to the center of the room and positions him on his knees. Stepping behind him, he yanks his head back and places the knife to the guy's throat.

I stiffen when the guy's eyes meet mine. "Good luck." He smiles before Tyson runs the knife across his neck, splitting the skin like butter.

I slap a hand over my mouth to keep my gasp from being heard. No one realizes I'm here expect for the dead man that has blood gushing from his neck wound. A gargling sound fills the room as his body convulses.

Tyson lets go of him and the guy drops to the floor, a pool of blood growing larger by the second as he bleeds out. "I'm going to go shower. Meet me in my office after you've cleaned this mess up," he orders.

I run up the stairs on shaky legs and exit the basement. I walk on autopilot to the wait station. The club has opened since I've been down there, and the blinding lights make it feel like I'm walking uneven. Or maybe I am. I stop, placing my hands on the bar. Bowing my head, I close my eyes and try to gather my thoughts.

All of these years, I really thought Tyson killed my sister. Even my brother tried to tell me that he hadn't. But I didn't want to believe Miller.

But what if Tyson hadn't? What if he was innocent and someone went after her because of him? I've never thought of it that way. Like me. Who have I pissed off? No one. But why would someone want me dead? It doesn't add up. Because the guy was right, no one thinks Tyson loves me so why would my death matter? Just to make him relive Whitney's death maybe?

"Couldn't handle it, huh?" Bethany laughs, seeing the look on my face.

I lift my eyes to Beau, and he gives me a sympathetic smile. "I

329

tried to help you," he says before giving me his back to go grab an order.

Bethany comes back to place an order and I look over at her. "You can have my table," I say, and turn, giving her my back. I make my way to the elevator and go up to the apartment.

FORTY-ONE

TYSON

Senior year at Barrington University

I enter the house, shoving the door open. Her car wasn't outside. "Whitney?" I call out, but there's no answer. "Whitney?"

I'm pushing doors open, yanking blankets and comforters off beds, trying to find her but don't see her anywhere. The place looks somewhat abandoned. Cabinets open, but nothing in them. Old furniture in the front living room. "Whitney?" Where the fuck is she?

I come to the last door in the four-bedroom house, and it's locked. "I'm kicking this open," I warn, just in case she's on the other side, my adrenaline pumping that something really is wrong. Whitney has been over the top but she's never this dramatic. And I'd hate to be downplaying something that's really wrong.

Lifting my foot, I slam my boot into the door, splintering the wood and I enter the room. There's a bed in the middle with nothing more than a blanket wadded up and covered in blood. My eyes drop to the floor, and I see her lying there on her back, arms out

331

to her side and eyes closed. I drop down beside her and place my fingers to her neck. "Whitney? What the fuck?" She's got a pulse. Barely.

Without wasting any time. I pick her limp body up in my arms and carry her out of the house. Ryat is already waiting in my car by the curb.

The passenger side door opens when he sees me carrying her. "Fuck."

"Drive us to the hospital," I bark, and he's already opening the back passenger door for me to crawl in with her. "It's okay. You're going to be okay," I whisper to her, sitting in the back seat. Her body lies in my arms, blood runs from her broken jaw and busted nose. "I promise ..." My voice cracks and I clear my throat. The fact that her clothes are covered in dirt, shirt is ripped, and her jeans undone tells me all I need to know. Not to mention the bruises around her neck.

What the fuck happened? Who the hell was she with? I haven't spoken to her in two days. How long had she been there and how did she get there? I didn't see her car anywhere.

"Almost there," Ryat announces from the driver seat while taking a curve so fast, I feel the rear end fishtail, jerking us around.

"I'm sorry." I rock her back and forth as if that will bring her back to life. I never meant for this to happen to her. I'm her Lord. I'm supposed to take care of her. They promised us protection. They failed us.

"Ty ... don't—"

I tune him out. "It's my fault." I pull her lifeless body into me, her arm falls to the side and lands on my thigh. Lowering my face to her neck, not giving a fuck if I get her blood on me. I've done my fair share of killing people to know that she's fucking gone. Whoever did this to her wanted her dead.

. . .

I STAND IN THE SHOWER, MY HANDS ON THE WALL AS I WATCH the blood disappear down the drain. The man in my basement got to me. His words about my wife dying in my arms just like Whitney.

I've spent every second of every day over the last ten days trying to find out who stabbed my wife. Yesterday, the guys finally got a hit. The man I stabbed in the basement the night the fight broke out had finally felt safe enough to make a move and contact a friend. The guys brought him in tonight.

Someone wants my wife. I thought that maybe she was stabbed by accident. But everything holds some kind of significance. The question is, do they want her alive or dead?

It could be her father or Collin. One of those *if I can't have her, you can't either* type of situations. Or it could have nothing to do with her and everything to do with me.

Ryat told me this could happen. That her father could come after her to get to me. *But why?* He would only do that if I loved her. If he truly thought that taking her from me would hurt me.

I married her for a reason, and it wasn't to fall in love with her. It was for revenge.

Right.

I turn off the water and step out of the shower. Drying off, I wrap the towel around my hips and step out of the bathroom and come to a stop. Lake stands in the bedroom.

She hasn't spoken to me much in the last ten days. She's avoided me, and I've allowed it. Mainly because I felt bad. I'm a man, and I failed her. I might have forced her to marry me, but I'm still her husband. No man likes to fail. Especially me.

"Lake—"

"You gave me one table," she growls, interrupting me.

"You're still in recovery." Gavin gave her the clear, and I wanted to break his fucking neck. She's not ready.

"I'm fine." She rolls her eyes. "Next thing, you'll be saying that I should quit."

I just stare at her.

"Tyson." She steps toward me. "You can't be serious."

I reach out, cup her face, and her eyes soften, leaning into it. "It's not safe. Not right now."

She pulls away, and my hand drops to my side. "So you're saying you care if I live or die?"

"Of course, I fucking care." My eyes narrow on her.

"Since when?" She gives a rough laugh.

I ignore that question. "You're fired. And that's that." Walking past her, I go over to the dresser and open it to grab a pair of boxer briefs.

"So you force me to work here dressed like a whore, then you fire me?"

I look up at her in the mirror, and she's glaring at me, hands on her hips.

"What am I supposed to do, Tyson?" she demands. "Just sit up here and wait for you to speak to me? Huh? Only see you when you want to fuck me?"

"No," I growl.

"Then what the fuck am I supposed to do with my life?" she shouts.

"Stay alive," I answer. "And you can't do that if you're out there getting stabbed."

She snorts. "Jesus Christ, Tyson. That is such bullshit, and you know it." She angrily shoves her shorts down her legs, unsnaps her leotard, kicks off her shoes along with her fishnets, throwing them to the floor. Standing naked behind me, I turn to look at her.

My eyes drop to the fresh wound on her side. Gavin said her stitches would dissolve, so she doesn't need them removed, but it's still red and bruised. Walking over to the bed, she yanks back the covers and crawls into it. She jerks them up to cover her body and glares at me with her arms crossed over her chest.

"What are you doing?" I ask with a sigh.

"This is what you want me to do, right? Wait here naked for you?" She arches a dark brow, and I fist my hands. "Why don't you just tie me down and leave me here until you're ready to use me."

"Laikyn," I growl, irritated with her and myself. She thinks that way because that's the way I've treated her.

"That's what I'm good for." She shrugs. "Except don't knock me up." Giving a rough laugh, she adds, "Because I'm not good enough to birth Tyson Crawford's child."

"Lake!" I bark.

"But my sister was," she goes on. "She was good enough to fuck and knock up."

I run a hand down my unshaven face. "I don't have time for this."

"Then maybe you shouldn't have forced me to marry you." She shrugs. "Then you'd be free to fuck whoever you want."

I want to rush over to the bed, wrap my hand around her neck, and strangle her. Tie her to the bed and leave her there while I go to work, knowing when I return, she'll be begging me to fuck her. But I can't. Not now.

So instead, I turn and exit the bedroom, slamming the door shut behind me, and head to my office.

LAIKYN

HE TURNED AND WALKED OUT OF THE BEDROOM. I DON'T know why I'm surprised. Or why I fucking care. After I saw him kill that guy down in the basement, I wanted a fight. Something about the way he killed him for me makes me question everything.

It wasn't like when he killed Walter because he touched me, or

Collin because I sat on his lap. It was ... different. It wasn't a *don't touch what's mine.* It was a *you hurt what's mine, and I'm going to make you pay for it.*

I hate how much it made me feel loved. Violence does not equal love. A Lord kills for his fucking oath, that doesn't mean he loves it. But I've never seen a Lord hate what he does. They've been conditioned from a young age to accept torture and death as their life. Their grandfathers did it and they watched their fathers do it.

In a world full of evil, they are taught to be the best.

So I tried to piss him off. Afraid he'd know that I saw him downstairs. That I might think he actually cares about me. It's stupid, really. To think he'd care what I feel anyway.

Getting up, I hear my phone ding. I open it up to see it's a text.

> BLAKELY: Hey, girl. How are you doing today?

She and Ellington have both been texting me ever since I was stabbed. I'm guessing Tyson told Ryat and Easton what happened. Then they told their wives.

> ME: Good.

What else is there to say? *Hey, I'm doing great. Just got fired from my job and now I'm pretty much on house arrest because my husband thinks someone wants to kill me. But he hasn't told me that. I just overheard him while he was killing a guy.*

It pings again.

> BLAKELY: That's great to hear. Let me know when you're feeling better and want to get out and about. I've still got to do some shopping for the babies, and I owe you a lunch.

Biting my bottom lip, I try to think of how to respond to her. I can't go out and be seen with her, or anyone for that matter. Not after what I heard that guy say to Tyson earlier. I can't put anyone else in danger. Ryat already threatened me. I'd never be able to live with myself if anything happened to her or the babies because of me. I'd let Ryat kill me if I was the reason something happened to his wife.

I start to type back a response to tell her that I'm not sure I'm ready to go out just yet but stop myself. My heart beginning to race. "Shit!" I never told Tyson about the pictures on my other phone that's in my locker.

Hurrying out of bed, I throw on a pair of cotton shorts and a tank top and then run downstairs. I run into the locker room and unlock it. Yanking the door open, I freeze when I see the phone isn't in there.

Where the fuck did it go? I know I put it back in there after I charged it long enough to come on. It's been ten days since I saw it. I haven't been in here since then.

Shutting the locker, I lean against it and sigh. Now what the fuck do I do? I can't tell Tyson that my father gave me a phone and then I lost it.

FORTY-TWO

TYSON

Senior year at Barrington University

I enter the hospital with Whitney in my arms and am met with nurses. Ryat called while on our way. "Gavin," I rush out. "I want Gavin."

"I'm sorry, but he's not here." They take her from me, laying her on the gurney. They start to wheel her away, and I follow after them.

"I want..."

"He's not here," a nurse says, slamming her hands into my bloody shirt, pushing me to a stop. "But I promise Dr. Finch is just as good." Then she turns and takes off after them, leaving me alone.

I pace the waiting room, my bloody hands fisted in my hair, trying to put the pieces together. I didn't see her phone, but she had called me from it. No car. No purse. Her clothes were torn and dirty, but there wasn't any dirt on the floor. Just blood.

Then there's the question of the baby. Is she really pregnant? If so, is it mine? My mind is racing, and so is my pulse. I can't focus.

"Ty?"

My head snaps up to see Ryat standing, he nods to a doctor that's walking our way. I can see it written all over his face. She's gone.

I've been sitting at my desk for three hours now in my office, my mind on that day once again. I've accomplished nothing but staring at a wall.

"Boss?"

I look up to see Colton staring at me expectantly. They've changed out of their bloodstained clothes after burying my latest victim.

He and Finn both stand there, hands in their pockets, waiting for an order. I don't know what to say. I don't know where to start. The most rational thing to do would be to put my wife in a jail cell with twenty-four-hour guards. She'd hate me, but at least she'd be alive.

"Go through his phone," I finally say. "Every text, every picture. Every fucking person he's called, I want to know about it."

They nod.

"He's not a Lord," Finn mentions.

"What about it?" I snap.

"How would he know so much if he wasn't one, sir?"

That's a good question. He could have been guessing, but he was spot-on. "He has to know someone. Check any connections to a Lord in my senior class." I order, but even I know it's a long shot. Not many knew what really happened, and the ones that do would never speak of it.

LAIKYN

I SIT AT THE MAIN BAR, JUST STARING AT THE MIRRORED WALL behind it. Watching the lights bounce off it to the point it's blinding. They're giving me a headache, and the music is so loud I can't even hear my own thoughts.

How does Tyson not get tired of this life? I never got to go out and party with my friends and get drunk off my ass. After my sister died, I was pretty much on house arrest. My parents were afraid that something would happen to me. But having to be here every night makes me think that was a good thing now.

I've been sitting here just staring at nothing for over two hours now. I no longer work here. He fired me. What else am I supposed to do with my life? Sit here day in and day out doing absolutely nothing?

And I'm trying to remember that damn phone. Where did it go? Who the fuck has it? And why would they want it? Maybe my father came back and picked it up. But what does that mean for my initiations? He said the Lords would contact me on it. Now I've lost the fucking thing.

"Want a drink, Lake?" Beau shouts over the song playing.

I'm about to shake my head when the other bartender who replaced Walter bumps into him and tells him, "She's not allowed."

"I'd love one."

"I wouldn't if I were you." The guy shakes his head at Beau while pouring some liquor into a shot glass.

The red light by the phone on the wall behind him starts to light up, and he turns around to pick it up. Holding it to his ear, he nods a few times before hanging up and then leans in to say something in Beau's ear. Then he walks out from behind the bar and runs up the stairs. I watch him run across the breezeway and then disappear, knowing he's going to Tyson's office.

"So how about that drink?"

He tosses a shot glass up in the air, and it flips a few times

341

before he catches it. "What would you like?"

"Surprise me." Not like it's going to matter. I just want to numb my thoughts and erase the fact that I've fucked up.

"Drink or shot?" he questions.

"Shots."

He raises a brow. "As in more than one?"

I nod.

I SLAM THE GLASS DOWN, GASPING AT THE BURN IN MY throat. It's on fire. Feels like I've swallowed lava. I shove the empty shot glass across the bar, and it tips over, rolling on its side. Beau catches it before it falls off the edge.

"Another." I nod to him.

He laughs. "I think four is enough. They all haven't even hit you yet. Tyson will kill me if I have to call him to carry you upstairs." Then he turns away from me and walks over to a couple.

I sit back and watch them. She's a pretty blond, looks like a Barbie doll replica with her hair up in a high pony, a pink sequinned dress, and perfectly done makeup with winged eyeliner. He, however, looks like a gym rat. Muscles too big for his shirt, and the guy doesn't even have a neck.

It makes me think of the woman from that night I waited on her. What she thought of before she died. I wonder the same about my sister. Was she scared? Did she have time to cry? Was it quick? I pray that when I die, I don't see it coming.

She smiles at the bartender and nods when Beau responds. The guy bows his chest and starts to point at him, but she places her hand on his chest, tapping it before he takes a step back.

I watch in fascination at how the little contact has such an effect on him. He's obviously the jealous type. I get it. I can see why people are that way. Why they don't want to share what they have. I've never felt that way until I found out that Bethany has a thing for my husband.

Beau seems to ignore it and goes to make their drinks. The woman turns into the guy she came with. He cups her face and lowers his lips to hers, devouring her in front of everyone as if they're the only two in the room.

He turns her around to where her back is up against the bar, and he presses her into it.

My thighs tighten, and my breath quickens when she lifts her left leg to wrap around his hip. His hand drops to her thigh, and I see him slide it up to her ass, pushing her dress up in the process. She stops the kiss, pulling away and tilting her head back, and his lips go to her jawline.

Heat rushes up my spine as I watch them practically fuck right in front of me. Tyson was fucking me multiple times a day to nothing for the last ten days. My body is begging for some kind of physical contact.

"Here you go," Beau yells, and the guy pulls away from her.

She slumps against it, wiping the corners of her mouth while the guy hands Beau a card to open a tab. Whatever concern he felt toward the cute bartender, now gone. Because she reassured him that she belongs to him.

Men aren't that complicated. I'd never had the chance to be with one before Tyson, but it's not hard to see how easily they can be manipulated.

I turn toward the bar and place my elbows on it while my hands fan my face. I look up at the mirror and see I'm flushed.

"You okay, Lake?" Beau notices and frowns. "Need some water?"

I shake my head and straighten my shoulders. "Another shot."

He frowns. "Lake, I don't think..."

"Just one more. Please?" I stick my bottom lip out.

He smiles. "One more. Then you're cut off."

343

FORTY-THREE

TYSON

I sit at my desk, signing papers, when I hear my door open. "I'm busy." I dismiss whoever it is, not in the mood to deal with anyone tonight.

"Too busy for me?"

I look up to see Lake leaning up against the now closed door. One ankle crossed over the other, hands on her hips, and a naughty smile on her face.

She wears a pair of white cotton shorts and a black tank top with her black Vans. Her hair is down and straight, and she has no makeup on her face. She looks absolutely stunning.

I lean back in my chair and look up at Andrew. "We'll finish these later."

"Yes, sir." He nods and starts to walk toward the door. She pushes off it and steps to the side so he can exit.

"What are you doing, Lake?" I ask. Last I saw her, I left her in our bed, naked and pissed off at me. That was hours ago.

She walks toward my desk, one leg crossing in front of the other, hands still on her narrow hips. She comes behind my desk and shoves my chair back to give her enough space to come between me and the desk. She hops up onto the surface, and I stand from my chair.

Placing a hand on either side of her, I lower my face to hers. Her eyes are heavy, her cheeks flushed. She drops her eyes to my lips, and hers part, letting out a heavy breath. I can smell the cinnamon—Fireball. She's been drinking. "Are you drunk?" I ask.

She reaches up, and her hands grip my button-up. I allow her to yank me even closer, my lips almost touching hers. Tilting her head down a little, she looks up at me through her long dark lashes. "Yes, sir."

Fuck me! I let out an audible growl at her answer. My cock instantly strains against the inside of my slacks.

My hand shoots up to wrap around her delicate neck, and she sucks in a breath. I stand to my full height, my free hand tangling in her hair. I pull her body into mine, her ass now at the edge of my desk. "What did I tell you?" I don't know if I'm more pissed she's been drinking, or that she's been down in the club. I fired her because I didn't want her down there. I want her safe upstairs in our bedroom.

Instead of answering, her tongue comes out and runs along my lips, making my body tense.

She pulls away, lips parted, and whispers, "Punish me."

I don't have to have years of training as a Lord to know this is a fucking trap. She's up to something. "You're still recovering," I say, trying to remind myself why I haven't touched her in days. It's been so fucking hard. Every morning that I wake up and she's next to me naked. Her body just begs me to take it. Or when I crawl into bed at night, and she rolls into me, wanting to snuggle in her sleep. She doesn't even realize she's doing it, but I hold her in my arms while she sleeps, and I find myself hoping she dreams of me.

"I'd feel better if you'd fuck me." She leans in, kissing my lips once again. "Remind me I'm your whore, Tyson."

I growl, and my dick reminds me that it's been a living hell not being able to fuck my wife. But she's not ready. She needs more time. I pick up my office phone and call the main bar once again. When Andrew picks up, I tell him to send Beau upstairs.

"What are you doing?" she asks when I hang up.

I lift her up off my desk and sit her in my chair, then I walk over to the door and open it, waiting for Beau. He walks in moments later. I slam the door shut and he turns to slowly face me.

"What's going on, boss?" he asks, looking from her to me.

"Did you serve my wife alcohol?" I know it was him because Andrew had been up here with me.

He swallows. "I did, sir."

"Tyson." She jumps to her feet.

"Take her home," I order him.

"What?" he asks, blinking.

"Tyson—"

"She's drunk," I bark, interrupting her. "Drive her home in her SUV and take an Uber back."

"Tyson..." He steps forward, and I hold out my hand, stopping him.

"Either take my drunk wife home right now, or you're fired." I look over at her, and she's got her arms crossed over her chest, glaring at me. She stumbles back into my chair and lets out a huff.

He nods. "I'll take her home."

"Give us a moment," I tell him, and he steps out of my office. I walk over to her, and she gets to her wobbly legs and goes to storm past me, but I grab her upper arm, bringing her to a stop. Her eyes narrow on mine. "Don't wait up, little darling."

Her eyes soften, and she leans into me. "Is this a punishment?" she asks as her eyes grow heavy. She's about to pass out any second.

"No," I answer, frowning. "This is for your safety, Lake."

"I saw you," she whispers.

"Saw me do what?" I push some dark strands behind her ear.

347

"Kill that guy in the basement."

My hand pauses, my eyes on her clouded ones. "Lake—"

"Why?" she asks, licking her lips. "Why do you care what happens to me?"

I'm not the guy that her family made me out to be. Although, I can't say I've tried to make her think any differently. "I've always cared," I answer honestly.

She's too drunk to remember this conversation tomorrow. She'll wake up even more mad because she'll be at our house, where I've got more security than this place. Plus, I've got people constantly there, living on the property. Eyes on her twenty four seven. I should have never let her come here. Put her out in the open like I did. Someone is after her, and now I have to put her in hiding.

"Sir?" Beau calls out behind me.

I lean in and kiss her forehead. "I'll be home soon, little darling." Taking her hand, I walk her over to Beau. "Take her upstairs to get her things." She will need some clothes, her cell, and car keys. "Then take her straight home. Text me when you drop her off and get your ass right back here."

"Yes, sir." He nods and then I watch her get on the elevator, her head down, staring at the floor. She can't even look me in the eyes, and my chest tightens.

I hate that she's mad at me, but as long as she's alive, that's all that matters. And I'm prepared to fucking blow anyone away who threatens her life. Once everyone is eliminated, I will make sure she understands how much she means to me.

LAIKYN

For a week, I've been locked in OUR house. I haven't spoken much to my husband, and he hardly comes home. Now I know why he lives at the club. When he does show up, it's around five in the morning most days. And then he spends hours of his day in his home office. And then he leaves around six in the evening to go back to Blackout.

If he's mad at me, he hasn't shown it. There hasn't been any anger, yelling, or hurtful words. It's like we're my parents—married for most of our life and ignoring one another. And still no sex. Gavin has come over twice to give me a checkup, and both times he told me everything looked great.

Another night alone in this house. Our home. It feels weird being here after spending so much time at Blackout. And the more time that goes by that he makes me stay here, the more and more anxious I grow about the damn cell phone that my father gave me.

I enter the spare bedroom and turn on the light. I look over my wedding dress that William had put in a glass case. He asked me yesterday where I wanted it to go in the house. I didn't have an answer for him. It wasn't what I wanted, but does that even matter? It is a pretty dress, and I'd hate to just burn it. Although setting it all on fire would make me happy.

Walking over to one of the boxes, I open it to find all the candles along with the champagne flutes from the hotel room. If I could go back, I'd take that drink that he offered me after the wedding. Who knew he'd cut me off afterward?

I open the other box next to it and see something inside that catches my eye. It's a small vial of liquid. My teeth grind when I realize I've seen it before. It was quick, but I remember it.

FORTY-FOUR

TYSON

I enter the house and yawn. I'm exhausted from running back and forth between the club. This is why I stay there. It's just easier. It's been a long day and night. I'm tired as fuck and just want to get a quick nap in before I have to get up and do it all over again. I've had Lake hiding here for a week now, and I'm no closer to finding out who is after my wife as I was when I sliced that idiot's neck open in the basement.

Walking through the living room, I sniff. The smell of food hits my nose and I take a left into the kitchen.

I see the formal dining room first; it's got five tapered candles lit in the center of the table. They're the candles from the Cathedral. The ones lit during our wedding ceremony.

Two plates are set across from one another. I walk into the kitchen and see her pulling a dish out of the oven. She sets it on the counter and turns to face me. Giving me a big smile, she drops her eyes to the floor before slowly meeting mine again.

"I wanted to make you breakfast. I hope you're hungry."

I'm not, but I say, "It smells lovely." It's also six in the morning. Did she even go to sleep last night?

Licking her lips nervously, she removes her apron from around her waist and folds it neatly on the counter. "Would you like a drink?" she asks, sliding her hands down her black dress. It's got a high neck and comes to her knees. It's not revealing in the sense that her tits and ass are hanging out, but it shows every curve her body has to offer. My hands itch to run all over it.

"Yes, please."

She goes over to the island and pours me a glass of whiskey. Bringing it to me, she holds it out.

I throw it back in one gulp, and she takes it from me. "I'll get you another one. Go take a seat. It'll be ready in just a few minutes."

I walk back over to the table and sit down. I'm not much for the romantic atmosphere, but I won't lie and say I'm not excited that she stayed up for me to get home. I've mostly ignored her the past week. I come home bloody from beating some guy in the basement. And she's passed out asleep in our bed when I get up and leave.

I undo the top button of my shirt, my skin starting to feel hot as she enters the formal dining room, carrying the dish.

"You okay?" she asks, her brows creasing. "You look flushed." She places her hand on my forehead, and her frown deepens. "God, Tyson, you're burning up."

"I..." I clear my throat and undo another button. "Think I'm coming down with something." My eyes get heavy, and my head bobs a few times. My neck unable to keep it up.

"You should lie down," she suggests.

"Yeah." I stand from my chair, but my knees give out, and I fall back into it. It feels like time stands still as everything slows. My eyes meet hers and I see her lips move, but I don't hear anything over the blood rushing in my ears.

I blink a few times, the room starts to sway, and I place my hands over my eyes, trying to rub them. But my hands fall to my sides, and my head falls forward.

LAIKYN

I SIT DOWN IN THE SEAT BESIDE HIM AND WATCH HIS EYES close, and this time, they stay closed. I smile, reaching out and grabbing a grape and popping it in my mouth.

I drugged him. I had already placed the drugs at the bottom of his glass before he even got home. I then poured the whiskey into it; he didn't even notice.

Teach him to drug me again.

I get up from my chair and grab the rope out of the drawer I put it in. I pull his chair away from the table. It scrapes across the floor, hurting my ears. I bend down, bringing his arm to the side and tie it to the back leg. Then I repeat the process to the other. There aren't armrests so this will have to do. I grip his shirt and rip it open, the buttons flying across the marble floor.

Then I sit down and make my plate. I'll eat breakfast while he's out. When he wakes up—who knows when that will be—I'll play with him like a toy. We'll see how much he likes being taken advantage of and humiliated.

AN HOUR LATER, I'M STILL SITTING AT THE TABLE WHEN HIS head pops up, and he sucks in a deep breath.

"Well, hello there." I smile at him.

"What?" He yanks on the rope, his head dropping to survey his situation. "What the fuck?" He yanks on them, the chair rattling from his force.

I pray to God it holds him because if he gets loose, I'm fucked.

"Lake," he growls, his eyes meeting mine. "Untie me right fucking now."

I tilt my head, my lips puckering in thought. "I don't think so."

"LAKE!" he shouts, his chest rising and falling fast. He takes in a deep breath. "If you don't..."

"What are you going to do?" I stand, and his eyes shoot daggers up at me. I walk over to him and straddle his legs.

He stiffens when I drape my arms over his shoulders. I can feel his body vibrating with rage. I start playing with his hair, and he yanks his head away. I grab it and yank it back, and he bares his straight white teeth, growling at me.

I lower my face to his. "It sucks knowing that you're helpless, doesn't it?"

He doesn't answer.

I get up off him and look down at his slacks. Bending over, I unzip them and reach inside, pulling his dick out. He's not hard, but I didn't expect him to be. Men like Tyson have to be the ones in control. They make the rules, the final decisions. But I have a feeling if I start playing with his dick, it'll be inevitable.

I drop to my knees, and he shifts in the chair. I bite back a smile and look up at him as my tongue runs across the head of his pierced cock. His head falls back, giving me a view of his defined jaw. I can see his Adam's apple bob when he swallows, and his dick swells in my hand. I wrap my lips around the tip and push it into my mouth.

"Lake." My name is breathless on his lips, and his head drops to look back down at me. His eyes are on fire, but his jaw now slack. Lips parted as he sucks in a deep breath.

"Tell me to suck your cock, *baby*," I order softly, using a nickname that I know he'll hate. Tyson isn't the kind of guy that you call baby or sweetie. No, you kneel and call him sir or god. Fuck, I'd call him *daddy* if that's what he was into. But he's not in charge right now. I am.

354

"Suck my dick, Lake," he orders. "Swallow it. I want to hear you choke on it."

I smile and lick up his now hard shaft. I have a plan as to why I tied him up and am still giving him what he wants. I have to do this part in order to get to the point I have to prove.

I take him into my mouth, and he lifts his hips, pushing it farther down my throat and making me gag. I should have tied his damn body to the chair as well.

"Fuck yeah," he groans. "That's the sound I've been wanting to hear."

I hate that my pussy throbs at his words. I'm supposed to be in charge here.

I suck on his dick, stopping here and there to swallow the saliva. I've never done this before—taken control. I'm not into being messy.

His leg muscles stiffen against my body, and I pull my mouth away, my hand taking over, and I quickly run it up and down.

"Fuck, Lake. I'm coming."

I hold his dick in place as cum squirts from his cock up and down his chest. Some covering my hand. I pull it away and run it over his thighs on his slacks.

I stand to my full height and look down at him. His heavy eyes start narrowing on mine when he realizes I won't untie him. "Enjoy breakfast, baby." I turn and exit the formal dining room laughing.

FORTY-FIVE

TYSON

I yank on the rope, but it's useless. She didn't tie them incredibly tight; I've just got whatever she gave me still in my system. So I'm going to have to get out a different way.

Bending over, I pick the back two legs up off the floor and slam them down, breaking them in the process, and the rope falls off my wrists. The room still sways a little, but I'm able to stand and have full function of my limbs.

I run out of the formal dining room just as she looks over her shoulder, hearing me. She screams out as I grab her hair and yank her to me, spinning her around to face me.

Holding her hair, I shove her face into my cum-covered chest, smearing it all over her. Then pull back on her hair. "That's more like it."

Her eyes are closed, face scrunched. I drag her back into the room and shove her facedown over the side of the table. Reaching down, I grab the rope and double it over, making a quick single-column tie along her forearms, her arms parallel to each other. I allow the excess to fall down her back, knowing I'll need the extra rope. If done correctly, it'll look like a snake head with a hissing tongue—a loop at the top—that I will also need to use.

I slap her ass hard enough to leave an instant print. "My turn."

I wish I could say I didn't like what she did to me. I'm not a fan of not being in control, but my cock has a mind of its own, and when she dropped to her knees, I couldn't stop how hard I got if I tried. It had been too long. Almost three weeks and I couldn't hold out anymore.

She knew exactly what she was doing. And I'm going to remind her who's in charge.

I walk out of the formal dining room and back to my study. I open the safe and grab something that I'm going to need and head back to the formal dining room.

Walking around the table to where her head is, I gather up all her hair and some sticks to her wet face. I gather it at the back of her neck and tie it with a rubber band that I grabbed off my desk to get it all out of the way. I'm going to use it. Reaching into my pocket, I remove the shorter piece of rope, making a slip knot and wrapping it around the rubber band in her hair, and then separate the two pieces, wrapping it around it again to tie it off. I yank on the rope, lifting her head in the process and making her hiss in a sharp breath, and I tie it off to the rope around her arms, securing her head in place and up off the table.

I lean down, lowering my face to her level. She's breathing heavily through her nose, her eyes still closed. "Look at me," I order.

She keeps her eyes closed, and I reach up, slapping the side of her face. Not hard enough to leave a handprint but definitely enough to sting. She whimpers, opening them up and then closing them just as quickly.

"I won't say it twice, Lake," I warn.

Prying them open, she blinks rapidly. Cum covers her lids and lashes.

"I hear cum burns the eyes," I say. "Let me help with that." I take the napkin off the table and wipe both of her eyes roughly, wiping some of it away but not all of it off. "Now look at me."

Her eyes flutter open, and they land on mine. They're red, irritated. I reach up, grip her chin, and squeeze, forcing a whimper out of her lips. "Leave them open," I order, then wipe what little cum covers her nose to clean the area. I need it dry for this to work. Lifting the metal clamp, I place it over her now clean nose, blocking her air.

Her lips part, sucking in a breath. "Tyson," she cries. "I'm sorry."

"You will be," I tell her, and she sobs, fighting the restraints.

I shove two fingers into her mouth, moving them around, and she sticks her tongue out. "I'm going to fucking remind you who I am, Lake." I've been soft on her. Taking it easy, forgetting why I married her in the first place—to make her my slut.

She gags when my fingers reach the back of her throat, her body jerking.

I stand up and grab one of the candles out of its holder and then lean back down. I slide it in her mouth, and her eyes widen as I hold it in place. It's not quite at the back of her throat, but it's close. "Bite down," I order. "Gently."

She closes her teeth around it, spreading her lips wide open in order to breathe around it since I took away her ability to breathe through her nose. "Do not bite through this candle, Lake. Or I will punish you."

She whimpers, tears forming in her eyes.

I stand and grab another candle that hasn't been lit yet. I run it along her cheek, picking up the excess cum, coating the end of the candle, then walk behind her. I hold it in one hand while the other goes to her pussy, running my fingers over it. She moans, and I easily slide two into her cunt. "Look how wet my little whore is. Did sucking my cock get you all worked up, darling?"

359

She whimpers, and I remove them before opening her wide and running the cum-covered candle over her wet cunt. Then I very slowly push it a couple of inches inside her. "Don't let that fall," I order and watch her thighs tighten, knowing she's holding it in place.

She'll remember this lesson for days to come. I'm going to make sure she's sore as fuck. Every muscle clenched and well aware of her punishment.

I undo my belt from around my slacks and yank it free of the loops. I fold it over and slap it across her ass, making sure to avoid hitting the candle sticking out of her pussy.

Her body tenses, and a cry fills the room. I do it again in the same spot watching the red mark cover her flawless skin. I do it again, lower this time across her thighs.

She's sobbing around the candle now, and I drop the belt to the table next to her and pick up another candle that is lit.

"I love that you brought home the candles from our wedding," I inform her. "We can put them to good use," I say even though I know her mother sent them with her stuff. Bringing it to hover over her ass, I tilt it, allowing the wax to drip where I just smacked her. Letting it burn her already irritated skin.

She screams, legs jerking.

I tilt it again and let it drip over the other cheek.

She's shaking, her cries filling the room, and I lower the lit candle under the one inside her pussy, lighting it.

I plop down in the chair and watch her body shake, watching the flame grow higher. It will start dripping down her legs and onto her skin. It's going to burn like a bitch. They make candles for this specific reason—wax play. But that's not what this is about. It's supposed to teach her a lesson.

LAIKYN

I taste the wax from the candle in my mouth, my teeth leaving bite marks in it. I try to concentrate on not biting through it like he said, but it's so hard not to. My ass is on fire from his belt, and my pussy is clenched as tight as I can, trying not to drop the candle. It's lit. I can feel the heat. I'd rather not burn my legs if I drop it.

I told him I was sorry, and he said I would be. I should have never thought I'd get away with what I did. It's not like I was going to run away. I have nowhere to go. It was just to show him that I could be a dick too. Guess he's proving me wrong.

My neck is pulled back at an odd angle by my hair, I have a headache, and my shoulders are screaming from how tight my arms are secured behind my back.

Blinking, I see him come to stand in front of me with a knife in his right hand. He leans down, eye level with me, and he holds the tip to my cheek. Drool slips out of the corner of my lips from how I have to hold my mouth open.

He slides the blade down the side of my face ever so gently. I feel the sharp edge cutting away his cum from earlier. "I wish you could see how pretty you look with my cum covering your face while you cry."

I hate that he tells me I'm pretty when I know I look the worst. It makes me feel special. Something that I know I'm not.

I cry out when I feel the first drip of wax from the candle that is in my pussy fall onto my thigh. My legs shake.

Standing, he walks out of sight, and my pussy clenches when he pulls on the candle inside me, trying to hold it in so it doesn't fall and burn my leg. But when I realize he's removing it, I relax a little.

The tip of his cock pushing against my cunt makes me whimper. His hand slaps my ass that is already on fire from his belt, and my body jerks, fighting the restraints.

He pushes into me, hard and fast, shoving my hips into the

side of the table, making me scream around the candle that's still in my mouth. He doesn't take it slow or gentle.

He's brutal, fucking me as a punishment. I'd beg him to let me come if I could, but instead, I just take it like the good girl I want to be.

His body slaps mine, hitting my burned and reddened ass. It hurts in the best way. My pussy is dripping as much as the wax on the end of the candle that hangs from my mouth. If I could beg him, I would, but I'm unable to. Fuck, I'd crawl to him right now if he'd give me the chance. Anything to show him how devoted I can be. A promise that I'm going to willingly be his.

Men like Tyson Crawford need a sacrifice, and he's made me realize that I'd willingly be that for him. I've become addicted to his touch, the sound of his voice, and the way he fucks me... Goddamn, it's unholy. But I'd gladly kneel for my Lord and let him use me however he wants.

He shoves his cock into me and lowers his body over my back, pinning my tied arms between us. The action makes me arch my neck even more since my hair is connected to them. I cry out around the candle and watch the wax start to run down from the lit end that is now up in the air.

He removes the clip from my nose, and I suck in a deep breath just as his hand grips my throat. I can hear his heavy breathing in my ear. It makes my pussy tighten around him, and he growls, his hand tightening, taking what little air I had away. I don't try to fight him. No need to. I live for my Lord, and I trust him with my life. "You feel so good, little darling." Pulling his cock out, he shoves it forward, the table rattling from his force. Tears slip from my bottom lashes while I feel the drool run down my chin. "God-damn, Lake." He does it again, and my vision starts to blur from his hand around my throat.

He begins to fuck me hard, slamming my hips into the edge of the table while I start to feel light-headed. My skin tingles, every muscle pulled tight, and my mouth starts to go slack, the candle slipping from my lips.

Tyson's voice is in my ear, but I can't make out what he's saying. The room is spinning, my eyes growing heavy. I'm floating, and heat rushes over me, making me shiver.

Just as my eyes fall closed, he lets go of my neck, and I'm soaring as the orgasm takes over me. I've never come so hard before. It's euphoric. Dots dance in my vision, my body shakes uncontrollably, and I'm gasping when I come back to reality.

I don't have the strength to open my eyes, but I feel the rope being removed and my husband lifting me off the table and into his arms. I lie in them, a smile on my face and wondering what I can do to be punished again. Because I've come to terms with being disobedient so he can remind me that he owns me.

WE'RE LYING ON OUR BED AND HE'S SOFTLY RUNNING HIS fingers along the red marks on my ass. "Where did you get the drugs?" he asks.

"They were the drugs you were going to use on me," I answer honestly. Don't want him mad at me for buying drugs. If he hadn't had them, I wouldn't have found them.

His hand pauses, and his eyes meet mine. "I was never going to drug you."

"I found them in the bedroom." His frown deepens. "Here in the spare room. They were in the bag from our honeymoon suite."

He lies still as a statue, eyes on mine.

"What is it?" I ask, sitting up.

"Nothing," he answers softly.

"Tyson?" I ask as he gets up off the bed.

"Lake, I never had drugs with me that day or since then."

"The basement..."

"I have them in the basement in case I need to use them on someone, but I've never purchased any type of drug that I planned specifically to use on you," he growls.

"So how did they get here?" I ask.

"I don't know," he answers.

"Quit lying to me."

"Lake—"

"God, do you think I'm this fucking stupid?" I get to my feet as well, ignoring the tightness in my muscles from what he did to me in the dining room. "Do you really think that I'll believe everything you say?"

His jaw ticks, and he looks away from me. I slowly walk over to him and cup his face. "Tell me. I can handle it. Promise."

His eyes search mine, and I hold my breath. "Luke."

I frown. "What does he have to do with this?"

"He was there at the hotel earlier that day before the wedding. They must have belonged to him."

My hand drops from his face, and I take a step back, my breath catching in my throat. "He was going to drug me?" I whisper. "How..." I swallow. "How do you know he was there?"

"I followed him," he says truthfully. "Watched him for days leading up to the wedding. He was there that morning when he dropped off your bag that your mom had made for him."

I go to open my mouth to ask if he killed Luke, but I decide not to. Of course, he did. It doesn't matter anymore. He's long gone. Men like Tyson don't have competition. They eliminate anyone in their way.

FORTY-SIX

TYSON

S he stands before me naked, her beautiful body marked from my hand and belt. The cum is completely off her face from earlier. Fuck, she's perfect.

I reach out and cup her face. Drugs. Luke was going to drug her. I'm not surprised. Lots of Lords give their chosens or Ladies drugs. Makes them easier to fuck. I've never been that guy. I'm not into fucking an unconscious woman.

I've wondered ever since she was stabbed if I did the right thing by making her marry me. As she stares up at me right now, I realize I did. She may never know why I married her. But I do.

But if there's one thing I do know, it's that your enemies will use what you love against you. And the gorgeous brunette who is staring up at me right now is the easiest target to get to me.

Love? It doesn't sound so foreign anymore. If loving someone means you'd burn the world to protect them, then I love her. It was never supposed to be this way. Me and her. But it doesn't matter why or how we got here. Not anymore.

Sliding my hands into her hair, I gently tilt her head back, and her eyes search mine nervously as I lower my lips to hers, needing to taste my wife.

She opens for me, her hands wrapping around my waist as I deepen the kiss. Showing her that no matter what happens from here on out, I will protect her. That means doing things that she won't like. I'm not going to treat her any differently. To the world, she's my whore. My useless fuck toy that I use however I want. And that's exactly what I'm going to let them think. She doesn't need to love me back. In fact, it's better that she doesn't.

Lots of people mistake lust and love. The difference is love demands a sacrifice. And that's what I did when I changed our futures three years ago. The fact that Luke was going to drug her the night of their wedding just proves that forcing her to marry me was the right call. I'm not sure how much she gave me, but it wore off pretty quickly. If she had been given the same dosage I took? She could still be out. Add the fact that I was able to get hard and it tells me everything I need to know—he was going to give her GHB.

Pulling my lips from hers, I watch her heavy eyes slowly open as she takes in a deep breath. I rub my thumb along her parted lips. "I'm going to shower and then head back to the club," I tell her, hating how she frowns at my words.

I'd love nothing more than to tie her to our bed and play with my wife all day, but I have a job to do. Someone wants her dead, and I need to kill them before they can get to her.

Her hands drop to her side before she turns and crawls back into bed. With all the strength I have, I turn and head into the bathroom to get ready for a long day.

LAIKYN

I LIE IN OUR BED, UNABLE TO SLEEP. MY MIND GOING NINETY miles an hour. There's still so much that I'm keeping from him. And I'm more afraid now not to tell him, than I am of him finding out.

I'm still in our bed but sitting up with my back against the headboard when he exits the bathroom freshly showered. He pauses when he sees me. "I figured you'd be out already."

"I need to tell you something." I swallow the knot in my throat, getting it over with.

"Okay."

"But you have to promise me you won't be mad at me," I rush out, sitting up straighter, my hands fisting the sheets in my clammy hands.

He crosses his arms over his chest, and leans up against the doorframe to the bathroom. The white towel sits low on his hips, showing me his impressive six pack and hard chest.

I drop my eyes to the comforter to keep my mind clear. "I lost a phone." I look up at him through my lashes, and he frowns. His eyes go to the one he gave me on my nightstand. Licking my lips, I add, "I lost a phone that my father gave me."

He pushes off the doorframe. "What the fuck do you mean a phone your father gave you?"

"He came to Blackout—"

"When the fuck was he in the club, Lake?" he demands.

I get up onto my knees, unable to sit still as his eyes narrow on mine. "The night of our dinner at the Minson Hotel."

"Jesus Christ," he hisses.

"I tried to tell him that you'd be mad. That you'd find out."

"Why didn't you tell me?" he barks.

My teeth clench. "You expected me to trust you?"

"More than him," he growls through gritted teeth. Running his hand through his hair, he knocks off the excess water and sighs heavily. "So you're saying you've had contact with him this entire time?"

"No." I shake my head. "Not at all. He said I'd receive my initiations on it."

His eyes snap to mine. "I told you; you wouldn't have an initiation."

"My father said you wanted me to fail."

"Why the fuck would I want you to fail?" he shouts. "God-dammit, Lake." His chest is heaving, his abs flexing.

I get even more nervous when he begins to pace the large room. "What was I supposed to believe?" I whisper.

"Tell me," he demands, "what else did he say?"

"Nothing," I answer hoarsely.

"Lake." His voice sends a shiver down my spine. It commands an answer, and he's not going to repeat himself.

"He told me I was a disgrace." Tears start to sting my eyes, unable to meet his. "That the Minson name would have been better off if I had been the one to die." I wipe my clammy hands on my bare thighs. "I just wanted to do something right for once."

"Lake." He sighs my name.

I sniff. "But I even fucked that up."

"What did you do?" He sits on the edge of the bed, his hand coming up and pushing my hair off my face, but I keep my eyes on the comforter.

"I forgot about it. Or maybe I wanted to avoid it." I've been trying to figure out how I could forget something so important. Maybe my mind chose to forget about it because I've known that Tyson was the side I needed to choose. "I remembered the night of the fight. I had checked it right before my shift started, and it was dead. So I used Starla's charger just long enough to get it to come on." I swallow nervously.

"And?" he asks softly, taking my hand in his.

"It had pictures."

His hand tightens on mine. "What kind of pictures?"

"Of me and you at the party at the house of Lords. Then pictures of me the day that I went out and had my hair done and bought my car."

"No texts or calls?"

"No," I answer, and he lets go of me to stand. "Why would they call or text me?"

"They don't send pictures for initiation, Lake."

"How am I supposed to know that?"

"Because I told you that you didn't have to do one," he responds tightly.

"Every Lady has to—"

"You're not every fucking Lady," he shouts, interrupting me.

"Why am I special?" I yank my hand from his and stand from the bed. "Huh? What have I done that warrants me a pass?"

His jaw clenches, and he looks away from me, refusing to tell me anything, and I let out a snort. "That right there is why I didn't believe you to begin with because you never tell me anything."

"The less you know, the better," he mumbles. "Where is the phone now?"

"I told you, I lost it," I answer. "I put it back in my locker, went to work, and that fight broke out. I went to go check it my first night back to work, but it was gone."

"You mean it was stolen." He runs a hand down his unshaven face. "Who all knew you had it? Just your father?"

I bite my bottom lip and lower my eyes to the floor. He places his fingers under my chin, forcing me to look at him. "Lake," he growls.

"I don't want to tell you," I answer honestly, and I'm surprised he looks more hurt than pissed.

"I need to know because someone has a phone knowing that it's yours. They can be pretending to be you."

I didn't think of it that way. Taking in a deep breath, I whisper, "Bethany."

FORTY-SEVEN

TYSON

Senior year at Barrington University

"Tyson Crawford?" *My name is called, and I look up from where I stand next to Lake holding her hair while she vomits into the trash can. Her shirt now covered in her sister's blood from making contact with mine.*

"Yeah?"

"Tyson Crawford, you are under arrest for the murder of Whitney Minson..." The cop walks up to me and yanks me away from Lake while reading me my rights.

"Wait—?" Ryat tries to jump in, but the other cop pushes him out of the way.

I'm shoved face-first into the wall, my arms pulled behind my back where the cop proceeds to cuff my wrists.

I look over to see Lake staring at me, color drained from her face from just getting sick and tears running down her cheeks. She shakes her head as she sobs, throwing her hand over her mouth.

The cops confirming what she already suspected.

"He didn't do it!" Ryat shouts. "I was with him..."

"Ryat," I bark, cutting him off, and the cop pulls me from the wall and grips my upper arm. He's pulling me through the hospital as Ryat follows us, already dialing a number on his phone.

I SIT AT MY DESK ON THE SECOND FLOOR OF BLACKOUT AS A knock sounds on my office door. "Come in," I answer.

The door opens, and Bethany steps into the room. I had her come in early before her shift starts this evening. "You wanted to see me, Tyson?" She practically skips to my desk after looking around for who I can only guess is my wife. But she's not here tonight. She's at our home, in our bed asleep. I know this because I just checked the cameras in our room.

"Have a seat." I gesture to the couch.

She plops down and crosses one leg over the other. Placing her arms along the back of the couch, she adjusts her hips to press her chest out. It's the exact same spot I fucked her mouth just months ago when Ryat and Blakely walked in on me while I had my cock down her throat.

The thought makes me think of my wife and how I'd never let anyone watch me fuck her. I've always preferred an audience. And with Whitney, it was required of me.

Make it public.

But with Laikyn, I don't want them to see what I do to her behind closed doors. The fact that no other man has ever been allowed to do what I do to her just makes me that much more protective of what's mine.

"Do you have anything to tell me?" I ask her. Getting to my feet, I walk over to stand in front of her.

She looks up at me, her brown eyes widening in fear before she licks her lips and shakes her head softly. "No, sir."

Sir? I almost snort at the change in her tone. "I won't ask again," I tell her.

Her arms drop off the back of the couch, and she leans forward, running her hands through her hair, all of a sudden on edge.

I don't want to ask her about the phone directly. I want to see what information she'll give up first. There might be other things she knows.

"Bethany," I bark, and she flinches.

"I didn't have a choice," she rushes out.

"A choice to what?"

She stands too, and I take a step back, putting some space between us. "Mr. Minson came to me and told me he needed to talk to Lake. What was I supposed to say? No?" She shakes her head.

"You could have come to me," I grind out. "Told me. Instead, you helped him get into this club. My club!"

"He threatened me."

I snort. "With what?" I hold up my hand, stopping whatever bullshit she was about to say. "It doesn't matter. You're fired. Clean out your locker and get the fuck out of my club."

"Tyson." Her hands grip my shirt. "Please, you don't understand..."

"I understand that I can't trust you. And that's enough. Get the fuck out, Beth."

"Tyson?" She grabs my arm, pulling on it, and I yank it out of her hold. The force makes her trip forward, her body running into mine. "Please?" She begins to cry.

She knows me well enough to know that I don't give a fuck about her tears. She was one of Whitney's friends. They were both chosens at the same time. They weren't extremely close but hung out often at the house of Lords. Whitney would have never let her parents know she was friends with Bethany because they would not have approved. So the fact that her father is using her makes me more than worried.

"How did he know he could come to you?" I question, pushing her to sit back on the couch. If she doesn't want to leave, then I'll get as much information out of her as I can. "What did you do that he thought you would cross me?"

She sniffs, dropping her head to look at her hands in her lap. "He found my number in Whitney's phone after she passed."

"And?" I ask tightly.

Wiping her tear-streaked cheeks, she whispers, "I slept with him."

"Of course, you did."

She glares up at me through her watery eyes. "It was years ago. I went over to her parents' one night to see Whitney, but she was out with Laikyn and their mother. I was drunk, and we had sex. He said if I didn't help him, he would show the video of us to everyone."

"You let him record you?" I grind out, but I'm not surprised. Guys like Frank Minson always make sure they have some kind of leverage against you.

"I didn't know he had cameras in his room," she growls.

"What else has he had you do?" I ask, walking back behind my desk and sitting down for some more space. I push my keyboard to light up my computer and see my wife is still napping in our bed. I shut down the screen and look at Bethany expectantly.

"He had me follow her. He said he knew that you'd be at your house before the house of Lords party. So I waited outside and took pictures. Then I was at the party with..." She trails off, lowering her eyes to her hands in her lap.

"Who the fuck were you there with?" She has not married a Lord yet. I'm not even sure she ever will. Not all chosens become Ladies. Just like not all Ladies were once chosens.

"Miller," she responds softly.

I'm unable to hold my chuckle in at that.

Her brown eyes narrow on me. "Did your wife tell you that her brother spoke to her while there at the party?" I stiffen, and then she's the one laughing. "Didn't think so." Standing, she brushes off her leotard as if it's dirty from our conversation, then she walks to the door.

"Bethany?" I call out.

She stops and turns around to face me with a smug smile on her face. I remove the cell phone from my pocket, and I lay it on my desk. Her face instantly falls when she sees it. I broke the lock off her locker when I got here earlier and found it. "Tell him you lost it."

Without another word, she turns and exits my office, and I sit back in my seat. My hands come up to run through my hair. Why is my wife still keeping secrets from me? I'm damn sure going to find out.

I ENTER OUR BEDROOM WITH A WHISKEY IN MY HAND. I needed a drink. It was a long night—three fights, lots of drunks, and one guy passed out in the bathroom in his own vomit. Then I hauled a guy downstairs and beat the shit out of him because I was just in the mood to smash someone's face in. He was the unlucky bastard. On top of all that, Bethany is no longer working there and neither is my wife. Bethany had been picking up Lake's sections.

The longer I've thought about what Bethany said, the angrier I've gotten at my wife. I don't know why. It's not her fault that she feels she can't talk to me. She told me earlier in this very room that she felt she couldn't trust me or my intentions. Her father told her I was setting her up for failure. He's filling her head with bullshit and trying to get between us. Honestly, it wouldn't take much, considering how our marriage started.

Soft light filters through the floor-to-ceiling windows, giving me a perfect view of my naked wife lying in our bed. She's on her side, facing me. One hand underneath the pillow, the other stretched out to my spot. The covers shoved down to her lower back, showing me part of her chest. She looks so peaceful right now. I hate to wake her up and piss her off, but I want, no, need to know exactly what her piece of shit brother said to her at the house of Lords party.

When did he even get the chance to talk to her? She was with me the entire time other than when she went to the bathroom. My hand tightens on the glass of whiskey. Surely that's not when he spoke to her, but when else could it have been?

She returned from the bathroom with Blakely and Ellington, so she couldn't have been in there too long with him if that's the case.

I make my way to our bathroom and get undressed, needing a shower to wash off the night before I crawl into bed with her and wake her up.

FORTY-EIGHT

TYSON

She starts to stir as I sit in the chair by the window, finishing my drink. I thought about tying her down to the bed, gagged and blindfolded. Just to watch her squirm as she woke and realized she was at my mercy, but I decided against it. I like to watch my wife's eyes go wide when I catch her in a lie. Or the sound of her breathing picking up when she realizes I know something that she hasn't told me.

I'd much rather punish her after I get the information I want to hear.

Rolling over to face me, she snuggles into the pillow. Her eyes still closed and still half asleep. Wanting to refuse to wake up and greet the day. It's not even seven yet, so it's still early.

I take a sip of my whiskey, the ice in the glass clinking, and her eyes spring open, landing right on mine. A soft smile spreads across her pretty face as she speaks. "Hey." Her voice is soft, showing just how drowsy she is. It instantly makes my cock harden. "How long have you been home?" She sits up, pushing her back into the headboard.

I take another drink, and she frowns. "I fired Bethany last night."

She drops her eyes to the comforter and sighs heavily. I open my mouth to speak, but her words make me pause. "Did you sleep with her?"

"Why the fuck would I sleep with her?" I growl, angry with my wife. Not only for asking that dumbass question but also for lying to me. She's trying to deflect.

Her eyes narrow on mine. "You've done it before."

"Yes, but ..." I pause when I realize what she means. I may be pissed at Lake, but I'm not going to let her think I've had an affair. "I haven't fucked anyone since I made you my wife." I won't tell her right now, but she's the only woman I'll ever need.

"She—"

"She fucking lied to you." I interrupt her. "I watched her on the camera, and she hid out in the locker room while you waited on her tables."

Letting out a long breath, she looks away from me. I get back to our previous conversation.

"But before she left my office last night, she informed me that you spoke to your brother at the house of Lords party."

She looks away from me, her jaw sharpening.

"Why didn't you tell me this yesterday when you told me about the phone?"

"Because it didn't matter," she answers tightly.

"Everything matters when it comes to you," I say honestly. It always has. She just doesn't know that. But why would she? I've never made her feel that way.

Her eyes meet mine, and I can't tell if she's mad or disgusted with my words. Usually, I can read my wife pretty easily. But she's getting better at hiding from me.

"It was in the bathroom, wasn't it? Where you spoke to him?"

Her eyes drop to the bed. "Yes."

"That's why you were so mad with me at the party," I growl, and she hangs her head. She had gone to the bathroom in a good mood and then came back to the table with a new drink and barely spoke to me the rest of the night. Until we were in the bathtub together and I demanded to know what her problem was. "What did he say to you?"

"He stormed into the bathroom, demanding to know what I was doing." I frown. "I told him I didn't know what he meant. He said he had seen the hotel room." She swallows. "I argued that I didn't have a choice. He asked if you held a gun to my head. Or a knife to my throat. When I said no to both, he then asked me if you tied me down and raped me." Her voice is soft, barely over a whisper. "When I said no, he asked if I had learned anything from Whitney. That even though she loved you, she knew nothing would come from it. I said it wasn't like he tried to stop the wedding, and he said he did what he had to do. I said the same thing. He then argued that I didn't have to come on your cock." Her eyes meet mine, and her cheeks flush.

I just stare at her, unblinking, but my blood is boiling. If he knows she came that day after our wedding, then they had cameras in the hotel room. He said he saw the room; he wouldn't have known she got off just by seeing the blood on the bed. I don't think she's put that together yet. But why the fuck would her father want cameras in there to watch her and Luke fuck? He was already going to see that she had, in fact, remained a virgin for Luke after they checked out the next morning.

"Anyway." She drops her eyes once more when I don't say anything, and goes on, "He said that I was acting like the slut you were turning me into, hanging all over you in front of everyone. That you don't love me or give a fuck about what happens to me." She shrugs. "As if I ever thought anything different."

"Lake—"

Her eyes snap up to mine, and she gasps.

"What?" I ask, sitting down on the side of the bed.

"He also told me that our dad had a plan, and I wasn't going to fuck it up." She nibbles on her bottom lip nervously. "Do you think that had to do with the phone he gave me?" I don't answer because I honestly don't fucking know what he could have planned. "I swear I never used it. Just saw those pictures and that was it. I never texted or called anyone on it," she rushes out.

"Lake." I cup her face.

Her bottom lip starts to tremble. "I promise."

"Calm down," I tell her. "I believe you."

She lets out a shaky breath and nods softly. Her pretty eyes swimming with unshed tears. "Come here." I let go of her face and pull her into my lap. She curls up and wraps her arms around my neck. I wrap mine around her small body and hold her tightly to mine.

I wish she would have come to me, but I understand why she felt she couldn't. She's never felt safe with me. Running my hands down her bare back, I feel her small body start to shake, and I hold her tighter. Hoping that she realizes just how much she means to me. That all she needs is me. "Lake—"

My cell phone ringing interrupts me and she pulls away, lying down under the covers while I stand and remove my cell from my pocket. "Yeah?" I snap when I see it's Colton.

"We've got something. On our way over."

I hang up, not even bothering with a goodbye, and run a hand down my face, letting out a long breath. "The guys..."

"Go," she mumbles, sniffing.

Sitting down on the edge, I reach out and gently brush hair off her face. "I won't be long," I assure her, and she looks up at me through her dark lashes. Leaning down, I give her a kiss on her forehead and then stand. I close the bedroom door and make my way to the front door in time to let them in and then lead them to my study on the second floor.

"This better be good," I say, falling into my chair. I'm exhausted and want to crawl into bed with my naked wife.

Colton walks over to my desk and drops a folder down on it.

"What is it?" I ask.

"We found something." Jenks is the one who answers. He picks up the remote and turns on the big screen hanging on the wall and goes to the Blackout footage.

LAIKYN

I pull into the parking lot of Blackout, bringing my car to a screeching halt when I see Tyson's car parked by the back door.

He's not supposed to be here.

When he left me in our bed an hour ago with his cum dripping out of my pussy, he kissed me goodbye and said he had to do something with Colton and Jenks and would be home late.

I'm guessing by the way his car is parked, he had to drop by and grab something. My eyes scan over the black Continental GT. It fits him so well—dark and deadly, powerful and expensive.

My eyes drop to the license plate on the back that reads BLAKOUT. Anyone who doesn't know he owns this club would think that's what he calls his car. Either way, it fits.

I slouch down in my seat, making sure my lights are off as I hide tucked back in the far corner when I see the back door open, and he steps out. I lick my lips while I take in his black button-up and gray slacks. He's got the sleeves rolled up to showcase his tan forearms. God, he's so fucking gorgeous. His hair is still messy from my hands pulling on it earlier while his mouth was between my shaking legs. His five o'clock shadow looks darker under the dimly lit parking lot lights.

He holds the door open, and I watch Colton, Jenks, Finn, and

Alex all exit. They allow the door to close and stand around Tyson's car as they have what looks like to be an in-depth conversation. I've never asked what they do for him, and after I watched them tie down Collin, I'm guessing it's whatever the fuck my husband wants.

Servants come to mind. Tyson tries to pretend he owns Blackout for the fun of it, but I see the way he runs the place. This is his palace. His home.

Tyson's not the kind of guy who wants you to think he rules the world. No, he's the type of man who doesn't give a fuck who does. He's not afraid to go toe-to-toe with anyone. And I'll bet on him every time.

He nods his head a few times, and I watch Alex and Jenks turn back around. Alex places his wrist under a keypad, and the door pops open. They enter, and I watch my husband fall into the driver's seat, start up his car, and drive off as Colton and Jenks go to a black Escalade.

I turn on my lights and find a parking spot as close to the back entrance as I can and head inside.

"Hey," I say to Beau over the thundering bass.

He turns to look at me. "Oh, thank god, Lake. We could use the help."

I figured. I'm going insane being locked up in the house. At least here at the apartment, I had the club downstairs. I don't want to just sit around the house waiting for my husband to come home. I can help him out here.

Beau turns and picks up his cell from underneath the bar and types out a message, then nods to me. "When will you be ready?"

Smiling, I remove my jacket, and he grins back at me when he sees I'm dressed and ready to go.

The club is packed like usual. I've got my section plus half of Nicki's. She had to go home because she was sick. If I'm being honest with myself, I'm not feeling all that well either. I'm just so tired. My body exhausted.

It's been three days since Tyson fired Bethany, and I've overheard him talking on his phone about how hectic it's been here. With her gone and another sick, they're all having to pick up the slack.

I've been here for an hour and haven't had a chance to breathe. I'm ordering some drinks from Beau, sweating my ass off in the packed club.

"Lake?" I hear my name being called out.

"Yeah?" I turn to see a blonde who I don't know standing behind me. "Can I get you something?" I ask, wondering if she's sitting at one of my tables.

"There's a woman in the bathroom asking for you." She points back at the hallway toward the women's restroom.

I frown but leave my tray and turn to follow her. We make our way to the women's restroom, and I open the door to see a familiar face standing in front of one of the sinks. "Bethany?" I ask, going over to her. "Are you okay?" My hands go to her arms. Her brown eyes meet mine, and she's got a black eye along with a cut lip. "Jesus, what happened to you?"

"I need to speak to Tyson." She crosses her arms over her chest, running her hands up and down her arms nervously.

"He's not here," I tell her, and she begins to cry. "What's going on?"

"I messed up." She bows her head, and her shoulders start to shake.

"What did you do, Bethany?" If she knows she did something wrong, then it must be bad.

"I ... I'm sorry," she cries, burying her face in her hands.

"How about we call him?" I offer. "You can talk to him, okay?"

"He won't talk to me." She sniffs.

"We'll call from my cell. It's in my locker. Come on." I grab her hand, not letting her say no, and pull her out of the restroom into the flashing lights and pounding bass. We make our way down the hallway to the locker room, and we step inside. I open my locker and pull out my cell. "Here." I pull up his contact, press call, and hold it out to her.

She sniffs a few times, trying to calm her breathing. Putting it to her ear, she shakes her head and hands it back.

I put it to mine. "You've reached Tyson. Leave a message."

Beep.

"Hey." I turn my back to her and take a few steps away to put some distance between us and lower my voice. "Don't be mad, but I came to Blackout tonight to help while you're out and I don't know what's going on, but Bethany is here and wants to talk to you. We're calling from my cell, but I'm going to put it back in my locker, so when you call back, call the club. I'll have her sit at the bar and wait. She's crying and very upset." I hang up and turn to face her.

"I told you he won't talk to me." She rubs the tears underneath her eyes.

"He'll call back. Come sit at the bar while you wait to talk to him."

"Lake?" She pulls me to a stop.

"Yeah?" I ask, looking at her.

"I'm so sorry for everything I've done."

"It's okay," I tell her.

"No, it's not. I wasn't nice to you." Her watery eyes drop to the floor. "I just ... I just couldn't tell him no."

"My father?" I ask, trying to be supportive but also needing to know who the hell she's talking about.

She shakes her head, wrapping her arms around herself, and I know she's lying. She's not going to tell me anything because she wants my husband.

"Who, Bethany?" I growl, getting irritated. Maybe she's just trying to piss me off and doesn't really want to talk to Tyson at all. "What did he want?"

The door opens, and Starla enters. She runs to the trash can and begins to throw up. Once she's done, she wipes her mouth with her hand. "Something is going around."

"Come on," I tell Bethany, pulling her out, and we push our way to the bar.

I know I've got everything out of her that I'm going to get. Tyson will have to get the rest. Thankfully, a nice man offers her his seat, and I tell her to stay right there while I add more tables to my section to help Starla.

FORTY-NINE

TYSON

We've just gotten out of town when I hear my cell going off and alerting me of a message. I see I had a missed call from Lake a while ago. I must have had bad service. We're out in the middle of nowhere. I hit call to listen to her voicemail.

"Hey." Her sweet voice fills my ear. "Don't be mad but I came to Blackout tonight to help while you're out, and I don't know what's going on, but Bethany is here and wants to talk to you. We're calling from my cell. I'm going to put it back in my locker. When you call back, call the club. I'm going to have her sit at the bar and wait for your call. She's crying and very upset."

"What the fuck?" Ending the call, I immediately dial Blackout and wait for someone to pick up. It rings until it stops. I dial it again. Finally, on the fourth ring, someone answers.

"Blackout," Beau calls out into the phone.

I want to demand why the fuck my wife is there, but he's not going to know, so I get to the point. "Hey, Lake called me. Said Bethany wanted to talk to me," I say.

"Yeah, she's at the bar. One sec. I'll get her."

"Ty-son," her broken voice says moments later.

I refrain from rolling my eyes. Bethany isn't my favorite person right now. "What do you want, Beth? And why are you at Blackout?" If she wanted to call me, she could have called me from her own cell. I'm not sure I'd answer, but she could have left a voicemail herself instead of using my wife. Bethany isn't stupid. She knows how to use people to her advantage, no matter how well she's able to play the victim.

"I'm sorry." She begins to cry.

I sigh, running a hand through my hair. "I'll be back at Blackout in a couple of hours. Stay at the bar, and I'll come get you." I left Alex and Jenks behind to keep an eye on the place, so I'll have them add babysitting her to their duties. "We can talk in my office, okay?"

"Tyson?" Colton hollers at me, and I nod at him to give me a second.

"Bethany?" I bark out, not having time for this right now.

"It'll be too late," she whispers, sending a chill down my spine.

"What'll be too late?" I demand.

Click.

"Bethany?" I shout out at the silence. Pulling my cell from my ear, I look at Colton. "I've got to go."

"What's wrong?" he calls out, he and Finn already heading toward me.

"Stay here. Get it done," I order, and then I jump back into my car, starting it up. I squeal the tires heading back into town, praying that this is one of those times she's just being dramatic.

I dial Alex's cell, and he answers immediately. "What's up, boss?" The sound of the music coming from the club makes it hard to hear him.

"Where the fuck is my wife?" I growl, my hand tightening on the steering wheel and shifting in my seat.

"I sent you a text that she was here."

"I didn't have any service," I snap, and take in a deep breath. "What the fuck is she doing?"

"She's on the floor working. Starla went home because she was puking in the locker room, so Lake took over her tables."

"Keep an eye on her. Don't let her out of your sight."

The only sound is the bass filling my car as he's silent for a second and then I hear him slamming a door shut, the music fading. "What's going on? I'm watching Lake right now on the cameras in your office. She's at the bar getting drinks from Beau."

"Bethany is there," I inform him. "Called me crying. She's up to something. Said she was sitting at the bar—"

"She's not there," He interrupts me.

"Fucking find her. Now." I shout.

The sound of a knock can be heard over his phone. "Once sec." I hear the music filter into the room once more. "What's up, man..." The phone goes dead.

"FUCK!"

LAIKYN

I walk over to the bar and place an order for a table of eight when I see Bethany walking over to the cage. Beau comes over to me and I yell over the music. "Did she speak to Tyson?"

He nods. Good, I feel a little better now. But looking back over at her, I watch her remove her shirt so all she has on is her bra.

"Give me a water, please." He hands me one. "I'll be right back," I tell him, and leave my tray behind.

Going over to the cage, I reach through the metal bars and tug on her jeans. "Bethany?" I shout.

She bends down and smiles at me. Whatever she said to Tyson must have helped because she looks much happier now. "Here's a water." I hold it up with my free hand.

Opening up the cage, she reaches for it but grabs my hand and begins to pull me in. "Oh, no. I can't..."

"Come on, Lake." She pulls on me as hands push my ass, lifting me into the cage. I catch sight of the guy shutting it behind me, closing us inside.

I try to look for Beau to get his attention to let him know I'm up here, but the bar is swamped.

Spinning me around, Bethany reaches up, gripping the bars my back is pressed into, and leans her face into mine with her lips by my ear. "Live a little before you die."

"Bethany..."

I feel wetness on my leotard and look down to see something on my uniform but the flashing lights make it hard to see. "What the ..." Did she shoot me? Stab me? My hands frantically grab at the material and then I see it's blood on me as my heart pounds in my chest. My breath catches as I run them all over my chest, neck, and arms, trying to find out what's going on, but all it does is smear the blood around.

My stomach sinks when I see her smiling at me.

All I can think is that I wish I would have told Tyson that I loved him at least once. Because the look on her face tells me all I need to know. I'll never be seeing him again.

FIFTY

TYSON

My cell rings through my Bluetooth as I fly down the highway. I'm hoping it's Alex because he hasn't answered my last twenty frantic calls back since his phone went dead.

Ryat lights up my screen, and I hit answer. "Hello?"

"Thank God." He sighs. "You're okay, you guys got out?"

Panic grips my chest. "What do you mean *got out*? Got out of what?" I ask in a rush as I speed up, going well over a hundred and fifty.

This Bentley GT will top out at two hundred and eight miles an hour. I'm pushing it to get there. The only thing going for me is that it's after two o'clock in the morning, so I'm not having to mow people over on this highway.

He's silent for a long moment. "Ryat?" I bark. "What the fuck are you talking about?"

"Where are you?" he rushes out, and I hear his car door open and close before the roar of his engine fills my speakers.

"Headed to Blackout. Lake went in tonight and then Bethany

called me..." I trail off, not getting into what's going on at the second. I want to know what the fuck he's talking about.

"Fuck," he hisses.

"What the fuck is going on, Ryat?" I demand. I can't get ahold of Jenks either. He and Alex stayed behind, and no one is answering the club phones.

"There was an accident. It's on the news. Prickett called me—"

"What kind of accident?" I interrupt him, my stomach dropping. *What did you do, Bethany?*

"There's a fire at Blackout. People are trapped inside."

***

Before I even reach the club, I see flashing lights where I know Blackout is located. Veering off the highway, I don't even slow down as I come up to a red light. I blow right through it, not giving two shits if I get hit or hit someone. I'm taking my chances because there's hardly anyone out on this side of town anyway, at least, until the clubs close and the drunks are going home.

My heart races as I come up on cop cars, ambulances, and fire trucks. Bringing my car to an abrupt stop, my body jerks forward, and the tires squeal. I smell my brakes burning, or that could be the club on fire in front of me.

I jump out and run through the packed parking lot that looks like a triage center—littered with people and first responders.

"Lake?" I yell out, running through the parking lot. "LAIKYN?" I spin around, looking for her, but she's nowhere to be found.

"Tyson?" I hear my name and turn around to see Beau. He's sitting in the back of an ambulance. His left arm is wrapped with a white bandage, and he's soaking wet.

"What the fuck happened?" I demand. "Where the fuck is Lake?"

"She..." He takes in a ragged breath. "She was in the cage..." He begins to cough, and a paramedic places an oxygen mask over his face.

I turn to look at the building that is still on fire and run toward it.

"Whoa. You can't go in there," an officer yells as I run past him. "Stop him."

The flames light up the night as firefighters try to get it under control. The roof is ablaze, the smoke trailing off into the dark sky. My adrenaline is pumping. All I can think is to get inside and find her. I can feel the heat from here, and the water they're spraying to try and put it out hits my face.

I'm almost to the back entrance when I'm hit from behind and knocked to the ground. A guy is yelling in my ear while he's on top of my back, pinning me face down. But I can't understand what he's saying. All I know is that I have to get to her. If she's not out here, then she's inside. I slam my head back, making contact with his, and then the weight is off me. Getting to my feet, I begin to run again just as I'm hit from the side.

We roll a few times before I'm on my back and an officer straddles me. I punch him in the face with a scream, feeling my knuckles crack. He's wasting my time. "Get the fuck off me."

I hit him again. And then again. His blood splatters across my face before his unconscious body falls down on top of mine, and I roll him off onto the wet parking lot.

Just when I get to my feet, I fall to my knees, unable to move. I swear I hear her scream out for me as more officers rush over.

FIFTY-ONE

TYSON

I'm pinned down, my chest pressed onto the hood of a cop car, when I hear Ryat's voice.

"What the fuck is going on here?" he shouts, coming over to me and the five cops that it took to put me down.

"Stay back—"

"Uncuff him right fucking now!" Ryat barks out, interrupting the cop.

"He beat the fuck out of two of our officers. And then threatened to shoot another with his own gun." He scoffs.

I'm shaking and not because the fuckers tased me, but because I can't do anything. My hands are tied. Literally. They've got theirs all over me, keeping me down. If I could just get them off, I'd run into the building. The cuffs won't stop me.

I watch Ryat pull his cell out of his pocket and make a phone call. He's pacing back and forth next to the car before he takes a few more steps farther away and begins to speak quickly into his cell.

Pushing against the car, I try to lift their weight up off me. But

I hear a gun cock and then feel the barrel at the back of my head. "Don't fucking move, Tyson. Or it'll be the last thing you do."

My teeth grind. I can't save my wife if I'm dead. I know she's alive. The one thing about them stopping me is that I was able to think about it.

This was a ploy. My club didn't burn down by accident when I was away. No, they wanted her here without me. If she's not out here with the others, then she's been taken. They want me to think she's inside burning.

Don't get me wrong, I was going in even if I wasn't going to be coming back out. I'd risk my life to save my wife's. Because there's still a small voice in the back of my mind saying that she's in there. Someone wanted to kill her to hurt me. That's what would hurt the most—having to live the rest of my life without her.

This isn't the Lords' doing. They'd never take Blackout from me. It's personal, which means they'd go after my wife.

I saw Alex and Jenks right before I got tased, both beat the fuck up but alive. They were jumped by two men, both in masks. They looked like dogs with their tails tucked between their legs because they think they failed me by not saving my wife. But the reality is, I failed her. She wasn't their responsibility. I didn't have time to discuss with them, but I sent them to my house to make sure it wasn't next. I need it to stay standing. I can access Blackout footage from my home office.

"You have a phone call," Ryat says, sounding much more cheerful as he walks back over to us and hands his phone to the guy who's got the gun to the back of my head.

He huffs, repositioning the gun so he has one free hand. "Hello?" Pause. "Sir... Yes. Yes, I understand." He hands Ryat back his phone. And a long silence follows before he says, "Uncuff him."

They growl, annoyed that whoever Ryat called probably threatened their career. The first cuff unlocks, and I pull my hands around to my front, not even bothering to wait for the second.

Pushing off the hood, I spin around, rip the gun from the officer's hand and shoot him in the chest. The sound of the gun going off echoes through the packed parking lot and the officer falls backward onto his back. "Fuuckk," he groans, gripping his chest and rolling to his side.

"Jesus, Tyson," another one spits out, falling to his friend's side. "What if he hadn't been wearing his vest?" he barks, looking up at me.

"That's what I was hoping for." I remove the magazine and toss the useless gun to the ground beside him.

"I'm sorry, but your wife is gone."

I turn to see the officer I shot now bent over but up on his feet, glaring at me.

His eyes look over the flames that heat up my back. "There's no way anyone left inside could have survived."

That right there is why the Lords don't cooperate with the police. They can't see the bigger picture. My wife is alive. The question is, where the fuck is she? I'm going to find out.

I turn to Ryat, and we walk closer to Blackout. It's still up in flames. "Whoa." He runs in front of me, his hands on my chest. "We both know she's not in there." He lowers his voice. "This is a ploy, Ty. I know it, and so do you." He speaks what I was just thinking but still. There's always that small chance.

I run my hands through my hair, realizing I still have that one cuff on my wrist. "What if she is, though?" I ask through gritted teeth. "Would you take that chance with Blakely?"

He looks away from me, sighing, knowing his answer would be the same as mine. "Tracker." His large eyes come back to mine, snapping his fingers. "You've got a tracker, right?"

I yank my cell out of my back pocket and pull it up. "It shows the alley," I say, and we run through the back parking lot to the side alley. This tracker is on point. It could be at the bottom of the ocean, and it would show me how many feet deep it is.

We enter the dimly lit alley. "Lake?" I call out. "Laikyn?" I'm shouting while I breathe heavily. Glancing at my cell, I come to a stop. "This is where it says she is." Lowering my hand, I look at the ground, and my blood runs cold when I see her tracker by my shoe. "GODDAMMIT!"

FIFTY-TWO

TYSON

My wife has been missing for two days, and I'm losing my goddamn mind. Literally. I haven't slept, haven't eaten. I'm to the point where I'm seeing shit. It's fucking with me. But every time I close my eyes, all I see is her begging me to find her. To help her. So I stay awake. Fueled by anger and desperation.

A desperate man is a dangerous one. I never understood why a man with nothing to lose is to be feared. Have you ever met a man with everything to lose? They are the ones to fear. They will do whatever it takes to make sure they keep what is theirs.

I haven't received one text or call about a ransom. Not like I expected to get one. They don't plan on giving her back to me. They want to make me suffer. See how far they can push me until I hit my breaking point. I'm going to burn the fucking city down. That's how far I'm willing to go.

Ryat brings his car to a stop, and I get out, shutting my door. I don't even bother trying to be quiet. I kick in the front door and enter the apartment; Ryat enters behind me with his gun drawn.

"What the ...?" The guy jumps up from the couch, dropping his beer.

I rush him, taking him down to the floor as the girl who was sucking his dick screams at the top of her lungs.

I punch Beau in the face, knocking him out, and go for the girl. Grabbing her hair, I pull her over to the kitchen area and shove her into a chair. He's a senior at Barrington this year, so he can get his dick wet. But I know she's not his chosen.

"Please," she sobs, "don't do this."

Ryat pockets his gun and removes the backpack off his shoulders and pulls out the duct tape. He helps me hold her down while I secure her wrists to the arms of the chair and then her ankles to the legs. I finish her off with tape around her mouth while her muffled cries fill the room.

Once I feel she's secure, I pull the chair into the living room and turn her to face the couch. Then I pick up an unconscious Beau and tie him up as well. Sitting him up on the couch, we wait.

**

He opens his eyes; they look around unfocused for a few seconds before he realizes that he's tied up. His eyes meet the girl's that is duct taped in the chair and he jumps to his feet. I ram my elbow into his face, and he falls to the couch, groaning into the cushion.

I grip his hair and yank him to sit as I lower myself to the glass coffee table and rip the tape from his mouth. He sucks in a deep breath. "What the fuck, Ty?"

"Where is she?" I demand.

"I don't know."

I punch him in the nose, feeling a crack on the bone.

"Je-sus," he cries out, leaning forward, blood now dripping from his face onto my shoes.

I go over to the table and grab the duct tape. I then walk back to the couch and wrap it around his head just like I did hers, silencing him.

Tossing it to the floor, it rolls under the coffee table. I make my way over to the girl, and she drops her head, sobbing behind the tape on her face.

I gently push the blond hair off her shoulder and then pull her head back, forcing her to look up at Beau. "It's okay," I tell her, and she breathes heavily through her nose. Tears run down her face, and she squeezes her eyes closed. "I'll make it quick," I say before grabbing either side of her face. Her eyes pop open, and I twist, breaking her neck.

I let her go. Her head falls forward, and Beau starts screaming through his tape.

"That was the only kindness I'm going to show tonight," I say, sitting down on the coffee table to face him. I know she was part of it. The camera didn't lie. I was able to access the cameras inside of the club from my home computer. I saw everything right up until the fire started. She lured my wife to the bathroom where Bethany was. The how and why doesn't matter. It happened, and now we're moving on. Now all I care about is finding Lake. Every second she's missing is a second that I could lose her forever.

"Where the fuck is my wife?" I ask him, reaching up and yanking the tape off his lips.

"Please..." He looks at the dead blonde behind me. "I didn't do anything," he cries.

"What *did* you do?" I ask, knowing he had a part in it.

"Bethany came to me. Said I needed to get out of the club. That something was going to happen. I didn't know." He sobs, rocking back and forth, his arms tied behind his back.

"Who was she?" I ask, referring to the dead girl behind me.

"She came with Bethany. That's all I know." He hangs his head. "I swear I didn't know anything would happen to Laikyn."

I punch him in the face just for mentioning her name, pushing him down onto his side in the cushions. "In the parking lot, you told me that you saw Lake in the cage. Why didn't you help her out of the club if you knew something was going to happen?"

"Because I didn't know *what* was going to happen," he growls through bloody teeth. "I already told you that."

Standing, I go over to his kitchen and start opening cabinets. I find what I want and go back to the couch. He gets up to run, but Ryat grabs his arm and forces him to his knees in the middle of the living room.

"No!" he shouts before I begin to wrap the cling wrap around his face, making sure to cover it all from his forehead to his chin. Ryat releases him and pushes him to the floor, and we both watch him flop around like a fish out of water, trying to breathe with his hands duct-taped behind his back along with his ankles.

The clear plastic wrap sticks to his tear-streaked and bloody face. His chest heaves and he bucks wildly. When his movements start to slow, I kneel next to him and push my fingers into it, breaking a small piece around his lips so he can suck in a breath.

"Who and where did they take my wife?" I ask calmly, but inside I'm on fire. A burning sensation that I can't put out. I hate feeling helpless, and I hate it even more that I have no clue what is happening to my little darling. Is she being tortured? Raped? Is she dead? She's innocent. So whatever is happening to her is because of me. They are making her pay because I love her.

Until she's back in my arms, I'm going to burn every person that helped take her from me.

"I ... don't know." He sobs, rolling onto his stomach. The cling wrap so tight on his face it's got his eyes closed, and cheeks squished, smearing the blood on his skin.

Standing, I pull out the flask and pour it over his legs.

He kicks around his taped legs. "What are you doing?" he rushes out, unable to see.

I take the lighter out of my pocket and bend down, lighting the gasoline I just sprinkled on his legs, setting him on fire.

His screams fill the room and I stand back, watching him try and roll around as the flames lick up over his skin. I didn't drown him in it. The plan is to make it hurt, fucking painful. Fire is unpredictable, but one thing about it is that it can be quick. And that would be too easy for him. He deserves to suffer like I know Lake is right now.

The smell of his burning flesh fills the room, and I smile as I watch him try to put it out but it's not going to happen.

Ever so slowly, the fire crawls up his legs and catches his T-shirt. I walk over to the girl and light her on fire as well. I'm not going to go through the trouble of removing them from her apartment and burying them behind the Cathedral. I'm going to leave a trail that says *I'm looking for my wife, and anyone who stands in my way will burn.*

This is my statement to anyone who had a hand in taking my wife. I'm coming for you.

We fall into Ryat's car, and we watch people start to run out of the apartment complex as flames start to crawl over the building. I'm not sorry for what I'm about to do. For all the bodies I'm going to leave in my wake.

Why? Because the villain doesn't give two shits about the world. All he cares about is the one thing that calms his demons, and that person for me is Lake. If I don't have her, they take control, and all they know is to destroy.

Ryat holds up a cell phone and I take it from him. It belonged to Beau. I pull up his messages and start to read over them. It doesn't take me long to find what I need.

FIFTY-THREE

TYSON

My wife has been missing for five days, and I'm no closer to finding her. I thought I was losing my mind, but I've officially gone manic. Lack of sleep will do that to you.

I pace the room, my bloody hands down by my side. Some mine, mixed with others. "Where is my wife?" My voice is as rough as I look. I can't even remember the last time I showered or ate something.

"I ... I don't know."

I swing, my fisted hand connecting with the guy's jaw, making him cry out like a little bitch. I've always preferred to fight with my hands rather than a gun or a knife. Hand to hand is so much more personal. It sends a message that I'm not afraid to fuck myself up, and I'll take anyone down with me.

"And you?" I walk over to the other man hanging from the ceiling. His arms tied above his head as he still rocks back and forth from the last fist to his stomach. "Still don't know where she's at, I suppose?"

His head hangs back, his body pulled tight. He's naked and

covered in blood. I took a knife to his leg a few hours ago just because. He'll hang here like the piece of rotting meat he is until I get what I want or decide to kill him.

"She's ... dead," he grinds out.

I refuse to believe that. It wouldn't make sense for whoever has her to kill her. I'd give up my life for her. That has to be their plan, right? A trade? Me for her? Otherwise, why would they take her from me? "You better hope not."

I punch him in the throat and his body jerks in the chains while he coughs and sputters. "Beau sent you a text the night of the fire. Told you that Lake was at Blackout. Why?"

It's ironic that the two guys I was chasing down the night of the fire are the same two who were at Blackout. I don't have concrete evidence that they had help in kidnapping my wife, but why the fuck would they care that my wife was up at the club? I don't believe in coincidences.

Neither of them says anything, and I pop my split knuckles while Ryat sits over in the corner of the room, straddling a chair backwards with his arm lying across the top. He's helped me the last few days. After I set Beau and his bitch on fire, we've watched these two for two days. It was all I could take. They weren't leading me anywhere and I was tired of waiting.

Lowering my hand, I twirl my bloody wedding ring, my body so tense I'm about to snap like a rubber band.

"Did you contact Bethany and tell her that Lake was there?" I demand, trying to put the pieces together. None of it makes sense. Beau messaged them that my wife was at the club, but their phones had nothing to Bethany. How did she know Lake was there?

These two have to be the ones who took Alex and Jenks out. They both said they were attacked with men wearing masks. Lords' masks. My security guards are Lords, but they're juniors this year. They've worked for me since I opened the club. I don't see why they'd want to double cross me now unless someone got to them. But then again, I didn't think that Beau would do that either and look what he did. They're all working for someone, but who?

I look over at Ryat, and he shakes his head at my silent question. Nothing on their cell phones other than the message from Beau. So they have to have more stashed somewhere. I'll go into the house of Lords after I finish them off and tear their rooms up until I find what I want.

Marco and Steve hang side by side, silently whimpering like little bitches. If you're going to piss off someone that you know will chase you down and torture you, you better be ready to get your ass fucking beat to death and take it like a man.

"Who the fuck took my wife?" I scream, my voice bouncing off the concrete walls and floor.

They stay silent as they swing from their chains. I begin to punch the one I'm standing in front of over and over. His body rocks back and forth from each blow. My body is vibrating with rage. I'm pretty sure it's the only thing keeping me going at this point. I'm afraid if I lie down, I'm going to pass out for days, and I can't afford to lose that much time.

I have to keep going. I have to keep demanding answers.

My bloody and sweaty fist slides across his chest, and I lose my balance. I fall to the floor and slowly get to my shaking legs.

I hear the sound of the chair scraping across the floor of Ryat's bunker as he gets to his feet. Since I no longer have the basement at Blackout, Ryat is letting me use the bunker that he has in the middle of the woods behind his house. I needed somewhere to bring them for the time being. I wanted answers, but it's getting me nowhere.

Looking over, I see Ryat now standing there, both of their cell phones in his hands. Turning, I make my way up the stairs, and he turns off the lights, shutting them in behind us. We walk silently through the dark woods to his house. The lights from it filter through the large floor-to-ceiling windows showcasing the backyard.

Once I get inside, I go straight upstairs and undress. When I step into the shower, my body shakes with madness. Placing my bloody hands on the wall, I bow my head. I want to fucking explode.

"Where are you, little darling?" I ask desperately as my throat closes up on me.

All I ask is for her to please be alive. I can handle anything else. I just need to get her back and we'll figure the rest out together.

Does she think I've given up on her? That I don't fucking care where she is or what is happening? Probably not because I haven't made her believe otherwise. The last time I was with her was different. I felt it, and I know she did too, but did I tell her? No. I just expected her to know.

She lies underneath me in our bed while I hover over her. My tongue licks my lips, wanting another taste of what my mouth just did between her legs. Fuck, she's so addicting, I want to devour her over and over again.

Her hands fall from my hair and lay down by her side. She's panting, eyes heavy, and perfect lips parted. "Tyson," she whispers, arching her neck.

My eyes drop to her collar, and I smile, knowing she belongs to me. What started out as a symbol of ownership is now an oath of her devotion. She'll never take it off. I may never turn it on again, but she'll wear it regardless.

"Yeah, little darling?" I lower my lips to her slick neck and lick up to her ear before biting down on it.

She cries out, and her arms wrap around my torso to run her nails down my back. I reach between us and grab the base of my dick. I spread her legs wide open with mine and push into her soaking wet cunt, loving the way she tenses underneath me when a gasp falls from her lips.

"Fuck, Lake." I groan, loving the way she lets me in. She's so fucking tight that it takes my breath away.

Her legs shake as they cling to me, and I lean up, my hand wrapping around her slender neck, and pin her down while I start to fuck her. I've never been the kind of guy who wants to make love to his wife, and Lake isn't the type of woman who wants her husband to go soft. She likes to be pushed to the point it's painful. Her body comes alive for me when she gives me full control, and I love pushing her to see how far I can take it.

FIFTY-FOUR

TYSON

I walk downstairs, fresh out of the shower. I've been staying with Ryat and Blakely. I think it's a way to keep an eye on me, but I don't want to go home. We hadn't been staying at our house for long but just the thought of going there, knowing I'll be without my wife, makes me ill. Having to see her clothes in our closet makes me sick to my stomach. Or having to lie in our bed by myself while her pillow smells like her shampoo. I can't do it.

So I've been here. Letting Blakely pretend to take care of me. She tries to get me to eat but I just push it around my plate while she watches like a hawk.

She never stops crying. I know she and Lake haven't gotten really close over the last couple of months but the fact that she's pregnant has also added to her emotional state.

I miss my wife, but I'm not going to sit around and cry about it. I'm going to make people bleed until I find her. I'll let myself feel something other than rage once she's in my arms again.

Entering their kitchen, I see a familiar face already sitting at the table. He pushes his full plate to the side. "I need to talk to you," Gavin states.

I sit down across from him, and I watch Blakely cover her mouth at the smell of the food.

"I spoke to the coroner yesterday. He said that out of the ten bodies he received from the fire, only one was burned beyond recognition."

"Which was?" I ask, but I already have an idea who he's going to say.

"Who they assumed to be Bethany," he answers.

I watched the cameras and saw my wife with Bethany in the cage before the fire started. They were still in there together when the fire took out the footage.

"Well, he just called me about thirty minutes ago with the DNA results."

I sit up straighter, knowing that the Lords put a rush order on it. They want answers just as much as I do. "And?"

"They confirmed it was her."

I bang my fisted hands on the table, making it rattle, and Blakely sucks in a deep breath. I was hoping that she was still alive. Bethany is the one who could lead me to my wife. But with her dead, I may never find Lake. *I'll never stop looking, little darling.* Which also means that whoever was in on this wanted Bethany dead so she couldn't tell anyone what really happened.

I thought this could be Lake's father, but I've had eyes on Frank since the fire took place, and there's nothing that would make me think he had a part in this. I've also had eyes on Miller. Colton, Alex, Finn, and Jenks are busy but haven't seen one fucking thing. So if they are involved, they've got someone else doing it for them. I'm afraid if I go after either one of them, they'll make sure she's dead if she's not already. As much as I want to kill them, I need them alive a little longer. Just until I find her. And if they had anything to do with this, they will burn as well.

"After Jimmy called me, I did some digging of my own," Gavin goes on. "The night of the fire, a Bethany Pace was admitted to a private hospital, the psychiatric ward about thirty minutes outside of town."

"I don't understand," Blakely says slowly. "You said DNA matched her body at the morgue."

My heart starts to hammer in my chest. Ryat sits up straighter. "Do you have access to this facility?" he asks Gavin.

"Legally? No. But I know someone on the inside, and he can get us in."

I jump up to my feet, the force making the legs of the chair scrape across the floor.

"I'll drive." Ryat jumps up as well. He's kissing his wife bye, and I'm already heading toward his garage with Gavin.

Ryat enters behind us and grabs Blake's keys to her SUV off the key ring.

FIFTY-FIVE

TYSON

We pull up to the back of the facility, and just like Gavin promised, a man waits for us. He lets us in.

"Where is she?" I demand, my heart is in my throat. I'm not sure what I'm more afraid of. It not being her, or it being her and seeing what kind of state she's in. Why here of all places? If they wanted her hidden, they could have found better places to hide her. That's what makes me think this is a trap, but it's not going to stop me from falling right into it. Or it's a way to keep me chasing my own tail. They don't want her found. No, they want her to themselves. My biggest fear is that she's already out of reach.

"She's down here." He points down the hallway that we enter. "Third door on the right."

I barge into the room to find a brunette lying in a bed. All she wears is a hospital gown that's open down the front. Her arms are down to her sides, brown leather cuffs wrapped around them to keep her restrained. Her legs are also pulled open with matching leather cuffs around her ankles. Another comes across her bare chest, pinning her down to the bed. She has bruises on her gorgeous face and a small tube down her nose. There's no blanket to cover her up.

"La-ke." My voice cracks when I run over to my wife. My hands cup her face, and her skin is ice cold. "Lake, little darling, I'm here. Wake up," I say, shaking her a little bit but nothing. Her eyes are closed, and I pry them open to see they're dilated. "What's wrong with her?" I demand, letting go and starting to remove the restraints around her wrists. Ryat works on her ankles. Gavin picks up her chart that is attached to the end of the bed.

"They've got her sedated," the guy who snuck us in answers.

"Why?" I snap, placing my arm under her back and lifting her limp body up to mine, trying to close the gown around her for what little warmth it may provide. "She's freezing," I bark out, and Ryat goes over to a cabinet. Opening the door, he finds a blanket and hands it to me to wrap around her.

"I don't know. I'm not on her case," the kid rushes out.

"Why didn't you help her?" I demand.

"I couldn't touch her." He shakes his head quickly. "She has a very strict team that was assigned to her when she arrived. I wasn't even aware of who she was until Gavin called me," he urges. "They've had someone watching over her most of the time."

"Get me the nurse who is here and assigned to her," I snap at him. He turns and runs out of the room.

I lay her lifeless body back down, tucking the blanket up underneath her and running my hands up and down her to warm her up. "I'm here, Lake. I'm here."

The door opens, and the guy returns with another man wearing blue scrubs. "You can't be in here," he growls, looking at her and then to us.

"Is her jaw broken?" Gavin asks.

My head swings to him. "Why the fuck would you ask him that?"

"Is her jaw broken?" he asks again, looking up at the man in scrubs.

"No," he finally answers, squaring his shoulders as if he's getting an attitude.

Gavin looks back down at her chart. "Then why is her jaw wired shut?"

"What?" I snap. I turn back to my wife and pull up her top lip, and my heart stops at what I see. It looks like braces. Individual brackets on her teeth with wires running up and down diagonally, keeping her upper teeth tied to her lower teeth.

"She was biting," the guy responds. "Drew blood."

I lift my head to look at him.

"Restraints?" Ryat growls. "She's sedated, for fuck's sake."

"She was combative." He lifts his chin.

I grab the nearest thing to me, which is a silver tray sitting on top of a rolling cart, and raise it, slamming it into the side of his face. "I'll show you combative."

He's thrown backward where he falls to the floor, landing on his knees, and I kick him in the face, blood splatters everywhere. I pick him up by his hair and slam his face into the end of the footboard, making it rattle. Falling to the floor, he cries, holding his now busted face.

I stand to my full height, breathing heavily. My adrenaline racing. Gavin walks over to Lake and looks at her mouth. "Can you get them off?" I ask, trying to calm my racing heart.

"Yeah. There doesn't seem to be any screws. It looks to only be on the outer surface of her teeth. But I'm going to need help."

"Meaning?" I shout, fisting my already busted knuckles.

"Meaning, I'm going to need an OR. A private one. I can't take her just anywhere if we don't want whoever dropped her off here to find out where she went."

"The Cathedral isn't an option." Ryat sighs.

There is a triage set up there underneath the building, but

Gavin is right. We can't take her anywhere that a Lord could possibly find out we have her. And any other hospital will have too many eyes on us. Even if Blackout was still a standing structure, the basement wouldn't be equipped with everything he'd need for her surgery. It barely had enough when she was stabbed.

"I know a place," I say, pulling out my cell and sending a text.

> ME: I need your help.

He responds immediately.

> Anything you need.

"Transport isn't going to be easy. We need to keep her sedated for now. If I wake her up, she'll be in a lot of pain," Gavin goes on. "Not to mention she can't open her mouth right now to talk. She'll get upset, and the last thing you want is her sobbing while her mouth is wired shut."

I kick the guy again just as he was trying to get to his feet.

"I can get you an ambulance," the man who helped sneak us in offers.

"No. They're equipped with GPS. That way dispatch can send the closest unit when an emergency occurs." Gavin shakes his head. "Ryat will just have to drive us." He looks at the guy. "I need a bag. Get me supplies. So that I can take what I need for her to get us there."

"Be right back." The kid runs out, obviously knowing what Gavin is going to need.

The guy on the floor moans in pain, and I kneel down beside him. "Who brought her in?" I demand.

"I don't—"

"Who the fuck brought her in?" I grip his hair and shove his face into the floor.

He spits out blood. "A man..." he cries. "He carried her in."

"Who the fuck was it?" I shout, my heart pounding and body vibrating with a rush of adrenaline. I want to slit his throat, but that would be too easy of a death for him. Plus, I need information, and right now he's my only option.

"I ... don't know."

"What do you know?"

"She was kicking and screaming. He forced her onto the bed while he had us restrain her. She was screaming for help."

I punch him again because I can. "Go on."

"She bit him. Deep enough that he needed stitches. He hit her so hard it knocked her out." He spits blood out onto the floor. "He demanded the doctor wire her jaw shut and sedate her. She's been out ever since."

"So you just did whatever he told you to do?" I punch him again.

He doesn't answer, instead, he leans forward, blood dripping from his now busted face.

"I'm going to remove her feeding tube and catheter," Gavin states, and I nod as if he was asking for my permission. A fucking feeding tube? She's been here what, seven days? My wife has lost a week of her life because they had her sedated and I couldn't find her.

The door opens and I look up, expecting to see the guy helping us return with a bag, but it's not him. Silence falls over the room as big brown eyes meet mine. She inhales sharply, looking over at Lake and then back to me. "Tyson." She holds her hands up.

I want to smile with satisfaction, but I can't. Not with the state my wife is in. Instead, I lunge at her, and she turns to exit but the door opens, forcing her to stop. I grab her dark hair and yank her back into the room. "What the fuck are you doing here?" I growl in her ear.

She struggles in my grip. "Let me go."

"Sure." I shove her into Ryat, and he spins her around, wraps his arm around her throat and holds her in place so I can look her in the eyes. "How did you know she was here?"

Her lips thin, and eyes narrow on me. "Fuck you," she spits out.

"Let her go," I order, and Ryat shoves her toward me. I wrap my hand around her throat, and squeeze. Harder than I should, but I can't stop. No one could pry my hand open right now. I want to see her eyes pop out of her head like a cartoon. "You'll pay for what you've done," I warn her.

She struggles. Her nails dig into my skin, cutting me. She can claw my eyes out for all I care. I'm not letting her get away with this. For what she's done to Lake. I will make sure every single person who knew what was happening to my wife pays. Doesn't matter if they had a hand in it or not.

FIFTY-SIX

TYSON

I hold my wife in my arms while she's unconscious. I know Gavin was right in keeping her sedated, but I want to see her eyes. Hear her say my name. Hold her and tell her that she's safe.

I need to know she's okay. I need to know what happened to her, no matter how bad it got.

"We're here," Ryat calls out.

I look up as we pull through the old wrought iron gates. He drives down the curvy two-lane road before we come to a stop in the circle drive.

Gavin and Ryat jump out of the SUV and open the back hatch for me. I crawl out with her in my arms, and a guy I've known since my freshman year at Barrington comes out, of the building with two other men and a gurney.

"A room is already ready for you," Saint states, looking at Gavin.

"Thank you. Bramsen," he calls to the kid we brought with us.

"What about her?" Ryat asks, yanking the girl out of the back by her hair. She tries to get free of his hold, but he jerks her head back so hard it makes her knees give out and she falls to the gravel.

I lay Lake on the gurney, and before I can even kiss her forehead, Gavin is already wheeling her inside. I turn to Saint. "I need a room."

He smiles. "Follow us."

Ryat yanks her up by her hair, and she screams into the gag. I walk over to her and pick her up, placing her over my shoulder and carrying her inside while she kicks and screams nonsense.

We make our way inside and down a hallway. Saint holds open a door, and we enter the cold concrete room.

I drop her squirming body to the floor, and she goes to roll away, but Saint places his boot on her back, holding her down to the floor. Leaning his weight on that foot, he places his elbow on his bent knee. "What did she do?"

"Let's find out," I say and reach down, yanking the tape from her mouth and pulling out the gag.

The sound of her sobbing echoes throughout the room. Like I give a fuck what she feels. Her tears aren't going to do shit. I sigh dramatically. "What am I going to do with you?"

"We could use a new toy." Kashton chuckles, entering the room. "Our latest one is pregnant and currently out of commission." He frowns, disappointed by that.

"I think Carnage would be too good for her," Ryat states.

"Oh, we can be very creative," Kashton tells him with a smirk.

She jumps to her feet, and I grab her hair, yanking her head back, making her scream. I forgot how much I like that sound until now. And I'm going to make her do it to the point she loses her fucking voice.

LAIKYN

I LOOK DOWN AT MY BLOODY HANDS, AND THEY SHAKE. THE lights flash, making my vision blurry, and I try to take in a calming breath while "Panic Room" by Au/Ra blares through the club.

I'm pushed back into the bars, and my hands come up to stop Bethany from knocking me down. "Beth—"

Her eyes are on mine, but they look ... vacant. "Bethany?" I holler over the music as her legs give out. My arms wrap around her, and I try to keep us both from going down. The cage isn't big enough for us to sit down in. "Bethany? Are you okay?" I feel more blood on her back, causing my grip to slip. "What the fuck is going on?"

The door to the cage is yanked open and a hand grabs my arm, causing me to release her. I'm removed from the cage and pushed down onto my hands and knees. I'm screaming, trying to figure out what the hell is happening, but no one can hear me over the music. A hand fists my hair, and I'm yanked up. The person stays behind me as they shove me through the crowd with their hand in my hair.

I take in a deep breath of fresh air once we're outside. "Let go of me." I try and fight them, but they let go of my hair to wrap an arm around my waist and pick me up off my feet, carrying me toward a white van parked in the alleyway on the side of the building.

I begin to scream for anyone to hear me. My hair is in my face. The arm around my waist tightens, and the doors on the back of the van open, then I'm shoved inside.

Someone sits on my back, pinning me down, and it restricts my air. It smells like urine and tobacco. So strong it makes me gag.

"Is it done?" someone barks.

"Yep. It'll be burned to nothing in no time," another answers.

I get up on my hands and knees, only to be kicked in the side, forcing me back down. I cough, my breath knocked out of my lungs. My hands are grabbed and brought behind my back, and something wraps around them.

"Turn her over," a man demands.

I'm shoved onto my back, my arms now underneath me, and I scream as loud as I can, hoping that someone on the other side of the van can help me. I'm thrashing around like a fish out of water, kicking and bucking the best I can to keep their hands off me as my heart races. Panic grips my chest, and it makes it harder to breathe.

"Keep her mouth open," the first guy orders.

I clamp my mouth shut but a hand grips my cheeks tightly, making me cry out as they're pinched, fingernails digging into my skin.

"That's it." Something is shoved into my mouth, placed behind my teeth, and I realize it's a gag of some sort. My head is lifted as the leather tightens on my cheeks before I feel them fasten it shut.

They let go of my head and I shake it, a sob racking my body as tears run down both sides of my face.

I'm yanked to a sitting position, and someone drops to the floor of the van to sit behind me. A hand grips my chin, forcing my head back. Saliva already runs down my open mouth. I go to pull my legs to my chest to protect my body, but he wraps his legs around my waist from behind, tightens them to the point it pushes mine down. He hooks his ankles over my thighs to hold me in place.

My wild hair covers half my face, and the strands are stuck to my tear-streaked skin. Some in my mouth.

A body comes to stand in front of us, a black boot on either side of my pinned legs. He kneels, and I try to yank my face away from their touch when they reach out to gently move the hair from my face, but the hand on my chin prevents me from going anywhere.

"Hey, Lake." Familiar eyes meet mine, making my heart skip a beat. His eyes drop to my chest, and he yanks on my leotard exposing my bare chest to the room.

I try to pull away, thrashing around on the floor of the van, but the guy behind me holds me in place. He reaches out and massages my breast. His fingers move to pinch my nipple and I scream into *the open mouth gag, spit flying from my mouth. "I've got so many plans for you. You're finally going to know your worth."*

"What about her collar? Want to remove it?" the guy behind me asks. "Cut it off?"

"No," he barks. "You try to cut it off, it's going to electrocute you and possibly kill her."

I whimper.

"We don't want that, do we, baby? Not yet, anyway." He hooks his finger into it and pulls my neck forward. The tip of his nose now touching mine. "We'll leave it for now."

How does he know about my collar? Has he been watching us? Seen Tyson use it on me?

His eyes lift to look at the guy who sits behind me. "Hold her down."

"I've got her." The guy chuckles in my ear. "She's not going anywhere." He releases my chin to wrap his arm around my throat, restricting my air, and I arch my neck to try and breathe.

The one in front of me drops to straddle my already pinned legs. He grips my cheeks and holds up a pair of pliers. I scream once again, my body trying to fight them but even I know there's no hope. "This is going to hurt, Lake. But you can thank your husband for it." Then he shoves them into my open mouth.

FIFTY-SEVEN

TYSON

"Tyson?" Gavin enters the room, and I jump to my feet. It's been three hours since we arrived, and I haven't been given any updates.

"What is it?" I rush out. The fact that I finally found her hasn't helped me. There's still so much that I need to know about the time she's spent away from me.

"I've removed the wires, but I found something interesting."

"What is it?"

"She had a tooth missing. It had been pulled."

"That's where I had her tracker." Never once had I thought that someone would think to look there. "Someone removed it."

"You put a tracker inside her tooth?" Kashton chuckles, nodding his head in approval. "That's pretty brilliant, man."

The Lords have put trackers on their chosens and Ladies for years. I wanted one where not everyone would think to look. I've seen women get a knife to their neck to have them removed.

"How did they know where it was?" Saint wonders.

"Good question." Kashton leans against the wall, crossing his arms over his chest. "Who all knew where you put it?"

"No one. Lake didn't even know." I run a hand through my hair. She was so confused as to why I took her to the dentist after our wedding, but I wasn't going to tell her what I was doing. I didn't want her to know where it was. Or that I had one on her at all. I wanted to see what my wife would do if given the chance at some freedom, and she never once tried to run from me.

"The dentist is dead." Ryat and I did our research the moment we found her bloody tooth in the alleyway of Blackout. There had been a fire. *How convenient*. The question is, how did they know to go there?

"Gavin?" The guy who helped us—Bramsen—runs down the hall to us and my pulse quickens at the concern on his face.

"Is she okay?" I step forward. Maybe thinking that something has happened.

He looks at Gavin and gives me his back to speak to him. Gavin turns back after nodding a few times. "Lake is pregnant," he tells me.

"Congratulations, man." Kashton slaps my back, but my eyes stay on Gavin.

He frowns and asks me, "Why do you look surprised?" Gavin looks over at Ryat and then back at me.

"You did a test?" I ask. "On Laikyn?"

"No," Bramsen answers. "Well, yeah. Not here, though. I remember them ordering one when she was brought into the psych ward. She was adamant that she was not pregnant, but the man insisted that it be done."

"It wasn't on her chart," Gavin tells him.

"I know. I had a friend of mine check before we left. I received the text while we were in surgery and just saw it." His eyes meet mine. "Your wife is, in fact, pregnant."

"Why wouldn't they put that on her chart? Why would it be a secret?" Kashton asks.

"She can't be." I shake my head in denial. It has to be a mistake. "She's on birth control. You put her on the shot."

"Who did?" Gavin asks.

"You did," I growl, tired of playing this damn game.

His frown deepens, and he steps into me. "I haven't seen her."

"I messaged you the morning of the wedding," I say, pulling my cell from my pocket. "Gave you the time and hotel and asked you to meet us there to administer the shot." I go to our conversation, and it's the last text between us.

He pulls his cell out and shows me our texting history. He does not have what my cell has. "Tyson, I didn't..."

"You didn't, but you sent the kid..." I trail off.

"Who?" Gavin demands.

I give him my back, running my hands through my hair. "FUCK!" That motherfucker tricked me. "Jackson," I growl.

"What does he have to do with this?" Gavin asks, knowing who I'm referring to.

"He was the one who showed up at the hotel and administered Lake's birth control," I snap. "He said you were in surgery and that you sent him." I even called Gavin the moment the kid told me he sent him. Gavin's phone went to voicemail, so I figured he was in surgery.

"I'm sorry, Tyson, but I did no such thing." Gavin shakes his head.

Somehow, Jackson intercepted Gavin's cell and made sure he gave Lake something else? What the fuck was in that shot? But why? And how the fuck did he know where we were? "Where is he? I want him here. Right now!"

"I'll call him." Gavin scrolls through the numbers in his cell, trying to find Jackson's. "I'll ask him to meet me here."

"He'll know it's a setup," I say and look at Kashton. No one comes to Carnage to *hang out*. And the Lords know that the Spade brothers have their own medical staff. So why would they need Gavin here?

Kashton pops his knuckles. "Tell him you need help, and you're sending him a car. I'll go pick his ass up."

Gavin nods and walks away, giving us his back while placing his phone to his ear. I step into Bramsen. "Does my wife know?"

He shakes his head. "As far as I know, she was already sedated by the time they got the results."

LAIKYN

I'M COUGHING UP BLOOD. THE SPIT FLIES FROM MY MOUTH AS the van comes to a stop. I'm pulled from the floor where I was shoved facedown after they ripped my tooth out of my mouth. It hurts so bad; I can't stop sobbing. Which just makes the throbbing worse.

"Let's go, bitch." My hair is grabbed, and I'm yanked from the van. I'm tossed over a shoulder and carried away as I fight the bastard but am unsuccessful.

I'm thrown onto a gurney, and I kick and scream as I'm pushed down a hallway. The bright lights that hang from the ceiling pass quickly as if they're running. A hand reaches down to press on my chest, and I lift my head to bite down on it. They shouldn't have removed the gag.

That grants me a slap to the face so hard my eyes fall shut. "I want her sedated," he barks out as I'm pushed into a room. "Right now. Knock her the fuck out."

I'm shoved over onto my side, my hands all of a sudden free, and I use them to push off the bed. I run for the door, but it's quickly closed, and I'm picked up off my feet. I'm screaming at the top of my lungs while I see people just standing around watching this man throw me down.

He gets up on the bed, straddling me, and pins my hands down by my head. "Fucking sedate her! Now! And where the fuck are the restraints?"

"No. No. No." I can't fight them off if I'm sedated and restrained. Where is Tyson? Was he in the fire? I saw it. The club was burning when we finally drove away in the van. I can still hear the screams coming from inside. Or maybe it was me that I heard when they yanked out my tooth. Arching my back, I suck in a deep breath. "TYSON!"

Someone else grabs my wrists, letting him release them. Instead, he wraps both hands around my neck and starts to choke me. I buck my hips, thrashing underneath him from side to side, but my arms are secured down to my sides. Then I feel hands on my legs, pinning them down as well.

"You know..." He lowers his face to mine. "He might have actually done me a favor. You may be worth something pregnant."

No. I'm not pregnant. Tyson wouldn't let that happen. I don't want that to happen. And this is the exact reason why. No one is coming to save me. No one even knows I'm alive.

He shoves my head into the mattress before letting go and gets up off me. I gasp, sucking in breaths, my lungs burning.

I yank on the restraints, realizing they've got me tied down to the bed, and any piece of hope I had that I might escape this is smothered. My chest so tight he might as well be sitting on top of me again.

"I want her sedated until I say otherwise. And get that pregnancy test done." He barks out orders, and people run in and out of the room.

"I'm... not..." Deep breath. "Pregnant."

He leans over my bed and grips my tear-streaked cheeks. "You better pray to God that you are. Otherwise, you're no use to me." His hand drops to my chest and it reminds me that I'm still topless.

431

He grabs my breast painfully before slapping me across the face, making me cry out. "A worthless bitch is a dead bitch."

His hand lowers to my black booty shorts and I can't fight him as he cuts them off me. I'm sobbing when his fingers move my underwear to the side. "I guess if the results come back negative, I can fuck you until you're pregnant." He kisses my tear-streaked face when his fingers enter me. "Either way, I'm going to make you useful."

His lips move to the side of my lips to kiss me again, and I lean into him, sinking my bloody teeth into his flesh. The last thing I hear is his scream before his fist hits my face.

THERE'S A BEEPING SOUND IN THE BACK OF MY HEAD THAT won't stop. It's driving me crazy. Among other things. Like the throbbing in my mouth. My cheeks hurt, and my teeth ache. Is that even a thing? Was I punched a few more times once I was knocked out? It's like a constant feeling of pressure, gripping my face.

"Lake?" I hear my name off in the distance. "Lake, little darling."

My heavy eyes open, and I flinch.

"That's it, Lake. Open your eyes. Look at me, Laikyn."

I see shapes of various sizes, but they're blurry. And then dots, bright floating dots that seem to move every time I blink. The room spins so fast it's like I'm rolling down a hill and can't focus on anything.

Something warm is on my face. Hands maybe? My head falls to the side, and I swallow, making me flinch. My tongue feels heavy. Why does my head hurt so bad but everything else feels so numb? Is it because I'm tied down? Is that why I can't move my body?

"Look at me, Lake."

I blink again or maybe my eyes were already closed and they

open. A familiar set of baby-blue eyes comes into focus. Mine instantly start to sting as my breath catches in my heavy chest. If I'm dreaming, this is the best dream I've ever had.

"Hey." Tyson leans down and gently kisses my forehead. "Don't cry, Lake."

I sniff.

He lets go of my face and he crawls onto the bed with me. He places an arm underneath my back, and I turn onto my side, not caring how bad it hurts, and bury my face into his shirt. His scent envelops me. "I'm ... sorry," I manage to say, my throat tightening and my hands gripping the material, but I can feel how weak I am.

"You're safe, Lake. You're safe." He rubs my back, and I begin to sob. "I'm right here. I've got you."

The act makes my head throb worse. That headache intensifying. But I feel that dream start to slip. A wave washing me out to sea, pulling me from him. I try to hold on but it pulls me under, and I'm unable to swim fast enough to break the surface.

FIFTY-EIGHT

TYSON

She cried herself back to sleep, or it could have been the drugs still in her system. Either way, I was thankful for it. Lake needs as much rest as she can get for her and the baby.

Baby.

She's pregnant. I can't even tell her I'm happy about it. Not yet. We have no clue if the baby is alive, and I don't want to tell her anything until we know. And I won't know much until I've got Jackson in my hands, telling me what the fuck he did and why he did it.

Why would someone want my wife pregnant? It can't be the Lords doing. I gave up my ranking, but if I had a son, he would still have a high ranking. He would fall back in line with my bloodline, and then add the Minson blood, and he'd be powerful. Hell, even if we had a daughter, she'd be placed with the highest-ranking Lord there is when she's of age. That's the exact reason why Lake didn't want kids. She doesn't want to bring a child into a world where their life will be dictated by the Lords.

But I don't see the Lords setting that up. It would benefit them, of course, but they didn't know who I was going to marry. So why would they force a child? It doesn't make any sense.

A soft knock sounds on the door before it opens, and Ryat enters. He looks at my sleeping wife in my arms and then at me. "Kash is back."

I go to get up but pause, not wanting to leave her.

"Go." Bramsen enters. "I'll stay with her."

He's proven himself to be helpful, and I need answers. So I unwrap myself from her arms and stand up off the bed, covering her up with a blanket. Walking over to him, I get in his face. "If anything happens to her, I'll carve your eyes out with a spoon and then force them down your throat. Do you understand?"

Honestly, there's no safer place for her to be right now. No one fucks with Carnage. Saint, Kashton, and Haidyn keep this place in line.

He nods quickly, giving me his word. "I promise, I'll protect her, sir."

Exiting the room, I follow Ryat down the hallway to an elevator. We take it down to the basement. I was just here recently, dragging Sin's dumb ass out of it. But I get it. Why he'd sacrifice himself for his wife. I'd do it too without thought.

Ryat pushes a door open, and I find the guy standing in the middle of the room with his back to me. "Why the fuck are we at Carnage?" he demands, looking at Gavin.

"They needed our help," Gavin lies to him.

"He fucking punched me." Jackson points over at Kashton, who leans against the concrete wall, crossing his arms over his chest and smirking.

The Spade brothers live to fuck people up. It's what they do best.

"That's the least of your worries," I say, and he spins around.

His face instantly falls. "Fu—"

I punch him in the face before he can even finish the word, knocking him back a few steps.

"Just wait…" He places his hands out in surrender, and I punch him again. This time, he falls to his knees. "I can explain," he rushes out before gasping.

Picking him up by the back of his shirt, I slam his face into the concrete wall and hold out my hand to Ryat. He places a pair of handcuffs in it, and I place them on Jackson. Yanking him from the wall, I spin him around. "What the fuck did you give my wife?" I yell in his face.

"Noth—"

I punch him again, and his head snaps back. He falls to the floor, blood pouring from his busted face. I press my boot into his neck and lean on it, applying weight. "What did you give my wife?"

"Gon-adotropin," he spits out.

Removing my boot from his neck, I kneel next to him. "What the fuck is that?"

"It's…" Cough. "A hormone to help you ovulate."

I stand, and he rolls over onto his side to alleviate the pressure on his arms cuffed behind his back. "What about the morning after pills you gave her?"

He shakes his head and I fist my hands. "Why and who wants my wife pregnant?" I demand.

"I got a call." He coughs as blood flies from his busted lips. "To go to the Minson Hotel."

"From who?"

"Frank Minson." He coughs some more and my body tenses. "He was in a panic. Said that Luke was missing and that he had been informed you were to wed Laikyn."

Ryat's eyes are on me, but I keep mine on Jackson. "Go on."

Sucking in a deep breath, he adds, "He told me to make sure you knocked her up."

"He hates you," Kashton speaks. "Why would he want you to get her pregnant?"

History repeats itself. She will die in your arms just like her sister did is what the fucking bastard said in my basement after Lake was stabbed. I wasn't sure what he meant until now.

Senior year at Barrington University

I SIT AT THE METAL TABLE INSIDE THE INTERROGATION ROOM *at the police station. They brought me in and left me here for three hours now. My hands are cuffed to the table, and I'm still covered in Whitney's blood. My T-shirt now dry and stuck to my skin.*

Big watery blue eyes keep flashing in my mind. The look on Lake's pale face as she stared at me with horror that I killed her sister. As if I was too good of a person to do that. I mean, I've done it before, so why not now? What makes her sister so special? I didn't love her. I was told to make it look like I loved her. It had to be public and over the top. Borderline obsessive.

The door bursts open, and my father enters followed by our family attorney.

"Murder?" he demands. "Jesus Christ, Tyson. It's all over the news. Do you have any idea what the fuck you've done to our family name? To my reputation?"

I remain silent.

"Call them?" he commands to our attorney. "Call the fucking Lords and get him out of this mess."

Hansen removes his cell from his pocket, dials up a number and then places it on speakerphone. He lays the phone between my cuffed wrists as the ringing on the other end fills the small room. "Hello?"

"Get my son out of here," my father snaps.

The Lord clears his throat. "It would be wise for you to leave the room, Senator."

"I'm not going—"

"Get out." I interrupt my father.

His eyes narrow on mine. "Ty—"

"Get the fuck out!" I shout, not in the mood for his shit. I don't need him here. I was eventually going to get one phone call, and it sure as fuck wasn't going to be to him.

He turns and exits, slamming the door. "What do you want?" I ask, getting to the point.

"Son, you've put yourself in a tight situation." He doesn't ask me if I killed her, and I don't waste my breath telling him I didn't.

"That's rich, considering you're the ones who put me here," I grind out.

Silence follows before he speaks. "I'm not sure what you mean..."

"You promised us protection. And you failed. Both of us." The Lords are supposed to protect their own. As long as we do as we're told, we're rewarded. That's why we take our oath. If they were to turn their backs on us, there would be no society. We would outnumber the founders and burn the whole thing down. We'd destroy them.

"I don't know—"

"Quit fucking lying!" I shout, yanking on the cuffs. "Either get me out or let them book me."

"I don't believe you," I decide to say to Jackson, not wanting him to know how close to the truth he is. I go to kick him.

He rushes out, making me pause, "Mr. Minson threatened Luke with his life. He was not allowed to fuck her after the wedding."

I frown. "That doesn't make any sense. That's why he gave

Luke the room." It was to prove she had remained a virgin. She needed to bleed for him.

He shakes his head. "No. He gave Luke the room to make sure she stayed a virgin."

"How would he have known?" Ryat wonders.

"Cameras," I answer. Lake told me that Miller had mentioned her getting off on my cock. "He had cameras in there."

"So her father watched you fuck his daughter? That's pretty fucked up." Kashton shakes his head in disgust.

"Why was her virginity so important?" Ryat asks.

"I ... don't know." He begins to cry, knowing he's not giving me enough information.

FIFTY-NINE

TYSON

My wife lies in her bed, sleeping. I sit on the couch while Ryat stands next to me. He's typing away on his phone to his wife while I stare at mine. Ryat puts his phone away and looks down at me. "What's the plan?"

"She needs to stay here," I say, watching her readjust herself in bed. She's still pretty out of it for the most part. We arrived six hours ago. And although I have some people to torture before I kill, I want to be here with her when she wakes up again. I lower my voice to make sure she doesn't hear me. "They confirmed her pregnancy at the hospital. That won't stay quiet for long."

"You think no one will look for her here?" he inquires.

"I think it's the safest place for now."

He looks over at her closed door and then back at me. "You trust them?"

I nod. The Spade brothers do some fucked-up shit here, but they wouldn't harm my wife. Or my unborn child. "Yes."

"We bring you an update on the fire that claimed the life of ten people earlier this week at Blackout," a reporter says on the TV.

Ryat grabs the remote and turns up the volume a little bit for us to hear. "Remember when we showed this clip…"

It goes to the night of the fire, and reporters are already littering the parking lot along with all the first responders. My Bentley comes squealing into the parking lot. It shows me running toward the building. Then the cops knock me down. We fight. I'm in handcuffs. Then it skips over to me pushing the cops off me and shooting one of them.

"We can now confirm that Laikyn Grace Crawford, Tyson Crawford's wife—the only living daughter to Frank Minson—was, in fact, inside the club when the fire took place and was pronounced dead at the scene. But no official report has been released as to how or where the fire started."

Ryat turns it off. "So that was their plan?" He snorts. "To make the world think she died. A horrific death at that? Burning?"

"Seems so." *It's worked before.*

"But why?" he continues. "How does her death benefit anyone?"

"It's not about benefiting *them*. Whoever it is wants to take her from me." *It has everything to do with me and nothing to do with her.*

"You think it's her father?" he asks. "We knew he'd retaliate. If not him, then who else could it be?"

A sniff gets my attention, and I turn around to see Lake sitting up in the bed, her watery eyes on the blank TV. Slowly, they meet mine, and the first tear falls from her bottom lashes, rolling down her bruised cheek. "Luke," she whispers.

"What does he have to do with it?" Ryat asks.

Her eyes meet mine. "He was the one who pulled me out of Blackout."

We both stiffen, glancing at one another. "Luke was there? At Blackout?" I clarify. *No. She's not remembering clearly. It couldn't have been him. It had to have been her father.*

"Thought you had guys on him?" Ryat asks me.

"They've been searching ever since the day of the wedding. He's been MIA," I say. Ryat doesn't know that Colton, Alex, Finn, and Jenks work for me. He knows I've hired some men to do my dirty work, but that's as far as his knowledge goes. When they never came up with anything, I pulled them from the surveillance.

"I thought you killed him." She speaks softly, her heavy eyes dropping to her hands in her lap.

I sigh, wishing I would have. I had a hunch he'd lead me to something important. I was wrong.

"Why would he wait so long?" Ryat goes on. "You two have been married for months now." He looks at her. "Did he say anything to you?"

She nods softly. "There were two of them. But I never saw the second guy. He stayed behind me." Her shoulders start to shake. "Luke dragged me out of the club and threw me in a van. They gagged me, where I couldn't close my mouth, and pulled out my tooth."

My hand tightens on hers. I've been going crazy wanting to know what happened to her while she was away from me. Now that I watch her break down reliving it, I want to tell her to stop.

"Said I could thank my husband for that." Deep breath.

My chest tightens.

"Then they took me ... somewhere." She looks around, as if to see if it's the same place she remembers. "Luke carried me inside while the other stayed behind. He said that I better hope you knocked me up. That I'd finally know my worth. I told him that wasn't possible."

I haven't had the chance to tell her she's pregnant yet. I look at Ryat, and he frowns. "So both her father and Luke wanted you to knock her up? Seems fishy to me," Ryat states.

"What?" she asks, wide-eyed. "My father wanted me to get pregnant too?" Her eyes meet mine.

"So it seems," I say vaguely, not really believing anything Jackson has to say right now. But some of what he said did make sense. Miller knew things he would have only known if he had been there in the very room with us. But Jackson also said that Frank had only given Luke that room to make sure she remained a virgin. And then sent him to give her fake birth control. So what is it? Stay a virgin or get pregnant?

She buries her face into her hands, and I crawl onto the bed with her. Wrapping my arms around her shaking shoulders, I pull her into my body while I rub her back.

Her sobbing fills the room, and my chest tightens. The world thinks she no longer exists. I'm not sure if that's what they had planned or if that was just what they wanted me to think. Either way, I'm going to find out.

LAIKYN

THE PAIN ISN'T AS BAD AS IT WAS LAST TIME I OPENED MY eyes, but I still feel sluggish and weak. I'm warm, something hard pressed against me.

Opening my eyes to the dimly lit room, I blink a few times before I realize it's Tyson in bed with me. His arms curled around my body. Taking a quick look around, I see Ryat has left us alone.

I snuggle into my husband and close my eyes once more, trying to keep the tears at bay. I didn't think I'd ever see him again. Or anyone, for that matter. I'm flooded with emotions. I sniff, burying my face into his T-shirt, hoping I don't wake him, but when I feel his lips on my forehead, I know I've done just that. "You're okay, little darling," his soft voice says.

It's like a dam, breaking and I can't hold the tears back anymore.

"I've got you," he whispers. "I'm here."

"You ... found me," I choke out.

How did he find me? How did he save me? I was sure I was going to die. Or pray that Luke would just kill me. I couldn't live a life without Tyson. I wouldn't want to know a life without being his wife. Even if that's all I am for the rest of my life, that's enough for me. His Lady.

"I would have never stopped looking, Lake," he assures me. "Never."

"Thank you," I whisper, swallowing the knot in my throat.

"Don't thank me, little darling. It's my job to protect you and I failed you. I'm the one who's sorry." His chest vibrates against my cheek at his words. "It'll never happen again."

I lift my face from his shirt, and his baby-blue eyes meet mine. He cups my wet cheek, and his lips gently touch mine in an innocent kiss, but it makes my breath catch. Pulling away, his eyes are back on mine. "I love you, Lake."

"I love you." My lips tremble as I say the words, but they're the truth. I'm in love with this man who forced me to marry him. The only regret I have is that I wish he would have made me do it earlier in my life so I could have spent more time with him. Because even I know this isn't over. Luke is out there looking for me, and when he realizes Tyson saved me, he'll come after both of us. And what are the odds we both survive?

I'M SITTING UP IN BED WHILE TYSON SITS NEXT TO IT, TYPING away on his cell. It's been ringing nonstop since he turned it on a couple of hours ago. I'm finally feeling better. My eyes aren't as heavy as they were, and my head isn't pounding as bad. Just a dull ache now, but my jaw is still sore. Tyson explained to me what had happened and that Gavin removed the brackets from my mouth. Thankfully, it didn't damage my teeth. They should start feeling better soon, and he's bringing in a dentist to replace the tooth Luke removed.

Fortunately, your mouth is the fastest healing part of your body.

"Where are we?" I ask Tyson. He hasn't offered up the information, so I'm not sure if I'm allowed to know or not. I've lost count how many days we've been here. I feel like I slept through at least a few of them.

"Carnage," he answers, his eyes meeting mine.

My eyes widen. "Tyson—"

"The Spade brothers are friends of mine, Lake," he assures me, his eyes going back to his cell as it rings again. He answers it, and I lie back, letting out a long breath.

The Spade brothers—although not blood-related—are Lords. Well, they were once. I'm not sure if they still have a title. I've heard talk over the years that Carnage is where you come to die. It's a prison of sorts. They torture you. It's equivalent to an animal playing with its food before it eats it.

I guess I can see why Tyson brought us here. No one would have the balls to come here and check. The question is, how long do we have to hide out?

"Tyson?" Gavin asks, entering the room.

My husband looks up and nods once before ending his call. "Give us a second," he tells Gavin who nods and exits.

I look over at Tyson. "What's going on?" I ask him.

He sits next to me on the bed and takes my hand.

I sit up straighter. "What's wrong?" I ask, my heart now racing. His face is a mask, hiding his true thoughts from me. I hate when he does this. "Tyson—"

"You're pregnant," he interrupts me.

"I'm sorry," I say, my throat closing up on me.

"Lake," he growls, both hands grabbing my face this time. "Why are you apologizing?"

446

"You don't want children." The first tear runs down my cheek, and he wipes it away with his thumb.

"You're right," he states, and my chest tightens. "I didn't want children"—he moves closer to me, his face now inches from mine—"with just anyone."

I sniff.

"But you? You, Laikyn Grace Crawford, are my wife. And you having our child would be the greatest gift in this world."

I sniff again, and fresh tears fall from my bottom lashes. He leans in, kissing my lips gently, but I don't kiss him back.

His hands drop from my face to my stomach. "Don't be sorry, Lake, and don't doubt that I want this child. I want it just as badly as I want you. Okay?"

I nod my head, unable to speak. My throat closes in on me. Luke got his way. But how? Had they been planning this since day one? I want to be excited that I'm pregnant with a man who I love and loves me back, but to be pregnant now? It just proves what I have been trying to avoid. This is supposed to be a special moment in our lives, and once again, someone is trying to take it away from us.

"I'm going to get Gavin," he tells me. "He's going to do an ultrasound to check on the baby."

Getting up, he makes his way over to the door and opens it to see Gavin standing in the hallway waiting. He enters and gives me a soft smile that I can't force myself to return.

I understand what we're doing. He's going to check and see if the baby is okay. I'm shaking. It's funny, I've been so against bringing children into our world that now I'm afraid I won't be able to give my husband something he wants. What if something is wrong with our child? What if something I did hurt the baby? I chose to go into Blackout and work that night. It's my fault if something is wrong.

Gavin pulls up the gown that I wear while making sure the

blanket stays down around my waist. "Normally, this early into pregnancy, they'd do a transvaginal ultrasound, but we'll try it this way first," he tells us. "If there's no fetal heartbeat, we'll try vaginally."

Tyson takes my hand, and I grab it while he places his other one of top of ours. Cold gel is placed on my stomach and on the end of the wand.

I lean back and take in a deep breath as he places the wand on my stomach and the screen on the monitor starts to show a black-looking distorted video. He presses a few buttons on the keyboard, and then I hear it.

The sound of a heartbeat has me tearing up.

"Well, that's interesting," Gavin says.

"What is it?" Tyson asks, leaning forward. His pretty baby-blue eyes are glued to the screen. There's fear in his voice that I've never heard before.

Gavin looks over at us. "Hear that?" He turns the sound up louder, and the swishing sound fills the room.

"It's a heartbeat," Tyson states, looking at him.

Gavin smiles. "It's *two* heartbeats." He points at two different spots on the monitor. "Congratulations, Mr. and Mrs. Crawford. You're having fraternal twins. I'd say you're about seven weeks along. Maybe eight. Not surprised, though. Jackson confessed to giving you pregnancy enhancement hormones. It could result in multiple pregnancies or it could have no effect whatsoever. No way to tell, really. And the fact that you only received one dose..." He trails off, watching the monitor.

"What?" My wide eyes go to my husband, and he gives me a sympathetic smile with a reassuring hand squeeze. His way of silently telling me he'll fill me in later.

Gavin pulls the wand from my stomach. "Everything sounds and looks good, but I'm no OB. I'd suggest you see one as soon as possible. I have one I can suggest if you'd like."

"They're okay?" Tyson asks once more.

Gavin nods. "I'll leave you two alone. Get some rest, Lake." He pats my arm. "You're going to need lots of it."

He exits the room, and Tyson's eyes meet my watery ones. A big smile lights up his face, and he leans in, kissing my forehead tenderly as the tears flow down my face.

Taking my hand in his, he holds it, and I frown when I look down at them. "Why did you take my wedding ring off?" I ask.

The smile drops off his face, and he looks at my hand. "I didn't."

SIXTY

LAIKYN

A week I've been stuck in this room. Away from the world with nothing but silence. Any time I turn on the TV, I see my picture plastered all over it. Along with the other nine that passed away that night.

People have gone to what's left of Blackout and started shrines with flowers, pictures, and candles. I just want to scream that I'm alive and that someone tried to kill me.

If I'm being honest with myself, I think it was my father. I wouldn't put it past him. He's a man of action, and Ryat was right. My husband publicly humiliated him. His name. Degraded my family.

Why kill Tyson when he can just kill me? I'm the easier target. The trash that needs to be taken out. I'm the child who betrayed the Minson name by falling in love with the enemy. But I can't figure out why my father hates him so much. I don't believe that Tyson killed my sister. But what I don't understand is why would my father send Luke to do the job? Why not have the balls to kill me himself? Maybe it's my mother. He doesn't want my mom to think he killed her daughter.

I look up when the door opens, and my husband enters. He's wearing a plain white T-shirt and jeans with a pair of Nike's. It's weird seeing him so casual. Tyson always dresses in slacks and button-ups when working at Blackout. Ryat brought us some clothes last night, along with new cell phones.

I was surprised that it actually had Blakely's number in it. That he's going to let me talk to his wife. I guess since I'm officially dead, I'm no longer a threat.

Tyson comes to stand next to me and lowers a tray to the bed. "Hungry?" he asks, leaning down and gently kissing my forehead.

"No," I say honestly, staring at the pudding cup. My eyes fall to my hand, and I numbly run my thumb over where my ring once was. It's gone. Luke took it. I know it's just a ring, but I want it back. Why take it? Just because I don't have a ring doesn't mean I'm not married. He did it out of spite, and I hate him even more for it.

Tyson frowns but doesn't push it.

My collar is also gone but Tyson explained that he removed it for my surgery. He also made it sound like I'll never wear it again. I've been stripped of two things that I never wanted but now don't want to live without.

"Tyson?" A guy pokes his head into the room. His bright-green eyes go from mine to my husband's. The man is covered in ink, from his jawline to his knuckles. He wears a long-sleeve T-shirt with the sleeves rolled up, but you can tell there's more under the material. I've never met him, but I know his name is Saint. "We've got an issue that needs your attention."

"What is it?" I ask, wondering what he means. Ryat comes and goes; Tyson hasn't left, and these three guys come in and out of my room to talk to him privately. I know my husband is keeping secrets from me but why?

"I'll be right back," Tyson tells me, avoiding my question. He then kisses my forehead before turning and exiting the room.

I jump up and put my shoes on that sit by the bed. I'm going crazy in here, and I'm tired of being in the dark. I can only spend so much time taking a shower and watching TV. I deserve to know what's going on and how long this will be my new life.

Opening the door, I catch sight of the back of them walking side by side down the hallway. I wait for them to turn a corner before I gently shut my door and follow them. Once in the hallway, I take a quick look around, and it doesn't look anything like a hospital outside of my room.

It's cold but brightly lit. Lights hang from the ceiling as I run down the hallway. Coming up to the corner, I turn and slowly look around to see them getting into an elevator. I see it's lit up to go down. I wait for it to close and then run down to the staircase next to it.

I make my way down to the lower level, noticing we were on level two. I gently push the door open and let out a long breath. I can see it puff out from my mouth. The temperature is even colder down here, making me shiver.

They push open a door and enter a room. I tiptoe and come up to it. There's a window at the top, and I try to lean up on my tiptoes to see through it, but it's frosted. "Dammit," I hiss.

When I go to turn the knob, a hand grabs my arm, making me scream out as I turn around.

"You look lost," a man says to me. He's one of them. Kashton is one of the three Spade brothers. He's also covered in tattoos. "What were you doing?" he asks.

I jerk my arm out of his hold. "I'm looking for my husband." I had overheard Ryat ask Tyson if he thought I was safe here, and he said yes. After I watched him on TV fighting off the cops in the parking lot of Blackout when the club was on fire, I know my husband wouldn't put me in any danger. Not now.

Kashton smirks and reaches up. I gasp, thinking he's going to pin me against the door, but instead, he uses his hand to open it. I fall backward into the room.

"Let me go," the man growls, and the hairs on the back of my neck stand up at the sound of his voice. I've heard it before. Recently.

"You're not going anywhere," Tyson tells him, shaking his head.

"You can't keep me here forever." The guy circles around, watching Saint and my husband as if one of them is about to pounce on him.

"Not until you tell me everything you know," Tyson informs him.

"I don't know shit!" he screams, the sound bouncing off the concrete walls.

"That's not true." I step forward, speaking.

At the sound of my voice, Tyson's eyes meet mine. They're cold. Unforgiving. They narrow on me as if I'm the one in the wrong here. "What do you mean, Lake?" my husband demands.

"That's him." I point at the guy slowly stepping back into the corner of the room. Wide eyes on mine.

"Yes, the nurse who pretended to give you a birth control shot," Tyson snaps at me.

I shake my head. "No. I mean, yes, but..." Swallowing, I look back at the guy. "He was the one who helped Luke." It was loud in the club when Luke dragged me out of it. I was confused, my ears ringing. I didn't recognize the guy's voice in the van then, but now I do. Maybe because less time has passed since I was with him last. But I know for a fact it was him.

Tyson turns to face him, taking a step closer. "You were with Luke?" The guy that I remember by the name of Jackson doesn't answer. "You've been here for a week, and you didn't think to tell me that you helped kidnap her?" he screams.

He goes to run out of the room, but Saint grabs the back of his

454

T-shirt as Tyson steps in front of him, punching him in the face and knocking him to the ground.

"How did you know where her tracker was?" he commands, hovering over him. One shoe on either side of Jackson's head. "Huh? How the fuck did you know, you son of a bitch?" He steps away only to drag him up by his hair and slam his face into the wall. I watch the blood splatter before he falls to his knees.

"I waited ... downstairs in the lobby." He takes a deep breath. "After I administered the shot ..." Blood pours from his face, and his shaking hands come up to wipe it away the best he can. "I followed you guys to Walls—"

"So you killed him," Tyson growls. "Went in after we left, got the information you needed, and killed him."

"No." He shakes his bloody face. "I just reported what I saw."

"To who?" my husband demands. "Luke?"

He nods, sniffing.

"Was it really Frank who called and told you to administer a fake birth control shot?" Jackson remains silent, and my husband kicks him, forcing Jackson to roll across the floor. "Fucking answer me," he roars.

"Noooo." Jackson begins to cry, holding his bloody face.

"Who the fuck was it?" he asks through gritted teeth.

"Luke."

"If Luke knew where her tracker was, then why did he wait so long to go after her?" Saint wonders, and Jackson just shakes his head, not knowing the answer to that.

TYSON

HE WANTED TO MAKE SURE I KNOCKED HER UP. BUT I KEEP that to myself.

Fucking finally, I know who is behind all of this. I figured that's who it was, but now I've got somewhat of a confession. *It's enough.*

I grab my wife's hand and exit the room with Saint right behind us. He locks the sorry piece of shit inside.

"You think they're working together?" Saint asks, referring to our other prisoner that we have in the room next to his.

I shrug. "Possibly."

"Who?" my wife asks, but I can't tell her. Not yet.

Saint looks over my shoulder, and I see Ryat coming down the hallway to us with a phone and car keys in his hand. "Found it," he states. I've had him searching high and low the past few days. "But it's dead."

Of course, it is. Nothing is ever fucking easy.

"I'll charge it in my office," Saint speaks.

"I'm going to take Lake back to her room, then I'll meet you two in there." I pull her down the hallway to the elevator.

She remains silent as I help her into the bed and pull the covers up to her chin. Rolling over, she gives me her back and sighs heavily. I know she's mad at me. She just helped me identify Jackson as Luke's accomplice, but I'm still keeping secrets from her. It's best this way.

I exit her room, giving her a second to take everything in. She's got too many questions that I can't answer. But I can show her. That requires proof. I already know Lake isn't going to believe what I say. And why should she?

Walking into the Spade brothers' office, I see Saint sitting behind his desk, the phone lying on it plugged in. Ryat is over on the couch, typing away on his.

Going over to Saint's desk, I plop down in the chair, and the picture on his desk catches my attention. It's of him, Haidyn, and Kashton with his chosen back when he was a senior. They were all four really close. He loved her more than he loved anything else on this planet. But the Lords had other plans for her. I tried my best to help her, but in the end, I just hurt them all even more.

I guess you can say that she's the one who got away. It turned their lives upside down and into the men they are now. "Still no luck?" I ask.

He looks up at me and follows my eyes to the picture. "None." Sitting back in his seat, he crosses his tatted arms over his chest and looks at Ryat, probably wondering how much he knows about their story. I don't think he knows anything, though. If he does, he hasn't told me.

"One of these days," I assure him.

He chuckles softly. "Even if we found her today, we wouldn't be able to collect her." His eyes go to the door and then back to mine. "The guys aren't ready. She'd be dead in a matter of hours."

I have no doubt the Spade brothers would tear Saint's chosen in half if ever given the chance. "And you?" I question. "Would you be okay with that?"

Saint looks away once more, a tic in his jaw. "The punishment would fit the crime," he states. "We're all about punishment here at Carnage."

I snort, knowing exactly what he means. Picking up the cell, he hands it to me, and I press the button to turn it on, seeing it light up. I begin to go through the messages and smile at him.

"Find what you wanted?" he asks.

"Yeah. Exactly what I wanted." My eyes meet his. "I'm going to need another favor." Then I look at Ryat. "From both of you."

SIXTY-ONE

LAIKYN

I wake to a loud noise. Sitting up in my bed, I notice it's dark in my room. Not a single light is on. It was when I closed my eyes earlier. "Tyson?" I call out, blinking to get my eyes to adjust.

Getting out of bed, I place my hands out in front of me as I walk toward where I think the door is. I feel the wall and then a light switch. I flip it on and let out a deep breath. Turning around, I scream when I come face-to-face with a man dressed in dark jeans and a black hoodie. He's got a mask on, making my heart leap into my throat.

A Lord's mask.

It's solid white with black lines all over, giving it a cracked look. The eyes have black circles, and the lips are the same. He's got his hood up and over his head. "Ty—"

His hand comes out to wrap around my neck and pins me against the wall. My heart races as I reach up and try to shove him away, but he only pushes his hard body farther into mine. His mask-covered face goes to my neck, and I suck in a deep breath when I realize my collar is on my neck. My thighs tighten at the thought he put it on me while I was sleeping.

The fact he has that power over me makes me wet even though I know he won't use it on me. I'm pregnant. But maybe once I have the babies ...

"Beg me," he whispers in my ear. His deep voice is deliciously dark, making goose bumps rise along my skin. "Beg me to stop, little darling."

Why would I want to beg him to stop? This is what I've wanted. My body needs him. Now more than ever. "Please?" I whisper, knowing I'm begging for it and not the other way around.

The hand around my throat tightens, and then loosens in a subtle warning. My hands come up, and I try to push him off me, but his strength is unmatched. "Pl-ease." I gasp. "Please ... don't hurt me." I try to be as believable as possible, feeling like this is some kind of test. If it is, I'm determined to pass.

"What if I want to?" He gives a dark chuckle at his own question, and my legs buckle, but he holds me up.

"What ... what are you going to do to me?" I swallow, my body begging him to fuck me as I push my hips into his. Clearly failing at being the victim he wants me to play.

"Whatever I fucking want."

I whimper, my breath catching.

He lets go of my neck, spins me around, and pushes the front of my body into the door. His body holding me captive. A hand grips my hair, yanking my head back, and I cry out at the sting. He shoves something round and rubber into my mouth, and I don't fight him as he buckles the ball gag at the back of my head.

My tongue explores the smooth rubber as saliva pools around the large ball. My arms are pulled behind my back, and I whimper when he cuffs my wrists together, cinching them tightly to make it hurt. Turning me back to face him, he cups my face, and my eyes are closed while I try to catch my breath.

"Look at me, little darling," he demands.

Opening my heavy eyes, I look up into the white mask. I hate that I can't see his eyes. A Lord's mask is to keep him hidden from the world.

"That's more like it." He runs his knuckles down my cheek, and I pull my face away.

He grips my jaw and shoves my head into the door, making my nipples harden. He steps into me, and I cower. The fear of not seeing his face is turning me on more than it should. Even though I know it's him, my imagination still runs wild. Is he going to hurt me? Fuck me? Tie me up and leave me?

"I wanted to gag you at our wedding," he admits shamelessly, and I blink as my heart pounds in my chest. "I was hoping you'd fight me then so I could use that collar and leash on you. Watching you crawl to me would have been so sweet."

I whimper, my hips pushing forward into him, and I can feel how hard he is. My thighs as wet as the drool starting to run out of my gagged mouth.

Cupping the right side of my face, he slowly runs his thumb over my bottom lip, smearing the drool.

"I'm in the mood to use my wife," he growls, and the words make my pussy clench, loving the reminder that I'm his. No one else has ever held that title, and I'll make sure no one else ever does.

He yanks me from the door, opens it, and pulls me into the hallway. I try to pull away and go back into the room, my heart now racing with fear. I don't want anyone to see me like this. As much as I enjoy it, I'm too embarrassed to let someone see me so vulnerable.

His laughter fills the cold hallway as he drags me down it. "I want to show off what's mine," he adds. I try to dig my heels into the floor, but I'm powerless. He walks me onto an elevator, and it's filled with my heavy breathing while it starts to carry us up.

My hands fist, pulling on the metal cuffs, and the drool drips onto my chest from the gag. A muffled moan escapes, and his soft chuckle tells me he heard it.

The door slides open, and I look wide-eyed at what resembles the Cathedral. But I know it's not. It's on a much smaller scale but looks almost identical.

He drags me down the aisle between the pews and to the altar. Several long pieces of black rope lie across a table. Turning me to face him, he pulls out his pocketknife and flips it open.

I hold my breath as he places it inside the collar of my shirt and cuts down the middle before yanking it off my body. My nipples are hard, and I shiver at how cold it is in here. Then he's shoving my cotton shorts down my legs along with my underwear until I'm standing naked before him. Like always, he's fully dressed. It's not fair that he gets to hide his body from me.

He picks me up and sets me on the Lords' table. I'm shaking, my breathing erratic and my pussy fucking soaked. He grabs my hair at the base of my neck, avoiding the buckle on the gag, and forces me down on my stomach. I close my eyes, knowing I'm about to serve my Lord.

For all I know, I'm about to be his sacrifice, and that's why he married me. You don't get to rule the world without shedding some blood along the way. The sad part is, I'd gladly do it.

TYSON

I PICK UP THE FIRST PIECE OF ROPE AND SLIDE IT underneath my wife, stopping it at her upper chest. I wrap it around her upper body and arms, bringing it to her back and tying it off with a knot. Then I take the extra rope down to her elbows, tying them together as well.

She moans, her body rocking from side to side, testing them. I smile. She won't be able to move once I finish with her. Removing the keys from my pocket, I undo the cuffs and toss them to the side. I don't need them right now. I continue with the rope around her wrists as I order, "Interlock your fingers." She does as she's told, and I slap her ass, making her jump. Rubbing the now red spot, I murmur, "Good girl." She lifts her hips in the air, begging me to lower my hand between her legs, but I don't. This is about me. Not her.

Tying her wrists together, I stand back and admire the rope wrapped around her flawless skin. "So perfect," I praise her, and she whimpers.

I pick up the second piece of rope and do the same to her legs, tying them together on her upper thighs, above her knees, and then her ankles. She wiggles her body around, and I imagine how soaked her cunt is for my cock. I wish I had the time to bury my face between them, but I don't. We're on borrowed time as it is.

We broke her out of the psych ward a week ago. People know she's missing by now. Luke is MIA and I've got two people who won't tell me what I want to know. The rest of the world thinks she's dead. As much as I wish to keep her safe, I don't want her to have to live a life where no one knows she exists.

I take the last piece of rope, loop it around her tied ankles, and then pull her legs, lifting them off the Lords' table and tying the excess to the rope wrapped around her upper arms, securing her in a hog-tied position.

Tying it off tightly so she has no way of getting free, I walk around to stand at the end of the table by her head and look down at her. Removing my mask, I smile at her as she looks up at me through her lashes. "Now I play with my wife."

SIXTY-TWO

LAIKYN

He reaches down and undoes the buckle to the gag. Pulling it out, I gasp as the drool runs out of my mouth. "Tyson—" I yank on the ropes that have me tied so tight that I'm unable to move other than rocking forward to back.

"You're hog-tied, Lake," he says, reaching his hands out to cup my face, and I lean into it. "You've been kidnapped. And must be restrained so you can't run away."

I moan, and he smiles. "You want that, little darling? Want me to set you free and chase you down?"

"Yes," I answer, and my voice sounds as desperate as my body feels. My tied thighs are soaking fucking wet from what he just did to me.

He chuckles. "I'll add that to the long list of things I'm going to do to you over the next fifty years of my life." My face falls to the table, and when I wiggle my tied arms, it pulls on my legs. His hand grips my hair and yanks my head up, making me cry out. His free hand goes to his jeans, and he unzips them before pulling out his pierced dick. He's hard. My pulse races as my pussy throbs, and my lips fall open without even being told. My jaw is already sore from the gag, but I don't care. I'm in desperate need to be used.

"That's a good girl, little darling. I'm going to fuck this pretty face of yours until you're crying big, beautiful tears. Then you're going to swallow."

I stick my tongue out like a needy slut as he holds his cock just inches from my face. I can see the precum on the tip, and I ache to lick it. The cold table and room have my nipples hard, the rope around my chest rubs against my breasts, and I fight to relieve the pressure in my limbs. It's all too much. I feel like I'm about to come just like this. Tied up and on display for my Lord.

"Aren't you?" He lets go of his dick and slaps me.

I gasp at the sting on my face, but my tied thighs are coated in my own wetness. "Yes," I breathe, trying to nod my head but can't since his other hand is still tangled in my hair.

"Good girl." His hand goes back to his dick, and he slowly strokes it. "Now open wide and cry for me, Lake."

I do as I'm told, my neck cramping from the position he has me in, but it's long forgotten when he slides his cock into my mouth. I suck on the tip, practically begging him to give me more.

"Fuck, little darling." He groans as he pushes forward.

I open up for him, and he hits the back of my throat, making me gag, my body jerking. He pulls out, and I gasp in a breath before he pushes back into me. The force makes my body rock back and forth on the table.

He holds it in place, his cock so large it fills my mouth and constricts my breathing. I'm gagging as tears fill my eyes. I fight the restraints, trying to move away, but he's got me pinned right where he wants me.

Pulling all the way out, I swallow before sucking in a deep breath. He slaps my face again. "Don't fucking close your mouth."

I nod the best I can and blink as the tears clear my blurry vision, falling down my cheeks.

He slides back into me, gentler this time, and I moan around him. The vibration making him let out one of his own. His hand in my hair tightens, and the one guiding his dick into my mouth moves underneath my neck, gripping it tightly. "I'm going to fuck you now, Lake, and you're going to take it like the fucking needy whore you are."

If I could talk, I'd say *yes, sir*. But I can't, so I lie here on a table inside of a cathedral, tied down and face fucked as if I'm a sacrifice to a high power. And you know what? I don't even care. I'd gladly serve my Lord because that's what a Lady does.

TYSON

I COME DOWN MY WIFE'S THROAT AND PULL OUT. THE cathedral fills with the sounds of her soft cries and gasps for air. I don't even give her a chance to recover before I stick the ball gag back into her mouth, fastening it in place.

Her body is slick from sweat and shakes uncontrollably.

I place my hard cock into my jeans and zip them up before grabbing what I need. "Smile for the camera," I say, holding up the cell phone.

Her watery eyes widen, and she shakes her head before she gives up the fight, and I take the picture. Lowering the phone, I make sure to take a close-up of her face to get the tears that run down her cheeks. She's been in this position for well over thirty minutes now. I can hear her whimpers as she struggles with the rope.

I take one more, then slip the hood over her head. She screams through the gag, her small body struggling even more with the darkness.

I press record and walk around the altar, making sure to get every inch of her naked, tied-up body. I get close to her face so my hand isn't in the video and yank the hood off before I pull back and get a good look at her. Then I end the video.

She lowers her head to the table the best she can and breathes heavily through her nose. I pocket the cell and place my forearms at the edge of the table, lowering my lips to her ear. "I'm going to tie you up like this later, and I'm going to stuff that tight cunt with a vibrator and your ass with a butt plug, and I'm going to sit back and watch you drool all over yourself while you come over and over."

My wife moans.

I reach out, wrapping my hand around her throat, pressing her collar into her neck, and smile at her heavy eyes. "You'll love it, little darling."

She blinks, fresh tears running down her cheeks. I lean in and kiss them. "Maybe I should leave you here a little longer."

She shakes her head, and I laugh. "It's not up to you, is it, Lake?"

Blinking rapidly, she speaks unintelligible things around the ball gag. Reaching up, I grip her long dark hair at the top of her head and yank it back, making her whimper. I lower my face to hers. "Just because you're pregnant doesn't mean I'll take it easy on you. I'm still going to fuck you like the whore I know you to be." The thought of her carrying not only one but two of my children turns me on so fucking much.

I can't wait to tie her to our bed at home and fuck her until she's begging me to stop and then holding her in the bathtub, washing her body for her when she's too weak to do it herself. I want to bring her breakfast in bed and help her get ready for the day. But then I also want those gorgeous blue eyes to cry for me while my cock is buried inside her. Taking her however I want, whenever I want.

Her heavy breathing continues to fill the quiet cathedral. The Spade brothers may be Lords, but they were not placed out in the world. They run Carnage like a prison. It's their own personal city. They have a smaller replica of the Cathedral where the Lords hold all their rituals and traditions. It came in handy for my plan tonight.

Cupping her face, I say, "Look at me." Her watery eyes lift to meet mine. "Are you wet, little darling?"

Nodding, she sniffs, and I bet if the gag wasn't in her mouth, she'd beg me to fuck her. But instead, I place the hood back over her head, securing the drawstring in place.

SIXTY-THREE

TYSON

SAINT: Package is five minutes out.

I read over the text before pocketing my phone. Looking up from the front pew, I watch the naked woman struggle in the rope displayed on the Lords' table. She's been there for over an hour, waiting, screaming nonsense into her gag.

My wife is pissed at me, but it's nothing new. It's also something I'm more than willing to live with.

Ryat enters from the side door that leads back to the hallway and office. "Done."

I nod. "Package will be here any minute."

He runs a hand through his hair nervously, and I wait for the inevitable. He doesn't make me wait long. "You sure you want to do this?" His green eyes slide to the table at the sound of her gagged sobs and then back to mine.

Do I want answers to who took my wife away from me? Abso-fucking-lutely. Does that mean she may hate me the rest of her life? Yes. But I can live with that. I've been her husband while she hated me, and it didn't bother me. I won't let it now.

Sighing at my silence, Ryat adds, "I hope it works."

It will. It has to. "Bring in our guests," I tell him. "Place them in the front pew."

Walking away, he goes back through the door but returns seconds later with our two guests we brought with us from Carnage. They're both dressed in black cloaks and white masks—just like the Lords do when they gather here to perform some ritual or tradition.

The only difference is they've got their hands cuffed behind their backs and gags in their mouths. Jackson's is full of an inflated ball gag—just like the one I used on my wife. I wanted him as silent as could be. The woman has tape over hers.

Ryat pushes them both to sit in the front pew. I can tell which is which just by looking at them. The woman is significantly smaller, so the cloak swallows her up. Ryat sits between them. If need be, he has to make sure they don't get up and try something.

The sound of the front doors squeaking alerts everyone that our package has arrived. I straighten my shoulders as a set of dark eyes meet mine. He's at the far end of the aisle, but he's slowly walking toward me.

I want to smile but don't, too much could go wrong at this point. "Tyson." He draws out the single word and then snorts. "I should have known it was too good to be true."

Shrugging, I place my hand on the edge of the Lords' table. His eyes drop to it before meeting mine. I see the apprehension in his.

"Is she your wife or mine?" I question as her tied body trembles. She's been in this position for quite some time.

He fists his hands and takes a step back.

"Go ahead." I cross my arms over my chest. "Have a look."

Reaching out, he unclenches his hand and grabs the drawstring holding the hood on. He pulls it gently, untying it, and his eyes rise to mine. He yanks it off, showing off our main guest—his wife.

I look at mine who sits in the front pew next to Ryat. I wish I could see her face, but I can't through the Lord's mask. But by the way she jumps to her feet, I'm glad I placed tape over her mouth because she's screaming into it.

LAIKYN

I'M EXHAUSTED, BODY STILL SHAKING FROM THE WAY TYSON used it in the cathedral at Carnage. I lie in the passenger seat of his Bentley, eyes closed and pussy soaking wet. He brings the car to a stop, gets out, and picks me up out of the passenger seat.

Opening my eyes, I notice we're at the Cathedral. The same one where I became his wife. He starts to take the stairs, and I look over his shoulder to see Ryat pull up into the dark parking lot and get out of an SUV I don't recognize. He goes to the back and opens the hatch. He's reaching into it when Tyson enters the building, and I can no longer see.

"What are we doing here?" I ask, my tongue as heavy as my eyes.

"We're having a confessional," Tyson answers, walking me down the aisle to the chancel. It feels like it's been years since we were here saying our vows.

I wrap my arms around his neck and bury my face into it as well. I open my eyes moments later when he sets me down. I look around to see we're in an office. I'm sitting on a leather couch, and he kneels in front of me. His hands on my shaking thighs.

"Why?" I wonder.

He stands, leans over, and gently kisses my lips. That's as much of an answer as I'm going to get. I know my husband well enough by now to know when he's going to keep secrets from me.

"We won't be here long," he assures me, pushing my tangled hair behind my ear. "And when we're done, I promise to fuck you."

I groan. "Please."

He chuckles at how much he got me worked up. The door opens, and Ryat enters. He tosses a cloak and a Lord's mask on the couch beside me. "Our main attraction is in place," he informs my husband.

Tyson nods and reaches into his back pocket, removing a pair of handcuffs, and Ryat hands him a roll of duct tape.

I swallow nervously, shifting on the couch. "Ty—"

"Stand up and put your hands behind your back, Lake," he commands, interrupting me.

My wide eyes go to Ryat but all he does is turn and exit the room, closing the door behind him.

I know that Lords restrain their chosens when they perform their vow ceremony, but Tyson said we're here for confessional. You don't perform the ritual when you're already a Lady.

"Lake." He growls my name, and I get to my shaky legs. Staring up at him as he cups my face. "I love you, remember that."

My eyes widen at his words, my fear tripling at what the fuck is going on. But he lowers his lips to mine and kisses me. Hands fisted in my already tangled hair, he's possessive, stealing what little breath I have left. My body softens, mouth opening and allowing him to deepen the kiss.

When he pulls away, he spins me around, yanks my hands behind my back, and cuffs them together before I even have the chance to speak, still trying to catch my breath.

"Turn around," he orders, and the moment I manage to face him once again, he's placing a piece of duct tape over my lips. It's wide and covers both my upper and lower lip along with my cheeks.

I whimper, my heavy eyes looking up into his while he rips off another piece. His bore into mine when he places that one on as well, placing it diagonally, overlaying parts of the first one. I *don't know why, but the act is more intimate than the kiss. Maybe it's because I'm horny as fuck and want him to use me. He rips another one off and places it diagonal again, opposite of the last.*

Stepping into me, he cups my cheeks and runs his thumbs along the tape, pressing them into my lips, making sure I can't wiggle my mouth to get them off.

Once satisfied, he runs his knuckles down the side of my taped cheeks and over my neck. My pulse races, and he smiles, feeling it.

Removing his cell, he opens it up and I feel the collar unlock. He takes it from my neck, and I watch him pocket his cell. I feel naked with it gone. I've worn it for so long that it started to feel as natural as wearing my wedding ring. Now both are missing.

He then steps back, grabs the cloak, and places it over me before putting the mask over my face. "When I'm ready for you, Ryat will bring you out." He helps me to sit back down on the couch and then he exits, leaving me alone, taped, cuffed, and hidden from the world that thinks I'm dead.

THE BLOOD RUSHES IN MY EARS, MY HEAVY BREATHING FILLS the mask, and I jump to my feet to run to the Lords' table, but the back of my cloak is grabbed, and I'm yanked onto my ass in the pew. "Stay the fuck seated," Ryat growls in my ear.

Now I understand why my husband taped my mouth shut, and as much as I try to talk, it's impossible. Every time I move my mouth, the tape pulls on my skin. He covered most of my face for a reason—to keep me silent.

My wide eyes shoot to Tyson, and he's already staring at me. No ounce of remorse in his eyes, just fucking emotionless. He knew! He fucking knew all of this time?

"What do you want?" Luke growls, and my husband gives him his attention. "My wife for yours?"

Wife? Tyson had called *her* Luke's wife. I yank on the cuffs, my body thrashing in the cloak. No. It can't be.

Tyson arches a brow. "You think this is a trade? I've already got both of them."

My eyes drop to the woman once more, and there's no denying who she is. *It's Whitney!* My sister. My dead sister.

I can only see a side view of her, but she's hog-tied and naked on the Lords' table. She's screaming, thrashing in the ropes. Spit flying from around the black ball gag in her mouth.

"Our main attraction is in place," Ryat had said in the office.

He tied her up in the same position he had me tied up in at the cathedral at Carnage. He took video of me, pictures of me, had a hood over my head, my collar.

My eyes fall to her neck, and she's wearing my collar. Jealousy courses through me like my insides are on fire. That's mine. Why did he give it to her? How long has he known she wasn't dead?

"Then what the fuck do you want?" Luke shouts, the sound of his voice echoing through the large cathedral, and it makes me flinch.

The sound of the doors opening behind me at the entrance squeak, and Luke spins around to face whoever has joined us. I try to look over my shoulder, but the mask prevents me from seeing out of the eye holes.

"What the fuck is this?" Luke barks, and then goes to run toward the door that Ryat brought me through that leads to the office, but Ryat jumps up from the pew beside me, throws off his cloak, and points his gun at Luke's face, bringing him to a stop. Slowly, Ryat removes his mask, and Luke curses.

"How the fuck did this happen?" Luke demands. I feel like he's talking to himself more than anyone else. He turns to the Lords' table and leans down into my sister's face. "How the fuck did you let this happen? You had one job." He slaps her. "All you had to do was make sure she stayed in that fucking psych ward!"

Tears run down my taped cheeks at the betrayal I feel. From her, my husband, Luke. I mean, every-fucking-body seemed to have known that she was alive but me. Hell, Tyson let me think he killed her years ago. Why didn't he tell me the truth?

Ryat moves toward the Lords' table as Tyson grabs the back of Luke's neck and slams his face down into the side of the table. It knocks him to his knees.

SIXTY-FOUR

TYSON

Ryat helps me get Luke into a chair, and we zip-tie him to it. I look up to see Kashton plop down in the pew next to my wife while Haidyn sits down in the pew behind her. Saint walks over to the other witness I had Ryat bring from Carnage.

He knocks the mask off Jackson, yanks him from the pew and drags him over to the Lords' table. Hitting the back of his legs, Jackson falls to his knees, and he screams behind the ball gag in his mouth.

I slap Luke across the face, trying to get him to focus. The poor guy is dazed. "Wake the fuck up. You're going to tell me what I want to know."

"Fuck ... you." He spits out blood.

"Let's start with the obvious. How I found your wife." I grab Whitney's hair, yanking her head back, and she looks up at me through her bloodshot eyes. "I found my wife sedated, tied to a hospital bed in a psych ward, and jaw wired shut. And you can believe my surprise when Whitney here entered the room. The only thing she was surprised about was that I was there. You said she had one job? I highly doubt that was all she did."

Looking up, I see Haidyn sitting behind my wife, and I nod to him. He reaches around her and removes the Lord's mask. Her watery eyes are on her sister. They meet mine, and she shakes her head, fresh tears rolling down her face. She doesn't want to believe it.

"Yes, little darling." I shove Whitney's head down into the table. "Whitney knew where you were and wasn't going to tell a soul where to find you. But then again, a dead girl is meant to be forgotten. If you don't know she exists, then she can't tell secrets."

Lake drops her head, her body shaking as she sobs behind the tape.

"Then we have Jackson here. He told me all kinds of information." I leave it vague because I want Luke to sweat it.

"I'm not telling you shit." Luke shakes his head.

I figured he'd be this way. That's why I have Whitney here. Otherwise, I would have never let my wife see her sister was still alive. I kept her hidden, tied up in a cell next to Jackson's at Carnage for this very reason for the past week. I didn't want to break Lake this way, but I'll do whatever I have to do to protect my wife. I had to weigh my options. And my wife's safety will always win.

Removing the gag from Whitney's mouth, she openly sobs, her body struggling in the rope. After I fucked my wife's mouth in the cathedral at Carnage, I brought her here while I had Ryat bring Jackson and Whitney. I then sent the video and pictures to Luke from Whitney's phone that I took of my wife. I had Ryat tie up Whitney the same way, making him think it was my wife when he arrived. All I needed was a second of surprise.

"Don't you fucking say anything," Luke yells at her. "Keep your mouth shut."

She can't right now over her sobbing, but I have something that will help her get under control. Removing my cell, I unlock it and turn on my wife's collar that I had placed on Whitney.

She goes silent as her body shakes from the shocks. Turning it off, she sags the best she can in the tight ropes. I do it again, and she tenses.

"I can do this all night," I tell Luke, ignoring my wife yelling into her tape. "But I don't need to." Stopping it, I lower myself at the end of the Lords' table to meet her eyes. "Were you going to sell my wife?" I ask.

She closes her eyes tightly, and I grip her face, squeezing it as hard as I can, knowing it'll leave prints afterward. "YES!" she cries, and I let go of her.

"Fucking bitch..."

I punch Luke, cutting him off. My wife's face is white, drained of all color, and her big, beautiful tear-filled eyes are on mine.

"Please let me go," Whitney begs. "Please—"

I pull out my knife and hold it to her neck. "Let you go?" Laughing, I shake my head. "You were going to sell my pregnant wife, and you think I'm going to just let you walk away?"

She gasps.

"Thanks for that, by the way." I smile at Luke. "She's giving me twins." I turn back to Whitney. "You took her away from me. And you must pay for that. Nobody takes what's mine and walks away."

"Please!" She shouts, "Lake—" Whitney tries to look over at her out of the corner of her eyes, but she can't see my wife with how she's positioned. "Please, don't let him do this to me."

"My wife can't help you," I say truthfully. Lake could beg, cry, and plead with me, but this is one thing I'd never give her. It's also another reason I made sure she couldn't speak. "You will die here like the fucking bitch you are."

Pressing the knife into her neck, she rushes out, "Ashtyn."

The Cathedral falls eerily silent, and I look over at Saint, who is already heading straight for us. I step back, and he takes the knife from me, flipping her onto her back. She screams as the hog-tied position smashes half her folded body underneath her on the Lords' table. He wraps his hand around her throat and pins her down. The knife now pressed into the side of her face.

"What the fuck did you just say?" he growls.

She tries to catch her breath. "Ashtyn … I know where she is."

He squeezes her throat so tight it cuts off her air, and she flops around the best she can.

"Bullshit," he spits out, pushing the tip of the knife farther into her face, breaking the skin.

Her face is turning blue, her lips white. The struggle starts to lessen, and I place my hand on Saint's arm. His wide and wild eyes meet mine. "I want her dead, but just in case she knows something useful, she's better alive for now."

He lets go of her throat and removes the knife, stepping back. She rolls onto her side and gasps for breath. "If you're lying…"

"I'm not," she cries. "I promise." She's choking out sobs.

We both look over at Luke, and he's staring straight ahead. He gives her away. The fact that he hasn't said anything means he knows the truth. Whitney isn't lying.

Haidyn gets everyone's attention as he jumps up from the pew behind Lake, walks down the aisle, and slams the double doors open when he leaves.

I look over at Kashton, and he's staring at Whitney, face white as a ghost.

"Even if we found her today, we wouldn't be able to collect her," Saint had said to me in their office at Carnage. *"The guys aren't ready. She'd be dead in a matter of hours."*

I step into Saint. "You can take Whitney with you. Get whatever you need out of her when you're ready." I owe the Spade brothers for what I cost them.

His eyes meet mine. "I'll make sure the punishment fits the crime," he says, referring to the part she had in my wife's life. "And after we get what we want from her, she'll be dead. Like she's supposed to be."

I nod, stepping away from the Lords' table.

Whitney starts to scream, her shrill cries making my ears ring. "LAIKYN! Help me. Please." Saint picks up the gag next to her head. "No. No. Please, Laikyn. Please help me. They're going to kill me—"

Saint shoves the gag into her mouth, and I hold her head up, helping him while he buckles it so tight that the leather digs into her cheeks. He then picks her up, grabbing the rope that ties her ankles to her shoulders, not giving two fucks if he breaks anything carrying her like that with her weight. "Grab Jackson," he barks out to Kashton.

We discussed earlier that he would take him to Carnage. I no longer have Blackout where I would torture men in the basement. I don't want anyone at our home, and I can't stay here at the cathedral forever.

Kashton grabs Jackson but remains silent, following Saint.

"Your turn," I say, facing Luke.

Ryat places what I want in my hand, and I shove it into his mouth before he can fight me. I fasten it behind his head and then push on the two metal pieces on either side, and it pries his mouth open wide. He thrashes his head, and I do it again. Each time it pushes his mouth open more and more to the point tears are running down the side of his face.

I yank the chair over to the pew that sits opposite of my wife. I plop down and look at Luke struggle to talk in front of me. "It doesn't even matter why you did it. All that matters is that you did it. So..." Ryat hands me the backpack he brought, and I remove what I need. Luke's wide eyes go from mine to Ryat. He mumbles unintelligible words around the metal gag, and I smile. "You took something from my wife. Now I'm going to take all of them from you."

LAIKYN

I'M PULLED TO MY FEET, SPUN AROUND, AND THE CLOAK IS yanked over my head. My wrists are uncuffed, and then the mask is removed. I wrap my shaking arms around myself. Strong hands turn me back to face the altar, and Tyson cups my face.

"Don't touch me," I shout, my body shaking uncontrollably.

"Lake," he says tightly. "I know we have a lot to talk about."

"Talk?" The word knocks the wind out of me. "Talk about how my dead sister is alive."

Tyson steps in front of me again, and I try to shove him out of the way, but he picks me up and spins me around in his arms, carrying me up the aisle he once forced me down. "Put me down!" I scream just as he sets me on my feet at the end by the double doors. "What did you do?" I demand, punching his chest. "What did ... you do?" I begin to cry, my legs trying to give out on me, and he wraps his arms around me to hold me up. I'm crying so hard that I'm choking.

My eyes catch sight of Luke barely breathing, head hanging forward, and all the blood that drips from his open mouth and onto his shirt.

Then I feel it. The bile starts to rise in my throat. My chest heaves, and I begin to gag. Tyson yanks me over to a trash can. Grabbing my hair, he grips it tightly while I wrap my hands around the edge and vomit into it.

It's like the day at the hospital when I found out she died all over again. I dry heave for a few seconds, and then I push off the trash can. He lets go of my hair, and I fall to my ass by the doors, pushing my body into the wall. I bring my knees to my chest, wrapping my arms around them. "You knew she was alive," I whisper, rocking back and forth.

"Lake." He kneels in front of me, forearms resting on his jean-clad thighs. "Little darling."

"Don't call me that." I whimper, tears stinging my eyes. "It's all been a lie," I say, more to myself than anyone else. "Why?"

"Listen to me, Lake," he says calmly.

My eyes are on his hands in front of me as they rest on his thighs. It's not the blood that covers them, but his silver wedding band that makes me want to vomit some more.

"Your sister—"

"You knew?" I can't help but ask. Fresh tears sting my eyes, and it blurs my vision. I thought he killed her, and now I find out he knew she was never truly dead. Why lie to me? Or why would he let me think he killed her when he knew she was still alive? I don't understand. It doesn't matter, he handed her over to the Spade brothers. They will torture her for whatever information they think she has about Ashtyn, and I'll never see her again. She was right in front of me, and now she's gone. "You knew all this time that she was alive?"

"No. I suspected but never knew for sure," he answers and reaches out to me.

I pull away, but he grips my arm and yanks me to my feet. "Why wouldn't you tell me? Any possibility of her being alive would have been better than knowing she was dead."

He frowns as if that thought never crossed his mind.

"Is that why you married me?" I demand, pulling myself free of his grip.

"What?" he barks out, getting equally angry.

"Because you wanted to make her jealous?" I've been trying to figure out why he married me. This has to be the reason, right? So it would get back to her, and she'd come running to him? That's why he kept her from me.

He glares at me, jaw sharpening. "You can't be serious."

"Why did you marry me?" I shove his chest. "It was because of her, wasn't it?" I'm shouting, my body vibrating. I knew there was a reason, and she must have been it.

He reaches into his pocket and removes a cell phone, shoving it into my hand. "What ... whose is this?" I ask, sniffing.

"Look at the messages," he commands.

My shaking fingers open the first one, and I gasp when I see it's a picture of me. I'm at the house of Lords party, sitting at the table with Tyson, Ryat, and Blakely. Sin and Ellington had gotten up to go greet a friend of theirs. "I don't understand," I whisper.

"This is Whitney's cell phone," he tells me.

"No."

"Fuck, Lake." He yanks it from my hands. "How much proof do you need?" He shows me another picture of me working at Blackout. "She sent the pictures to your phone."

"She couldn't have," I argue even though I see one of the same pictures I had seen on my phone. "My father gave me..." I trail off, my watery eyes meeting his, and his face softens.

Cupping my cheek, he whispers, "I'm sorry, little darling. I wish it wasn't true."

"My father knew." My voice cracks.

"I went through her phone." He speaks softly. "The day of our wedding, Luke contacted her, informing her that I was marrying you. She was here within a matter of days."

I wrap my arms around my shaking body.

"I tried, Lake. I tried to get tabs on her. To get ahead of it, but they were very quiet. I had men on Luke twenty-four seven, tracking him, and they never made contact with one another."

"You said they're married." I frown. "How could he have married me if he was already married to her? I don't understand."

SIXTY-FIVE

TYSON

I'm sitting in my room at the house of Lords when my cell rings. It's a blocked number. Not unusual. The Lords always hide their identity. "This is Tyson," I answer.

"I've got some information for you."

I sit up straighter and turn off the TV so I don't have any distractions. "What'd you find out."

"They're married. Or at least were."

"No."

"Yep. Three weeks ago. To Luke Cabot."

I'm not surprised. She's nothing but a lying, vindictive bitch who will do whatever Daddy tells her to do. "Thanks, man."

"Hey, Ty. I'd watch my back if I were you. Her father is trying to set you up for something."

"I know." When two families merge, especially powerful ones, there is always a big scene made about it. It might come a week later, but it comes nonetheless. That's what we do. We show off our power, our wealth. Why hide the fact that Luke is her husband?

. . .

"He was never going to be married to you, Lake," I say truthfully.

"Was he going to stand me up?" She frowns, not understanding. Why would she? Lake doesn't know what kind of man Luke really is.

I grab the backpack Ryat brought and pull out the file, holding it to her.

She opens it up and gags when she sees the pictures. I reach out for her, but she takes a step back, eyes still on it. "What ... this is her?" Her wide, watery eyes meet mine. "Tyson, this is the girl."

I nod, following her as she walks to the pew closest to the doors and falls down into it. I stand in the aisle, bloody hands shoved into my jeans. "Who did this to her?" Tears fall down her cheeks. "W-hy?" Her voice cracks on the single word.

When I don't answer, she looks up at me. Her eyes go to Luke who still sits tied to the chair at the front by the altar. "He did this?"

I don't answer.

"Why would he do this to her?" She angrily wipes the tears from her eyes.

"Because she was at Blackout," I say simply. Four women have gone missing over the last six months from Blackout. Only one had been reported. The others never will. They're long gone. On a boat or on a plane. They've been sold to the highest bidder and will spend the rest of their life begging for death to come sooner rather than later.

"Bethany told me Frank blackmailed her into sending pictures of you, but she lied. It was Whitney." She shakes her head, and I nod. "I found the pictures on Whitney's phone. Your father said you would receive initiations on the phone he gave you, but that was a lie. He gave it to you to gain access inside of the club." My wife is staring at the floor, unable to meet my stare at the fact she believed everything her father told her. "Frank wanted to know what was going on, on the inside of Blackout because he knew that Luke and Miller were taking girls from my club."

My eyes are on hers, and her head snaps up at those words.

"They wanted attention on Blackout. They wanted to frame me for the disappearance of all those women. They had tried before and failed." Her brows pull together, confused by that, but I'm not going into detail right now. "They thought this time would be different, but their plan backfired because you forgot about the phone." Her father didn't gain anything from it. So, Whitney followed Lake around, took pictures, and then sent them to her, hoping to get a rise out of her, but again, it didn't work as planned.

"He was targeting you?" my wife wonders, but before I can answer, she jumps up and runs down the aisle.

"Lake." I follow after her, but she's quick. The moment she reaches him, she knocks over his chair. He makes a gurgling sound of drool and blood as I pick her up with an arm around her waist, spinning us around. "Get him out of here," I bark at Ryat who hasn't left yet. "Put him downstairs in the basement. I'll take care of him in a minute." He deserves to suffer a little longer.

I set her down in the front pew, and her watery eyes meet mine.

"Was he targeting you because you married me?" she asks, licking her wet lips.

I sigh, running a hand down my unshaven face. Technically, her father started way before I married her, but that doesn't matter right now.

"Why did he care that I married you if he wasn't going to?" she wonders, her face scrunched with confusion and anger that she can't understand it.

I can't say the words. My tongue is all of a sudden heavy, my mouth dry. I wanted her to know how sick these people were, but now that I've found out what they had planned for her, I can't do it.

"Tyson?" She snaps my name. "Why did he care..." Her voice trails off. "The honeymoon suite." Her eyes search mine, and I keep my stare as blank as I can. "My brother said... Oh my God, were there cameras in there? If I wasn't going to marry Luke, then why would there be cameras in there?" She nibbles on her bottom lip. She's getting warmer. "Then Luke told me that I better pray I was pregnant. Because I'd finally know my worth. Whitney..." She chokes on her sister's name. "You asked if she was going to *sell* me..." Her voice trails off, and her eyes meet mine. They fill with fresh tears before they spill over her bottom lashes and roll down her gorgeous face. "You saved me," she whispers brokenly, her shoulders shaking.

I reach out and cup her tear-streaked face, and her chest heaves. "Take a deep breath, Lake."

"Why?" she gasps.

I don't know if she's asking why I chose to hijack her wedding or why Luke was going to pretend to marry her only to sell her body, so I don't answer. She covers her face with her hands, and I pull her into me, holding her tightly while she clings to my bloody clothes.

I wasn't innocent. I married my wife for revenge. I always suspected Whitney was still alive, but I had no proof. But I never thought making Lake my wife would bring Whitney out of hiding. Or save Lake from a life of slavery.

They gave up one daughter to offer up the other. I wanted to rub it in their faces that Lake was a whore—my whore. I fucked her every chance I got, any way I wanted. She needed to crave me. Want me. Need me. It would only work if I trained her to serve me.

The collar I gave Lake was the very same collar that Luke had purchased for Whitney as her wedding gift. I saw it in her bag when she came over to see me at the house of Lords. When she pretended to love me. I was pretending too, but I wasn't trying to set her up for something.

I made sure Lake wore it for the wedding, my not-so-subtle hint that I knew what they had done three years ago. Just another way to show off my bride.

Pulling away, she sniffs and wipes her face free of the tears. Her bloodshot eyes look up at me. "Can we go home?"

I give her a smile, pushing her dark hair back behind her ear. "I need to go talk to Ryat for a second. Will you be okay by yourself?" I'd offer to take her downstairs with me, but I don't want her getting sick again. I'm not sure if that was the pregnancy, nerves, or the fact that she saw her *dead* sister. It could have been a combination of all three.

She nods. "Yeah." And rubs her hands on her bare thighs.

I kiss her forehead. "I'll only be a second, and then we'll leave."

LAIKYN

I sit in the front pew, staring at the chair knocked over by the Lords' table and the blood that covers it and the floor. Tyson pulled out all of Luke's teeth. One by one with a pair of pliers. I'm going to hear his screams every time I close my eyes for a while now.

But nothing will compare to the woman I saw mutilated and thrown into a grave. She was unrecognizable. But I knew it was her because I recognized the folder that Tyson had shown to Collin in his office the morning after he fucked me in the ass.

I can't help but feel responsible for her. If I had said something to Collin the morning he showed up at Blackout with the other cop, maybe they could have found her and saved her in time. But who knows if he had a hand in the poor girl's disappearance.

491

Would I have ended up like that if Tyson had not married me? Probably. I reach up and the loss of my collar makes my breath quicken. My sister had it on when the Spade brothers carried her out of here. I need something to replace it. It doesn't have to shock me, but something to show the world that I belong to Tyson Crawford. I'm his Lady. The ring—that I'm still missing—isn't enough. Wives wear a ring to show they're married. I need something more. Our marriage isn't traditional, but I wouldn't have it any other way. Not like I put up much of a fight anyway.

I wish I knew then what I know now. I would have let him put that collar, leash, and gag on me. I would have crawled down this long aisle, leaving a trail of my drool behind me to be his whore in front of my family just to piss them off. Embarrass them.

Tyson sacrificed his life for me—his future, his career. Everything. I could never give him that. I have nothing on that scale to offer. He even lost Blackout because of me. When will it end? When will I stop costing him his life? What he's worked so hard for?

The sound of the double doors opening have me spinning my head around, but I don't see anything there. I stand. "Hello?" I holler, my eyes searching the entrance.

The Cathedral is eerily quiet. Creepy when it's empty. The stained glass windows howl from the wind outside. The old wood creaks. It's cold, sending a chill down my spine.

"Tyson?" I call out, thinking that maybe he had to go outside for something. But still nothing. Wrapping my arms around myself, I walk over to the door that I know leads to the hallway and office. I'm not sure how to get to the basement, but I watched him go this way so it's a start.

I turn the knob and open the door but quickly take a step back as I scream in surprise. "What are you doing here?" I ask, rushing out.

"Luke called me." His dark eyes look around the Cathedral. "Where is he?" His eyes fall to the blood, and his jaw sharpens.

I take another step back, but it's putting me farther away from the door, which is where I want to be.

"Where is he, Lake?" he snaps.

"I ... I don't know," I stammer.

"You always were a shitty liar." He reaches for me, and I jump out of the way, running around the Lords' table, but he leaps onto it and jumps off, managing to grab my hair. Yanking my back to his front, I cry out, and he shoves me to the floor.

I glare up at him as he smirks down at me. "Why were you so mad when I was forced to marry Tyson when you knew the wedding to Luke wasn't going to be real?" I'm so tired of not knowing the truth. Of having to guess and be way off.

He snorts. "It's funny that you think anyone would want you, Lake." He reaches for me again, and I kick out my foot, making contact with his knee. Grunting, he lunges for me and yanks me to my feet with a hand around my arm and pulls my back to his front.

"Because he was in on it."

"Ty—" My brother slaps his hand over my mouth, spinning us both around to see my husband has joined us, gun drawn and pointed right at Miller. I want to cry in relief, but I have to try and take a calming breath through my nose.

"Let her go, Miller," Tyson demands with his arms out, gun trained on my brother.

"God, isn't this poetic." Miller laughs. "You couldn't save Whitney, and now here you are, not able to save your wife."

Does my brother not know our sister is alive?

"Let. Her. Go." Tyson's voice is controlled, but I can see how tense he is from where Miller holds me hostage, and it makes me even more nervous. That my brother might be able to kill me.

"If you had just stayed the fuck away..."

"You know I couldn't walk away. Not after what happened to

493

Whitney." Tyson shakes his head. "You had to know I'd take the only thing left."

I flinch at how Tyson speaks of me. Like I'm nothing to him. But even though I know I started out that way, things have changed now.

"But you fell in love with her." Miller snorts, ignoring Tyson. "God, you're as pathetic as she is." His fingers pinch my nose, and I kick my legs out, twisting in his grip, but he closes the distance between us and the Lords' table. Smashing my body into the side of it, he limits my struggle.

My eyes grow heavy, my body betraying me.

"Miller—"

"You will not beat me!" my brother roars, interrupting my husband. I feel something being pushed into the side of my head. Tyson tosses his gun to the side, and it slides across the floor, then he lifts his hands in the air.

"You want me?" he shouts. "I'm right here."

"You just had to take her from us," my brother growls, his body vibrating against mine. My arms fall to my side while my chest heaves, desperate for air. "Gave your life up for her. How fucking pathetic."

"I'm right fucking here!" Tyson is screaming, his words full of rage and desperation.

I blink, and it's hard to open them.

He steps closer, and my brother steps back from the table, but I don't have the strength to fight.

"Miller." Tyson's eyes are on mine. They're large as he takes small steps closer to us. Needing to get to me. "Let her go."

The pressure to my skull is released, and then I feel it in my side, digging into my ribs.

"You want me? Do it!" Tyson screams. "Fucking do it. Shoot me, you son of a bitch."

Tears well up in my eyes, and I beg him to stop, but no one can hear me.

My brother laughs. "I'd rather you know what it's like to lose the only woman you've ever loved than die."

My eyes fall shut as a calmness washes over me.

BANG.

SIXTY-SIX

TYSON

My wife drops to the Cathedral floor as the shot rings out. I rush to her, falling to my knees. I pick her up in my arms, my hands instantly covered in blood. "Lake?" I cup her tear-streaked face. "Lake, look at me."

She gasps, sucking in a breath, and her eyes pop open. I pull her to me, and she wraps her arms around my neck as sobs rack her body.

I kiss her hair, and she pulls away. Her eyes fall to my bloody arms, and she begins to shake. "It's okay. You're okay," I assure her.

Her wide eyes meet mine, full of panic, and her face drains of color. "You—"

"I'm okay."

The sound of a mumbled cry comes from beside us, and we look over to see Ryat handcuffing Miller while his bloody body lies on the floor. He was able to get a shot off in Miller's shoulder without hurting Lake. I knew he wouldn't let her go, and he wouldn't talk much longer. We had run out of time.

"Let's go, you piece of shit." Ryat yanks him up and drags him out of the Cathedral.

I help her to stand on shaky legs and start to walk down the aisle to leave, but she pulls me to a stop. "What?"

"I'll wait here." She wraps her arms around herself. "Please," she whispers when I go to reach out to her again. "I need a second." Her eyes drop to the floor.

"Okay." I nod, give her a kiss, and run outside to help Ryat load him in the back of the SUV.

I make a quick call to Saint, giving my wife the time she needs. Hanging up, I pocket my cell and enter the Cathedral to find her standing at the altar. I walk down the aisle and come to the front. Watching her stare at the Lords' table.

"Lake—"

"Why did you waste your life?" she asks softly, interrupting me.

I don't respond. Instead, I tilt my head, confused by what she means exactly.

"Why did you waste your life?" she repeats, and when I still don't answer, she adds, "On me." She turns her back to the altar to face me. "You could have had any woman in the world. Why me?" Her bottom lip starts to tremble at her words, and I hate that I ever let her doubt my intentions. I could treat my wife like my own personal slut but still make her feel loved. I chose to make her fear me and hate me instead. That was so stupid of me. I reach out and cup her soft face.

She knocks it away, and I grip her chin, forcing her head back while I push my body into hers, pinning her up against the table. The softest whimper comes from her perfect lips, making me smile. My wife reacts better to force than tenderness. She likes to be taken, but even before I came into her life, she was groomed for that. She was always meant to serve, and her father saw to that. "You're right, Lake. I did waste my life."

The first tear runs down her cheek, and I hate how broken it makes her look. She's so lost and confused. "I wasted the last three years plotting my revenge against your family—how I was going to make them pay, and you know what?"

"What?" she growls, trying to pull out of my hold but is unsuccessful.

"Every scenario I came up with always brought me back to you," I say truthfully. "Killing them was too easy. The best revenge is served over and over. Years and years of torture. You were the one thing I could take from them. And you know what I regret the most?" I don't let her answer. "That I didn't make you my wife sooner."

Her face falls, eyes soften, and she inhales sharply. My free hand comes up to cup the other cheek. I lower my face to hers, close enough to kiss but don't. Instead, I stop and whisper against her lips, "I'd choose you, Lake." If you want the Lords to give you something, then you have to give in return. I gave it all up for her.

"Tyson—"

I gently place my lips on hers, and she opens up for me as I slide my hands into her hair, tilting her head back and devouring her.

She wraps her arms around my neck, and my hands drop to her thighs, picking her up. Walking forward, I set her on the Lords' table. Her heavy eyes slowly open to look up at me through her long lashes.

"The question is, Lake..." I run my thumb over her parted lips. "If you had the choice, would you pick me?" Her answer doesn't matter really, considering she's already mine, and I'm not giving her up for anything.

Dropping my hand into my pocket, I pull out her wedding ring. Her eyes widen when she sees it.

LAIKYN

"Yes." The single word is out of my mouth before I can even think about it.

He arches a brow in question, clearly not believing me. Some would say it's stupid because I didn't get to choose. Tyson did that for me months ago in this very spot. I'm his Lady. He's my Lord. And I am to serve him for the rest of my life. I was always drawn to him. Obsessed with him. I wanted what my sister had. And although I wasn't given a choice, I'd pick him a thousand times over.

Tyson Riley Crawford is the kind of man that women dream of. And I'd gladly never wake up.

I hold out my hand, and he slides on my ring. I want to ask where he found it, but I'm guessing it was on Luke. The bastard probably took it after he kidnapped me from Blackout.

Fuck him and Miller. I refuse to allow anyone to come between me and my husband. I'm his wife, pregnant with his children.

I push on Tyson's chest, and he takes a few steps back, giving me some space. I reach down, grabbing the hem of my shirt and pulling the material up and over my head. I wasn't wearing a bra; I also don't have any underwear on. I dressed for easy access after he tied me up naked and fucked my mouth.

"I choose you," I say, feeling the butterflies in my stomach at the way his eyes devour my chest. He's starving, and I want to be his offering. I'd willingly be his sacrifice. *Make me yours.*

Stepping into me, he lowers his hands to my shorts, and the zipper can be heard over my heavy breathing. The denim material drops to my feet, and he grabs my bare thighs and lifts me, setting me on the Lords' table. I spread my legs wide for him to stand between them before wrapping them around his hips.

My hands go to his jeans, and I unzip them, needing him right here and right now. I need a reminder that I'm his. "Show me." My voice is desperate, my hands needy. I don't know why I need the reassurance. I'm his wife and carrying his children, but that's not enough. Tyson was right. He's trained me to be his whore, and I need that from him. Before tonight, it had been days since he's fucked me. I thought I was going to die and that I'd never see him again. And after everything I've learned tonight, I need him. "Show me that you choose me."

He growls into my mouth when I reach into his boxers and pull out his dick. He's as hard as I am wet. "Lie back," he murmurs against my lips.

Taking in a shaky breath, I lie back onto the cold Lords' table that once held the dagger he cut me with and our candles. He lifts my already shaking legs over his shoulders as a flash of lightning outside illuminates the Cathedral. His eyes are on mine when he pushes into me, making me cry out as he stretches me. No foreplay, we don't have time for that.

He wraps an arm around my thighs, holding them together, and he starts to thrust harder, making the Cathedral fill with my moans and cries.

My back slides against the table, my hands going to my hair, and I tighten my fingers around the strands, pulling to the point my scalp stings. "Oh God..." My voice trails off as the sound of our bodies slapping fills the large space.

I'm breathing heavily, body already shaking with anticipation when he pulls out, and I sag on the table. He grabs my ass, yanks me off, and spins me around, pinning my hips against the side of it.

Wrapping a hand in my hair, he yanks my head back as he slides into me, spreading my soaked pussy, and a whimper escapes my lips when his piercings hit just the right spot from this position.

He leans over my back, and I hear his heavy breathing in my ear. "Say your vows, little darling," he orders roughly. "Remind me that you belong to me."

"I vow." I manage to get out as my hips hit the Lords' table. My hands reach out in front of me, needing to hang on to something, but there's nothing there, so I slap them on the surface.

"You vow," he growls before his teeth sink into my neck, making my breath hitch and my body break out in goose bumps.

"We vow," we both say, and my eyes fall closed as his free hand wraps around my waist and holds me tightly as the ground comes out from underneath me.

WE'RE IN HIS CAR, THE LIGHT FROM THE DASH ILLUMINATING the inside. It's still dark outside. Looking at his clock, it shows a little past four in the morning. The rain hasn't stopped, but it's now a steady drizzle.

"Guess we're not going home?" I wonder when I realize the direction we're heading.

"Sorry, little darling. We've got to go back to Carnage."

"How long do we have to hide out there?"

He lets out a long sigh, letting me know I won't like the answer. Reaching over, he grabs my hand, interlocking our fingers and placing them on my leg. "Bleed On Me" softly plays by Daniel Seavey.

My eyes fall to them, and I see the red diamond on my finger. It's as red as the blood that still covers him from Luke and Miller. "Did Luke have my ring?" I ask.

"Whitney did."

My teeth grind. "Why the fuck did she have my ring?"

"The only thing I can think of was she removed it while you were in the hospital."

"The Spade brothers are going to kill her," I say, and I'm not really sure how I feel about it. Like, I'm not upset, but should I be? My sister who I loved let me think she was dead for the last three years. She tried to hurt me. She knew I was married to Tyson and had no intentions of telling him where I was or how to help me. I would have never done that to her.

"When they get the information they want," he agrees.

"Do you believe her? I mean, how would she even know who Ashtyn is, let alone where she is?" They weren't the same age. If I remember correctly, Ashtyn was a little older. I knew all of my sister's friends, and I don't remember her even mentioning Ashtyn. I only know the name because of Saint. But then again, Bethany acted like she knew Whitney, and I had never met her before either. "I thought Ashtyn was dead," I say, and give a rough laugh. "Apparently, no one really dies."

"She was supposed to be," he says.

I look over at him and ask, "How do you know?"

His baby-blue eyes briefly meet mine. "Because I'm the Lord who was supposed to kill her."

SIXTY-SEVEN

TYSON

Sophomore year at Barrington University

I sit on the couch. The girl lies face down on the floor, hands still tied behind her back and she's crying around the tape on her mouth. Miles Hopper sits next to me, recording her with his cell phone. Something about material to jack off to later.

The front doors slam open. The sound of them hitting the interior walls echo through the house, and Miles jumps to his feet. I stay on the couch with my arms fanned across the back.

"What the fuck are you doing here?" he demands, watching the three men enter the family room. He spins around to look at me. "What did you do, Tyson?"

I don't answer because it's obvious what I did. I sent a picture of the girl to her Lord. I believed the girl when she said she didn't know anything. Her mother did, but her? I wasn't given any information about her.

Saint removes the pocketknife from his back pocket and cuts the zip tie around her wrists and yanks her to her feet. He rips the tape

505

from her mouth, and she sobs, wrapping her arms around his neck while she stands up on her tiptoes.

"You can't take her," Miles growls, then turns to face me. "We have a job to do."

"And we did it." I nod to the dead mother.

"She's supposed to be dead," Miles snaps. "Everyone in this house must be taken care of. If her brother isn't here in thirty minutes, I'm going to fucking gut the bitch." He turns around to face Saint but is met with the end of his knife. Saint stabs him in the neck and then pulls it out. The girl places her hands over her ears as Miles gurgles nonsense before dropping to his knees, and Kashton takes her in his arms to comfort her.

I stand and shove my hands into my front pockets. "You understand what this means?" I ask him. My eyes going to the sobbing girl. Haidyn takes her from Kashton and picks her up with his hands on her thighs. She wraps her legs around his waist and buries her face into his neck, still sobbing. I look back at Saint, waiting for an answer.

He nods, putting the bloody knife away. "I owe you." Walking over to Haidyn, he rubs her back, and she turns, facing him, and like a child, he takes her from him and walks out the door.

"I don't understand," my wife whispers. "Why were you supposed to kill her?"

"Because she is Luke's half sister."

She gasps, pulling her legs up underneath her ass, and turns in her seat the best she can to face me, her other hand coming to lay over our joined ones. "What...I—"

I smile at her lack of words and explain a little more. "I was sent to do an assignment for initiation. Me and a fellow Lord were supposed to take care of everyone in the house. Well, I was just as surprised as you were when I found Miles dragging Ashtyn into the living room. I knew her from the house of Lords. She was Saint's chosen."

"I've heard the rumors." She nods, referring to Saint and Ashtyn. "What did you do?"

"I killed her mother."

"Tyson." She gasps in horror as if the thought of me killing a woman is too much to handle.

"You know how you get a woman to trust a man?" I ask, looking over her quickly.

Her brows pull down at my question. "No."

"You send a woman to do the job for you." The silence that lingers tells me she doesn't understand, so I elaborate. "He would find a girl that he wanted, send his mother to talk to her, get close to her, then she would help him drug her and take her."

"Oh my God." Her hands tighten on mine.

"But there was never anything said about Ashtyn. The Lords had a description of the mother. That wasn't a chance I wanted to take."

"So..." She thinks about her words for a few seconds. "You knew all the way back then that Luke was involved with kidnapping and killing these women?"

"No." I shake my head. "Luke was never mentioned."

"But you said it was her half brother."

It's complicated. "Ashtyn had a brother. The Lords thought that it was him because of the mother's role she played." That's where things got tricky. For some reason, her brother didn't come to save them that night, so who knows what the fuck he was into. After I killed their mother, the Spade brothers took Ashtyn into Carnage and hid her away from the world. But that didn't go as planned either. She fucked them all over. There are days I bet they wish I would have just killed her when I had the chance. But *if* Whitney is telling the truth, they will get their chance, and Ashtyn may be dead soon anyway.

"So Luke and Ashtyn have the same mom?"

"Yes." I nod. "Brenda—their mother—had an affair with Luke's father." I wave my hand in the air before placing it back on the steering wheel. I don't know the specifics and never cared to. Some Lords trade their wives like fucking baseball cards. It's not uncommon for orgies to take place during certain Lord events. "But this wasn't figured out until years later. After we completed our assignment, the kidnappings and killings stopped. For a while."

LAIKYN

I WAKE UP IN A ROOM I'VE NEVER BEEN IN BEFORE BACK AT Carnage—no more hospital bed. Thank God.

Black silk sheets and a big fluffy comforter. The carpet a dark gray like storm clouds with a black area rug. The dark curtains are pulled open to showcase the floor-to-ceiling windows that overlook the woods. Nothing but trees for as far as the eye can see. The clouds cover the sky, making it look gloomy and gorgeous at the same time.

Two white leather barrel chairs sit with their backs to the window, facing the room with a round glass table between them. A matching couch sits at the foot of the four-post Alaskan king size bed. The walls are as dark as night with shiny inlay designs. It's beautiful.

Sitting up, I look over at the double doors to the right that open, and my husband exits the en suite bathroom with a towel low on his narrow hips. I smile when his eyes meet mine.

"Good morning, little darling," he says, walking over to me. Leaning over, he kisses my forehead while his hand goes to my stomach. "How do you feel?"

I always knew I wanted a family. Kids with a man who wanted

me and our children. But I never stopped and thought about how much of a turn-on it would be for that man to ask such a simple question. Or how much my heart races when he touches me. "Good."

His hand rubs gentle circles on my stomach, and I spread my legs for him. A playful smirk appears on his handsome face. "Does my wife want to be fucked?"

"Yes, sir." I lift my hips, my hands going to my breasts.

He groans, his fingers lowering to run over my pussy. I'm already wet, needing him. "Beg me, Lake," he commands, and I gladly oblige.

"Please, Tyson." I kick the comforter off my legs, making sure nothing is in his way. His free hand comes up and wraps around my throat, pinning me to the bed but not cutting off my air. I wrap my hands around his wrist. "I need you." Licking my lips, he enters a finger into me, and I lift my hips off the bed once again.

Removing it, I move onto my side, pushing my ass to the edge of the bed, hoping he takes the hint.

He laughs, and I'm not even ashamed of how desperate I am for him. He runs his fingers between my ass, applying pressure as he leans over the bed, his lips almost touching mine. "Want me to fuck that ass again, little darling?"

"Yes," I breathe, my pulse racing at the thought. He told me in the bathroom at the Minson Hotel that I'd beg him to fuck me. "Please ..." I wanted to laugh then, but I understand what he meant now because I would beg this man to do the most depraved things to me. I'd crawl on my hands and knees and beg him to make his little darling a whore.

"Do you want me to stretch it beforehand or make it hurt?" he asks, his finger moving to my wet pussy, and I groan, wanting more of him.

"Make it hurt." I whimper the words, unable to hide my embarrassment. I loved the way he fucked my ass last time. Fuck, the humiliation that comes with it after he's done with me. I know my husband will hold me in his strong arms and tell me how good I was for him.

I'm dying to be his good girl.

A knock sounds on the door, and I sag, rolling onto my back. Grabbing a hold of the covers, he yanks the comforter up to my neck. I sit up, gathering the fluffy material, and hold it to cover my chest while he walks to the door, not worried that he's only in a towel. Opening the door, I see Ryat standing there. "Everything is good to go."

Tyson nods. "Give me ten." He then closes the door, and I allow the comforter to drop to the bed, exposing my chest to him, hoping he gets the not-so-subtle hint.

"Does that mean you're not going to fuck me?" I stick out my bottom lip. I know my husband, and he'll want more than ten minutes in bed with me.

He chuckles, coming around and kissing my lips tenderly. "Always so fucking needy." His hand drops to my breasts, and he pinches my hard nipple, making me gasp while leaning into him. "Later. I promise." He pulls away and looks down at me. "I want to take my time using my wife."

My cheeks flush, and my pussy clenches. *Fuck, I'm so horny.* Is it the pregnancy? The adrenaline from everything that's happening? I don't know but I also don't care as long as he gives me what I want. "May I come with you?" I ask, knowing he's going somewhere inside of Carnage with Ryat. He's probably waiting outside the room for him.

"Not this time." He shakes his head and I cross my arms over my chest.

"Are you going to see Whitney?" I wonder. The thought of him seeing her doesn't sit well with me, no matter the situation. I trust my husband with my life. He's earned that. But her? I no longer trust her and am afraid she'll try to hurt him. Who knows what kind of plan she had with Luke and our brother that we aren't aware of.

He was in the process of putting a T-shirt on but turns and faces me, his face giving nothing away. It makes me feel stupid that I even asked. Of course he's going to. So I think of a reason as to why I would ask that.

"Will you get my collar back?" She already tried to take my ring. She doesn't deserve anything that he gave me. It's mine. He's mine. I refuse to share with her. My entire life was altered after she *died*, so I refuse to let that happen now that she's decided to come back from the grave.

He arches a dark brow. "Missing your collar, little darling? That's a surprise." Walking back over to me, he grabs a hold of my chin and tilts my head back, my hands go to his wrists. He drops his lips to mine and kisses me, taking my breath away.

"It's mine," I say breathlessly, my heavy eyes opening to look up at him. "I want it back."

He just smiles, finishes getting dressed, and leaves me. Lying down, I fan my arms out and let out a deep breath. I guess I can get out of bed and clean myself up. I'm starving and who knows how long he'll be gone.

SIXTY-EIGHT

TYSON

I meet Ryat outside of the bedroom door and we make our way downstairs to the basement where the Spade brothers took our guests late last night.

Opening the door, I find Luke tied down to the table with leather straps. His eyes are closed, and I wonder if he's dead. When Lake and I finally returned this morning, we went straight to the bedroom. I was in the mood to fuck my wife, not torture this sorry bastard. I knew he would be waiting for me this morning.

Walking over to the countertop on the far wall, I pick up what I want, and I look up when the door opens to see Sin enter. "Saint said you'd be in here."

"What are you doing here?" Ryat asks with a smirk on his face.

"I had to meet Gavin," he answers vaguely, and only I know what he's referring to. As far as I know, he and Elli meet him here several times a week for updates.

"Well, you're just in time for the show." Ryat chuckles.

Sin walks over and looks down at a naked Luke. I wanted him as humiliated as possible. "Branding?" he inquires.

I didn't plan on stripping him of his Lord's brand, but I guess that's always an option. "Not right now." I shake my head and begin to release the restraints. "Grab an arm and help me get him up."

Ryat frees his legs while Sin and I each grab an arm. We drag him off the table to the center of the room. "Hold him up," I say, and Ryat takes my place to help Sin out. I remove the handcuffs from my back pocket and cuff his wrists out in front of them. Then I reach up to grab the chain on a spool, hanging from the ceiling and yank it down. I attach the link on the end around the center of the chain and yank. The process releases the chain, pulling his arms up above his head, holding him up by his cuffed wrists.

Stepping back to get a better look, Sin crosses his arms over his chest and smirks over at me. "This looks somewhat familiar," he jokes.

I snort, fucking bastard. He's lucky he's alive.

"I don't even want to know." Ryat shakes his head.

Luke groans, his head bobbing a little and I walk over to the counter and pick up the next thing I want. I grab the end and let the rest unravel to the concrete floor. Walking over to him, I reach up from behind him, and I place it between his lips and wrap it around his face and arms that are up by his face multiple times.

His body jerks, mumbled words filling the room. Once I've decided there's enough, I reach out, and Ryat hands me the pliers, and I cut it off where I want it.

Walking in front of him, I look into his wide eyes. "Good morning, Luke. Glad you could join us."

He looks around the best he can, body fighting the cuffs, but there's nowhere for him to go. He's here because this is where I want him. Otherwise, he'd be dead and buried in the cemetery behind the Cathedral. I reach out and tug on the barbwire that I wrapped around him, making sure it went between his busted lips.

Sin gets closer to Luke's face and frowns. "What happened to his mouth?"

"Tyson yanked his teeth out," Ryat answers.

"Oh, man." Sin laughs darkly. "You must have really fucked up."

I step into Luke, gripping his chin, not caring if I cut myself on the barbwire, and say, "I'm going to wrap your entire body in this shit, and then we're going to watch you squirm and fight while you cut yourself open. Just like you did to all those women."

Who knows how many will never be found. Or how many he sold that wish death would come. It makes me physically sick to think of where my wife would be right now if she wasn't upstairs, naked in a bed, waiting on me. What he would have done to her. Or allowed others to do to her. And the fact that she's carrying my children, I want to shoot this fucking bastard between the eyes, but that would be too quick of a death. Not enough pain. I want to see him bleeding, sobbing like the bitch he is, begging for his death. I've prided myself on being a patient man, so now is the time to be one.

I swing, my fisted hand hitting his face, making his body sway in the chains. My hand instantly stings, but it feels good. I do it again. His body jerks while it hangs from the ceiling. Spit and blood fly from his mouth, and he makes gurgling noises, unable to speak. The barbwire not only splits my hand but his face as well.

"Ty—"

I hit Luke in the ribs this time, cutting off Ryat. I don't want a voice of reason right now; I want to fucking kill him. I hit him again in the stomach, and he doubles over the best he can. Blood is flying, my hands slippery and burning. The skin splits more and more every time I make contact, but that won't stop me.

I hit him again and again. I'm panting, body vibrating with fucking adrenaline. He touched her, hurt her, planned on selling her. That deserves fucking violence.

Heart pounding and gasping for breath, I step back, and my bloody hands drop to my sides as I watch his body convulse, his chest heaving and openly sobbing. Walking over to the counter, I ignore the look that Ryat and Sin give one another, wondering if I've lost my mind.

I haven't. My head is clear. I know what I have to do. And when I'm done, I'm going to go crawl in bed with my wife and remind her that I will do whatever needs to be done in order to protect her.

Grabbing the roll of barbwire, I grab the end and let it unravel as I walk back over to him. He shakes his head the best he can, and I smile. I'm going to decorate him like a Christmas tree and then watch him squirm. It won't kill him. It's not razor wire. It's going to dig into his skin, but not slice him open. It's going to hurt like a bitch and make him wish he was dead.

LAIKYN

I'M WALKING THE HALLS, LOOKING FOR A FUCKING PLACE TO eat. I know there's a kitchen around here somewhere because Tyson brought me food when I was in the hospital room. It was good, too. But we're in a different building now. Carnage is a fucking city all on its own.

Turning a corner, I jump and let out a scream when I run into someone. "I'm so sorry," I rush out when I see it's Saint. My eyes drop to the snake tattoos that wrap around his neck, and I rub mine. Just the thought of them makes it hard to breathe as if they're tightening, cutting off his air.

"Lost?" he questions.

"I'm, uh ... hungry." I stumble over my words. There were stories that I heard about the Spade brothers over the years. They are what nightmares are made of.

I've always believed evil walks the earth, and they are the devil times three. Just because I know Tyson trusts them doesn't mean they don't scare me. I feel sorry for Ashtyn if she really is alive, and they find her. Hell would be better than Carnage.

"Fourth floor," he states, and then walks past me. He doesn't bother to show me the way, as if he doesn't have an extra second of his time to give me.

I turn around and watch him pass on by. He wears a pair of black jeans and a black long-sleeve T-shirt with the sleeves rolled up, showing the ink on his arms as well. "Wait," I call out, and then curse myself when he stops and turns to face me.

"What, Laikyn?" he asks. The sound of my name on his lips makes me shiver. His voice is as cold as this hallway.

"Do you know where my sister is?" I ask, wrapping my arms around myself.

He doesn't answer. Instead, he crosses his arms over his broad chest and leans against the wall, his eyes on mine.

I take a step back, all of a sudden feeling stupid that I asked. Why would he tell me?

"He's right, you know," he says, and I lift my eyes to meet his through my lashes, frowning. "In wanting to keep you from her."

I swallow the knot in my throat.

"She can't be trusted." He pushes off the wall.

I step forward. "Don't I deserve to know why?"

His brow furrows. "Does it matter? She was willing to throw you to the wolves and let them eat you alive while she planned to take what was yours. That's reason enough to want her dead."

Take what's mine? Was that why she watched me when Luke locked me away? She wanted to make sure I was long gone before she moved in on my husband? Not sure how she planned on that working. Tyson wasn't even sure she was still alive at that point. And how would she be with Tyson if she was married to Luke? His words were meant to make me stay away from her, but they just make me want to speak to her even more.

"Don't you want to know why Ashtyn left you?" I question.

517

I'm reaching because I don't know their personal story, but he's curious. Otherwise, my sister would already be dead.

His body goes rigid, his face morphing into something evil that makes my breath get stuck in my lungs. He slowly strolls toward me, and I can't make my legs work to run away. Stopping inches from me, he glares down at me. "Wanting to make someone pay for what they did, and wondering why they did it are two very different things. And one of them doesn't fucking matter."

My hands fist, getting annoyed. I let out a huff and take a step back from him, needing the space.

"Oh, come on, brother." A man speaks from behind me, and I jump, pressing my back to the wall so I can see both of them. It's Kashton. "Let her see her sister."

My eyes fall to the tattoo of a woman dressed as a nun on his arm. She's got a ball gag in her mouth, drool and makeup running down her face and an upside-down cross on her cheek.

"It's not worth it," Saint states.

"Saint?"

We all turn to look, and I see Gavin standing at the end of the hallway. His eyes go from me to Saint. "A word please?"

Saint walks off and leaves me alone with his brother. Kashton's blue eyes are on mine, and I look at the floor. "Come on. I'll take you."

"You will?" I ask, skeptical.

He doesn't answer. Instead, he turns, and I find myself following him. We make our way down a hallway to an elevator, and I stay silent, back in the corner while he leans up against the wall. His eyes on his cell while he types out what I'm guessing is a text.

It comes to a stop, and we exit. We've got to be in a basement. Nothing but concrete walls and floor. The ceiling is low, and some lights hang from it. Kashton is tall enough that they almost hit him

in the head. We approach a set of double doors and he pushes them open.

Entering the next room, I come to a stop, gasping at what I see. Two men hang from the ceiling. Each one has blood running down their naked bodies, arms tied behind their backs, heads hanging down, eyes closed. They look dead. "What ...?" I whisper, walking over to them. "Why are they ...?"

"Tyson had Ryat bring them over from his place," Kashton informs me.

"I don't understand." My voice is a whisper. *I know them.* Why are they here of all places?

"Tyson killed Beau."

"What?" I gasp, looking at him wide-eyed.

He smirks, obviously getting excitement from telling me this information. "While he was trying to find you, he went to Beau. Killed him and that dumb bitch of his. Then went through his cell to find that he had texted these two when you arrived at the club."

I remember watching Beau pull his cell out from behind the bar and sending a text when I told him I was ready to work. My eyes go back to the two security guards I know from Blackout.

"Anyway, they helped Bethany out with setting the club on fire. Tyson was torturing them at Ryat's until he found you. Then had them brought here." He walks over to one of them, pushing on his bloody shoulder. The guy lets out a moan from his taped lips as his body starts to sway back and forth.

I take a step back, my hands going to my face when I realize he's hanging from a meat hook embedded in his back. My stomach starts to turn, and I give them my back. "I'm going to be sick," I mumble to myself, but I hear Kashton chuckle at my unease.

"Come on." He starts to walk to a door at the other end of the room, and I rush through it when he holds it open for me.

This room is different than the last, and I look over the bars on

519

the floor. I frown. "What are those for?" I ask, unable to stop myself.

He looks over his shoulder and comes to a stop, answering, "Those are the pits."

Pits? I stand over one. There's a hole dug out of the floor, like a mini, square bathtub. But they have bars running across the top with three holes in them. The one in the center is bigger than the one on either side of it.

Looking up at him, I step away, not wanting to know what they put in there, or why. He smirks, turns, and opens another set of double doors. We're in a new hallway, and there are doors on either side. It's deadly silent down here. Nothing but my heavy breathing fills the dimly lit hallway.

It reminds me of a prison. One where they put you in solitary confinement. No light and no interaction with anyone. Just left alone with your thoughts and voices, causing you to go crazy.

"Here we are." He comes to a stop at one of the doors. He reaches down and punches in a code on the outside keypad, and it unlocks.

My wide eyes look at him, and I have a moment of panic.

He checks the large watch on his wrist, and it looks out of place next to the nun tattoo. It's a black and silver Patek Philippe—expensive and classy. My father has one like it. "I'll give you five minutes to find out what you want to know. Then you're done." His blue eyes meet mine as he drops his arm to his side. "I have no problem dragging you out of there."

Swallowing, I nod and turn to step into the room. It's freezing cold and looks just like the hallway, nothing but concrete.

Looking over my shoulder, I make sure he doesn't lock me in here, and I see him leaning against the wall, arms crossed over his chest, eyes on me.

"Lake?"

I jump and turn to look at the room, seeing my sister step out of the corner. I swallow nervously when I see she's naked, chains around her wrists that connect to the wall behind her. Now I understand why he didn't shut the door; she can't escape even if she tried.

"Whitney." My voice is rough, all of a sudden dry.

"Thank God, Lake. Please..." Her wide eyes go from mine to the open door. "Please get me out of here."

"I can't do that," I say honestly. I don't have that kind of power.

She bares her teeth, and the chains rattle as she yanks on them. "They've got me chained like an animal." She holds up her wrists to show me the thick metal wrapped around them with padlocks in place. The links so short that she can't be more than two feet off the far wall. If she were to sit down, her hands would have to rest in the air. This isn't the Minson Hotel & Resort, for sure.

A quick look around tells me there's no bed, not even a cot. There's no food, water, or blanket. Just her, chains, and my collar around her neck. The sight has my heart racing with jealousy. I want it. Saint said she was going to take what was mine. She's already accomplished that. I know Tyson put it on her for a reason, but I hate the satisfaction that she has from that one little thing. "Where have you been?" I decide to ask.

Her face grows red with anger. "Laikyn! Get me out of here."

"Whit—"

"Where is Tyson?" she demands. "TYSON?"

I cover my ears, his name echoing in the small concrete box. "He's not going to save you," I tell her, shaking my head. "Not after what you did—"

"What I did was what you deserved," she interrupts me.

I take a step farther into the room at her words. "What I deserved?" I ask, breathless as if the wind was knocked out of me. "I didn't do anything."

She snorts. "I saw you, Lake. The way you obeyed every order he gave you." Her eyes look me up and down with disgust. "Like an obedient bitch in heat," she spits out. "And Bethany filled me in on what I didn't see."

I open my mouth to say I didn't have a choice, but Tyson and I have moved past that. Early this morning when he had me bent over the Lords' table—the very same one she had been hog-tied on —we took our vows by choice. "He chose me." I lift my chin with pride. "And I choose him."

I'm proud to say I'm Laikyn Grace Crawford.

She throws her head back, giving a manic laugh that sends a chill down my spine. "You think because he fucks you, you're something special?" She shakes her head, and her matted hair hits her face. "He'll never love you, Lake. You're just another worthless bitch to him."

I tilt my head to the side. "What's that make you, Whitney?" Her eyes narrow on me. "He put you here. Alone. Your husband is dead." If Luke isn't by now, he will be soon. "So what does that make you?"

She lets out a feral scream, her body shaking violently. "You fucking bitch!"

"You've been dead to me for three years, Whitney." Her eyes widen at my words. "You're still dead to me now."

"You don't deserve to have what I had," she cries. "I fell in love with him, and Dad made me let him go."

"You set him up," I growl. "You let the world—you let me—go on believing he killed you. For fuck's sake, Whitney, people thought you guys were engaged and you were expecting." I remember Collin and his friend talking about it at Blackout.

"Speaking of baby..." Her watery eyes drop to my stomach. "You're welcome."

I step forward, my hands going to my flat stomach. "What do you mean, you're welcome?"

"It was my idea to have Tyson knock you up. Once Luke realized you'd no longer be useful to him."

Useful? There's that word again. "Why would you do that?" I ask breathlessly.

The cruelest smile I've ever seen graces her bruised and dirty face. "Because I knew he'd fuck you every chance he got." She steps forward, the chains pulling as tight as she can from the wall. "I wanted to give you the greatest gift in the world." I swallow the knot in my throat. "And then take it away from you."

Tears sting my eyes, and I shake my head at what she did. "I never did anything to you," I growl.

"You took him from me!" she shouts.

"He was never yours to begin with!" I scream, my lungs burning. "You might have had a chance with him, but you blew it. Now you can rot here while I remain his wife carrying his children." Her eyes narrow on me. "I hope it eats you alive to know that he loves me. That he married me." I smile, feeling at peace that it doesn't bother me. Giving her my back, I move toward the door when her next words stop me.

"He won't want you once he finds out that you fucked Luke."

My pulse begins to race at her words. "I'd never cheat on my husband. I'm not you."

Her face goes red with rage. Taking in a deep breath, she lifts her chin like she's not chained to a wall, and a smile spreads across her face that makes her look crazy. Like she should be in a padded room with a straitjacket on. I guess she's not far from it. "If Tyson doesn't already know, he will soon. I'll make sure of it."

I step closer to her, my hands fisting. "I'd never cheat on my husband!" I scream this time, my body vibrating with violence. I want to get close enough to beat the shit out of her, but I can't. I won't put my babies in any position where she can harm them.

"After Luke knocked you out in the hospital bed, he fucked you."

"No." I shake my head, refusing to believe that.

She gives a rough laugh. "Yes. He wasn't allowed to after your *wedding*, but you were no longer a virgin, so it didn't matter anymore." She steps forward, and her arms are pulled behind her due to the shortness of the chains. It doesn't seem to bother her. "If you weren't already pregnant, he was going to make sure it happened."

"No." Tears sting my eyes once again. A part of me knows she's telling the truth, but I don't want to believe it.

"I recorded it." She smiles at me, and my heart stops. "We needed a video to share for those who would bid on you."

My chest is so tight that I can't breathe. Tears run down my face, and she watches them as she steps back into the darkened corner as if satisfied with hurting me. I don't want to believe it. Tyson showed me her phone. The texts. If there was a video on it, he would have shown me. At least told me what happened. "You're ... lying." I manage to get out through my trembling lips.

"Why don't you ask him yourself?" She lifts her chin, and I turn to see Tyson standing in the doorway.

He's covered in blood, face hard as stone, and eyes narrowed on mine. He's mad that I'm in here. I don't expect him to understand why I needed the closure, and although she gave me more than I wanted to know, I got it. Like I told her, she's dead to me.

He looks away from me, and my stomach drops. Panic gripping my chest. "Ty—"

"I told you." She gives another laugh, and I'm gasping for air. I can't breathe all of a sudden.

Shoving my way past him, I exit the room and make my way back down the tight hallway as my sister's laughter fades the farther away from her cell I get.

SIXTY-NINE

TYSON

I enter the bedroom we're staying in, kicking it open so hard that both doors hit the interior walls and bounce back, slamming shut. "Lake?" I call out, chasing after her. She beat me to the elevator and up to the room. Seeing the bedroom is empty, I make my way to the en suite bathroom.

I shove them open too, and she's already stripped off her clothes and stands in the shower, her cries filling the bathroom.

With my clothes on, I open the door and step inside. She just found out she was raped, so I don't want to strip down naked in front of her. "Lake—"

She slaps me across the face, cutting me off. Before I can recover, she does it again. "Little—"

Slap.

"You knew." She's screaming at me, her voice shaking. "When were you going to tell me?" She shoves my chest, and I wrap my arms around her, spinning her around and pinning her back to my front.

Her knees give out, and I lower us both to the shower floor.

She cuddles up in my arms, and I run my hand down her hair while kissing her head.

"You ... knew." She trembles in my arms, and my chest tightens. Telling her the truth won't matter. It's not going to change what happened to her.

THE DOOR OPENS, AND I LOOK UP TO SEE GAVIN ENTER THE room with Saint. Gavin's eyes drop to my cut and bloody hands before meeting mine. "I've been trying to get ahold of you."

I nod. "Been busy."

He looks over at Luke hanging from his chained wrists and speaks. "I see that." Reaching into his pocket, he removes a cell phone and holds it out to me. Sin takes it for me because my hands are covered in blood, holds it in front of me and presses play.

My wife is thrown onto a hospital bed. Luke gets up and straddles her, pinning her wrists down by her head. "Fucking sedate her! Now! And where the fuck are the restraints?"

"No. No. No. TYSON!" She screams for me.

The male nurse with the blue scrubs on who I killed grabs a wrist from Luke and places it in a leather cuff attached to the bed and secures it down to her side. Luke wraps his hands around her neck and chokes her while the guy continues to make his rounds, securing her other arm and both of her legs.

"You know..." He lowers his face to hers. "He might have actually done me a favor. You may be worth something pregnant." He shoves her head into the mattress before letting go and gets up off her.

She gasps, sucking in breaths, yanking on the restraints, realizing they've got her tied down to the bed, and you can see the life drain out of her face. All hope gone.

"I want her sedated until I say otherwise. And get that pregnancy test done," he barks out the orders, and people run in and out of the room.

"I'm... not..." She sucks in a deep breath. "Pregnant."

He leans over the bed and grips her tear-streaked cheeks. "You better pray to God that you are. Otherwise, you're no use to me." His hand drops to her bare chest. He grabs her breast before slapping her across the face. She cries out. "A worthless bitch is a dead bitch."

His hand lowers to her black booty shorts, and she fights him as he cuts them off. She's sobbing when his fingers move her underwear to the side. "I guess if the results come back negative, I can fuck you until you're pregnant." He kisses her tear-streaked face when his fingers enter her. "Either way, I'm going to make you useful."

His lips move to the side of her lips to kiss my wife again, and she leans into him, sinking her bloody teeth into his flesh, and he screams before his fist hits her face.

Her body goes limp, her cries now silent, and he wipes the blood from his face. He undoes his jeans, jumps up on the bed, and spreads her legs the best he can while they're tied down. And then he fucks her. Her body moves with the bed as he leans down, grips her hair in both of his hands, and spits on her face. "Fucking bitch. I'll make sure you're worth something."

He's coming inside her in a matter of seconds, then gets up and zips his jeans. "Clean her up," he barks to someone and exits the room.

Whoever holds the camera walks farther into the room to stand beside the bed. "You won't be needing this," a female says, and then I see a hand in the shot, pulling Lake's wedding ring off. Whitney's laughter fills the room as she turns, leaving my naked wife restrained and unconscious, her face covered in Luke's spit and his cum leaking from her pussy.

· · ·

I REALIZE I'M SHAKING WHILE I HOLD HER TO ME. THE VIDEO ended, and I couldn't breathe. I went to run out of the room, looking for my wife when Saint told me that Lake was down in the basement with Whitney. I was too late. The fucking bitch told her what Luke had done.

"I'm sorry, little darling," I whisper, my tongue heavy and throat closing on me.

The sound of her sobbing makes my chest ache. I can't comfort her. Nothing I do will be enough to take away the pain.

The thing is, I had a feeling Luke did this. I had Gavin run every test possible on her here at Carnage once we got her here. And when the rape test came back negative, I was relieved, but he said too much time could have passed. That it may have not caught it. I hate that he was right.

IT'S BEEN TWO DAYS SINCE I SAT ON THE SHOWER FLOOR AND held my sobbing wife. She hasn't spoken to me since. Not one word.

She's shut down. Gavin is on standby. He said at any time, night or day, just call him, and he'll be here to start a feeding tube and IV for fluids. She's not eating and won't drink anything. Just lies there in bed staring at the wall. I'm not even sure she'd put up a fight if I called in Gavin to help her.

I'm going crazy. Almost as bad as I did when she was taken. Because once again, she's gone. She's right there at arm's reach, but she's not there mentally. I don't know what to do for her. How to pull her out of where she's gone to hide. I want to give her time, but I also hate to see her suffering like this.

I gave her a bath last night, and she silently cried while I washed her. I half expected her to hit me, slap me, or punch me in the face. But she didn't. Instead of pushing me away, she clung to me.

I've spent my day with Luke today. I woke up this morning, kissed my wife, and went down, needing to blow off some steam. She needs the tender side of me right now, not the *I want to make you bleed* side.

Gavin taped my cut hands, and even those are bleeding through because I can't not use them. I step out of the shower and dry off. Entering the bedroom, I see she's in bed where she's been, and I put on a pair of boxers before I crawl in next to her. I've always slept naked with her, but I no longer do. I don't want her to feel uncomfortable around me. I've based our marriage on sex, and now I don't want her to think that's all I want from her.

She rolls over onto her side, facing me, and I reach out, gently running my taped knuckles down the side of her pretty face. I hate it. When I close my eyes, I hear her screaming my name. I see her lying there fighting for her life. Then I see him hit her, knocking her out and raping her while his spit covers her face.

I did that to her. I allowed Luke to take something from her that I can't give back no matter how much I make him suffer.

"I've decided," she speaks, her voice rough since it's the first thing she's said in two days.

"Decided?" I ask softly.

"I don't want to see the video."

Is this why she's been so quiet? Because she's spent the past forty-eight hours debating if she was going to watch her sister's husband rape her and spit on her face? I hate to tell her, but I wasn't going to let her see it.

"If that's what you want." I push her dark hair behind her ear for a better view of her gorgeous face. *I just wish for once in my life I'd get to choose something for me.* She once said that to me. I'll allow her to think this decision is hers. But the truth is, the video is long gone, and the phone destroyed. No one will ever see what happened to her. Gavin had told me that Bramsen found it back at the hospital. Whitney had two different phones. One she used to communicate with Luke and another one with no texts, calls, or emails. Just pictures and videos of victims over the past few years. The things on her phone made me sick, and I've seen some fucked-up shit. I've done some unforgivable things in my life, but to know that she helped makes me angry.

"Is that awful of me?" Lake whispers. "Am I ... a coward?"

Propping myself up on my elbow, I frown as she rolls onto her back, placing her shaking hands over her face. "Why would you ask that?" I pull them away so I can look at her.

She licks her trembling lips, looking over at the floor-to-ceiling windows, unable to meet my eyes. It's dark outside, so you can't see shit out of them. The first tear runs down the side of her cheek when she speaks. "Because I don't remember it. Other victims—"

"Lake." I cup her face, cutting her off, and fresh tears fall from her lashes when she blinks. "No."

"We've had sex since then." Her chest starts to heave. "I've ... begged you."

I grab her wrists and pull her to sit up. "Breathe, little darling," I tell her, needing her to calm down. She's all worked up, and I hate to see her hurting. She's fighting a battle that I didn't even think would be one.

She throws her arms around my neck, and I pull her into my lap, hugging her to me tightly and softly rocking her.

I understand what she's trying to say she feels. She went on with her life while other men and women have had to live with the nightmares and the trauma.

Am I glad she was unconscious? Yes. Do I hate that he's making her feel bad about herself for that? Abso-fucking-lutely. But the Spade brothers have assured me that I can keep Luke alive as long as I want and visit him as often as I choose. While my wife starts to heal and comes to peace with her decision, I'll remind him every fucking day that he has to live with his.

EPILOGUE

TYSON

I sit tucked back in the corner when my cell vibrates in my suit jacket. I pull it out to see it's a text from my wife.

Little Darling: Don't forget we have dinner tonight with our friends.

She thinks I'm at Blackout overseeing the progress of the new building. I'm not, but that's what I told her. The club is coming along quicker than I expected. The grand opening is in just a couple of weeks.

The Lords offered me my life back. The one I traded in for my wife. Truth is, I love my life the way it is. Does that mean I'll run Blackout until I die? No. But for now, it's what I want to do.

We made a public announcement and informed the world that my wife was alive and well, while carrying our children. We told them that she was recovering and we wanted privacy at this time.

I wanted the world to see that she is loved. That means everything to me. She deserves to be seen and heard. Her family had silenced her for so long, and I won't do that to my wife. She may be my whore in private, but she is my equal in every aspect of our lives.

As it turns out, more died in the fire than we were aware of. That's what we made the world to believe after Gavin helped me out with the men I killed while trying to track down my wife. The Lords didn't give a fuck who I killed, but when the body count grows as high as mine did, you have to give a reason for why they disappeared.

ME: I'll be home soon.

I pocket my phone when I hear an elevator ding, signaling the arrival of my guest. I stay seated, hands steepled and waiting. I've been here for over an hour. It took a little longer than expected but I knew it would happen nonetheless.

Laughter fills the room before a woman enters with a man. "I want a drink," she tells him.

He goes over to the bucket that holds a bottle of Louis Roederer Cristal Brut Champagne that he already had waiting for them. Handing her a flute, he then fills his own and throws it back, ready to get this party started.

Setting his glass down, he stumbles, and she reaches out to grab his arm, her drink untouched. "Are you okay?"

"Ye-ah." He blinks rapidly, his eyes darting around the room aimlessly, trying to focus on anything. After a few minutes, he falls to the floor and doesn't move.

I stand from my chair and make my way over to the light switch, flipping it on. She takes a step back, almost tripping in her heels she's so nervous.

Reaching into my suit pocket, I hold out the envelope to her. "Get the fuck out of here," I tell her, and she turns, running to the elevator, wanting to get as far away from me as possible.

Once I'm met with silence, I get to work.

Senior year at Barrington University

I sit in the passenger seat of Hansen's car as he pulls up to the Cathedral. It's three in the morning, and he just busted me out of jail.

After I yelled at the Lord to let the police book me or get me out, I was released and was told that I needed to see them immediately. So here we are.

I enter the Cathedral and walk down the aisle to see two Lords standing at the altar, masks and cloaks on. I fall down into the front pew, placing my arms across the back, still dressed in my bloody clothes. "You wanted to see me." My eyes look up to the loft and see the baptism pool is empty. "No water this time?" I snort. "Don't feel like drowning me today."

One steps forward. "Tyson—"

"Get to the point as to why I'm here."

"We failed you," the Lord on the left says, and my stomach drops at the words. The Lords never admit when they are wrong because, in their eyes, they never are.

"I ... I don't understand," I stammer, rubbing my hands on my bloody jeans.

"Son, we did not give you the assignment to take Whitney Minson on as your chosen. Or to dig into Frank."

I stand, running a hand down my face. "You did."

"No. You were tricked."

The wind is knocked out of me, and I fall into the pew. Bowing my head, I reach up and grip my hair.

"You're all over the news..." He trails off.

My father told me, but I haven't seen it.

"The State Senator's son arrested for pregnant woman's

murder..." I get to my feet and start to pace as he goes on. "They said you stalked her."

"Because I was told to make it look public," I shout. "You told me to make sure everyone knew she was mine." It was stupid, but you don't question the Lords. You do whatever they want, no matter how big or small.

"That you raped her." He goes on. "That you robbed that poor, innocent girl of her life. We can make it go away. And once we do, it'll be as if this never happened, but it'll cost you."

"How much?" I swallow the lump in my throat, knowing it won't be money.

"Your title," he answers.

I come to a stop and glare at their fucking masks. "You're telling me I've given you three years of my life for you to take it away?"

"Tyson—"

"Three fucking years and all you can do is fucking nothing?" My body vibrates with the anger bubbling in me. "How did this fucking happen?"

One of them sighs. "The best we can come up with is that Frank set you up."

My legs give out, and I fall into the pew once again.

"He wanted you to go to prison for killing his daughter. She either went along with it, or he had her killed."

I'm guessing the latter. She had been trying to set me up to get her pregnant. I highly doubt he killed his daughter just to put me away. No, instead, he'll make her live the rest of her life in hiding. I rub my hands on my jeans. "So ... I lose my title. Then what? You guys kick me out?"

"We are willing to give you Blackout. Free and clear. The land, the building. You remain a Lord, but you don't have to answer to anyone."

They might as well just cut my brand off. I snort. "A Lord is never free." Sitting back, I look up at them. "And Frank? What about him?"

"We can't prove—"

"I was fucking here," I grind out. "There were at least three... four Lords here." I try and rack my brain to remember. There were three. Two that helped me up the stairs and another one at the top of the loft. My mind isn't clear right now.

They remain silent.

"I've got text messages..."

"From an untraceable number," the one on the right states.

"Unbelievable." I give a rough laugh. I've got to give it to Frank. He fucked me over good. "And Whitney? You don't think she's dead?" If she's willing to go as far as getting me to knock her up, she's more than capable of faking her death, especially if her father helps her.

"If she's not, the world won't think any different."

My head snaps up to look at them, and they were serious. "You really think she's alive?" I question, and again, they say nothing.

Pacing, I stare at my bloody shoes as I walk back and forth. "I'll do it." What else is there for me to do? Prison for murder of a woman and an unborn child, or take what the Lords are offering me? Even if she wasn't, her medical records will show that she is. Word is already out that I did it. Even if they remove every video or news article from the internet, the Lords still know what happened tonight. If Frank did set me up, he'll make sure everyone knows what he wants them to think. "Under one condition."

"Son, you're in no position to negotiate." One of them laughs.

The other one holds up his hand and steps forward. "What is it?"

I come to a stop and look at his mask. "I get to marry whoever I want when the time comes."

Their masks look at one another.

"Free and clear. No initiations. No stipulations. Nothing. Who I want. When I want." If Frank wants to fuck me, I'll fuck him right back. *Big, blue eyes and long dark hair is exactly what I want to take from him, and I'll remind him who the fuck I am as I parade her around this town like an obedient slave with a collar and leash. I'll make his last daughter my wife, and she'll choke on the words that bind her to me.*

"Done."

"You set me up," I say, more to myself than anyone. "I can't prove it, but you had Luke, Miller, and Jackson pretend to call me for an assignment my senior year to make Whitney my chosen. You wanted me to come off to the public as an obsessed, stalker boyfriend. So when she came up dead, her phone pointed the cops directly to me." That's why I didn't find Whitney's phone on that day she had called me crying and lost. One of them had already handed it over to the cops, leading them right to me. It wasn't a hard sell really. I had a tracker on her cell. I had been texting and calling her for days. I said some really shitty things to her during the days she would go MIA. A few of my condoms with holes poked in them were found in her purse—it too, was conveniently not at the house where I found her. They were to be used against me as I was trying to knock her up so she couldn't leave me. I set myself up as the perfect suspect, playing right into their hands.

I stand next to the bed, arms crossed over my chest, and watch the man come to. I didn't give him much. Just needed a little time to get him where I wanted him—stripped down and naked. He was planning on getting fucked, but I have different plans for him.

He's on his back, spread-eagled with a gag in his mouth—he's here to listen, not speak. His eyes open, and he looks around aimlessly for a few seconds. They meet mine, and he begins to yank on the ropes, mumbling nonsense.

"We've been here before," I tell him, getting to the point. I've got somewhere to be. "Years ago. This all started because I filmed you with a woman in this very room. But you have to understand it wasn't my doing." I snort. "Like I care who you decide to fuck, but the Lords did care that you were pushing for more. Getting greedy." I remove the lighter from my pocket, and he begins to yank harder, screaming louder. "You wanted to be State Senator, and they wanted my father to have that position. So they had me set you up with a woman and film it."

I just recently found out that she was one of those women who went missing. "Miller and Luke killed her, didn't they?" I found out later that she was last seen exiting this hotel with a smile on her face. I sigh, hating the fact that what I asked her to do got her killed.

The best I can come up with is that Miller followed his dad. Saw him enter the Minson Hotel with her and then watched her leave alone. He followed her to the bar down the street, made his move, and she left with him, never to be seen again. She was among one of the many women whose bodies were never found.

"It's brilliant, really, that you use Minson Hotels for a front." Frank wasn't innocent. He may not have killed and sold women for money, but he knew what his son was doing, and he allowed it. "Your son and his best friend kidnapped women, brought them here, and put them in a room, and then they come and go as they please. They're registered under Minson or Cabot, and no one was the wiser. They've just vanished." They knew every camera angle, where to take them, what to avoid.

Pushing off the dresser, I light up the lighter and hold it over his skin, smiling as he thrashes on the bed. "I consider myself a reasonable man. A patient man. I waited three years to marry

Lake." I can't figure out why he made her wait until she was twenty-one to marry Luke, but it doesn't matter. Not anymore.

"You're as fucked as they come, watching me fuck your daughter." I flip the lighter shut, and he sags into the mattress. I pull out a knife, and his body goes rigid. "You will bleed on this very bed for me just like Lake did." I stab him in the hip and pull out, smiling as the blood starts to pour out of the wound. His mumbled scream makes my smile widen and his body shakes.

"It took me a while to figure out why it was so important that she remained a virgin before marriage." I stab him again in his upper arm, and he sobs. "Virgins are worth a lot when being sold." I run the tip of the bloody knife down his chest, and he tries to hold his breath to not move and cut himself. "Luke was going to drug her and sell her off to the highest bidder. But then I interrupted his wedding, and he knew I'd fuck her on our wedding night. Whitney informed my wife that it was her idea to knock her up. I didn't believe it when Lake told me." I roll my eyes. "Why would Luke and Miller go along with what she wanted." I frown. "But then I did some research and found out that pregnant women are worth as much, if not more." I push the tip into his stomach, and he sucks it in the best he can. "Breeding kink is big in the industry." I nod to myself. "I get it. No kink shame here." I hold my hands up, shaking my head, and he lets out a deep breath through his nose. "I love fucking my pregnant wife. But..." I push the tip back to his skin, right next to his flaccid dick. "Let's just say that I give you the benefit of the doubt, and you weren't aware of what Luke and your son had planned." I remove the knife and place it under his neck. His narrowed eyes meet mine. "And let's say that I don't even care that you tried to put me away for murder because I've moved on from that. Without you, I would have never ended up with the life I have now. That I love. All of that is excusable. What's not is that you still came into my club and threatened my wife. And that is unforgivable." I slam the knife into his stomach. His back bows, the rope pulled tight, and he screams into the gag.

It took Lake quite some time to tell me everything—from her father threatening her before our wedding, to slapping her—but one night she broke down and told me she didn't want us to have any secrets. She wants our family to be different than the ones we were raised in.

I agreed. I want to share everything with my wife, the good and the bad. I mean, she fell in love with me even when she thought I killed her sister, and she knows that I'll kill enough people to form an army if it meant keeping her safe.

My wife could tell me that she wanted to burn the world, and I'd be proud to watch her burn it down to nothing but ashes. In my eyes, she could do no wrong.

I stand, leaving the knife inside Frank. "With you dead, your wife will be handed down to another Lord. Your son is dead." I killed him off the other night. It wasn't worth keeping him alive. I was getting bored with him and his pathetic attempt to beg for his life. "Whitney... Well, she's been dead for years, right?" I laugh.

To the world she died, and soon, her body will be placed in the ground. That's if the Spade brothers leave any of it to be buried.

"So Lake will be left with your empire. Now, I'm not sure she wants it, but I've got our family to think about. Our twins—a boy and a girl. She's giving me the best of both worlds," I say with a smile. "Well, like I was saying, Blackout isn't what I want to leave them. I've got plenty of years to get Minson Hotels & Resorts how I want it to be before I hand it over to our children." Wrapping my hand around the handle of the knife, I yank it out, and his body shakes uncontrollably. Spit and blood flying out from around his gagged mouth onto his chest.

"But I've got to make a point." I pull the Zippo out of my pocket once again. "So I'm going to burn this one down and call it a loss." He shakes his head, as if I wasn't going to kill him. Leaning down, I place my face right in front of his as I speak, making sure he can hear me over his pathetic sobs. "It's the last warning I'm going to give the world that if you fuck with my wife, you'll burn in hell."

Using my thigh, I light it on my jeans and then toss it onto the bed, watching it catch fire.

EPILOGUE TWO

TYSON

Eighteen Years Later

I exit the master bathroom to find our bed empty. Frowning, I shrug on my button-up and make my way down the hallway to the kitchen. My wife stands at the stove cooking breakfast while our son stands next to her texting away on his cell.

"Good morning," I say cheerfully.

"Morning," he mumbles, not bothering to look up.

My wife's eyes meet mine, and she gives me a big smile. "Morning." Abandoning the stove, she walks toward me, and I meet her halfway. Pushing her dark hair out of her face, I cup her cheeks and lean down, giving her a long kiss, hoping she understands that I'm about to drag her back to bed and bury myself between her thighs. She's been mine long enough to know that I like to start my day with her screaming my name.

"Gross," Halston whines, and pockets his cell.

I pull away from my wife, smiling, and look around the kitchen and dining room. "Where's your sister?" I ask.

"She stayed with Annaleigh last night," he answers.

My wife goes back over to the stove to finish what she was doing. I pull out my phone and track Hartlyn's car but frown when I see it's in our garage.

"How do you know Hartlyn stayed with Annaleigh last night?" I ask Halston.

His baby-blue eyes meet mine. He's on my side. He and I are a united front in this house. We protect the women we love, and no matter how much he and his sister fight, he'd kill for her without thought. "Annaleigh picked her up last night. They were going to see a movie and then stay over at her parents'."

I pull up Sin's number.

> ME: Was Hartlyn at your house last night?

You can never be too careful. Lake would kill me if she knew I have a tracker on Hartlyn's car, but that's one fight I'm not afraid to have with Lake. She argues we have to trust them. *Fuck that shit.* I know what boys her age think about. I was once one, and in our world, you can never be too careful.

"I've got a meeting with Blakely today," Lake tells me as I put my cell away.

"What time do I need to be there?" I ask her. She and Blake are starting their own business.

After my wife had our children, she wanted to stay home with them. It was important to her that our kids grew up with a different life than we had. And I couldn't argue with her on that. As a parent, you want what's best for your children. We are still a Lord and Lady, and our kids will never be what society considers "normal."

They're about to graduate high school. Halston and Hartlyn plan on attending Barrington University. Halston wants to be a

Lord, and although my wife isn't happy about it, we've raised him and his sister to have a mind of their own. To make their own choices.

Choices have consequences. I've told him just like my father told me. I can only hope that he doesn't make the same mistakes I did. But if given the chance, I'd make them all again if it meant I'd get Lake in the end.

"Oh, you don't have to—"

"I wouldn't miss it." I interrupt Lake, kissing her on the cheek and slap her ass, making her squeal in surprise.

"I'm off to school." Halston rolls his eyes, grabs his backpack off the counter, and walks out of the kitchen.

"We love you," Lake calls out. "Have a great day."

"What about me?" I wrap my arms around her from behind.

"What about you?" She laughs.

"You know what would make my day great?" I ask, dropping my lips to her neck. "You and me in our bed."

"Mm-hmm," she mumbles.

"Your shaking legs wrapped around my neck...your cum on my face." She moans, her ass pushing into my hard cock. "My idea of a great day is knowing your cunt..."

Her cell phone rings, cutting me off, and **Blakely** lights up the screen. "I have to take this." Picking it up, she walks away from me. "How was your trip?" she asks in greeting. "Oh my gosh, that's awesome. I bet she's excited..."

I pick up a piece of bacon and pop it into my mouth while I listen to them talk about their meeting later on today. My eyes scan over my wife. She's wearing one of my T-shirts that hangs off one shoulder. I can see her hard nipples through the thin material, letting me know my words were affecting her, and a pair of cotton shorts. No makeup on and her hair up in a messy bun.

Fuck, she's so goddamn gorgeous.

I'm still obsessed with her. I can't keep my hands off her. I wanted to have more kids after the twins were born, but it just wasn't in the cards for us. I'd never say it out loud, but Luke did us a favor by having Jackson show up at the Minson Hotel on the day of our wedding. I love my wife and kids. Just when I thought I'd lost what future I could have, Lake gave me something I could have never dreamed of.

When she was a few months pregnant, I asked her what she wanted to do with her life. Tears welled up in her eyes when she answered. "Spend it with you." I reassured her I wasn't going anywhere. No matter what, she's stuck with me until the day I die.

My phone vibrates in my pocket, and I pull it out to see a text from Easton.

Sin: Does Hartlyn like coffee?

I frown as I read over it a second time but respond. What's that have to do with what I asked him?

Me: No. She hates it.

He reads it and responds immediately.

Sin: That's what I thought.

I'm about to ask him what the fuck coffee has to do with my daughter, but Lake gets my attention as she ends her call with Blake.

My eyes fall to her hard nipples once again, putting my cell away. *Sin can wait.*

Her eyes meet mine. "What?" she asks, nibbling on her bottom lip.

I walk over to her, grip her bare thighs, and pick her up off her feet. She wraps her legs around my waist as I carry her off toward our room while her laughter fills our home.

I've got two hours before I have to be at work. I took over the Minson empire years ago, and although I like my job, I'd much rather spend my days with my wife naked and tied to our bed, begging me to fuck her until she's so exhausted, I have to carry her to the bathroom to bathe her.

Kicking the bedroom door shut with my shoe, I throw her onto the bed, and she immediately sits up, grabbing the hem of her shirt and pulling it off. Then she's lifting her hips and pushing her shorts and underwear down her tan legs.

I reach over and open up the nightstand, pulling out what I know she wants. Standing in front of her still fully dressed, she lies back on her elbows completely naked, her beautiful blue eyes on mine, and the corner of her lips twitch as she fights the urge to smirk.

Her eyes grow heavy, her lips part, and her breathing picks up when she sees the collar. She still wears it for me every now and then, and I love how much she wants me to use her. "Are you ready, little darling?"

THE END

Thank you for taking the time to read *The Sacrifice*. Did you enjoy it? See where it all began with *The Ritual*.

Continue on for a sneak peek of *The Ritual*

. . .

Want to see where the Lords' started? Continue on to read **_The Ritual_** (Ryat's book)

THE RITUAL

USA TODAY & WALL STREET JOURNAL BESTSELLING AUTHOR
SHANTEL TESSIER

RYAT

I ENTER HER apartment, knowing that she's home alone. I made sure of it. Pushing her bedroom door open, I find her lying on the bed. She's on her back, her hands up by her head. Eyes closed and breathing deeply. Passed out.

She took the GHB.

I figured she would. People in our world are always looking for a way to escape reality. I needed another taste of her, and there are rules for a reason.

Walking over to the side of the bed, I pull the covers off her to find she had changed into an oversized T-shirt before it kicked in. I fist the material in my hands, thinking it belongs to her cheating ex. Yanking it up, I see she's got on a pair of black lace underwear. Letting go of the shirt, I place my hand on her flat stomach and slide the tips of my fingers into the fabric. Teasing myself.

My cock is hard, straining against my zipper. I want to fuck her so bad. Ever since I saw her sprawled out on the floor, I wanted to take her dark hair in my hands and shove my dick down her throat and make her pretty blue eyes cry.

The rules of the ritual are simple.

The chosen must offer herself. She has shown me interest by showing up at the party. If there was any doubt what she was doing there—my bedroom proved she wanted something. Even if it was just revenge on Matt. I'll take that. That's something I can use.

Typically, the chosen one and the Lord know each other. They've been friends, or they've dated. Few instances are like Blakely and me—when the Lord is forced to pick a certain chosen one. There are women at Barrington who would kill to be a chosen. Serving a Lord is an honor for them. Matt has kept her in the dark for a reason. He didn't want her to know what was going on. He thought it didn't matter, and she was a sure thing for him. Now that's no longer a possibility. So, his reasons for keeping her in the dark have changed.

I wouldn't say she would have been my first choice because I never thought of her like that. Is she hot? Yeah. But I knew she was off-limits. Even after I was given the order, I had reservations. That was until I started planting myself in her life. I've been following her for several weeks now. Then after the little taste she gave me—I've been salivating, wanting more. If I had revealed myself to her in my bedroom that night, she wouldn't have allowed me to touch her.

If the chosen one accepts, she is yours until you no longer have use for her. She won't remember that motherfucker's name after I have my way with her.

Slowly, I hook my fingers into her underwear and pull them down her tan legs, letting my knuckles graze her smooth skin. Gripping her thighs, I push them apart and crawl onto the bed to kneel between them. I look over her shaved pussy, bringing the fabric to my face. I inhale, my cock jerking in my pants. Fuck, I need to be inside her, but that can't happen tonight. Not yet.

The rules are clear, but they don't say anything about playing with her. They allow us just enough to hang ourselves. The Lords are always testing us.

I throw the underwear to the floor and slide my hands up the inside of her thighs to her cunt. I bite my lip, spreading her lips open for me. "Goddamn," I whisper, slipping a finger inside her.

She's not wet, but I didn't expect her to be. Bringing my finger to my mouth, I suck on it up to my knuckle and then slide it back in, gently testing the waters while my eyes go to her face.

Her head is tilted to the left, her dark hair covering her pillow, and her breathing remains unfazed. I reach up with my free hand and shove her shirt up farther to expose her chest to me. I smile at the fact she's not wearing a bra. Her breasts are fucking amazing. Round and firm, they fit in my hand perfectly with pretty pink nipples and small areolas.

Looking back down at her pussy, it's getting wetter. I remove my finger and add another one. She still doesn't move.

My girl has proven that I own her, and I can't wait to show her just what that means.

I start to get more and more aggressive. Her head moves to the other side, and a whimper escapes her lips. I didn't give her very much GHB because of her small size. I didn't want her to experience too many side effects. I just needed her to be drowsy and impaired to the point I could play with her. Plus, it can increase an urge for sex.

She arches her back for me, her lips parting, and I watch the way her nipples harden as her pussy tightens around my fingers.

I readjust myself on the bed, placing my left hand by her head. I lean all my weight on it while forcing a third finger into her tight cunt. My cock twitches with anticipation to be inside her. To be the first there. To own her.

Her breath catches, and I gently kiss the corner of her lips. "Beautiful."

"Ryat." She moans.

"Yeah, Blake. It's me," I tell her, and she whimpers. Even

drugged and only half-conscious, she knows I'm the one touching her.

I begin to finger-fuck her roughly while my thumb plays with her clit. Her body rocks back and forth, making her tits bounce and the bed squeak. She lets out a cry when her pussy clamps down, and she comes all over my fingers.

Something about having her like this—having total control over her body—is very powerful. Knowing she willingly took something I gave her without any knowledge of what it was. She's craving to be owned, to be dominated, to be mine.

I stop, and her eyes remain closed. Bringing my fingers to her mouth, I rub them over her parted lips, smearing her cum across them like icing. "Soon, little one," I tell her before I stick them in my own mouth, licking them clean. Tasting that fucking honey that I've been craving after she gave herself to me in my bedroom.

Pushing off the bed, I move to a sitting position between her shaking legs. I reach down and grab the collar of the oversized shirt and rip it down the middle. "I'll burn this," I say to myself, pulling her arms out of it, knowing that I'm one step closer to owning her and erasing any trace of Matt.

Reaching into my back pocket, I pull out the card and lay it on her nightstand. Now I wait.

ALSO PART OF THE LORD'S WORLD

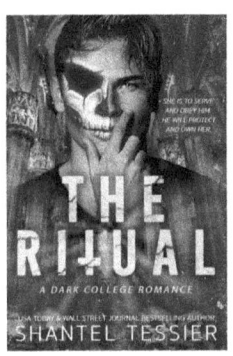

CONTACT ME

Facebook Reader Group: Shantel's Sinful Side

Goodreads: Shantel Tessier

Instagram: shantel_tessierauthor

Website: Shanteltessier.com

Facebook Page: Shantel Tessier Author

TikTok: shantel_tessier_author

Store: shanteltessierstore.com

Email: shanteltessierassistant@gmail.com OR darkangelcreationsllc@gmail.com

Shantel Tessier's Spoiler Room. Please note that I have one spoiler room for all books, and you may come across spoilers from book(s) you have not had the chance to read yet. You must answer both questions in order to be approved.

Milton Keynes UK
Ingram Content Group UK Ltd.
UKHW021355201024
2278UKWH00021B/65